HUNTED FOR THE PACK

CELESTIAL CLAIM, BOOK 2

NATALIA PRIM

WWW.NATALIAPRIM.COM

CONTENTS

To my family, friends, fans, and fellow freaks.
Thanks for taking this wild ride with me.

Monsters are real…and I may be one of them.

Reanne's future looms above her, while salvation may come from deep below.

New bonds are formed, old ones are tested, and a certain hidden past may be the key to solving the biggest question SteelTooth pack has encountered.

Cyan's race to repair his crumbling family is met with heated moments, as well as heartbreaking ones.

The unexpected driving force behind all of their problems reveals himself, and our players in the prophecy learn more truths than they ever wanted to know.

But nothing is as it seems in The Glade, and the moon is always watching.

Contains:

✓ Multi-pov ✓ Kïdnapping ✓ NC by non-harem members

✓ Shifted smex ✓ Gröup smex ✓ Inter-pack relationships ✓ Knïfe play

✓ Stabbïng ✓ Cüt play ✓ Bloöd ✓ Chöking

✓ Unique world-building ✓ A veritable buffet of pairings

⚠ Head to nataliaprim.com for all the "heads-up" info! ⚠

#LetTheGuysKiss #LoveIsLove

#IfYouClutchedYourPearlsThisAintTheBookForYou

Hey Reader! You've been warned. The story is about to begin. If you haven't read the content alerts and you still plow forward, don't attack me via ratings if you come up on something you don't like! If you have specific content questions, PLEASE reach out. I know what being triggered feels like, and if you're worried, I'm more than happy to help! #knowledgeispower

CONTENT WARNING

This book is intended for those over the age of legal adulthood. If you needed permission to buy this book, put it down right now and go finish your homework.

All characters depicted herein are adults and do some bad sh^t. Don't try this stuff at home. I mean, I guess you could, you're an adult, don't listen to me. Just be safe, 'kay? You die, there's one less darkling in the world, and that would suck.

REANNE

This cabin is barely held together, much like my heart right now. There hasn't been a lot of talking. I think Aeon and I are both in really bad head spaces, plus we had to focus on making this place livable. It clearly hasn't been visited in decades, maybe longer. Even so, it has all the basic things we'll need like a bed, a small, warped bench, one off-kilter counter with a basin, and a table with one chair.

It would be sort of cute if the bathroom wasn't outside. A literal outhouse. Aeon swears it's clean, but I will hold everything in until the last possible second before I try it.

We found a lantern, which we lit with the only match that wasn't moldy. It's set up on the table, which we dragged to the foot of the bed. Well, he dragged it. I was forbidden to touch it, in case it had splinters.

The bedding's been shaken out, the floor sort of swept with a leafy branch, he's just finished killing spider number eight, and I've gotten the last bit of webs out of the corner.

Now we're done. Now the emptiness inside comes back into focus. I place the balled-up rag on the table and slowly lower myself to the edge of the bed. Aeon crosses the room and drops down beside me with a heavy exhale.

It's deathly quiet in here, yet I can't think of anything to say. 'I'm sorry' seems pointless. I can't promise something like 'we'll go back soon,' because I have no idea when we'll leave. I already thanked him twice, to which he did nothing but nod. So, sitting here in silence for now is probably the best way to go. Except my stomach has other ideas, and rumbles, sounding like a monster in its own right.

Aeon's somber expression finally cracks into a small smile. "Yeah, me too. But there's nothing here. I checked twice. Even if there was, we probably wouldn't want to eat it. So, I'll have to go hunt."

"Oh." I stare at my joined hands, resting on my bare lap. Why is talking to him so hard all of a sudden?

He leans back on his elbows. "I don't want to leave you alone, though."

I glance over at his profile and his long, lean torso as he stares at the ceiling. "Plus...hunting was never really my thing. I can do it, don't get me wrong, but it won't be as fast, or as good as Korey."

His expression falls, and he copies my posture, bumping my shoulder with his. "Cheer up, ReeRee. We can just pretend we're doing that thing humans do, where you pretend to live like we do for a night, complaining about it the whole time."

A laugh bubbles up and I grin at him, an errant dust particle crossing his face. "You mean camping?"

"Yeah," he smiles softly, "that. Only we suck at it and forgot all the supplies."

"Well, if we were just humans we'd go home and get what we needed."

Both our smiles drop, mine dissolving into a wince, Aeon's twisting into a frown. "Sure as hell aren't doing that."

"I'm sorry. I know this is hard on you."

"Psh. It's harder on you. You left two mates behind. I'm with mine. All I left was..."

The other thing I left behind. Cyan. Even thinking his name makes my chest freeze. I'd rather go back to dead silence, but I have something else I need to ask.

"Do you remember when Mishka said my power would be changing souls? Or commanding them?"

"Yeah."

"But, then with Fen, he...I... and there's this darkness," I poke my chest, "inside and—" His eyes are wide, mouth slack. "Uh, never mind."

"No, no. Sorry." He smiles and grabs my hand. "It's a little scary, but I love you no matter what. And yeah, I wondered about that. I mean, what are souls anyway? What if that was his soul? Maybe you just...commanded it to the surface?"

I stare at him a moment before cutting my gaze to the wall, the memory of Fen's charred body forcing a shudder into my bones. "I guess that could make sense. I started feeling the darkness around him."

The cabin creaks, a gust of wind pushing through the logs, stirring up ancient dust.

It's another moment before Aeon speaks. "Was that the thing when you couldn't breathe?"

I nod. "I...think it's still here, Aeon. I can't feel it right now, but it didn't leave."

He tugs me into a hug, kissing the side of my head. "I wish I could protect you from everything. But I can't save you from yourself." I know he's right, and that's the scariest thing of all. "Besides, can we even trust Mishka about that, about anything when he did what he did to Cyan?"

I exhale forcefully, "I don't know. Can I...be honest with you?"

"Always, ReeRee." He kisses the back of my hand and gives my fingers a squeeze.

"What if I don't have a choice? You guys have no idea what I'll become, and if he does, if he can help..."

Aeon growls quietly. "I think I know what you're getting at, and it's a bad idea."

"What if I turn into a monster," I whisper, my voice catching, "and hurt you all?"

He teases my cheek with his knuckle. "What if you don't?"

When I don't answer, he lets his hand fall. "I really don't think you'll turn into anything. And besides, Mishka can't be

15

the only werewolf in the whole Glade who knows about this stuff."

I sniffle, staring at him. That's a very good point.

"Tell me this, do you want him or Cyan?"

"Cyan." The word rockets out of my body on pure reflex, and my heart leaps into my throat, a small smile hooking my mouth. "I really want Cyan."

Aeon's shoulders relax. "Then, it doesn't matter what Mishka might know. He's not going to help you. He's sure as hell not going to help Cy. Doing anything with him is a bad, bad idea."

He's right about this, too, I know.

"I'm just…so worried. If I don't go with him, he'll kill you guys."

"Cyan wouldn't let him get close enough to try."

Panic wells in my chest again as I cock my knee and face him.

"Aeon, you didn't see what I saw in his mind. There was this huge battle, and he's killed hundreds, maybe thousands of werewolves. He's tricky and smart. I didn't understand everything, but it was all dark and awful."

Aeon chews the inside of his lip. "Well, I've seen Cyan fight. And Cy's smart, too. Mishka won't be able to do a damn thing to us as long as he's around."

A tiny bubble of hope forms in my chest. "Do you really think so?"

He smiles, but it almost looks forced. "He won't let another Alpha hurt us. Period."

Maybe…maybe we should go back. If Cyan can keep everyone safe, then we could—ugh, but he wants to mate! I'm so scared of what might happen to me. Though, if I think about it hard enough, I guess I'd rather be scared with my whole makeshift family, than scared in a broken-down cabin with only one of them. I open my mouth to tell Aeon, but he chuckles, taking my hand.

"So, how does that work?"

"What?"

He makes a rolling gesture at my head. "The mind reading thing. Is it weird?"

"It's...different, for sure," I mutter, picking at his knuckle. "But it's just a surface thing. Whatever's being thought about right then."

"Oh. That doesn't sound so bad."

We stare at each other a second. No idea why I'm nervous about asking, but, "Do...you want to try it?"

His brow quirks, but after a second, he nods. I gently cup the sides of his face and press our foreheads together, sucking in a breath.

Aeon's mind is full of brilliant swirling colors, morphing to sort of embossed faces then flattening again. I see a gorgeous version of me, followed by Cyan, then Neo, which quickly fractures back into me again.

"Hey, it doesn't hurt."

I laugh. "Why did you think it'd hurt?"

"I dunno." He grins. "So, what do you see?"

"For starters, you think I'm way prettier than I am," I chuckle softly, leaning back.

"You're stunning, ReeRee." He gives me a soft kiss and my heart flips on end.

"Aw, thank you. Your thoughts are beautiful. Colorful. Super different than the others."

"Is that good or bad?"

I shrug. "Neither. It's just you."

"Huh."

It goes quiet again, and it's his stomach that breaks the silence this time.

"Right. I guess I'll be back with...something." He sighs and pushes to his feet. "Wish I'd remembered to grab the starter rock. That fire is going to take a bit."

I watch him walk until inspiration hits. "Hey, just because I'm a human who sucks at camping, doesn't mean I'm not resourceful." I stand and grab the lantern. "We can just stick the branch tip or whatever in here, get it started."

He smiles and rounds the table, taking my face in his hands. "You're so smart. I'm a lucky werewolf."

It would mean more if there wasn't such a vivid swirl of heartache in his eyes. But I smile back and accept the small kiss he gives me.

When he takes the lantern and heads outside, I follow, leaning against the doorframe. I shouldn't be watching him so intently, the way his muscles ripple, his hands, his focused expression, his cock and balls swinging. I haven't had anything sexual since before Mishka took Cyan's place and teased me until I thought I would die. True, that was only five or so hours ago, but I've been simmering since we got here, and now it's like a slow boil. Given that I can't masturbate, or I'll die, I don't really know what to do.

Because we haven't eaten in a long time, and I don't think Aeon is in the mood. His energy has been basically inert. I remember Korey saying something about the Betas only being Betas around the Alphas, and using their energy or whatever, but that convo seems so long ago now.

The fire crackles higher, heat licking along my skin. Aeon stands, satisfied, and I give him a round of applause, which earns me a genuine grin.

"Very nice."

"Thank you, ReeRee."

"If Neo were here, I bet he'd be beyond excited."

Aeon's face swiftly closes off, darkening as he closes the space between us. "I'll be back. Stay inside, okay? Unless you have to use the toilet but come right back."

He gives me a chaste, hard kiss and trots away, shifting to his werewolf form and disappearing into the forest.

What happened with them? They were so hot together during the group sex, dear Lord. The way they kissed around Cy's cock, all the moaning and—

My skin tightens, need surging through me. Ugh, damn it. I have to think about something else. Maybe Aeon will be back soon. I'll just have to beg him to help me, I guess.

Now it's just me, a fire outside, a fire in my belly, and nothing else. Literally nothing to distract me. What did Veikko do when he came here? Not a book in sight.

Of course, he didn't come here, judging by the state of it. I wonder why he has this place at all, if he stays in the clearing. Question for another time, I guess, when I'm not so turned on I could ride a doorknob. I stare at the fire for another few seconds, giving serious consideration to doing just that. Nah. The angle would be too awkward. Fine. I can wait. I close the door, spin around, and come face to face with an absolutely enormous, snarling, decayed werewolf.

He's emaciated and ashen, with sunken cheeks, dull solid black eyes, and swaths of damaged skin under missing patches of fur. His claws are fully visible, like the muscles have melted away, leaving the bones on display, and even his feet are missing the fur the others have.

I try to scream, but nothing comes out. I'm too scared to breathe. He hasn't moved, hasn't attacked. He's just here, taking heavy, labored breaths with his long teeth bared as he stares at me, hunched over, inches away.

He honestly looks dead, but that can't be ri—Oh, God. Are there zombie werewolves? No. No, I can see his heart thumping away under the thinning fur. But...he's unnaturally stationary. Aeon twitches constantly in his werewolf form, like his bones itch, or his skin is out of alignment, which is probably true on all counts. This one is only waiting. Watching. Testing the air with flaring nostrils.

I don't know what to do. I'm afraid to move. He's clearly starving, so maybe he thinks I'm food? But if so, why isn't he eating me? This is getting weird, I should say something.

"H-hello."

There isn't an immediate response. Then, even though he

doesn't move at all, a deep, slowly reverberating growl fills the room in reverse echo, bringing with it a warm, rich, heady energy. I recognize it in my core. Alpha energy. So strong it feels like it's pushing down on me, while lifting me at the same time. It burrows up from the floor through the soles of my feet, curls around my legs, slides up my hips, along my stomach, over each breast, and circles my neck until it dives under Veikko's mark.

I suck in a gasp, and my head falls back as pleasure zips through me. It doesn't make any sense, but it's like Vik is touching me, everywhere all at once. Then it stops.

A whimper escapes as I level my head, panting. He hasn't moved still, just staring at me.

Great, now I'm way worse than I was. And there's no one else here. I squeeze my thighs together and can't find any position for my arms that doesn't hurt.

It feels weird to hope a complete stranger gives me an orgasm. One who may or may not be alive, at that. Yet, I don't have a lot of options.

I try my voice again, and it still works, though it's much breathier. "Do you have a name?"

His eyes dart to the left in thought, and it's almost imperceptible, since they don't have the normal shine that eyes are supposed to have. They dart back, and my answer comes from the room again, all around me, an eerie echo.

"Kas...i...mir."

"Kasimir?"

The growl comes back, louder, and there's a flicker of life behind those dull black pools. His energy surges through me again, warming me, soothing me, and it feels like he's telling me everything I've ever wanted to hear in my whole life, even though he's not saying a word. I take a step forward on weak knees, my heart overflowing, my marks aching.

It feels like I'm falling in love, and that's terrifying, because my brain knows that's not possible, but my body thinks it's only alive for one purpose, and that's to do anything and everything it can to make this scary beast happy.

I'm so confused. And horny.

The energy burrows deeper into my cells until I'm a live wire, buzzing with desperation, but that's all he does. He holds me here, staring, waiting.

What am I supposed to do? Beg? Fine, I'm not above that right now.

"Kasimir—" the word chokes off as he stands to his full height, head mashed against the ceiling. He's bigger, wider than Vik by a sizable portion, which is scary enough. I purposefully keep my attention on his eyes only, and swallow, narrowly avoiding crumpling to my knees under the weight of the Alpha waves.

"Please," I whisper. "Please help me. I don't know why you're here, or how you got in, but my mate is gone, the Alpha I was with is far away, and I need…" Nope, it's too embarrassing to say out loud.

That flicker brightens more, turning the vacant black voids into a shimmering liquid umber. I couldn't look away now if I tried.

"Me," he rumbles like thunder, crackling against my skin, his mouth still frozen in that snarl.

"Yes, please," I gasp, trembling, clenching my jaw to keep my teeth from chattering.

"Only here…for you. Little…queen." The sides of his snarl pull back in a smile and joy drowns me.

"Tiny…soft…" The words swirl around me, dance through my mind, and all the questions I should ask vanish when he's suddenly eye level again. Tangible power thrums in the space between us as he reaches out, curling his cracked claws in until only one remains out.

"Mine." He touches it to the center of my chest, and stars explode inside me. My marks throb one after the other, faster and faster, until my clit joins the cycle. He drags the claw up and curls it around the back of my neck, leaving a thin, stinging line behind it. The pleasure is so intense I drop to my knees, screaming, moaning, bracing on the floor as the orgasm rockets through me, threatening to tear me apart.

His energy is everywhere, sliding down my throat, easing inside my clenching heat, and I soar from one peak to another, pulses of power radiating from the claw. It's too much, there's no break, but I don't want it to end. I'm worried I could die from it and can't think of any other way I'd want to go.

The door flies open, and everything stops. There's not a speck of Kasimir's energy left, and I wail in utter heartbreak at the loss. I wrench open my eyes and find only Aeon, saying words I can't hear, pressing kisses to my face I can't feel, cradling my numb body to his. The room is empty otherwise, no trace that anyone had ever been here.

But someone, or something was. My eyes slip closed, and all I want more than my next breath is to see him again.

When I blink back to awareness, Aeon's worried face is hovering above me. I'm on the bed, pinned in by his hands on either side of me, pushing down on the blanket.

"Reanne? Are you back with me yet?"

I nod, swallowing through shards of glass. So, it wasn't a dream. Or at least…I was definitely screaming.

He leans back, giving me space to sit up. My limbs feel like jelly, deliciously weak.

"What the hell happened?"

My mouth opens, but he cuts me off.

"I should have been paying attention. Should have made sure you were taken care of before I left. I'm so sorry. I really wasn't thinking."

"S'fine," I whisper, wincing. "There was someone here."

22

His hang-dog expression morphs into shock and anger. "What? When? I didn't smell anyone!"

I flip the blanket off and glance down. A thin red line snakes up from my sternum, and I trace the ridges of the fresh scab around the side of my neck, smiling. "He was real," I whisper again, this time to myself.

"ReeRee, what are you talking about? Who do you think was here? And what is that? Did you fall against the table?"

I shake my head. Though...I suppose that could have happened. I could have fallen and hurt myself and hallucinated the rest, but I really don't think that's it. Especially given how wet I still am.

Something Aeon finally picks up on with a deep sniff, exhaling a growl. "He...touched you?"

Well, the truth is not really, but also, holy hell yes.

"It sounded like you were dying, not coming."

Without warning, Aeon shoves my legs apart and slips his fingers inside, shocking me out of any leftover dream haze. He pulls out before I have a chance to enjoy it or be annoyed, and sucks my juices off, staring at me. His brows furrow. "This is only you. And there wasn't anyone here when I came in. Did you hit your head?"

"No. He said," I swallow again, glancing up, "his name was Kasimir."

Aeon blinks at me, laughs twice, and freezes. "Wait, you're serious?"

Nodding again, I try to swing my legs off the bed, but Aeon grips my arm, stalling me.

"Kasimir. You're absolutely sure?"

"Yes," I grumble. Why is he being so weird about this? "When you opened the door, he vanished." Saying it out loud makes it all seem even more unbelievable.

His hand slips off as I stand, wobbly. Though, I don't know why I'm getting up, there's nowhere else to go, nothing to do, nothing to look at. Defeated, I sit back down, and frown.

23

"Okay," he says. "I know you wouldn't lie to me. But you have to understand, ReeRee. Kasimir…"

I cut my gaze to him, and swallow at the wide-eyed fear.

"Is the first Alpha. The first one ever. Touched by the moon herself, made celestial. A god. It's a story we're told in pup-lessons. How the moon made The Glade, and nothing could live here until a big wolf broke through the barrier. He started to die, but the moon made him into what we are now. A few more came through the next cycle, and they were changed, too. The moon eventually grew jealous." His gaze goes a bit distant. "Man, I haven't thought about all of that in forever. There's more to it, but anyway, it's all just a legend, or…so I thought, anyway. If he was alive, he'd be, shit, thousands of years old. Maybe more. But he couldn't be. Alive."

My mind refuses to process what he's saying. The moon is a hunk of space rock, not a thinking being. "H-how do you know he's not? I thought you lived forever?"

He tilts his head side to side. "I mean, we can, if we're not snuffed out and don't accidentally decapitate ourselves somehow. And if we get hurt beyond what we can heal, we'll still die. But that's us, the non-alphas. It's pretty rare for an Alpha to live a long, long time, especially a mated one. Even protected by a pack. It's almost impossible to avoid, with the drive to rear pups, and pretty often those pups are driven to take over. It's sort of a cycle. So, they'd have to go into hiding…or join another pack…" He glances off into the distance like he's realizing something before focusing on me again. "Uh, maybe you can change that, who knows. Anyway, Kasimir died long ago. I don't know how, I never really paid attention. But that means he couldn't have been here, ReeRee."

"He was, he was here."

Aeon nods, touching the line on my chest. "I believe you. It just doesn't make any sense. And it sucks, because how can I be mad at a dead god for pleasuring my mate when I failed?" He laughs derisively, shaking his head and falling back against the mattress. "We knew you were special, but damn."

Not alive. But obviously not a zombie, since those can't disappear into thin air. Which leaves…

"So, he was a ghost?"

"Maybe. Maybe something else. A soul, raw energy, I really don't know, ReeRee. I'm just sorry I wasn't here when you needed me."

His brows tilt, bottom lip jutting out in an adorable pout.

"It's okay."

I curl against his side, stroking my hand down his stomach, seeking any of his spark, but there's nothing above the baseline mate bond. Even that's dull. Telling him Kasimir wanted to claim me would probably make things worse, so I keep that to myself.

"It's not," he sighs, tucking his arm around me, pulling me close. "But what is?"

Whatever is going on with him is seriously affecting everything. And I don't know how to help.

CYAN

I f I see one more tree that doesn't have Aeon or Reanne behind it, I'm gonna kill someone. Fuck that, I'm killing someone anyway. I don't even know what Mishka looks like, but I bet I could spot him twenty miles away. Can't be that much of a sleaze and not give off some kind of beacon.

I stop running at the edge of the DuskFall Pack's territory and shift back to man form, fighting the sinking feeling in my stomach. We've got no beef with Zaid and his people, but we aren't exactly pals. Aeon wouldn't have come this far. Wouldn't have risked Reanne like that.

Fuck. Fuck, fuck.

I grip the back of my neck and let my head tilt, watching clouds cross the moon. I can't keep looking tonight. I need to get back to my pack, do my fucking job, and sleep.

"Alpha Cyan."

Energy butts up against mine, not quite threatening, but absolutely not submissive. A wall of 'Don't do anything stupid and we won't fight.'

I twist to the left and spot Zaid ten or so feet away, tense and wary, with a guy on each side. A quick sniff tells me he's got a few other guys behind him, too, in the trees.

Smart. I'd do the same thing if I had more. As it is, I can't risk any of my numbers. Especially since Agnar already left. Bastard.

"Alpha Zaid."

I answer the energy with the same vibe, mostly because I'm too damn tired to get into any shit tonight, and if I get hurt, I won't be able to search tomorrow. Not with Reanne gone.

His shoulders relax slightly, and his pack shuffles out of the woods, headed back to their village. Zaid is an older guy, probably about the age my dad would be I guess, though I really have no idea. Black hair, black eyes, scraggled face full of scars. I think, if I remember right, his pup challenged too early and lost his blood right. Doesn't happen often, but it's a risk, since we only get one shot.

"Why are you here?"

"Looking for someone." I don't know how much is safe to tell them, but it isn't really their business anyway. If I hadn't come so close, they never would have known I was here.

"No one else has been stupid enough to come here," one of his flankers snarls, all teeth and bluster.

Zaid scowls with a heavy sigh and glares down at the young guy. "Gar. What did I say about talking?"

"Not...to."

"That's right. No talking. Go find your dad."

After giving me a comically angry glare, the kid storms off, and Zaid pinches the bridge of his nose. "Sorry about him. Garrin is..." he trails off and shakes his head, letting his hand fall. The wavy-haired guy left standing here is trying not to smile.

"But he's right. We haven't had any other visitors. Sorry."

There's a subtle, 'Okay, your time's up, good luck,' tone, which I can appreciate. It's rough for another seated Alpha to be this close to a pack. It disrupts everyone's energies, makes them jumpy. And if I stay too much longer, it could get dangerous.

I give him a terse nod and turn, but the other guy speaks up.

"Must be important, to risk coming this far. And at night." I twist back in time to see him step into a beam of moonlight and glance up at Zaid, clearly conversing. A whole parade of emotions crosses Zaid's face, the guy's too. Eventually, he turns a triumphant, dimpled grin back at me. "If you're willing, I can help, man. I'm a Tracer."

There's something heavy in Zaid's gaze, but also a hint of fear in the air around him. Whether he's worried the guy will get hurt, or that I'll attack him, I dunno. But that must have been one helluva conversation if it ended with someone in his rank being given permission to leave that fast.

I cut my gaze to Zaid and do something I've never done before. I push against his Alpha link, for permission to talk directly to him. It's a show of respect, which, to be fucking honest, not a lot of other Alphas deserve.

His brows shoot up, the fear fizzling away, and he nods, allowing me access.

Why you letting him go?

Zaid exhales. *Jakobe is miserable here.*

Oh, that explains it.

He feels displaced, Zaid continues. *Disrespected. He'll never be an Alpha since he lost the challenge, and his skill is of no real use to us. Even though I try to give him jobs, he knows they're meaningless. He's wanted to leave for a while, but I've held on. He says it's time. And I…agree.*

Damn, this is his pup? Poor guy.

Jakobe's smile falls as he passes a worried look between us. "I can do other things. I'm not a troublemaker. I'm not mated. I follow directions. Open to anything, man."

I eye Zaid and quirk a brow. *Why me? Why not just let him go on a Pack Hunt?*

He says…he likes your…vibe. It looks like it physically hurts Zaid to say that.

I can't help my smirk, but I wipe it away before Jakobe spots it.

I see. How many you got?

Thirty-nine. Three…no, two of those still pups. You?

Seven.

He grunts. *Tighter bonds. I miss those days. Jak will like that.* His gaze turns fierce. *Can I trust you?*

I know what he's asking. I can feel it. One Alpha to another, he wants to know if I'll fully accept Jak in my pack, protect him with my life like I do my other guys, give him a home, a purpose, make him family. Basically, if I'll do my damn job.

But he's also asking as a father, if his pup will be taken care of.

I don't see a pup like Zaid does, which is a good thing since I'm not a fucking pupkeeper. No, I see a grown ass werewolf, asking to join my pack, telling me he might be able to help find my Beta and my Aruna, and it's all I can do not to punch the ground in victory.

Even so, I get it.

You can trust me.

Zaid's shoulders fully relax, and he smiles as he grips Jakobe's arm. His eyes light up. "It's a yes? I can go?"

I hold up my hand, breaking the link with Zaid. "We've got a spare cabin, and you're welcome in SteelTooth, Jakobe, but in respect to your dad, I'll be honest with both of you. You gotta understand what you're coming in to. I'm in a dark fucking place right now. This isn't gonna be all rainbows and flowers and jerk circles. Two of mine are missing, and when we find them, I'm either hitting the mate cycle, or going to war on GrimBite, or both, so you need to be damn sure."

"Two? War?" Zaid's brows furrow. "Jak, maybe we should rethink this."

"Are you kidding? I can finally do something important. It sounds exciting. Yo, I mean, I'm sorry you're hurting, and war is bad and all, but…" His smile widens. "I'm ready, man."

He's practically vibrating. It's almost infectious.

Zaid grips Jak by both shoulders, forcing his gaze away from me. "Once you break pack here, you can't come back. Not while I'm alive."

"I know, Dad." He shrugs. "It's cool. Cyan's the best, I can tell already." He flashes his dimpled grin at me again.

Jeez, this guy.

Zaid's eyes land on mine, something knowing at the back of his glow. "You are pretty strong for an Alpha your age."

29

I thumb my nose and sniff as he rubs his hands down his face.

"Alright. If you're sure, Jak."

"Positiiiiive." He does this upper-back lean, thumbs-up move that makes me snort.

Apparently, that was enough to earn all 100% of his loyalty forever, because his gaze snaps to mine, pupils dilating as his energy lashes out like a whip.

It's different, getting a pack member this way. Not doing the whole wooing thing. Maybe I'll do it anyway later.

"Already acting more like your old self. I'm...glad." Zaid smiles, claws a crescent on his forearm, and after one more sad look, draws a slash through it.

I'm ready for the drop, and the second he's free, I send as much Alpha energy as I can spare, snaring Jak before someone else could. Not that I detect any other Alpha's dicking around, but I want to show his dad I meant what I said.

Jak's mine now. And in seven more moons, both he and Laz will officially be SteelTooth.

ΠEO

Cooking. More specifically, not burning another dish. That's what I should be focusing on. Not Aeon. Because there's nothing to focus on there. I don't like him. I mean, I like him, as a friend and a packmate, and that's all.

We've lived together for over ten years, but that's nothing special. Not like we live together, together. I've only been inside his messy cabin a handful of times. No reason to. I'm either here cooking, in my cabin sleeping and/or getting fucked, or in Cy's cabin, sleeping and/or getting fucked.

I hang my head, hands braced on the long wooden prep table.

And now I'm thinking about fucking and Aeon again. I give up. I miss him. I miss Reanne. I didn't know what it would feel like to be separated from a mate, and I have to say, it sucks. The part of myself I'd given her is gone, and there's an aching hole, deep inside.

Worst of all, Cyan's completely destroyed. He's been out hunting for them for hours. In the wrong direction.

I shoot another furtive glance at Veikko, sitting in the middle of his clearing, staring out at the river.

Even though I had my ears plugged and didn't hear where exactly, I could tell Vik was lying when he told Cy they went south. It was necessary, I guess, to give her more time, but he should tell the truth. Tell Cy where they are, so we can all be together again.

All of us. Together. Again.

I clear my throat and force the images away, slamming a hunk of rabbit down on the cutting board. Can't believe Vik was licking his back. What the hell was that about? I guess, the bigger question is, what the hell was up with Aeon's reaction?

I'm not stupid, I know Vik isn't into guys, so I didn't assume it was anything like that, but Aeon... what's that dead human poet's line? Something about protesting a lot? Whatever. The bottom line is, none of this matters because they're gone, and I miss them, and Vik and I are lying to Cyan, and my stomach hurts.

"It's a good thing that rabbit's already dead." Korey chuckles, tossing another loaded snare line on the far end. "Surprised the knife is still together."

I glance down at the absolute destruction in front of me and groan. "Damn it."

"Ah, if-if I may, I know a recipe for little pies that need meat in, uh, well, that condition."

Lazaros, Korey's mate and shadow, smiles at me from around his arm. "You would need, I'm afraid, an oven of sorts. But-but I could help you. With that. If you wanted."

"That's my little pup," Korey glances down at him and winks, sending a full body flush over Laz.

I focus fully on him. He such a small dude. Nice, from what I can tell, and clearly, he's got Korey wrapped around his finger, but I think he's just making up words at this point.

"Pie?"

He blinks at me several times before nodding. "Yes. Have you...never..." He glances around and hums. "I suppose, you wouldn't, with, well with the, ah, present facilities."

I arch a brow at him and slap a fresh rabbit carcass on the slab. "What's wrong with my 'facilities'?"

He shrivels back behind Korey, blasting out a Beta wave. "N-nothing, that's not, that isn't what I, it's very nice, I quite—"

I don't even have time to feel guilty before Korey scoops him in his arms, shushing and biting at his jaw and neck.

"Sorry, so sorry!" I call out to their retreating forms, as Korey carries him back to his cabin. "I'm having a really, really bad day!"

Great, way to go, Neo. No reply. That's fine. Just fine. Maybe while I'm at it, I can upset Veikko, too. Insult his carvings or something. His hair. Ugh. Now my stomach hurts worse and there's a mysterious recipe I can't find out more about until I get my attitude way under control.

"Pie," I grumble to myself, processing the rabbit. "Sounds stupid." Only it doesn't, it obviously uses meat, which means I'm sure it's amazing. Fuck, this heartache is going to kill me.

"It can be good."

I don't even bother to glance at Veikko as he settles his big body on the closest stump.

"You've had this pie thing?"

He chuckles. "I have. Pie is like stew, in that, it can hold varied ingredients, yet still be called the same thing."

I drop the rabbit in the pot and move to the next. "Huh."

"You are hurting."

My hand freezes around the knife handle. "Yeah." I let out a long exhale. "I am." Lowering my voice, I speak sideways. "We need to tell him."

"In time."

"Now, we need to now. You can't really think this is better for everyone, right?"

"It is better for Reanne."

The wind puffs out of my lungs. I know he's right. At least, that's what Reanne believes. I think she'd be better off mating Cyan now, and we can deal with whatever comes as a family. But I know it's not that easy. I know. I just want her back. And Aeon. Both. I want them both back.

"I believe he shares your feelings."

"What? Who are you…" I trail off at his knowing expression. "No, he doesn't, because there are no feelings to share, Vik. Veikko. Vikster." I punctuate each nickname with a stab on the table. "Vikkorino."

He hums.

"But if there were," I mutter sideways, adjusting my glasses, "they'd be pointless because we're not a match. You know, like that."

"Sexually."

"Damn it, Vik, I'm trying to—I'm not having this conversation."

His laugh rumbles out as he stands and grips my shoulder. Without another word, he tugs me into a hug. I stand here, stunned, glasses askew, mushed in his arms, waiting, determined to pop free and go back to being grumpy the second he lets me go.

But he's really warm. He tightens like a python when I breathe out, and weird, spiky energy seeps into my body. I go soft, tears forming, and even when I start sniffling, he doesn't let go. I drop the knife on the table, set my glasses beside it, and wrap my arms around his waist as far as they'll go, clutching at his skin.

I can't keep this up. It's only been a few hours and I'm falling apart. What if this goes on for days?

"We will give her a little longer. Then tell him."

"Okay," I mumble against his chest, sniffling. That's a less awful timeline.

"You need to be with Cyan tonight."

I laugh bitterly. "I can try, but I doubt that's happening."

"You both need it."

He's not wrong, I know that. But after today, I can't see Cyan cuddling up with me in bed, being gentle and loving. And that nearly breaks my heart most of all.

AEON

My mate has her hands on me, and all I can focus on is everything else. There's something wrong with my bond to Cyan, my bond to ReeRee. I should have picked up on her needs, no question. My running, apparently colorful, thoughts are no excuse for my damn nose not working. Or the need not coming through the bond. Did having Vik tend me mess something up? I know I wanted to jump Alphas in the moment, but I didn't. Right? No, I didn't.

Worst of all, I'm not able to make her feel better because we're too far away for my Beta energy to work. Unlike my replacement.

Anger and heartbreak swell again, and even Reanne's touch is starting to chafe. But I'm not an asshole, so I'm going to lay here and pretend I'm not broken.

"We can go back." Her voice is small and scared. I reach for my energy on reflex and there's nothing. It takes all I have not to shout or cry.

I'm not sure I'm ready to go back. I know I don't want to see Neo yet, and sure as hell don't want to see Lazaros in my spot. But, if that's what my mate needs, that's what we'll do.

"How about this? If you still feel the same in the morning, we'll go."

"Okay, that works. It's probably not safe to travel at night anyway."

"Yeah, tomorrow would be better. But whatever you want, I'm with you, ReeRee."

"Thank you, A. I love you." She squeezes me in a hug.

"Love you too, little snack." I sit up and rub her arm as I kiss her temple. She smells different. Really good, actually, but not like at home. Is it this cabin? Because we're not with the pack? Surely, she didn't get changed somehow…right?

My gaze hits that red line and uneasiness crawls along my back. I don't know what I think about all the Kasimir stuff. That's not a name she could pull out of thin air, and she had at least two, if not more, orgasms and didn't die, which means it wasn't her doing them. I mean, can she just orgasm spontaneously? Doubt it. No, she was definitely visited by someone. Someone who was making her come and messing with her energy at the same time. I'm just lucky as hell I got here before it did whatever else it planned to do.

I thought I knew how my world worked, but it's been one reality punch after another since we found her.

Her stomach growls again and she slaps her palm over it. "Sorry!"

"Shit. No, I'm sorry. I caught two fish, that was it. Was really easy, too. I guess I'm not as bad at hunting as I thought. I'll go get them cooking."

And who does cooking make me think about? I scowl at the wall as I launch off the bed. I grab one of the pans from Vik's counter and set it directly in the fire, because I have no idea what he cooked in it last, but it obviously wasn't ready to die.

This cabin makes no sense. Nothing in here screams 'Veikko' to me. It's all plain fabrics and minimalistic to an extreme. Not that he's a shiny guy or anything, but he does have an artistic eye. So, the fact there are no carvings or sculptures or driftwood, is weird. And there's nothing here for his herbs and stuff, either.

The door hangs open, so I hear her frustrated exhale.

"Do you think leaving was a bad idea?"

"No." That's an easy answer. I would have probably left on my own, so this worked out.

"Because he wouldn't have waited, right," she calls out again.

"You said that before, if I thought asking him would work, I didn't know him at all."

I did say that. Though, I was under the impression I knew Cyan then. Apparently, I don't, if he planned on replacing me after everything. I still think this was the right call, though.

"No, he wouldn't have. Once the Alpha mate drive kicks in, it's impossible to ignore. And when Cyan wants something, he gets it. So, until you're ready...we'll stay."

Or, until we starve to death.

Once the ghost of dinner past cooks off, I set the filets in, and...they burn almost immediately.

"Shit!" I grab at them with my fingers, hoping I can flip them, but they've already seared to the pan. "Fucking...how does he do this!?"

Now I'm missing Neo again.

Reanne rushes through the door, surveys the scene, runs back inside, and returns with the spiderweb rag.

"What is that for?"

"So you don't burn yourself!"

I stare at her wide eyed, earnest expression and can't help my chuckle. "I'm not worried about that, we can heal, and we're kind of tough, I just didn't want to burn your dinner."

"Oh." Her shoulders droop in relief. "That's okay, I'm sure it's fine. Let me seeeeohhheyy that looks...great!"

I snort and carry the pan inside, setting it on the table. "It's ruined, I'm not a pup. You don't have to lie to make me feel better."

She looks a little green for a second, holding her nose and stomach, but it passes quickly.

"Stop, it's amazing. Crispy fish is the way to go, didn't you get the memo?"

"The what?" I laugh, poking at the charred tail fin.

"The...memo? It's a little note you...never mind. Here, I'll prove it." She takes her nail and scrapes the fish until a semi-edible piece reveals itself. Daintily, she plucks it out and pops it in her mouth.

I know it's bad. I can smell it. But I'm watching her face like a hawk, trying my best not to smile.

"Ifs...good." She chews once, then again slowly, and swallows with a small cough. "See?"

I can't hold my laugh in any longer. "Your eyes are actually watering. If you're going to puke, aim it that way."

"No! I swear, no puking." She laughs too, eyes twinkling like stars. It's like a warm hug around my soul. I track her fingers again as she shovels another bite in, keeping her eyes on me. She quirks a brow as she chews and swallows, but when she sticks her tongue out to prove she ate it, desire sweeps through me. I grab her hips and pull her into a kiss.

"Mmph!" She laughs and pushes back a bit. "I have fish mouth!"

"I don't care. But fine." I cinch her to me with one arm and dig at the fish until I find a less burned bit, and eat it. "Oh," I cough and laugh. "That's awful."

"It's super bad." She belly laughs and grips my face, kissing me over and over. I back us up to the chair and sit, letting her straddle me as we make out. She grinds against my cock, teasing me with her slick, so I grip her hips, lift her, and bring her wet heat down on me.

She moans in my mouth, and we find a deep rhythm, rocking together. I can feel the faintest stirring in our mate bond, but nowhere near the level it used to be. I guess I have to be happy with anything at all.

I bring my focus back to her body, sliding against mine, her breasts bouncing as I buck. Those are almost my favorite part. I grab the right one and am about to suck on the left, but then I see Neo's mark, staring at me.

Damn it.

I lift her and drop her down on the bed instead, hovering above her so I can get a different angle. But my mate isn't stupid.

"Aeon." She runs her nails through my hair.

I grunt and bite at her neck, refusing to answer.

"Hey, do you…do you need me to hurt you?"

My eyes pop open, all my breath leaving against her skin. Even just being asked that by her has me hard as a rock again.

I kiss her neck and pull back, wincing. "So, seeing that… didn't bother you?"

"No." Her eyes widen as she shakes her head. "It was hot, watching you really enjoy yourself. That whole thing was almost hotter than the—"

She tucks her lips under her teeth.

"The what?"

"Mm mm."

"ReeRee!" I grin. "You just offered to hurt me for sex, but you won't tell me what you think is hot?"

She rolls her eyes toward the wall and pops her lips free. "The thing in the woods."

My eyes bug. "With the—"

"Yeah.

"When we were all—"

"Yesss," she hisses with a smile. "Anyway." Her hips roll, drawing my attention back. "Just tell me what to do or give me some hints. It'll be fun. We have nothing but time."

"How about this idea?" I shake out my muscles, calling up my beast as I growl, "We'll take turns."

5

JAKOBE

Man, this is the best. It's a nice night. Lots of stars. Got my bag of junk Dad couldn't let me leave without slung over my shoulder, just grinning at the moonbeams. I never have to see pity in anyone's eyes again. No more pointless jobs, no more fights, get to use my skill, live in my own place, maybe even find someone to be with. Hard to do in a pack full of people who only remember how you lost because you were dumb. Hate to say it, but I'm kinda glad Cyan's people went missing, or Dad might have never let me go. Love the guy, but, yeah, this is gonna be awesome.

Cyan keeps shaking his head, trying not to smile, but I say, if you're happy, no need to hide it.

"Are you on something?" He barks out, shaking his muscles.

"Nope. Glad I'm out of there. Hey, did you get that scar from your challenge? Guess you saw my dad's face, but I only did, like, half of those. That's alright, though, man. 'Cause that means I'm all yours. Yo, the pack's I mean. Ay, though, I'm not saying anything's off the table. I'm just happy to be here. Not here, but you know."

Cyan grabs his jaw and glances up, laughing. That's a real nice sound. Dad hasn't laughed in a long time. I think I make him sad. So, hey, that means this is an even better deal for both of us.

"What's your partner situation anyhow? You need anything, I'm your guy."

"I'm good on partners." Cyan's expression sours in a heartbeat. "Or will be, once we find them."

40

"I hear ya. I'm ready whenever. I napped earlier, so I could Trace all night. Up to you, Mister Alpha."

He snorts. "We're going home. Sleeping. Searching again in the morning. Now, shift so we can cover ground."

"You got it, man."

Cyan is cool as hell. Can't wait to meet everyone else.

"So, hey, you didn't say," I grunt, pulling off my shirt and shorts and stuffing them in my bag, "who we're looking for."

Cyan's gaze snags on my body for half a second before he scowls and glances away.

I pat my abs and grin. "Right? Moving rocks, man. Check these out." I twist my leg and show him my calf. "Nothing but muscle."

He stares at me, this funny half-smirk, half-snarl on his face. "I think she'll like you."

"Hey, alright, that sounds good. I bet I'll like whoever it is, too. You got a Nikta or something?"

"No, Jak. Actually, what do you wanna be called? Jak? Kobe?"

"Man, you call me whatever makes you happy."

"Fuck's sake." He squeezes his eyes with his fingers and sighs. "We're looking for my Beta and my Aruna."

"Oh, alright. Must be hard without a Beta. But you're holding it down! My buddy Corbet was hoping to be one of those. He started his Pack Hunt about a month ago, so, you know, I haven't seen him since, but I'm hoping he found a good one. You ever meet back up with any of your friends who left on Pack Hunt?"

Cyan squints at me. "How old are you?"

"Twenty-nine yesterday." I flex.

"Are…you…" His shoulders tense. "You were still a damn pup two days ago!"

"Hey, man, was. Not anymore. Besides, you know we get ready before then. You can't tell me you weren't fooling around by, what, twenty?"

His ears tint.

41

"Yeah," I laugh. "My man. I knew it. Bet you had 'em lined up."

"Can't believe you're so fucking young," he grumbles. "Can't believe I didn't fucking ask."

"Age is just a number." I grin. "I promise, I know what I'm doing."

He shakes his head again and shifts, but not before I see his smile.

"Woah," I breathe, taking a step back. "Dude…you look awesome!"

Cy's beast is solid black like the night, but his eyes are glowing gold. Totally scary looking. He's big, too, not quite as big as my dad, but bigger than I expected, which is great because that means I was right, he's gonna be the best Alpha.

He huffs a huge sigh and growls, "Shift."

I haven't mastered talking in my beast form yet, I've only had control over my shift for a few years. But I'm working on it. I'll get there. Not worried at all. Especially with a great Alpha like Cyan to learn from.

"Got it, Mister Alpha. Check this out. I'm almost as fast as you."

I call up my beast in record time and snag my bag off the ground, hooking it around my claws. Cyan is studying me again. Oh, man. I forgot he hadn't seen my beast yet. It's the first time I've felt self-conscious since we met, but that's not new. I know I'm different. Plus, my challenge scars are way more visible in shifted form, since they're on my thighs and we don't have as much fur there. But it's okay, I know Cyan won't say anything mean.

"You…are…red." He chuffs out.

See? I knew it, man. The best. Since I can't reply, I nod once, shrug, and give him a clawed thumbs-up.

I've never heard anyone laugh in their beast. Sounds like he's coughing, wheezing, and barking at the same time. It's a pretty funny sound.

He takes off through the trees, and I catch up quickly, staying as close to beside him as I can. We run for a long time, but it's okay, because the farther we get from my old pack, the lighter I feel.

The landscape changes a bit once we pass Kasimir Falls. Best fishing spot there is. The dumb things practically jump into your claws, you don't even need any hunting skills.

I wish I had his people's energy signatures, I could be tracing while we run. There's a bunch of different ones in the air, but I don't know what to focus on.

We keep going for another hour or so until we reach a break in the trees, and he slows to a walk. I'm glad because my legs are burning. That's more running than I've done ever. But I'd have kept going until I dropped, if that's what he said to do.

I guess this is my new home. I like it. There's a roaring fire surrounded by stumps, a guy with black hair hovering over a big pot, a huge guy with long white hair heading toward the far side of the village, and five log cabins spaced out around the area. I can hear the river, too. That's great, I love swimming.

Cyan sends out an Alpha wave as he shifts back to man form, and both the guys whip their heads around. I let the energy sift through me, loving how it feels, memorizing it. The more I can teach my body to pick up, the farther away I'll be able to trace him, just in case it ever comes to that. Not one to brag, but I'm a seriously awesome Tracer.

I drop my beast, too, grabbing my shorts and tugging them on as quick as I can. I don't have a problem with being naked, but it's better to keep my dick under as much control as I can. It tends to get in the way.

After I'm sorted, bag on my shoulder again, I wave over my head with a grin and follow behind Cyan.

"Hey, do you guys have bathrooms inside your cabins? We had those, but my friend, Corbet, he visited some pack way up north. You know they keep their bathrooms outside?"

I see that small, almost annoyed smile on his face again,

which makes me grin wider. I'm glad he likes me. If I can make him at least a little happier than he was, maybe perk all these guys up, then I'll really be a useful dude here.

KOREY

I know Neo is hurting, missing Reanne, but he shouldn't have been so short with Laz.

I carry my mate inside, kick the door closed, and curl up on the bed, spooning him. I know it hasn't been long, but I still can't believe how lucky I am that this adorable guy likes me.

Licking my mark, I hold his tiny body close. Sucks that Cy's not here, he could Alpha wave him and calm him down. I can't help but wonder if this is the sort of trauma my daughter will go through, after we rescue her. Suzette was always a spitfire, but apparently where Mishka is keeping them…isn't the best of conditions.

"I-I'm sorry, I'm fine, Sir, it wasn't, he's nice, I know he wouldn't," he trails off, and even though I hear his words, he's trembling from head to toe. He also called me Sir again, and I'll be damned if that doesn't make me hard as steel every time.

"Shh, I've got you, little pup. Nobody's hurting you ever again."

He whimpers and nods, resting his head on my bicep. I'm not sure he believes me, but I'll prove it.

I stroke his arms, his chest, his stomach, his hips, his thighs, everywhere I can touch. Except his cock. That I keep a watch on, because it grows as his trembling eases up, and I could play with that thing all day. Just not right now. Not when he's in a dark place.

He pushes his back against my stomach, arching his head a bit more, begging me to bite down. I'm not sure he's doing it on purpose, because his eyes are closed, brows furrowed, but I sure love seeing it.

Love my submissive little mate.

"Tell me what you need, pup," I murmur against his neck, brushing my beard along his skin. "Tell me how to make it better."

His cock bounces, a short sigh escaping his soft lips.

"That's, uh, that's good."

"Yeah?" I grin, dragging my teeth across my mark. He shivers and nods, wrapping his arm around my head.

But there's still something sad in his energy. I have an idea.

"You know how lucky I am to have someone as handsome as you?" I bite around the mark, teasing him, drawing circles around his nipple with the pad of my finger.

His skin flushes, heating under my touch. "N-no."

"The luckiest." I nuzzle his ear as he groans, cheeks a vibrant pink. "And I love your perfect little body."

I run my index finger along the bridge of his nose, over his parted lips, down his throat and down the center of his torso, stopping right above the base of his cock. There, I trace more small circles, barely touching.

"Bloody hell," he whines in a near-whisper and tangles his fingers in my hair. He bucks his hips, hoping I'll give him more, but I slide back up to his stomach and continue the circles there.

"Mmm, and that dirty mouth of yours. Your sweet tongue."

I get my reward when he grips my hair harder and twists his head back so that our lips meet. The slight change in position is enough to free my pinned cock, which springs down, and now rests under the curve of his ass, between his cheeks, the tip grazing his shaft. I lift his thigh a little and roll my hips forward, gliding my cock along his.

Each of his breaths is a pant, his exploration of my mouth more urgent until I pull back. He cracks his eyelids slowly, a desperate tilt to his cute, thin eyebrows.

"Please," he whispers.

"Please what?" I grin and nip his bottom lip. "Please keep telling you how amazing you are? Please keep sliding my cock like this? Okay, you've got it."

I'm really loving this, way more than I thought I would. Turning him into a panting, twitchy wreck that I'm the cure for is doing it for me on a whole other level.

He can't decide if he wants to nod, shake his head, moan, or touch me, so he does all of it at once, his hand abandoning my hair in favor of digging at my hip as we rock together.

"You smell so good." I kiss a path down his neck and lap at the mark. Each flick makes his hips snap, his tip glistening.

Fuck, I really want that in my mouth.

"Little pup, you know what I'm going to do now?"

He shakes his head, chest heaving, skin scalding hot.

"I'm going to suck that beautiful cock of yours."

The sound he makes is so needy, so desperate, I get chills. He scrambles to get out of my arms and is on his knees by my head in no time, gasping, cock weeping for attention.

Since my idea paid off so well, no reason to stop now.

"See? Look at that." I cup his balls and kiss the underside of his head. "It's so perfect." I lap along the length. "It tastes so good."

"Fuck, I can't—" he shakes his head, smiling even though he looks like he's in pain. *"I can't take it."*

"Aw, sure you can." I run my tongue along his tip, dipping in to grab his pre-cum as I give him a teasingly slow stroke. "You're doing such a great job."

"Oh, that's the end of me," he whines and shivers, thrusting in my hand. His head falls back, and right as my mouth closes over his tip, he explodes, painting the back of my throat.

I swallow him down with a happy hum and keep sucking until he pulls back with a hiss. He descends on me, kissing and licking my face, my neck, my chest. I roll onto my back, letting him explore again, but he's not slow about it this time. He scoots down and kneels by my hip, taking me all the way in his mouth.

47

"Damn," I groan, clutching the back of his neck. "That feels so good, little pup."

He whimpers something around my cock and his hips twitch.

A smirk tugs my lip up even as a moan escapes. One of the best parts of being a werewolf is how many times we can go.

"Keep sucking, I'm going to move you."

His eyes pop open, but he does as I said. I grip his hips and lift, adjusting us until he's lying on my stomach, his ass perfectly situated. His hard cock throbs, mashed against my chest.

He squirms, uncertainty rolling off him, so I pet along his lower back. "You're sucking me so well, I'm just gonna play with you while you do it."

He makes a choked sound and pulls off, twisting a look back. "What? How…are you, uh, with, I don't know…"

"If I don't start getting you ready, I'll never be able to fuck you. You want that, right?"

"I do," he nods. "I-I think I do."

"Oh, you do." I grin at him and bite his round cheek. His eyes bug, rolling back when I lick his balls. He thrusts back against me, but I was ready, and my tongue slips inside.

"Oh…fuck!" He tenses at first, but I mold his cheeks, squeeze his thighs as I work my tongue, and eventually he melts, back to moaning around my cock. I only have to stop once, when he sucks hard and I shoot my first load, then we're right back at it.

I tongue him until there's a puddle between our bodies he's thrusting in, then when he picks up speed, I quickly replace my tongue with my finger.

You would think I stabbed him with the way he freezes, but then I slide it back out a little and it's like I've unlocked every bit of pleasure in the world. He loses all control, arching and rocking, sucking me like a crazed man. I reach under him and stroke him with my other hand, and we come one right after the other, panting, chuckling.

I couldn't tell you what I expected at the start of all this, or at the end, outside of another few mouthfuls of my mate, but what I got was a wonderfully sweet moment, followed by a tear-soaked make-out session, followed by one of the best cuddle-hugs I've ever had.

We'd never leave this bed if we didn't have to, but Cy's energy ripples through the cabin. I kiss Laz's forehead and he sleepily blinks up at me.

"Cyan's back."

He bolts up with a stretch. "Blimey, I thought I dreamed that."

Off the side of the bed he goes, grabbing his pants. I stand, too, and for his sake, snag my shorts. We both stop and glance at each other.

"He's got someone else with him."

Laz nods. "But, n-not—"

"Nope. Come on."

We walk out together, hand in hand, Laz lagging behind as usual. Cyan and another guy are walking toward the fire, so we head that way too.

The guy's really muscular, but not bulky, with an easy smile, and mid-length, wavy, red hair, tucked behind his ears. Almost as tall as Cyan, too.

"Oh," Laz mumbles, "mercy."

My jaw clenches. I know it's dumb to be jealous or possessive in a pack, but it's one thing to share Laz with Cyan, that's kind of required. Another thing to think he finds some other guy attractive, when I've only got eyes for him.

I tug him along faster, keeping my strides small enough he can keep up, and we're at the fire just before they get there.

Neo is chewing the inside of his lip, arms crossed. Veikko is tense, frowning. I'm quite sure I'm giving off a major scowl, but all this guy does is smile wider and wave.

We're waiting for the introduction, but Cyan stalks right up to Neo and grabs his face, kissing him deep. He pushes him back against the prep table with his hips, and Neo whimpers, clutching at his waist. Energy is zipping everywhere, which is good. Neo needed this big time, I guess Cy did too. He pulls back and says something in Neo's ear which has his eyes widen and his cheeks flushing. After another kiss, Cy steps back in line with the guy and gestures.

"Jakobe. New pack member. He's Zaid's son."

Ohh, wow. That guy from DuskFall.

Cyan points to each of us in turn.

"This is Neo."

Jakobe steps up, smile still in place, and shakes Neo's hand. "Hey, man. That looked like fun. Love the glasses. And the stew smells awesome. Can't wait to dig in."

Neo smiles and nods. "Thanks. Welcome."

"That's Veikko," Cy continues.

"Look at this guy, that's an epic scar." Jak's eyes light up, posture changing completely as steps closer and shakes his hand too. "I bet I could do pull-ups on your bicep. Dude!" He doesn't let go immediately, the two of them staring at each other, until Vik pulls back with a throat clear.

I can feel Laz's smile against my arm, and his heating skin. I'm trying not to be upset, because if anyone needs to feel good about something, feel good at all, it's my mate, but...

"This is Korey and his mate Laz."

Laz does a small wave and ducks back behind me. Good. That makes me feel better, which makes me feel worse, because he shouldn't have to hide. Get it together, Korey. If Laz decided he wanted someone else in our bed, I'd do it without complaint, so I don't know what's wrong with me.

"That's a killer beard, man." His handshake is firm, grin widening. "You're like a big ol' furry bear. I dig it. Bet your hugs are the best."

I blink, an unexpected zing dancing down my back. "Uh. Thanks."

"They-they are," Laz mumbles.

"Right on. I knew it." Jak chuckles. "And you're good back

there, man, we can wave, that's alright. I'm just happy to meet you guys."

I almost growl that waving is as close as he'll get.

Cyan's smiling as he wipes a hand down his face. "Jakobe's a Tracer."

"Best one I know," Jak says with a smirking wink.

Neo shoots a wide-eyed look at Veikko, who returns it. Hmm. What's that about?

"First thing in the morning, he and I are hitting the ground."

"Yeah, so, I just need to get a feel for their energy from you guys, and you know, what they look like would be helpful. Probably have them found before lunch."

Cy pats Jak's shoulder, but there's still a glaring war happening between Neo and Vik.

"Vik said they ran south. That's why I was near your territory."

"About…that." Vik rumbles, finally glancing away from Neo.

Cyan's attention snaps to Vik, brow lowering.

"I gave Aeon the location of my cabin. Which…is north-east."

Jakobe laughs. "Hey, that's great, man! That'll make tracing them even easier."

Jak's not pack yet, and neither is Laz, so they aren't getting the full brunt of the angry energy Cy's pumping into the link.

"We'll deal with the lying to me later. I can't believe you gave Aeon," he growls, "directions."

Veikko's face contorts in confusion. "Yes?"

Neo's eyes slowly bug. "Oh, no. I forgot."

"What?" Vik passes a glance between the two of them. I have a sinking feeling in my gut.

"Aeon," Cy growls louder, rumbling deep, "has no fucking sense of direction at all!"

Neo grips his throat and drops down to a stump. "They could be anywhere…lost. Scared. Hurt."

It's the first time I've seen Jak without a smile, but he's still got a gentle expression. "Hey, no worries at all, guys. I've got this. Your man Jak's on the job. I'll find them. Like I told Mister Alpha, here, I'm amped and ready to go. I can start now. Just show me where to set my stuff down, and I'll head on out."

"No." Cy takes a long, deep breath and reins in his energy. "I need to rest, and I'm not sending you out alone."

"Alright, sounds good, man. Hey, which one of these cabins is mine? And I'm starving, you mind if I grab some of that stew?"

Neo shakes his head, but still hasn't moved. Veikko points to Agnar's old place, and Jak pats his upper arm as he passes by, his tone dipping. "Thanks, big guy, I'll be right back. Save me some, now."

He trots off, and silence descends. Laz grips my hand tighter. Cyan's chest keeps catching, fists clenching, before he storms off to his cabin, Neo's sad eyes watching him go. Veikko settles himself on a stump and scrubs his cheek, avoiding anyone's gaze.

And there's me. Still stressing about Laz wanting someone else, and now worried something bad might happen to Reanne.

I hope like hell they're alright.

REANNE

I watch in mildly scared fascination as Aeon's body shifts around me. I haven't seen them do it slow before. So far, it's been almost instant, but he's clearly putting on a show for me. He grows in height, in weight, in width. Coarse brown fur sprouting, his face morphing back into that scary muzzle, loaded with long teeth, and bunched, angry ridges between his dark eyes. Claws sprout out of his elongating fingers and toes as his hands, arms, legs, and feet lengthen. He adjusts so he doesn't slice into the mattress as a low, rattling growl fills the room, coaxing my ingrained prey response to life, filling my body with adrenaline and the need to run. There's nothing soft, or curved, or friendly about their wereforms. They are every bit monster.

It helps knowing who's inside the monster, keeps me from being utterly terrified. But he could kill me with one swipe, absolutely no doubt. Veikko was scarier, by far. Bigger teeth, bigger hands, angrier expression. I wonder idly what Cyan looks like fully shifted, but Aeon snaps his teeth, drawing my brain back to the present.

I rake my nails down his stomach, through his fur, over his muscles, around the base of his massive cock, then further, teasing his furry balls. He growls louder, thrusting again, and I whine, arching. This is so perfect.

His cock grows more, and it feels so good, stretching me, filling me. I moan, my eyes fluttering closed as I grab handfuls of his spiky scruff.

It should be wrong and it's definitely not normal, but oh my God, I love it. I think he likes it, too. He seems way more into it now, his wide, hot tongue making a slow path up my neck, sending curls of lust through me. He snarls in my ear, grazing it with his teeth and I squeal as chills shoot down my body.

He adjusts, covering my arms with his huge hands, dwarfing them. I'm pinned in place by his size, his grip. It's so unbelievably hot. He runs his tongue along my breasts, teasing my nipples as he thrusts again, hitting every pleasure spot, and it's not long before I come with a long, desperate, relieved moan. He chuffs a low, pleased sound, and adjusts his angle slightly, tongue traveling my neck, lapping my ear, thrusts never stopping, and I crash into another orgasm that leaves me satisfied all the way to my soul.

Eventually, I force open my eyes, only to find Kasimir's enormous, gnarled, damaged body, hovering above Aeon. He's easily four times his size, and from this position, it's like he's filling the whole room. I stop breathing, but Aeon doesn't notice anything, and keeps right on fucking me.

Kasimir braces his hands on either side of my head, nearly taking up both sides of the mattress. I feel the weight of him, the weight of his energy, the weight of his piercing gaze, even though the bed doesn't move. He's somehow avoiding any contact with Aeon, who is urging my body closer and closer to orgasm while Kasimir watches. I'm whimpering, now, moaning, grabbing at Aeon, eyes locked on the figure looming over us.

I don't understand how Aeon hasn't noticed, how they aren't touching. Either he's too high up, or…he really is a ghost.

I've been afraid a lot in my life. I really have. And until all this stuff started, I hadn't considered it an aphrodisiac. But the closer Kasimir leans, the more scared I get that he's going to do something, and the more turned on I become. I can't look away, even though I want to, even though it feels like I'm staring into some abyss, some danger I have no business seeing.

And Aeon is pounding me through it all, grunting, losing himself in it. I can feel him again, in our bond, in his mark. There's no way I'm going to stop him, to bring him out of this moment he obviously needs. I don't want to anyway, it feels too good.

That choice is taken away when Kasimir sends his Alpha wave through the room again, sizzling me from the inside out. I gasp breath after breath, pleasure skittering through my bones, as Aeon stalls, whips his head level and stares at me.

"He's...here?" He growls, hackles raising along the back of his neck.

I nod and scream as I arch back, my torso lifting off the mattress with the force of my orgasm.

Kasimir chuckles, or I guess what passes for that from a monster, and it fills the room in echo again.

"Beta," he rumbles, the sound cracking against the walls, rattling the furniture. "You...are deemed...worthy."

"Wh-what?" I shout, clutching at Aeon harder. More energy swirls in the room, and Aeon's eyes roll back. He starts thrusting again, harder, faster. Kasimir's energy licks along my skin, burrowing inside, touching every inch of me. I soar again, like I'm not on this planet anymore, like I'm just ecstasy from one end to the other.

Kasimir's massive head reaches Aeon's neck, and he takes the whole of it in his mouth, teeth piercing on both sides, blood dribbling out, staining his fur.

Aeon roars, shuddering, violent spasms rocking his muscles as he pounds. He unloads in me, blast after blast, filling me up. I scream again, the orgasm blanking my mind, leaving only white and static and pleasure.

Sound filters back in with a high-pitched whine as my chest heaves. Aeon is still pounding me, but he's shifting back to human, eyes closed, neck tilted to the side at an odd angle.

Kasimir unlatches once Aeon's shift is complete. A huge black tongue unfurls from between his jaws and traces along the closest set of bleeding puncture wounds.

A shockwave of power hits the room, and Aeon's eyes fly open. Kasimir repeats the same motion, healing the second set of wounds, blasting energy, but this time Aeon focuses on me. His pupils are huge, but he gives me his cute smirk, and my heart nearly bursts. He dives at my shoulder, hitches my legs higher, and somehow finds a new speed, railing me as he bites into our mark.

Colors run together, everything turning watery as I clutch the back of his head. Our mate bond is completely healed. Better than that, it's stronger than before. I lock eyes with Kasimir again, so grateful I can't put it into words. He lifts one of his massive hands and curls his claws in again, leaving just the one, which he touches to Aeon's upper back.

I'm not sure why I think this, or what possesses me to do it, but I grab his claw. It's ice cold, and just as solid as I am. The side of his jowl pulls back, and with my hand in tow, he rakes the claw down, digging into Aeon's back, splitting the skin open. It's shocking to see so much blood, to have it spill over, but the sheer volume of Aeon's desperate moan, the way he curls his hips, panting against my shoulder, lets me know it's exactly what he was hoping for.

I also know I could never hurt him this much on my own. Anything I could have muddled my way through would be nothing compared to being sliced open. Did Kasimir know that somehow?

The path continues down the rest of his back, until Aeon is shouting through another orgasm, sending waves of his energy through my mark, and bringing me to another orgasm.

He collapses on top of me, unlatching as he separates himself from Kasimir's claw. He lets out small groans as he lavishes my mark, each swipe giving me the familiar zings to my heart I'd forgotten.

I'm still holding Kasimir's claw, staring into his swirling umber eyes, and I could do it forever. He leans a little closer, runs a single lap along Aeon's wound, sealing it, and pulls away.

I grip harder, emotions welling. I don't want him to leave. He saved our mate bond, he gave Aeon what he needed. Yes, he's terrifying to look at, but the last time he took his energy away, I felt like I was being ripped in half, and I don't want to feel that ever again. I'm also weirdly jealous that he licked Aeon and not me.

"Our...bond," he reverberates through the room again, still not moving his jaws, "will be...forever."

The same claw that did so much damage, spilled so much blood, delicately traces my neck again, my hand still attached. He runs it down my cheek, smearing a tear into my skin.

"Mate."

The last word booms like a clap of thunder, shaking the house itself. My hand closes around nothing, and he's gone like the ghost he must be, only this time, I'm not ripped in half, I'm completely consumed with loneliness. It's a deep ache in my gut and a stabbing pain in my heart. I'm trying not to cry, because it doesn't make any sense, but it's also the most real thing I've ever felt.

Aeon kisses my tear streaks and my mouth over and over, holding me close, telling me he loves me. It helps, but only a little.

Because I can feel it now. The doorway inside me is cracked open, spilling in the faintest glow of light. The time to choose, to either take this power or die, is coming.

Soon.

ΠΕΟ

Cy's door slams shut, and I don't know what to do. Normally, Aeon would Beta wave him, but, since this is mostly about him to begin with…

Korey and Laz leave, too. Laz mumbles something and waves, Korey looks like his jaw is going to break from clenching. There's too much stress going on. We need Aeon.

Cy's kiss earlier was wonderful, and helped, otherwise I'd be an absolute wreck still, but it was for him, not me. Vik was right, I desperately need to be with him, need him to hold me. He's always been so good on picking up when I do, but he's everywhere at the moment, heart-broken, worried, wooing two new pack members at once. I know that, in my brain, but it still hurts that he hasn't noticed.

Veikko grunts softly, drawing my attention. When our eyes meet, he cants his head toward Cy's cabin.

"Yeah," I sigh. "But that leaves you out here to deal with Jak alone."

He shrugs.

"Are you sure you can handle that much one sided, happy conversation?" I smirk at him, and he grins, a wide one. I'm taken aback. He doesn't do that, really.

"He reminds me of an old friend."

"Huh. Okay."

I'm stalling again. I know it. Veikko knows it. That stupid whippoorwill across the river knows it. With a resigned sigh, I push to my feet, grab a bowl of stew, and make my way to Cy's cabin. I don't even make it over the threshold when his voice sounds.

"Not in the mood, Neo." His fingers mash against his temples, rubbing in slow circles.

It's like a slap in the face, so shocking I can't move from my spot in the doorway.

"…You're always in the mood."

He exhales and stares at the floor, crossing his arms. I unroot my feet, set the bowl on the table, and sit slowly beside him on the bed as cold truth settles over me.

"You just don't want to be with me."

He says nothing, but his jumping jaw muscle tells me everything.

"You want Aeon."

He doesn't deny it, scrubbing his face with a groan while I die inside.

"I don't think I can be gentle right now. And hurting you is the last fucking thing I want."

Okay. I can deal with that. Maybe.

"Then…" I rest my palm on his thigh. "You could lay back and let me…take over." One of his brows lifts before the other one, and he simply stares at me. Well, that I can't deal with. Offering the idea was bad enough, but him not answering is worse. "I…know I'm not him. I can't give you the same things, or take the same things"

"Neo—"

"And I know I don't really have that much more to offer, but I can at least take some of the pain away. Give you a release. It sort of worked out with the group thing earlier. If you're worried you'll hurt me, just…lay here."

There's uncertainty, apprehension in his eyes. It makes my stomach hurt again. I know I'll never measure up to Aeon and this is just proving it. Finally, he shakes his head, gripping the back of his neck as he levels a glare at the wall.

"I'll deal with it."

I can hardly breathe. He'd rather be in pain than have sex with me right now. I take my hand back and tuck it under my leg. We sit in silence for a few minutes, both staring at the wall, and right when I'm about to get up, go throw some poor critter on the chopping block and make a paste out of it, he speaks.

"This is fucking hard, Neo."

I glance at him, his tense muscles, the worried lines on his face. "I know," I murmur.

"And I don't have anyone to talk to about it."

Doesn't have... I try to swallow the hurt, because it won't help anything, but I still can't stop my tears from forming. Thankfully, he's too distracted to notice.

"Fucking Agnar. We talked all the time. He's gone now, apparently just waiting to kill me. I used to talk to Mishka, too, but he turned out to be a murder-happy psycho."

There's an almost hopeless pause, and I can't help feeling bad for him. He's been through a lot in a short, short time. We all have, though.

"Did you talk to Aeon?" I mumble it because I'm not sure I want to know.

"Rarely. But now he's fucking gone, too."

Wonderful. Everyone but me it sounds like. That's great.

"And Reanne."

I nod. That one, I'm not upset about. Airing all my feelings to her while Cy was unconscious was nice. It felt good to be heard. And she didn't judge me for them, either. In fact, she was supportive. She's really an amazing female, and I'm lucky to have her as a mate.

He rubs his chest, a pained smile. "Little thought siphoning beauty."

Oh, right. Yeah, I'm not sure I like that part. I keep watching, waiting for him to elaborate, but he doesn't. Okay, Neo, be brave. "You...could talk to me."

He snorts, and I almost leave.

"You don't wanna hear all these shit-ass thoughts."

He couldn't be more wrong. The idea of sharing with him makes me happy.

"What if I do?"

He stares at me a moment and shakes his head, expression grim. "Doesn't matter. I don't want you—"

And there it is. The truth. He doesn't want me.

"Fine," I cut him off, any hope of happiness gone in an instant, replaced with anger and heartache. "I get it. That's great." I stand, adjusting my glasses. "You know, I'm sorry I don't make you as happy as…as Aeon does. I can't read your mind, like Reanne. I can't give you long-winded advice like Agnar did. I can't carve you presents like Veikko, I can't hunt for you like Korey, I can't blast you with Beta waves like Laz, but damn it, I'm in here now. Me. I'm trying to make you feel better, they aren't. But it's fine. You don't want to talk to me, you don't want to be with me, you don't have to."

I turn to leave but he grabs my wrist, holding me in place. It's uncomfortably tight, still, I don't squirm away.

"That's not what I fucking said," he growls, sending a shiver down my back.

His fingers loosen and splay, sliding up the inside of my wrist, the inside of my forearm, ramping me up, making me hard, but I know it's for no reason. He's not in the mood for me. This is just to show he has that kind of sway over me, to make himself feel better, I guess.

"I don't want you…"

My gut twists, heart dropping to my feet. He doesn't have to say it again, I heard it damn well enough the first time. I'd want Aeon more if I had a choice, too, between the two of us.

"…to see me weak."

Oh. I blink, sniffling, processing, but still don't turn back around. "You're gentle with me all the time."

"That's different. That's a fucking master lesson in control. Shoving all this aggression and pain and power to the side so I can give you what you need? That takes strength. Talking about feelings?" He scoffs.

Boy, if I wasn't offended and hurt before. I talk about my feelings a lot. How weak does he think I am?

"And you didn't care if Agnar or Mishka saw you that way, because you liked them more," I bite out.

"I didn't give a shit what they thought because I don't like them a quarter as much." He stands, pressing his hard body against my trembling one, sliding his hand farther up my arm as his hot breath hits the back of my neck. "I care what you think, because...I love you."

I want to cry, to shout at him, tell him he sucks at showing it, tell him I love him too, even though he knows, and tell him love doesn't have to mean only sex. But I can't. He's pouring Alpha energy all over me, slow and sticky, like tree sap, and I can't do anything but stand here and revel in it.

He runs his teeth down the back of my neck, to the left of the bones. That side is his favorite, I don't know why, unless it's because it's closer to the heart. He nicks the skin and laps in almost the same motion, healing now, too, and damn I needed it. My heart swells, skin heating. We're both hard as stone, the length of him pressed against me.

I'm hopeful, desperate, but he stops. He staggers back a step and there's a weird hiccup in his energy. A void.

I spin and find him clutching his chest with one hand, his stomach with the other, face contorted in confusion and pain.

"What the..." he mutters and drops to the bed.

I rush over and grip his arms. "Are you okay?"

"No." He stares at his hands. "I don't know...I felt..."

He's pale, wide-eyed, and scaring me to death. "What?"

"Doesn't make any fucking sense," he mutters. "I felt Aeon..."

I immediately assume the worst and launch into a denial spiral. Nope. No, he's not dead. He's fine. Perfectly fine. Nothing is wrong. No. Because if he's not fine, then I can't accidentally on purpose kiss him again and that's happening, so he's fine.

Oh. Well. I suppose I know where I really stand on the side of this 'no feelings for Aeon' thing now.

"It's like I just bonded him all over again. I don't...fuck," Cyan grunts, scrubs his face, and grabs me around the waist, pulling me to the bed with him.

After wiggling us around, he spoons me, one leg heavy over my hip, pinning me down, his arm cinched around mine, mouth on my neck.

"Stay with me tonight," he whispers against my skin, small, fragile.

My eyes well up and I nod, pushing back against him as he pulls me in tighter, like he's afraid I'll vanish.

"I could never think you're weak," I murmur. "No matter what. And you'll find them."

He doesn't respond with words, he simply hugs me even tighter with his whole body, teeth bearing down on my skin in glorious possession. There's no more cutting, or healing, or energy, or ranks, or bonds.

It's just him and me, in a bittersweet, incomplete pile.

VEIKKO

B eing distanced from my mate is emotionally taxing. Cyan's fractured energy is distracting. The moon's cycle wears on, and time runs thin. I'm disappointed in myself for failing to remember such a glaring fact about Aeon, potentially causing them injury or worse. Are my memories so damaged? I have been making them for a long time. Perhaps too long.

Twice now, Cyan leaves and returns with a new pack member, someone uniquely suited to carrying out his true purpose, one I still don't think he's even aware of. Twice. And a Tracer... I've only met a handful in all my years. They aren't as rare as Born Betas, but it's not a skill one can be taught, it's a blood gift.

Were I still with The Sentinels, I would be crying apocalypse, heralding the end of times, with these instances being proof of how she's twisting things in her favor, manipulating everything so she can rule eternal.

Proof of the prophecy coming true.

I force the bitter ball down. It's still fresh, hard to undo centuries of rhetoric, of vows, of certainty. Even if I'm the one who put it all there to begin with.

It's so different to view these occurrences from the other side of the battle. From the side that wants Reanne to attain her true power, to mate with the High Alpha. They become proof of fate, of destinies intertwined. It's certainly a more hopeful viewpoint.

"Man, that cabin is awesome. Way bigger than where I was before." Jakobe slaps my shoulder and grabs a bowl, helping himself to the stew. "Just you and me, huh, big guy. All good. I bet you can hold down a conversation, am I right?" He winks one of his green eyes over his shoulder at me, friendly smile dimpling his cheek, and refocuses on the stew. "Guy your size, lookin' like you do, cool scar, I bet you have tons of stories."

I take an easy breath. Jakobe's chatter quiets my mind, keeps me in the present. Just like Eoghan and Agnar used to. I haven't thought of him in more than 600 years before tonight. They're so similar, I thought his ghost had come for me.

After Jakobe fills his bowl to the brim, he strolls over and holds it out. I don't take it, but he's not deterred.

"Aw, come on, now. You can't let me eat alone on my first night here. That's bad luck. Besides, you gotta be hungry. Takes a lot of food to grow muscles that big." He winks again and I blink at him but take the bowl with a grumble. Our fingers brush and there's a slight static pop, but he laughs and pats my shoulder again. "My man, I knew you wouldn't let me down."

He grabs another bowl, fills it only halfway, and kicks one of the stumps until it's right next to me. "Really nice night, isn't it? Goddess doesn't make mistakes, for sure. That moon's a beauty." He sits with a loud exhale and bumps into my side. "Truth out, I was hoping to get some alone time with you."

I let out a short hum and return the smile he tosses my way. I may have been hoping for that as well.

"So," he shoves a bite in his mouth and talks around it, staring into the fire. "About them stories. How's an Alpha with this much power come to be a member in someone else's pack?"

I choke on my bite and stare at him.

"Tracer." He clicks his tongue and points his spoon at the fire. "Energy's my bag, yo. Hey, though, I'm not judging," he continues after swallowing. "Cyan's cool as hell. But, dude." He eyes me finally, the firelight reflecting. "You're like a hundred times stronger than him. Easy. How are you keeping it all inside like that? You should be wooing pack members for miles."

I know my own strength, just as I know Cyan will pass me

soon. Whereas I might have been hesitant to answer the others, Jakobe is terribly easy to be around.

"Years of practice."

"You will talk to me! Alright!" He shoves my arm, laughing, and I smile. "So, yeah, I bet that was hard, man. Did your dad teach you? Or did you learn how to be awesome all on your own? My dad taught me a bunch of stuff, but nothing like that."

As they've done endlessly before, thoughts of my father lead me down a dark path. "This skill was born of necessity," I growl. "My father taught me many things, however. How to kill. How dangerous power can be, in the wrong hands. How power attracts those hungry for it. Most of all, the consequences of reaching for the moon, while neglecting those still grounded."

"Woah. That's heavy…but, hey, at least that all led you here, now, right? You got to meet me." He flexes, prompting my smile, pulling me back from the past.

"True." I set my bowl down and cross my arms, his eyes on me the whole time. "Jakobe…you must keep this a secret. From the others. From Cyan."

"No worries. I might talk a lot, but I can guarantee I know how to keep a secret better than the people I tell it to."

My laugh surprises me, and I clear my throat to mask it. Jakobe looks incredibly pleased with himself.

"Nah, I got you, big guy. You're a whole lot of Alpha, though, I gotta say." He shivers. "It's making me antsy." He clacks his spoon against his bottom lip, grinning slowly. "Making me wanna jump ya."

I'm not sure what my expression is, but he laughs and it's a happy, warm, rough sound. Infectious. I can't help but chuckle.

"It's all good, man. But, so you know, and in case anyone asks, your man Jak's down for whatever, whenever. I don't know where you sit on the whole thing, but I've got no preferences and I didn't leave anyone behind. I make a great third, fourth, fifth. Watching's fun, too." He takes another bite and stares into the fire, still smiling, letting the invitation float in the air.

I don't know what to do with it. While it's true Reanne won't always be in my bed, I'm not prone to urges I can't control. It's not an altogether off-putting idea, though. Now that Fen's darkness can never touch me again, it could be reasoned that a safe and sane pairing could further help. Jakobe's also attractive, but no decisions of any kind will be made tonight.

"Mmm! This stew is amazing. I'd have never thought to put carrots in it." He sets the empty bowl down on the ground and stretches. "Did someone have my cabin before? Or was it just waiting for me?"

I sigh, the memory weighing heavy on my heart. "Agnar used to live there. He…betrayed us. Left."

"Damn. Well, his loss, everyone else's gain, right? Oh, hey. That other energy with yours, is that one of the people we're looking for?"

"Yes. My mate. Reanne."

"That a guy? Girl?"

"A woman. Human. Or…was."

His brows raise and he faces me, his knees hitting my thigh. "Now *that* sounds like a story. I knew you had some!" He rubs his palms together. "I'm all ears, big guy."

What to reveal? I suppose the shortest answer is always best.

"She is an Aruna."

He nods, expression still the same. "Alright, I've heard the word before, yeah, but between the two of us, I don't really know what it is. I mean, I have an idea, I think, but I don't, know-know. Y'know?"

I lower my brow in confusion. A werewolf old enough to leave their home pack should know all of this.

Jak exhales, face falling a little. "I…challenged way too early. First time I shifted to full on wereform, boom." He chuckles, but it's without humor. "Didn't even have all my tail fur, so I don't know how I thought I was going to win. Anyway, after losing, I didn't care much about anything else. I'd never have my own pack, so none of that stuff mattered. Nothing did, really. I'm not up on all the little details. But it's all good, because you guys know lots, and I'll learn everything I need to, right here."

His usual happy, youthful spirit returns, that genuine, dimpled smile, and I envy him. I was never so positive, even in my pup days. Not that I remember many of them, now. His explanation makes sense, however sad it may be. It also tells me his former pack never found theirs, or I feel certain he'd know at least that.

"An Aruna is a seated Alpha's true mate."

Jakobe nods, watching me hungrily. I am afraid to admit that I enjoy his attention, that it is nice to be listened to. He seems content, so I continue.

"They are rare and difficult to find, a safe-guard said to be put in place by the goddess to keep our numbers in check."

"Rare like a green moon? Or rare like finding a guy you're interested in the second you walk into a new camp?"

He winks and sets his chin on his palm, grinning. My pulse races, fear tangling with odd excitement, causing me to lose my mental footing as if I am some hormone addled youth.

"Uh...green...moon." I clear my throat. "Aruna's are able to sate the beast and rear pups without dying."

Jakobe's eyes widen to an almost comical size, jaw falling open as he straightens.

"Seriously? And it's a girl? Never mind, yeah, has to be a— are you serious? So, he gets to...and she gets to carry..." He trails off, and even in the dark, even with the yellow-orange tint from the fire, I can see the bright flush hit his face.

He coughs and adjusts himself, shaking his head. "Man, oh man. Buddy, I've got to tell you. There's nothing hotter than a pregnant Nikta. All swollen and even needier. Whew. That's my...mmm. Yeah, so, we're definitely going to find her. I mean, we were before, because I'm awesome, but, you know."

I grunt because he is correct, they're stunning. Even though I haven't seen one in many, many years, it's something your body never forgets. And I have no doubt Reanne will be just as magnificent. In fact, I need to stop imagining it.

"And you're mated to her." He shakes his head again, jaw cocked, tongue toying with the corner of his mouth.

"Three of us are, so far. To assist in the Alpha mate cycle. Your father never mated?"

"Nah. But he wasn't waiting for his Aruna thing. He loved my mom, but Niktas die, that's what they do. He couldn't bring himself to mate with anyone, didn't want to feel that loss again, I guess. I mean, you know the Alpha urges and all, so he's got partners, like Cyan does. Like all Alphas, probably. 'Cept you." He cuts his gaze to me and winks. "Yet."

I smirk, and stretch my legs out, crossing my ankles. "I lead no pack, Jakobe. No need for them."

"Hey, man. Needs and wants are two different birds. Tell you something else, I've got a lot of both going on. You're not lacking for one or other right now, either." He grins, gesturing to my lap with his chin. "Unless that's where you keep your collection of trees."

I laugh and quickly change my position. "You were the one who brought up pregnant Niktas."

"Mmm. Yeah, I did. Not sorry about it either. But I don't think that's all you're worked up over. Tell you what, big guy. I'm going to my awesome new cabin, and I'm gonna take care of this. If you feel like coming," he pauses, grin widening salaciously, "you don't even need to knock."

Heat flashes across the back of my neck as he stands, and it spreads when he gives my shoulder a lingering pat on his way by. I twist and watch him walk, his gait smooth and confident.

I believe if I wasn't distraught over Reanne and her current condition...I might go. Though, what I'd do I have no idea.

After all, I am quite hard, and he is correct, it was not due only to thinking of Niktas. Watching Cyan, Aeon, and Neo was incredibly erotic, as well. But that was easier, because I was pleasuring her, taking my pleasure from her, all of which is safe.

Jakobe is an unknown. The biggest risk being, he has not joined officially, which means there is no solid Alpha bond on him. Yes, Cyan's energy is there, but were I to go to Jakobe, lay with him—my throat bobs—it could prove disastrous. I nearly bonded Aeon entirely on accident when I tended him, and there was no desire threaded through that encounter.

One of the myriad reasons I've stayed on the outskirts of every pack is to make hiding my true nature easier. Minimize the chances of someone bonding to me, or of being found out.

No. I cannot risk it. Not yet. My situation has not changed. I cannot be with an unbonded werewolf and maintain my secret.

And that must be kept from Cyan, even at the expense of my own happiness. Just as it has always been.

JAKOBE

I don't know if he'll show up or not, but I sure hope so. I'd love to see what he's packing. It should probably be scary how much power he has, but it's hot as a rock left soaking in the sun. And it isn't just the Alpha energy, neither. He's a solidly, great-looking dude. Definitely not how I thought my day would go when I woke up this morning.

I get he's all stoic and everything, and had some sort of dark past, but it's not the past anymore, man, and I say, he should be living happy in the now. Which might include some action inside this cabin.

Once I reach my door, I glance back, only to find the big guy staring right at me. So, I drop my shorts, right here outside the door and kick them inside as I stretch my back with a couple of twists. I'm still hard as can be, and he'd have to be blind in both eyes not to see this monster.

I can feel his energy spike from here. Yep, that oughta do it. I grin and head in, leaving the door open.

This place really is awesome. The bed is big and soft, the bathroom is clean, the table and chairs are just right, and I dig the carved bench along the wall. The two wall lanterns are different than the ones we use, but it makes sense. Every pack pilfers whatever they want or whatever they have access to when they go to the human world. I've never been, 'cause pups don't get to go, but I've heard stuff about it.

I fluff the pillows a bit and flop down on my back, scooting until I'm in the middle of the bed. After smushing the pillow a bit more, I tuck one hand behind my neck and grab my cock, stroking slow as I wait. He'll be here, I have no doubts at all now.

It's only another minute or two before his energy moves closer, pinging off my skin. Man, it's crazy. I wonder what it'd feel like if he wasn't keeping it all hidden.

I shiver again, and he keeps moving toward the cabin. I can hear his footfalls now, and I'm still slowly stroking when he stops in my door, his energy like a slingshot.

"Hey, big guy. Make yourself at home. I'd give you the grand tour, but I've got my hands full." I grin, stroking again as I do.

He doesn't come in, though. Not the whole way. He braces his back against the frame and faces me, his undamaged eye staring me down while he crosses his arms.

"Why…do you want me?"

"That's easy. Because I do."

He thins his lips. "That is not an answer."

I shrug, lazily stroking as his throat bobs. "It's the only answer I've got. Doesn't have to be some big meaning."

His expression melts into something much sexier, sending a bolt of lust straight through my cock. Man, I like this.

"It is too dangerous," he growls, so on edge.

"How's a little one-on-one time with me dangerous?" I stroke again, sliding my thumb over the tip, grabbing my pre-cum and dragging it back down with a wink. "I only bite if you tell me to. And besides, if you get much harder, you're gonna destroy those shorts. I don't know about you, but I can't sew."

He lets out a single chuckle through his nose, clearly fighting a smile. I call that a win in my book.

"At least sit down, so I can say I've had my first official visitor."

Yeah, I know what I'm asking. If he comes inside, he can't tell himself he was just passing by, that he saw by accident. If he comes in that door, he's admitting to me, to the moon, to himself, that he wants at least a taste of Jak.

My hand stalls when he locks eyes with me, heat racing through the room. "You are not bound to Cyan yet."

I smirk, stroking again. "You already forget what I am?" I gesture with my chin. "That chair on the right looks nice and comfy."

He rumples his brows and pushes away from the frame. Getting closer.

"What does being a Tracer have to do with anything?"

"It has to do with everything, man. Cyan can't bind me if I don't let him. Neither can you. Neither can anyone. Energy," I stroke down to my base, thrusting up at the same time, his eyes widening, "is my whole thing. I control the flow of it in my body. So, if you do ever want to link up with me," I stroke again, harder, and Veikko steps into the room, gaze locked on my hand, "you'll have to ask."

Sparks dart up my spine as he stares, and I'm so turned on right now it's crazy. The man's not even touching me.

"Is that true?" He's less growly now, that's a good thing.

"I've got no reason to lie. But, if you wanna test it out, please," I bite my lip, letting it pop free. "Go for it."

"I…"

He's got such a strange, conflicted expression. If he'd let me at that giant thing between his legs, I could make it all go away.

"You were letting it into you…on purpose?"

I nod, grinning. "Now you're getting it. I like you, man. A lot. And that wet spot on your shorts tells me it isn't all one sided. Why don't you take them off?"

His face flushes, and he scowls.

"Hey, you can leave them on, that's fine with me. No need to be grumpy, even if it's a sexy look on you."

"It is not that."

"Tell me what it is then," I murmur, cupping my balls with my other hand as his chest heaves. I've gotten off watching others have sex, but never at having someone watch me. Just another way this pack is the best.

73

"I...do not want to touch you. I do...badly. But I also...do not."

"Oh, alright." I grin. "So that makes two of us who don't know where you sit on the whole thing. That's cool too, man. We don't have to touch. If you wanna sit right there and watch while I jack off thinking about sucking your cock, we can do that."

He exhales a fast, harsh breath, energy filling the room. I let a little more into my body, learning the frequencies, soaking up the warmth.

"Mm. Let me put it this way, big guy." I pick up speed, groaning. "You're about to watch that, anyway, standing or sitting."

Instead of either, he white knuckles the wooden footboard, leaning his weight forward, a kind of open-mouthed snarl in place.

Man, this guy is good looking. And with his lips parted like that, now all I can think about is unloading right on his tongue.

My head falls back against the pillow, breaths coming faster. Vik's energy swirls around me, getting thicker. He really is testing. I fling the energy back and crack an eye at him, smirking. "Ah, ah. You didn't ask."

His brows launch up, the wood groaning under his grip. "It is true."

"'Course it is. Does that mean you'll let me at least see the thing I want in my mouth so badly? I mean, my imagination is obviously working, but I bet it's nothing like the real deal."

He slow blinks at me, before zeroing in on my hands again. He's really giving this footboard a bad night. Pretty sure at least some of it splintered. But it's all good, he's closer now, and his outline is really nice. I stroke faster, working my balls, rubbing my lower stomach, my gaze flicking between his cock and his tortured face.

I'd love his hands on me, but it's almost hotter, me wanting it and him just staring. I moan and he tilts his head to the side to get a better angle. That pushes me right over the edge. With a loud grunting groan, I shoot all over my torso, panting.

Wood cracks under his grip, and by the time I can open my eyes again, he looks like he's about to die. Man, I hate that. I hate that he's so worried about something. Just want the guy to feel good.

I'm gonna take my chance. If he leaves, I suppose that's on him. I won't take it personal. Especially since I know he might jack off thinking about what he just saw. Man, that's got me twitching again already.

I roll forward and knee-walk toward the end of the bed, slowly, still stroking. Don't wanna spook him.

Each inch I go, his muscles jump.

"I'm not gonna touch you," I whisper.

His gaze darts up to meet mine, full of maybe disappointment, maybe relief. Hell, maybe both.

"Just getting closer, that's all."

I don't stop until the only thing separating us is the footboard. I'm three inches away, stroking myself sort of against my body since I don't feel like jamming my dick on the wood.

He's breathing heavy, fast, his eyes locked on the cum sliding down my chest. Unh, that's hot. I can work with that, too.

I squeeze my head, milking a bit more, and swipe it off with my other index finger. His nose flares when I move it up between us, and his tongue darts out between his thick lips. I freeze. Damn, I want to feel that. I shiver and continue slowly up to my collarbone and wipe the drop there.

A strangled groan leaves his throat, his hands rotating around the top of the footboard. Oh, woah, that was a sexy sound. My cock throbs under my grip, thighs flexing to keep me upright, keep me from leaning forward and accidentally touching him.

Energy bounces between our bodies. I can't tell if he likes that or if he wants me to let it in and submit.

He seems to be enjoying what's going on now, though. Just not as good as he could be.

"If I asked you," I murmur, "to touch me. What would you do?"

"Leave," he breathes, barely audible, still staring at my hand's motion.

"What if I asked to touch you? What would you do then?"

"…Leave." It looks like the word is a knife in his heart.

"Alright, big guy. Then why don't you tell me what would make you stay? 'Cause it sure would be nice to spend a whole night with you. Even if we're just talking."

His gaze trails up until our eyes meet, his brows pinching in the middle. "You want my company for something other than sex?"

I can't help my grin. "Well, yeah. Why's that so surprising? Tell you what, you just give me a little while longer, watch me unload a few more times, and we can chat all night long."

"I was silent for over a century," he mutters.

What in the glade…why…no, *how* could anyone go that long without talking? Guy's probably bursting. Unless he's exaggerating. Yeah, that's probably it.

"Then your voice needs a workout. Good thing I got here when I did." I stroke faster, pleasure filling me again. "Just… keep standing there, just like that. I'm almost there."

His grip tightens, eyes flicking down, lips parting again. One day. One day I'm gonna feel that white hair of his on my thighs, that mouth on my cock, that tongue—

"Yeah," I groan, my chin tipping up.

My eyes fly open. There's hot breath against my throat, sending me into a tailspin.

"Fuck!" It's a thin, desperate sound, and I try my best not to move my neck while my hips buck, reveling in the fast rhythm of air hitting my skin.

He lets out a chuffing growl and chills spring up along my body. I just imagine his teeth sinking in, and I'm there again, moaning to the ceiling, coming on myself, staying as still as I can so he doesn't move.

Panting, head still tilted back, I slowly grab the top of the footboard, right beside his hand. He hasn't pulled back or moved forward, seemingly content to breathe in my scent.

"The only...male partner I had...was not by choice," he whispers.

Oh, man. Well, no wonder. That would have been really good information to have. Nothing I can't work with, though.

I smile and murmur, "Sounds like it's time you took that power back."

He pulls away and I level my head, only to almost bump noses with him. His gaze swings up to meet mine, flicking between my eyes, searching for something. But he doesn't run out the door. Another win in my book.

"I think," he says, swallowing, breath against my lips. "I would like to touch you."

I inhale deeply, grinning from ear to ear. "I'd like that too, big guy. Start anywhere you want. Nothing on me is off limits."

I expect him to touch lots of places, I know I want him to. I tighten my grip on the footboard in excitement, forgetting his hand is right there.

His thumb lightly brushes my pinky and I suck in a breath, tiny explosions setting off in my chest. He travels across the backs of all my fingers, our shaky breaths mingling, until he covers my hand completely, pressing down.

It's intense, and gentle, and still somehow possessive.

I can't make any words come out, which might be the first time that's ever happened. I'm too keyed up, focused on these sparks, this heat. His palm skates higher, over my wrist and forearm. I want to lean forward and taste his mouth so bad. My cock is throbbing again, but I'm afraid moving will scare him off. He gives my bicep a squeeze that makes my nerves jump, before trailing just his fingertips over my shoulder until his thumb lands on the spot where I wiped the last drop of cum.

Damn, that's hot. A groan slips out, zings of lust shooting to my cock. There's a tiny upturn on the corner of his mouth as he smears it along my collarbone. He lets his thick fingers dance up the back of my neck and along my jaw, featherlight. That same thumb rubs along my bottom lip, and before I can make ears or tails of what he wants me to do, he cups my cheek and eases his tongue across the same path.

He licked me. He actually licked me. He tasted my—

I moan and shiver, gripping the footboard tighter so I don't fall over. Alpha waves blast through the cabin as a deep, rumbling growl fills the space between us. Takes all I've got not to let the internal submission response take over. I might be able to control energies, but the guy's still an Alpha. The power is gone in a flash, hidden away again.

"Say something, Jakobe," he murmurs, brows mashed together as he traces the outline of my lip. "My thoughts are too loud."

The first thing that pops to mind comes tumbling out. "I'm looking forward to holding you while we sleep tonight."

His chest catches, his features twisting more, his voice a raspy whisper. "You would still want that if this went no farther?"

I exhale slowly and nod with a smile. "Yeah. I'd need to work a few more loads out, but yeah. I already told you we didn't—"

His mouth mashes against mine, hand tangling in my hair. I'm frozen for a moment, then open for his seeking tongue. He tastes as fantastic as I thought he would. We're passing groans back and forth, and he's desperate, gripping my head, molding my shoulder. He breaks the kiss, and I gulp air, my cock begging for attention as he licks down my neck.

"So since...oh...damn." He laps at my chest, my stomach, with hungry, forceful swipes, cleaning my cum off and making deep, rumbling sounds. It's almost enough to make me shoot again. Once he makes his way back to my neck, I remember my question.

"Veikko, since this does seem to be heading to a very happy place, you should know, if I was gonna die today and I had one final wish, it would be to have your cock in my mouth, so will you please, for the love of the moon, take off those shorts?"

He lets out a single laugh against my cheek and claims my mouth again. He grabs my hand with his other one, tugs it over the footboard, and presses it to his huge bulge.

I'm so happy I could dance. I moan in his mouth and hook one arm around his neck while I stroke him. Letting my fingers trail his waistband, I bite at his lip, living for his groaning breaths.

"Take one step back for me, so I can get over this footboard."

He does, and I vault over, dropping to my knees in front of him.

Honestly, he looks a little panicked, but he hasn't stopped me, so I grab the sides of his shorts and pull, slowly, revealing skin I have to taste. I lick along his hips, all the tender places that show themselves, until he can't take the tease anymore, and shoves them the rest of the way out, freeing his absolutely monumental, gorgeous cock.

"Oh holy—" I cut myself off, diving in for more than a mouthful with a loud moan. His hand lands light in my hair, a growling groan filling the cabin as he tenses.

Yeah, big guy, soak it all in. I worship him like he deserves, pulling out all the stops, taking him deep, scraping my fingertips down his thighs and up his stomach. Every one of his heavy breaths is a growl now, crossed over to beast even though he's not shifted.

Really damn hot.

The one thing that's different about this than any suck-off I've done before, is we haven't broken eye contact yet. He's fully focused in the here and now, and I could watch pleasure cross that face all day, every day.

His hips snap forward as I swirl my tongue, and I take it as far down my throat as I can. His shock and ecstasy as he cups the sides of my head are worth all the stars in the sky. But the best is when he starts thrusting, using my mouth just like I wanted.

I moan every time I get air, and stroke my cock until I shoot another load, this time toward him. I have to assume something landed on part of him, because his entire body trembles, a long growl sounding as he picks up speed, thrusting harder and harder until my eyes water, but we still don't break gazes.

He shoots down my throat with a roar, and I swallow, hard as hell again at the taste, at the feel of it, at the sight of him utterly breaking free.

With a quick move, his hands are under my arms, and he tosses me on the bed. I bounce, laughing and scramble backward as he rounds the side. I shouldn't have bothered, because he grabs my calves and pulls me to the edge of the bed slowly, eyes holding mine as he lowers to his knees and takes me in his mouth.

I'm dying, right here, right now. His hair is brushing against me, that hot mouth working some sort of wicked magic that has me grabbing at everything as I swap from whimpering, to groaning, to gasping and back again.

My muscles seize, the biggest orgasm of my life slamming through my body, and I shout, the last of me pumping into his mouth.

I push up to my elbows and pant like I've run the width of The Glade twice, while Veikko releases me with a slow final lick, placing warm kisses along the inside of my groin.

"Jumping jagflies," I exhale a long breath with a laugh as I run my fingers through his hair. "I think I owe you my life after that."

He chuckles against my lower stomach, and I sit all the way up, tugging his face toward mine for another kiss.

Man, oh man. I think this giant might have just stolen a little bit of my heart.

"Are you ready for some pro-level cuddling?" I murmur against his mouth, met by another of his deep chuckles.

He nods, so I scoot back to the head of the bed, patting the space beside me before opening my arm. "You get to be the small one tonight."

Incredulous is the best way to describe his face as he glances between himself and me. I only grin wider, flipping the blanket back.

"You know you want to. I promise you won't be less of an Alpha in the morning."

He scratches his jaw and glances away, a smile creeping up. "Fine."

"Alright," I laugh, making a bit more room and lay on my back. He settles his big body along side mine, scooting down so his head is on my chest. He has to curl his knees up to keep his feet on the bed, so I drape mine over top. Wrapping him up tight, I kiss the top of his head for good measure, and sigh happily.

He's tense until I start lightly scratching his shoulder, then he melts, hooking his arm around my hip and squeezing me.

"You want to talk or sleep?" I whisper. "I'm good for either, so whatever makes you...happy...hey, are you out already?"

No reply. Only deep breathing. Aww, the big lump. I drift off with a smile etched on my face, warm sparks skittering through my chest.

What a damn good day.

CYAN

"**M**orning, Mister Alpha." Jakobe's voice is barely a whisper, but it's already oozing happiness. Swear this guy is snorting moon dust or something. I blink, stuck in his doorway. I can't fucking believe what I'm seeing.

Veikko is here, inside a cabin, curled under Jak's arm. Not only that, he's naked. I blink, and blink again.

"Vik," I bark, startling him awake. He bolts upright with wide eyes, jostling Jak, who chuckles.

Vik doesn't say anything as he stares at me. Being honest, I don't know what to fucking say here either. I've never seen him in a bed. It's weird as hell. And I thought he was strictly anti-guy. I would have been too if I went through what he did. So, shocked about covers it.

"Morning to you, too, big guy." Jak gives Vik's bicep a kiss, which makes his cheeks flush.

"Morning," he mumbles, still staring.

He finally breaks eye contact with me when Jak cups his cheek and plants one right on his mouth. Vik is frozen for a second, then relaxes, letting a clearly hungry Jak takeover. It's hot, and I should have let Neo take care of me last night. My muscles are boiling, skin buzzing like I'm covered with bees. But we've got shit to do, and last night was not happening, so it is what it is.

Jak eventually pulls back and winks. "That's a way better goodbye kiss. Your man Jak's gotta go save the day, Honeybear. See you when I get home."

Vik's face twitches until laughter barks out and he shields his eyes with a groan. Even I can't help smirking.

"I am not your...Honeybear." Vik's face is so flushed he looks like he might explode.

"Alright," Jak chuckles. "You can come up with a better name while I'm busy today if you want. Tell me all about it at dinner."

He gives a truly embarrassed, smiling Vik another kiss and slips off the bed. After stretching his nice muscles, he tugs on his shorts, twisting his dimpled face to me.

"Ready to hit the underbrush, Mister Alpha. Just give me a few bites of food, and I'm all yours, man."

"No time."

I still can't look away from Vik. It's like I have no idea who he is.

"Aw, man. I'm no good on an empty stomach. There's got to be something left I can eat."

"Hunt on the way. We're leaving."

"Hey, you're in charge. You got it. Right behind you."

I stare at them for another second before stalking through the door and back onto the grass. My world has turned over too much lately for Vik to suddenly become domesticated.

Neo groggily makes his way from my cabin to the prep table, scratching the back of his head, hair in all directions. He glances over at me, and only gives me a small smile before continuing his path.

I hate this. He's hurting and needs me, but I have to find Aeon and Reanne, or it's only going to get worse.

I'm only going to get worse.

I could force him to come over here, but I could go to him just as easily. Neither's gonna happen, though.

Jakobe slaps my shoulder with a pleased exhale. "Haven't had raw food yet. Can the beast puke? Do I eat the bones too? What about fur?"

I pinch the bridge of my nose. "Just...go see if Neo has anything."

"You got it!" He trots over, and I watch as they interact, Neo's expression lightening, his real smile peeking through.

Vik clears his throat behind me. "He is a powerful Tracer. I advise you follow his lead."

"That what you advise?" I side-eye him and exhale loudly. "Yeah, I know. I felt it."

Really don't want to have a conversation, but since I'm standing here waiting anyway.

"You and him, huh?"

He makes a noise somewhere between a cough and a growl.

I face him, because I need to see this reaction head on.

"You know he was a pup three days ago."

Vik's eyes widen slowly, all his color draining away as he whispers, "Mother of the moon…every item I own is older than him."

I laugh, crossing my arms. "I think we all have something older. For what it's worth, he seems good for you. Reanne will like him."

He hums a short tone, and Jak trots toward us, wide grin on his face. Half-way back he hollers, "Honeybear! I brought you something!"

My laugh barks out again and Neo glances up, confusion giving way to wide eyes.

Vik groans, burying his face in his hands. "What have I done?"

He may be hiding his face, but I can see the grin peeking out. I'm glad for him, glad as hell, but it's still weird.

"So, are you…" I frown, shaking my head. Yeah, I'm not asking if the guy is cured or open for business or any fucking other thing. I just can't see Vik that way.

But he figures out what I want to know, because he sighs, still behind his hands. "No. Jakobe is—I had…have…no intention—I am not interested in anyone…else. I thought Reanne would be it for me. But he…"

"Good thing I brought him, then."

Vik lets his hands drop and eyes me. "Yes," he inhales, "Thank you."

I nod and step away, clearing room for my shift.

Jak hands Vik a hunk of jerky with a wide dimpled grin, green eyes sparkling up at him. "Check it out, I'd say this counts as me providing for you, big guy."

Vik slowly takes the palm sized hunk of meat, staring down at it as his brows pinch in the middle. I don't know why he's so sad about food, but Jak's swagger melts into concern, and he strokes Vik's arm.

"Hey," he murmurs, "this is just the start, Honeybear. If I didn't have to single-handedly be the salvation of the SteelTooth Pack, I'd stay right here and give you things all day. Woo you like you deserve."

I shake my head and call up my beast. Single-handedly, huh? The guy has ego to spare, for sure. But bet your ass if we run into a fight, it'll be me shredding faces, not him.

Vik levels his head, brows still working, and Jak chucks his knuckle under Vik's chin. "Don't forget, you can come up with a different nickname while I'm gone. I'll even be the small one tonight, if you want."

With a lightning quick movement, Vik grips the back of Jak's neck and ducks, claiming his mouth in a heated kiss.

I cut my gaze to Neo, feeling his longing, and find his eyes locked on me. I almost go to him, but Jak hums happily and pulls back.

"Now *that's* a send-off right there!" He slaps Vik on the ass and steps back with a wink, devouring the jerky in three bites, before calling his beast.

Funny. Shifted, he's almost eye level.

Vik stares at Jak, appreciation and a little something else in his small smile.

"Protect…them," I growl to him, gesturing to the camp as I send an Alpha command.

His expression hardens, and we stare at each other, a blip of weird energy coming off before he nods.

Dunno what that was, but I don't have time to care right now.

Jak and I take off, racing through the forest, northeast of the village. I keep Jak in my sights, which would be hard if he wasn't red, because he's not running in a straight line. We go a little way further and he veers left, repeating this time and time again until I can't take it anymore and Alpha wave him.

We stop and he faces me, tilting his head. I drop my beast first, and he follows.

"What's up? I'm hot on their trail."

"You're taking us in a circle. At this rate we'll end up going all the way around the damn village."

He shrugs. "I go where the energy flows, man. I can't tell you why it's doing this, just that it is, and it's getting a little bit stronger. I'm picking up the other line, too. Your Beta."

Rubbing my temples, I sigh and nod. Only Aeon could manage a circle when he means to go in a line.

"Okay. Let's keep going."

Jak glances off into the woods for a moment before facing me again. "There's another energy. Real faint. It's…nah. That's dumb."

"What? Fucking tell me."

"Well, it's like…it's almost like… So, this other energy curves first, then the Beta's does."

"What's that mean? Someone else was here?"

I don't know whether to be angry or scared.

Jak purses his lips and stares into the woods again. "Nah. More along the lines of…man, I swear it feels like he was being led, or…pulled, yeah. Yeah, that's what it is. I can't explain it, Mister Alpha. But that's what I'm picking up."

Angry and scared, then. I growl and call the beast, rolling out my shoulders. "Hurry."

"Right on. Good news is, I still feel them together so far."

Jak calls his beast back up, and we run again, the curve

eventually smoothing out. We're heading straight south now, back toward DuskFall territory. I can't believe I was in the right area. If I hadn't been so fucking tired, I could have found them myself. Maybe.

Jak scans the ground and the trees faster now, some of his steps zipping sideways, before coming back to a straight line. He cuts to the right and halts, glancing around before spinning to face me. He drops beast, concern on his features. "Man, there's lots of energy now. Three, maybe," he closes his eyes a second and nods, "four other werewolves."

"DuskFall?"

He shakes his head, and I snarl, hackles up, ready to rip whoever it is apart.

But I'm ripped apart instead, at least that's what it feels like. Aeon's connection to me goes ice cold, and I have no idea why or what it means.

I stumble, each pant laced with a whine, my beast fighting to stay in control as I dissolve into a heartbroken wail.

Jakobe grabs my shoulders, shaking me, talking, but none of his words get through. I only thought I knew pain. This is worse than anything.

After another few stuttered breaths, my beast roars back to life, rage fueling us both, and I steady my legs as I shout, "Find them!"

Jak swallows and steps back, calling his beast again, and leads the way, faster.

AEON

A noise wakes me just after dawn. I'm still curled up with Reanne how we fell asleep, her head under my chin, my fingers in her hair. I strain my ears but it's quiet now. Maybe it was just a bird. I pull her closer, breathing in her scent. But it's changed a bit more, unless I'm imagining it. There's an almost icy undercurrent. Hmm. Maybe being in this cabin with Kasimir is affecting her. I don't know if that's possible, but yesterday I would have told you a dead god can't give people orgasms. Yet…

Last night was intense. I believe he's real, now. I don't know how, but he fixed my bond with Cyan, and it's stronger than it was when we first connected. He fixed the one with Reanne, too, and it's thrumming between us.

"I wish there was a shower in here," she mutters against my skin.

"Thought you were still asleep." I snuggle her closer. "It's early."

"I know, but I'm filthy." Her arm pops up, stretching over her head, shifting her chest against me.

"Mm, I think you look great. Feel great, too."

She chuckles. "Yeah, I doubt that."

"I'm serious. I want to dirty you up some more. Give me a little while longer and I can."

She laughs but rests her hand on my side. "Aeon," she pauses, and I glance down at her head. "Are you…okay?"

I chuckle. "Great. Why?"

"You're not sad anymore?" Her chin tips up, catching my

gaze. "Angry about whatever it was?"

Oh. Right.

I refuse the thoughts, and smile. "I'm good, ReeRee. Our bond is fixed. I got to spend the night with my beautiful mate, having amazing sex. What's to be angry about?"

Her eyes tell me she's not convinced, but she kisses me anyway. "I'm glad, then."

"So, what's the decision?"

"I want to go back. I miss everyone too much." She tucks into a ball in my embrace. "I want to be with Cyan, I really do, but I'm...scared."

"I get it. We'll all be there for you, whatever happens."

I'm just glad she's not considering Mishka as an option, after what he did to Cy, and how he threatened all our lives.

She exhales loudly and scrubs her head against my chest. "Thank you, Aeon."

Sleep threatens, forcing my lids closed, but she's restless, and eventually sits up.

"I have *got* to get in some water. Since there's not a shower, maybe you can take me to the lake where you caught the fish?"

"Wouldn't call it a lake, really," I murmur, snuggling closer. "The waterfall sort of leads into a river. I guess the pond at the bottom might be a lake if you're tiny."

There's a pause before she pushes up to her elbow. "Veikko didn't mention a waterfall. Remember? Northeast, two-hundred something miles, between MoonMare Cavern and the Lake of Tears?"

My eyes pop open, brow twisting. "Huh?"

"No waterfall."

My mind zooms in a million directions as I sit up, almost bumping her head in the process. There is no lake near here, not that I saw.

Her eyes narrow as cold sweat drips down my back.

I felt pretty confident we were going Northeast...at the time. Damn it. I thought I'd gotten better at the directional stuff. And I didn't hear him give those landmarks, but I was a bit out of sorts.

Shit. I have no idea where we are. Which means even though she's ready to leave, I can't get us back home. Well, I maybe could eventually…as long as I didn't run headlong into the wrong pack's territory and get us killed.

Worse, since I didn't go the right way, that means this isn't Vik's cabin. What are the odds there'd be another one out here?

She figures out my screw-up before I have a chance to cover for it, her eyes widening. "Did we go the wrong way?"

I guess there's no point in denying it. "I think we did. I'm really sorry." I hang my head and rub my temples.

"It's okay, it's okay." She grips my knee. "We're still together, and this house was pretty abandoned, so I don't think anyone is going to show up and kick us out. If anything, they should be happy we cleaned it."

I cut my gaze up to hers, so soft and understanding. She really is the best.

"Yeah, you're right. I wonder who it belongs to, though."

"Me, too." Her stomach yowls and she groans. "Those few bites of fish from last night are long gone. I think food is gonna take a priority over getting clean now."

I nod. I'm long past hungry.

"I'll go catch a few more, and hopefully not burn them this time." We share a grin and a kiss before I crawl off the bed with a stretch.

I freeze. There's that noise again. Rustling, but now I can tell it's bigger than a bird. It could be nothing, but I need to make sure.

"What? What is it?"

I press my finger to my lips. She nods, and I creep toward the door, shaking out my muscles. Before I open it, I shift, only to have the mate link ping with faint need.

With a grin exposing more teeth, I twist back to see ReeRee, wide-eyed, a small smile on her face. I love that fucking me in beast form turns her on. It does me, too, way more than sex in man form. They're both good, but rutting into her, the way she looks under my claws…a shiver travels my body, spiking my fur.

Okay, that's enough of that. I don't need to get caught with my dick hanging out right now. I refocus on the door. I snatch it open and growl, but instead of anything menacing, I scare the living shit out of a fawn and doe, who bound away.

Good. Though, that would have been easy food. Now, I really do have to go get some breakfast.

"Nothing," I growl at her. "Going…for…fish. Then we…go home."

"Okay." She smiles and adjusts the blanket. "I'll be here."

I nod and only make it one step over the threshold before something lances my stomach, white-hot pain blasting through me.

"Ree…" I gurgle, dropping to my knees. My body jerks as claws dig into my sides, rip open my back, slice through my shoulders, and gash my throat.

I hear the snaps before I feel the spiderwebs of agony, and both my legs crumple. I fall flat, and it's only then I can tell how many are attacking me. Four werewolves. Four mauling one Beta who can't even make energy.

Blood soaks the mossy ground under me, and my limbs won't work. I blink too long, and Reanne's scream rouses me, but it's outside the cabin.

They're gone. They took her.

I try one last time to get my claws under me, but I fail and slip in my own blood, losing the beast altogether as I shift back to a man.

I've heard when werewolves die, we can't think of anything but the moon goddess, of returning our borrowed magic, but my final thought as everything goes dark is only about Reanne.

LAZAROS

I bolt awake from my blissful dream about putting different hats on Korey while we have tea somewhere surrounded by flowers. Good dream, very good dream. But something is off.

Instead of blasting the entire village with a Beta wave in fear, I manage to keep it in. I've gotten remarkably better at that, since leaving GrimBite. I suppose, yes, I'm rather proud of myself. Mishka demanded all the energy I had, every time he needed it, leaving me tired constantly. Yes, I know I'm a Born Beta, according to Korey, and that's why I don't need an Alpha, but that doesn't mean I'd prefer to be a tapped keg, as it were. Here, they don't need as much, barely any, really, with Aeon. It's been exceedingly nice, even just these few days.

Heartbreak blooms suddenly, spreading ice through my veins, and my eyes widen.

I can't explain how I know, not that self-awareness has ever been my strong suit, as if I have one, but something's wrong with—

"Reanne," I mutter, clutching my heart.

Korey's arm curls around my waist, a grumble in his throat about needing more sleep.

I'd grin if I wasn't scared out of what little mind I have left. I send a testing thought but get nothing back. Have to be within eyesight, I suppose. My gut wrenches in sorrow, pulling tears from my eyes. Blimey, she's utterly miserable.

Korey rustles again, lifting his head with a bleary snorfle.

"What's…" He sits up and cradles me close, nuzzling my cheek. "Hey, you're safe, little pup. Those bad dreams can't get you."

I couldn't love this man more. Even if he said he'd take me to the tippy top of The Spire just to carve me off a piece of the moon. Ah, okay. I might love him a bit more if he said that, but that's beside the point, I think.

"I-I'm fine," I sniffle, "it's not me."

He pulls back, brow lowering. Confession time, I suppose.

"So, as it turns out, the darling Reanne and I, share somewhat of a…connection. It wasn't very much, you see, and we didn't have long, barely at all, to explore it before she-they left, but, and please, do not pan— You're already panicking."

His wide eyes are locked on mine, chest heaving. "Is she okay?"

I wince. "She's not dead, if-if that helps. Otherwise, well, no, no, not at all."

"Shit." He scrubs his face. "Let me see if Neo or Vik can feel anything."

Oh, what a smart idea!

His gaze unfocuses a bit, worry lines forming on his so very handsome face.

"Well. I've succeeded in freaking Neo out. They can't feel any distress. She's obviously still too far away for the mate link. Which means there's nothing we can do. Cy's already looking for her with Jakobe."

I tilt my head. The way he said Jakobe's name is fairly synonymous with how one might refer to a blister which busted under duress and was then stabbed with a thorn. Either I'm imagining it, or—

"Korey, are you…are you jealous?"

"Jealous? Of that fresh-faced, red-haired, green eyed, overly friendly, muscular…" His angry growl gives way to a hefty exhale and a very pup-like tilt to his brows. "A little."

I chuckle, wiping my tears and curl up on his lap. I kiss his mouth over and over, followed by his scruffy cheeks. Once he's smiling, I pull back and stare him in the eyes.

"Korey, you're my love. You're my mate. I adore every massive inch of you, and no newcomer will change that. You're stuck with me until our tails fall off, I'm afraid."

"Hmm. I'm glad to hear that. You know I love you too, little pup."

I fight the heat that climbs up my back, because now isn't the time. But I do give him a sly smirk.

"He is a wee bit muscular, isn't he?"

Korey throws an exasperated hand out. "Seriously, those abs, how?"

I bark a shockingly loud laugh, covering my mouth in embarrassment as he fills the space with his own chuckle. Korey's abs are brilliant, his whole bulky body a dedication to muscles everywhere.

He tugs my hand away and kisses me soundly, until he pulls back, clearing his throat.

"Neo says to tell you he's still sorry, and he would love to know the pie recipe."

Guilt at my reaction strikes again. It's bad enough to have the feelings, but then I made him feel bad, too. Top notch way to make friends, Laz. Really.

"I'm rather looking forward to-to joining the link here. The pack. It'll be easier. Telling him things, I mean. My mind is, well, it's a mite clearer, than what, ah, comes out of my mouth. Usually."

"I love everything about that mouth." He bites my lip and grins. "Also, there's breakfast left."

"Fabulous." I climb off and tug on my shorts. "Today, I'm going to-to be strong."

Korey slinks off the bed like a hulking, erotic snake, and gathers me to him. I'm clay in an instant. He kisses his mark, sending a thrill through my limbs. "You're strong every day, little pup. Like a squall line."

"Ah, I thank you for that, but-but you're terribly wrong, I'm light snowfall, remember? But, e-even so, today's goal is simple. I will not wither. Well. That is to say, I won't wither without, you know, proper cause. Not to say I'm looking for any."

"Great goal. But if you do, that's perfectly okay. I'll bring you in here and take care of you again."

I chew my smile, unable to stop the shiver of desire from flushing my skin and calling up that dirty grin of Korey's.

"Or," he murmurs, nipping my ear. "I could just take care of this gorgeous, perfect little body now."

Oh, I can't breathe again. Hard as a mountain and aching all over. His fingers dance down my back and just graze the top of my ass when I'm filled with another wave of Reanne's pain.

It steals my breath and I push out of his embrace, clutching my stomach.

"Auch, whatever is happening, it's bloody awful."

Korey heaves a sigh. "Maybe you should tell Neo and Vik what you're feeling."

"Do you think they'll be mad? Or-or will they shout, possibly? If-if so, then perhaps, we could, uh, well, not."

"One second. Okay, there. I told them you had bad news, but if they acted like asses, they'd have to deal with me."

The thought of Korey standing up to Veikko and somehow not being squashed like an insect makes me chuckle. Terribly large men, the both of them, but Veikko is two or so feet taller and a foot or so wider. And much, much older.

Regardless, the protective sentiment is one of the reasons I love my mate so dearly.

"Thank you." I grin up at him and thread my fingers with his while we make our way to the door.

We both stall in the same step, Korey's eyes widening as his fingers clamp down on mine. But where Korey is able to remain standing like the pillar he is, my world crumbles out from under me.

The unfortunate bond still inside me blooms back to life, and any pride, happiness, resolve, freedom, and love I've managed to find dissolves into nothing as I drop to my knees in utter terror.

Korey lifts me, clutching me to his chest too tightly, but it doesn't stop the cold from seeping in. The tremble from rattling my bones. It's over. He's come for me.

Mishka is here.

REANNE

I have no tears left. I used them all on the run here, tossed between the uncaring werewolves who murdered my mate.

The image of his bloody, destroyed body is burned in my mind, like a nightmare I'll never wake up from. My sweet Aeon, who came with me even though he should have stayed behind. Who burned my fish and wanted to steal me a dress with pockets and gave me his only mate bond to save my life and let me see his beautiful thoughts even though he was worried and—

I guess I've got tears left, after all. Several drip down my chin, landing in the dirt below. I dig my fingers in the soil around them as another sob wrenches out.

I felt the moment his life left, because his mark burned like the sun, spreading through my torso, singeing the edges of my heart. It's the only thing it can mean. That's when I used the rest of my screams. No one cared though.

The werewolves dumped me on the ground in this giant tent, and I had no fight in me. I let them tie my hands and feet to this support pillar, limp, crying, and utterly defeated.

I've been here for a while now, waiting for whatever, or whoever's coming. I don't want to think about it, but I don't want to think about my mates, either, because I'll just worry. And reminiscing about school, or any of my life before is pointless, because I can never go back. The harsh reality is, there isn't much to think about that doesn't break my heart.

Feet shuffle outside the tent entrance, kicking my pulse into high gear.

They're careful. No one's talking where I can hear, so I have no idea where I am, who has me—nothing.

The door flap rips open, spilling blinding sunlight inside. I wince, twisting my head to the side. With my hands tied near my feet like this, it's all I can manage.

"So, this is what you look like." The man's voice is scratchy, mid-range, and full of venom. "I assumed an abomination like yourself would be ugly. No wonder they didn't kill you like they were supposed to."

The flap closes, and I blink the white spots out of my vision as the outline of a big body crouches in front of me.

"If I wasn't so disgusted by your very existence, I'd probably want to fuck you, too."

It's such a shocking thing to hear, I can't come up with a retort.

"But you're absolutely wretched." I flinch with a gasp when he spits on my thigh and growls, "Even that's too good for you."

I can't wipe it off or smear it on the ground with the way I'm restrained. It slides down, twisting my gut with shame and anger the whole way.

A faint echo of darkness thrums once in the center of my chest. The same thing I felt when I killed Fen. I grasp at it with my mind, but it's gone too soon.

The man comes into focus finally, but that doesn't help. His expression matches his words, a deep sneer on his rounded face under short brown hair, with thick shoulders leading to large arms.

But it's the shiny glint in his hand that draws my attention and has me attempting to scoot away. He flicks the dagger upright, twisting it. I'd say the ornate hilt was pretty, if I didn't fear for my life.

"To help me settle an argument, abomination. I think it's already too late, some think there's still time."

He thrusts forward with no warning, stabbing the blade into my side. I scream, the nerves around the wound burning and freezing at the same time. Pain radiates outward as hot blood trickles down in pulses with each of my sobbing breaths. I'd rather be dead than feel this.

With a disappointed grunt, he snatches the dagger free, and stares at it.

Tremors wrack me, and I jerk when he mashes his hand against the spot, wrenching another scream.

"I was right. Too late. You're already healing. Now, all we can do is keep you from escaping until it's time, abomination." He hefts a sigh and stands, kicking dirt on me in insult. I cough, grimacing.

"I…h-have a…name," I stammer out through pain-induced teeth chatter. I don't know where the will power to speak came from, but I can't take it back, now.

He glares at me with nothing but contempt. "Not anymore."

"Why are you doing this?" Tears run down my cheeks again.

"Because you should never have made it here." He drops back down to a crouch and grabs my jaw, bruising. "And we won't allow one Sentinel's failure to seal the fate of us all."

My stomach drops, fear stealing my breath. He must mean Veikko. Are these werewolves also Sentinels? If so, as twisted as it may be, they could have more information about what's coming. I don't think this guy is in a sharing mood. Their view of me is so different than Mishka's, though. Maybe I can use that. It might be a dumb idea, but it's the only one I have.

"The Vigils called me a savior."

I wince as his grip tightens.

"When did you speak with them? You've already been to The Spire?!"

"W-what? No—ah!"

He squeezes even harder, grinding his teeth with the effort, and I scream again. It feels like he's trying to dig his fingers through my flesh. He only stops because someone flings open the flap, blinding me again.

"Enough."

The flap closes behind him, plunging us back into the dim lantern light.

A heavy wave of dark Alpha energy pushes down on the room, and the mean man releases my jaw, dropping to a knee as he faces the other one.

"Yes, Yuli."

Wait…Yuli. Oh, shit. This is that other pack, the one…the one they came from, God, what's the name? I guess it doesn't matter.

"She hasn't spoken to the Vigils, nor been to the spire. Your skin would be melting, Filnir."

Filnir grunts, handing over the dagger. "Good point."

"Though," Yuli continues with slow, powerful strides into the room, spinning the blade, "why she's bluffing I don't know."

Filner grumbles something, but Yuli tuts, waving his hand and Filnir falls silent. Yuli smiles at me, but it's far from friendly.

"It's interesting to finally be face to face. Especially after all our conversations with Mishka. When I found out you'd somehow gotten away from the stupid humans we'd arranged to kill you the other night, I was intrigued. Went about meeting with that egotistical maniac to learn everything he knew."

"Watching him die will be fun." Filnir chuckles.

I suck at the air, fast breaths forcing static into my head. He set up the frat guys? And I shouldn't be feeling bad for Mishka at all, but I can't help it.

Without warning, Yuli spins and flings the dagger at Filnir, impaling him in the back of the neck.

I scream yet again, my throat burning, and Filnir struggles for only a moment before falling face first in the dirt. My stomach turns, every bit of me shaking in fear.

"W-why did—"

"To show you what a special weapon it is." He crouches and slowly pulls the dagger free, wiping the blood on the back of Filnir's head as he talks. "I'm sure by now you've heard and seen how werewolves can heal from almost anything. Something as minor as a blade in the neck? An hour, maximum, to be right as rain. But this is an ancient weapon, and it's taken a very long time to get it perfect. There's no werewolf alive it can't kill, and it would have solved our problem, halted this endless cycle then and there. But no. Someone interfered, and here we are. Luckily, you left this for my pack to retrieve." He taps the handle of the dagger with his ring finger as he faces me. "Or I would have been much, much angrier."

I have no idea what to think, and I'm too scared to say anything. I'm glad Filnir's dead, but there's a twisted part of me that wishes I'd been able to do it.

Yuli stands and strides through the space until he's directly beside me. "I hear you're the one responsible for Fen's death. I have to be honest...that put me in quite a rage."

Oh, that's right. Fen is from here, too! No wonder they're so angry with me.

"That was an accident, I swear." I won't say I'm sorry, because I'm not. But it really was an accident.

He lets out a soft chuckle. "That's where you're wrong, orphan. I think, deep down, you knew exactly what you were doing, and exactly how to hurt me."

My eyes widen, confusing bunching my brows. "How do you know I had no parents?" All that comes out is a faint whisper, but he hears me.

"You're always an orphan. Now, we need to establish a ground rule. If you speak a lie to me, from this point forward, I will cut out your tongue. It may grow back, it may not." He shrugs a shoulder. "If it doesn't, and you lie again, I'll cut off something else."

Oh my God. Whatever small amount of hope I had that he might be somewhat reasonable is gone in an instant.

"Do you follow?"

"Y-yes."

His steps take him to the other side of the tent, where he

grabs a bucket. He brings it closer, liquid sloshing over the edges when he drops it on the ground beside me. I flinch with a whimper, because I honestly have no idea what to expect.

"It's just water." He crouches in front of me, bringing his black hair, glowing blue eyes, and unnerving smile into sight. "I'm going to help you stay honest."

I'm about to ask how water could do that when he holds up the dagger. "You don't mind, do you?"

He plunges it into my thigh this time, and the pain is twice as bad as before. I can barely draw in a breath to scream, so what comes out is a gargled wail. He tugs it out slowly, skin tearing as he goes, seemingly transfixed.

"Wanted to see for myself." He smiles as he stares at the wound. "You understand."

I sob openly, the nerves around the wound crawling, searing. I glance down through watery eyes and can't believe how fast it's closing up.

"Hmm. That is something, isn't it?" He gently sets the dagger off to the side and dunks his hand in the bucket while my sobs turn to whimpers. "It's a shame we don't have more time. I think carving into you could prove…quiet therapeutic."

This guy is beyond twisted. And why am I healing so fast? Is it part of the powers? And even if I heal, it's still really awful to stab a person just to watch that happen!

I'm shocked out of my thoughts when a soaked, tepid rag lands on my shoulder. Yuli drags it down my arm slowly until he reaches my hand, then repeats the whole path again.

My body doesn't know how to process anything right now. There's too much input, everything magnified by the residual pain, shock, fear. Part of me appreciates being cleaned, part is terrified of what might be next, and another small part is hungry for the contact.

"What's your name?"

I blink at him, struggling to focus. "…Reanne."

He nods like he already knew, watching my face closely. After he refreshes the rag, he rubs it along my back in segments, scrubbing at who knows how much filth. I fight the part that wants to curl into his touch, soak up his warmth.

"Do you know what you are?"

"I…"

"Take your time," he murmurs, wiping along my side now, cleaning the blood and dirt.

My brain is working overtime, struggling to remember the full—

"Rigdis. Aruna Rigdis."

"Good." He smiles. "That's right."

No, I won't be weirdly pleased that he's happy. This is not okay, none of this is okay.

"Do you know who I am?"

Is that a trick question? I catch his gaze, but it's weird. Expectant, hopeful, yet already disappointed.

"Y-Yuli?"

He sneers, and I panic.

"Uh…an Alpha? A werewolf?"

"Enough." There's such a despondent rush of air behind the word I can't bring myself to look away. I wait for another question, but he just keeps wiping my body.

"Please, stop washing me," I whisper.

He ignores me completely, cleaning my leg now, with slow, methodical drags. All I can think is how glad I am the dirt-caked spit is gone.

Finally, he breaks his silence.

"Do you know where you were when we found you?"

He's moved to the inside of my leg, my inner thigh, eyes locked on mine. I'm holding my breath, fighting with the rising need, praying to any god or goddess or deity that will listen. He dunks the rag again, and moves to my stomach, rivulets of slightly warmer water running down.

"A cabin," I blurt on exhale. "With my…with my…"

God. Aeon. Tears form again, my chest hitching as I shake my head.

Yuli studys me. "Why are you crying?"

"They killed my mate," I shout, hanging my head as more tears fall. "Your wolves, the ones who-who brought me here."

He hooks a claw under my chin, the sharp point forcing it level as I gasp. His smile turns sinister. "They certainly did. It's a terrible feeling, isn't it? The black stain on your soul, the freezing hole that will never be filled again, no matter what you do, being unable to say goodbye. I waited to take a mate for longer than anyone, certain I'd die myself before I felt the loss of him. But no, here you are, taking from me, yet again. We're not even, yet. You have at least two more, from the marks I see."

I blink my tears away. Even? Fen was his mate? That makes what I did worse. But also, there was nothing but burning heat when Aeon died. Maybe I feel things differently than they do. And what does he mean taking from him again? Nothing is making sense.

Yuli smiles wider and frozen dread settles in my gut, but that echo of darkness thrums again, louder. He just threatened Neo and Veikko. I can't lose another mate, I won't survive it.

He dunks the rag again, rinsing it, before dragging it across my chest and dropping it back in the bucket. How is the water even warmer?

"Let's see if I can guess which one died." He trails his hot finger along Neo's mark and around the other side of my breast, and I recoil even as goosebumps pop up. "Was it this one?"

"No." I suck in a breath, my skin tightening everywhere.

He flicks across my nipple, a slight smirk forming as I jump, and continues his path to my neck. "This one?"

I shake my head, not trusting my mouth.

"Then that leaves," he slides along my collarbone until he reaches Aeon's mark on my shoulder. "This one."

He presses his thumb in the center of it, and I scream, the mark filling me with pain in response to an unfamiliar Alpha.

Yuli's smile is victorious.

He lifts his hand, leaving me panting, shaking. But he slides a finger down the center of my body, leaving a trail of frayed nerves in its wake. I arch even though I don't want to, nothing in my control anymore.

"You're really sensitive. So different from a Nikta."

His finger hasn't stopped moving, and I can't focus on anything else. It slips down my lower stomach, over my mound and teases along the lips. Whimpers peel out of my throat on every breath, tears of anguish leaking because this is the absolute last thing I want to happen.

"They don't feel things like this. They have emotions, sure. But sex is perfunctory for them. They only exist to give birth and die, they don't have to enjoy anything for that to happen. But this is...interesting."

My heart breaks, even as I rock forward, praying for more friction. What a horrible way of life for them. That can't be true, can it?

His grin is lustier now, a little awed. "You want me to touch you." He states it as absolute fact as his eyes hold mine in challenge.

I shake my head, tucking my lips under my teeth, but he keeps teasing, keeps stroking, and a shiver of need travels my body.

"If that's what you want," he murmurs, "spread your legs wider."

His fingers stop, just holding their position, hot against my skin.

Fuck, it's not fair. I don't want his touch at all, but I need it. I don't even know if this is a game or not. Shame and disgust battle, coming out in more tears as I ease my knees farther apart.

There's a distinct clench of his jaw, shock replaced by an angry sneer, finally masked with indifference as he tilts his head.

"That can't be for me." Rather than where I want it, he drags just the tip of his middle finger through my wetness, bringing it up in front of my face. I ignore it and glare at his furrowing brow. I guess it was a game.

"Tell me who you're thinking about."

"I'm not thinking about anyone," I snap, closing my knees with a jerk. I'll just be miserable instead. I can't believe I let myself fall for it.

But he slaps his palm on my inner thigh, gripping it tightly. The sting sends a pulse straight to my clit. "Hold out your tongue."

My eyes widen. Is he... serious about cutting my tongue out if I lie? But he's not holding the dagger!

I can't afford to risk it. I tremble from head to toe as I swallow. "I wasn't thinking of anyone, but that...is because of you."

His brows launch up, his mouth kicking into a smirk. "Interesting. Hold out your tongue."

"But..." Panic wells. "I told you the truth!"

He huffs a breath and grabs my jaw. I'm too shocked to react at first, and he gets his thumb over my bottom lip, snags the dagger, and wedges it against my teeth. I whimper, holding my mouth as wide as I can to avoid the blade.

"I won't tell you again."

Carefully, I slide my tongue far to the right and extend it.

His pupils darken, and he lets out an erotic growl as he wipes his wet, rough finger along the length of it. His gaze follows the motion, his own mouth open like he wishes he could do the same to himself.

"The taste of defeat. How is it?" His voice is a ragged whisper, angry and desperate at the same time. I don't want to think about that at all, but the slightly sweet flavor murders my resolve. I can't stop myself from wondering what he tastes like.

He takes that same finger and resumes his tormentingly light strokes, dagger still in place.

I hate that this is turning me on. I hate how the dagger being in my mouth scares me to death, but thrills me at the same time. I hate him. I don't even know who I am anymore, or why I'm responding to him like this. No matter how hard I try, I can't fight the arch of my lower back or my moan.

"So different than I expected." He chuckles darkly. "Unfortunately, you'll never get relief from me." He runs his finger in light circles, driving me insane as he slowly withdraws the dagger. All at once, everything stops, leaving me throbbing and ashamed.

"But it was fun to watch you beg. I think I know how you'll spend your time leading up to the ritual."

I swallow, my thoughts spinning out of control. "Ritual?"

He ignores me and stands, stalking from the tent through only a small opening this time.

"Wait. Let me go, please!"

Tremors shake my frame, my wrists and ankles aching from the ropes. Confusion, fear, desperate need, loss, all swim together inside me, as I wait again for whatever comes next.

I'm not waiting long. In a matter of moments, five men file into the tent and descend on me.

"What are you...ow!"

Two untie me from the post, while another has me by the hair, craning my head back. I tilt my eyes up and sickening panic fills me.

It's Agnar.

I open my mouth to scream, but someone shoves a wad of cloth in and quickly ties another around my head. I can barely make my tongue move, and all my wails are muted to the point they're hardly audible. His unreadable expression is the last thing I see before a blindfold is secured in place.

With pitiless hands, they yank me to my feet and force me further into the tent.

I'm held in place by my hair, while they secure my hands above my head somehow. There's no time to orient on my new position before I'm doused in frigid water. Sucking in air through my nose, I push to my toes to relieve pressure on my shoulders and wrists. Another bucket dunks over me, somehow colder, and I'm scrubbed everywhere all at once, rags scraping along my body like they're trying to flay me.

An unforgiving hand rubs a rough cloth back and forth across my overly sensitive clit, showing no mercy, no matter how I writhe away, and I scream through the forced orgasm. I doubt anyone could hear it. Or if they did, no one cares.

Just as fast as it all started, it stops. I hear the rags land in an empty bucket, and my hands are unhooked. I can't catch my breath, my now-clean skin burns from the violent attention, all my nerves aching as I tremble.

I'm led in a different direction. When my feet hit a softer texture, someone kicks at the back of my legs, so I fold and drop down to my hands and knees.

I'm restrained again, only this time, they separate my feet, securing each ankle to something else, while my joined wrists are connected elsewhere. A rope loops around my throat and they pull until I have to arch to keep from choking. It's tied off and they leave.

I want to cry, and it's hard not to, but I can barely breathe as it is, sobbing will only make everything worse. I miss my mates. I miss the cabins. I miss Cyan.

That name makes me cry anyway, no matter what I want. I should have let him mate me. If I hadn't tried to buy myself more time, I wouldn't be here now, and Aeon wouldn't be…his mark warms slightly, probably in response to my dying heart.

The only bright spot, if you can call it that, was the orgasm. It helped calm my insides, even though my clit is sore. I don't know which of them did it, but it was done in such a way that I don't think the others knew. I'm going to hold on tightly to the hope that maybe they aren't all completely awful people.

Or maybe they had no idea. If I'm so different than the females they know, that literally could have just been a bath.

All I can do now is wait. Again. Pray that someone finds me or has a change of heart and lets me go. Wallow in this awful heartbreak over losing Aeon, use it to nurture the growing darkness, in hopes I can send Yuli to the same place I sent Fen.

Aeon

The blackness fades little by little. How long was I out? Ugh, everything is heavy, nothing is working. Finally, my eyes peel open, and I blink in shock.

A gigantic, matted, decaying, almost fleshless werewolf looms over me, emotionless, swirling eyes peering down. My brain hazes and all I can think is, hey, it's Kasimir, before I slip into darkness again.

The next time I wake up, I'm slightly better. Awareness filters in, slowly, and I realize there's a huge tongue, smoothing over my wounds. Warm, heavy energy seeps in through my muscles, into my bones, mending and resetting.

"I…will…fix…this." His tone is commanding, reassuring, and I believe him. After all, he fixed my bonds.

There's a pop in my chest, my heart-rate soars, and I suck in a deep breath, tears of relief spilling out. Good, now I can go find Reanne. I try to sit up, but a single claw presses on the center of my chest, pushing me back flat.

"Not…ready," he rumbles, and I feel it rather than hear it.

"I have to find—" My speech is slurred, unrecognizable. Dizziness creeps back in and I close my eyes. Okay. He might be right. I'm not healed all the way yet.

I come to again a bit later, and he's still here, still fussing over me, claw still pinning me in place. The difference is now I feel fantastic. He pulls back his energy and warmth, leaving me with a chill, but otherwise, I think I'm completely healed.

"Thank you," I exhale with a smile. "Now—"

He's gone. I glance around, but it's just me. At least at first.

There's two sets of running feet, getting closer, and I call my beast...but it doesn't come.

What the hell?

I try again. Nothing. One more time, and still no answer. I don't have time to panic before two werewolves burst out of the tree line.

A red one I don't recognize and the other one painfully, beautifully familiar.

"Cy," I whisper, glad I'm already lying on the ground. How did he find this place? I'm so glad to see him, but worried, too. Is he mad? I bet he's mad. I'd be mad.

The second he sees me, he drops his beast and rushes to me, an Alpha wave blasting with such force I can't move.

"Aeon?!" He hits his knees beside me, scanning my body furiously. "You're not— I felt you...the bond—" He lets out a single hysterical laugh as a tear hits my chest. "I thought I was going crazy when it burned through me again, but you're..."

I don't have a chance to say anything as he cradles my face and kisses me in a frantic version of his hypnotic rhythm. His tongue demands entry, and I open to him with a whimper as he sends wave after wave of Alpha energy, filling every inch of me, until I'm buzzing, tingling all over.

I wrap my arms around his neck, hugging him tight. I can pick up on his threaded emotions again, and when I reflexively reach for my Beta energy to soothe him, it's finally there. I send an answering Beta wave, probably too much, but it's such a relief to be useful again.

His shoulders droop, and he pulls back. "You're really not dead."

I shake my head and shrug. "I was, or...I wasn't..." If I did die, does that mean Kasimir somehow brought me back to life instead of just healing my wounds like I thought?

A vein in Cy's temple throbs, jaw clenching. Uh oh. "And you're perfectly fine now?"

"Uh," I swallow at the renewed pressure from his Alpha energy and nod. "Yes?"

"Good."

With one move, he stands, grabs my shoulders, picks me up, and shoves me back against the cabin wall so hard the door rattles and something knocks loose inside. Pain twinges my spine as his forearm lands against my throat and he pushes in, eyes on fire. I knew he'd be mad.

"Why?" He shoves again, strangling my air, eyes wild. "Why did you leave me?"

"Reanne...wanted...time."

"The real reason!" He shouts as the guy behind him drops his beast.

All my suppressed emotions come boiling up.

"You...don't...need...or want...me," I choke out.

"The fuck?!" His eyes widen, full of confusion and fear as he lets up on the pressure.

I can feel his anguish, his rage, because he's pumping them through the bond at lighting speed.

My gut fills with guilt. Maybe I was wrong.

"Did you fuck with our bond yesterday? And don't fucking lie."

The only time I can come up with that he might have felt something like that was when Veikko tended me. I open my mouth to explain, but... I can't. I promised.

Damn, this is going to kill him.

"I did, but I decided not to," I mutter. And now I'm lying to my Alpha. I hate this.

All other emotions drain from his eyes, leaving only heartbreak.

"You brought in another Beta," I continue, clenching my jaw. "What was I supposed to think?"

"Hey...guys." The man glances around, confused.

"Not now, Jakobe," Cyan snarls.

"Alright, I hear you, but that other energy I felt on the way is craaazy strong here."

I don't know who this guy is, or what he's talking about, but Cyan doesn't pay him any more attention. He's glaring at me, water pooling on his lashes again.

"You are mine," he growls, pushing off of me. I suck in a breath, only for him to grab my throat and throw me back on the ground. He pins me down, snarling in my face. "That's not going to change. Ever! Not even when you die, do you fucking hear me? The bond went cold, and you know what I thought? Not, who am I going to replace you with, it was, that's it for the SteelTooth pack, because I don't want to be a fucking Alpha if you're not my Beta, Aeon!"

I can't breathe, my heart is overflowing.

"Leaving me is not an option." He drops down, anger vanishing as fast as it came, and presses his forehead to mine. "Our bond is forever."

I nod and tug him into another kiss, from which he jerks free.

"Why would you ever think I don't want you?"

"You...didn't tend me after you cut into my mark on Reanne." I hate the tremble in my voice.

His eyes widen, filling with regret, and I choke on a cry that escapes, shoving the rest down.

"Fuck, that miserable piece of—" He grabs my face, forcing my gaze. "Mishka was in my body. I would have never, *never* left you hurting like that. Were you frayed the whole time?!" His pitch rises, and without waiting for an answer, he dives at my shoulder and slices clean in.

I can't stop the broken moan or tell him that Vik already fixed it. But I can channel every bit of anger and sadness and hurt to a single point now, even if he didn't earn it all. Mishka.

Cyan covers me with a smoldering blanket of his energy, calming my frantic breaths, and unlatches. He laps at the wound, clutching my shoulders tighter. Nothing changes with my bond to ReeRee, not better, not worse, but everything changes with my hurt over Cy's neglect. I cover my face, another rough cry escaping.

"You're okay," he murmurs against my skin, "You're okay. The bond is okay."

I cry harder because this isn't how he normally is with me, and...I like it. It's a shocking realization after over a decade of my life being one way and one way only. Also a bit much after nearly not being alive to realize it at all.

It makes me think of Neo, and how it might not be so bad to have something gentle in my life for once, and that maybe I do like him, and maybe we could be something, which scares the hell out of me, because he might not like me that way.

"Aeon." Cyan pushes kisses along my jawbone before nipping my ear. "In case it isn't fucking obvious by now...I love you."

I blink several times, overwhelmed, and stare up into Cy's eyes as he leans back. But I can't answer. Can't tell him what that means to me. My gaze flits to the space above Cyan, my heart hammering. Kasimir is back, hovering above us both.

Jakobe's focus narrows in, but his eyes are still searching.

"Beta," Kasimir rumbles soothingly and I feel it through the ground. "I...will fix...it all."

Maybe he means he can make Cyan happy, or maybe Cyan has wounds he'll heal, like he did for me. Only, I realize that's not the case, when a single, giant claw hooks around Cy's neck.

He doesn't notice, still staring at me, waiting.

Why would he want to hurt—

I kick at Cyan, grip his wrist and try to wrench myself free, but Cy's too strong. My fear must reach some rational part of Cyan left, because his grip slacks enough that I can scream, "No!"

Hurt flashes across his features and he leans back. "What?"

It gives me the needed space to launch upward, throwing him off balance. I don't have time to think about anything except he can't be killed. He has to mate Reanne. I dive forward, not even bracing for what Kasimir might do to me.

Jakobe lets out a straining, pained grunt, muttering, "There you are," and Kasimir's form turns, right before I make impact.

Cyan lands on his back, with me on top of him, breathing heavily, not dead. Very not dead.

"Young Tracer," Kasimir hisses, clearly unhappy. "You… cannot…withstand this…power."

Jakobe smirks, trembling, sweat on his brow, palms out in front of himself. "I don't have to, man."

He jerks his arms down and Kasimir's form wavers, stretches, twists, until ribbons of him snake down to the ground.

"You…fool!" Kasimir roars so loud the trees shake, and twists his head all the way around to face Cyan as his ghost body thins. "Find the…queen. We have…eleven…days."

The rest of him dives into the ground, taking all his energy with him.

Jakobe staggers back a step, big grin in place. "That's right! Whoo! Told you I'd save the day, Mister Alpha."

"What in the unholy fucking shit was that?!" Cyan shouts, shoving me off and stepping protectively in front of me with the same motion. "What queen? Eleven days to what? Where did he go?"

"That was Kasimir," I mutter, cracking my neck. "Pretty sure, anyway."

"Kasimir," he twists and stares at me. "Are you messing with me right now?"

"Apparently not. That's what he told Reanne his name was."

"The fucking first Alpha just pops up and you're acting like it's no big deal!"

"Well, it's not the first time I've seen him," I mutter.

"We'll deal with that later. Where the hell is Reanne?"

The red head pipes up. "Those other energies, the four werewolves? They're with her now."

My brows lift and I step back. "Yeah, she was taken. How do you know that? What are you?"

Jakobe dusts off his shoulders and gives a smug grin. "Only the best Tracer in The Glade."

"Taken?" Cyan growls. "Did you see who they were?"

I shake my head. "They ambushed me. That's when I…died. I'm so sorry."

I brace for shouting, for rage that I failed him and her, more disappointment that I left, but I get none of it.

He pales and grabs my face, mashing his mouth to mine. "You're not allowed to die again," he growls against my lips. "You're not allowed to leave my fucking sight again."

"Okay," I whisper, afraid to admit how much I like that idea.

He clutches my face tighter, wincing, before he wraps his arms around my neck and holds me close, kissing me harder.

"Fuck, I missed you," he groans, and the sound lights me on fire. He's hard as rock, grinding against my hip.

"So, you guys want me to go find her then? Or…" Jakobe's worried tone breaks our moment.

"Shit." Cyan's breath trembles, pain twisting his features as he pulls back. "No. We go together."

I scan his face. "You didn't have sex last night?"

"It's fine," he growls, pulling away.

"What about this morning?"

His scowl morphing into another wince tells me everything I need to know. Cold, dead fear pools in my stomach.

"Is…is there something wrong with…Neo? Did he get hurt?"

"No, he's fine, damn it."

Oh, thank the stars. I exhale and nod, gripping his waist. Still doesn't explain why he's in this state, but at least nothing happened.

"If I'd known you needed it, man, I'd have taken care of you myself before we left!" Jakobe steps closer, concern on his face. "Why didn't you say anything?"

"This," he cuts his gaze to me, "was more important. Now

we've got you, but we still need her. Apparently, we have eleven days before something, and a queen to find, whatever the fuck that means, so I have to wait."

I try so hard to keep my expression under control, to not give the slightest hint that I know anything, but, as always, Cy can tell.

He stares at me, wheels turning as his expression hardens. "Aeon," he growls. "What aren't you telling me?"

I crumble immediately, let out a nervous laugh, and swallow. "A lot, I think. We told you she's the Aruna Rigdis, but that means she'll be queen of the werewolves once she takes power. You and Mishka are both High Alphas, and she has to mate one of you or we all die, uh, what else…"

Cyan's energy is really weird right now, and he hasn't blinked at all since I started talking. I can't tell if he's angry or excited, or—

"When did you learn all that?"

Ah. Angry. I swallow again. "From Mishka. Before…you were poisoned."

"You couldn't be bothered to tell me that in the rundown after I came to?"

"We sort of got interrupted once we got to the part about Agnar. I'm sorry. Then everything got out of hand."

Cyan takes a deep, slow breath. "Leave anything else important off?"

"Not, uh, that I can think of. Two High Alphas. Mate or we all die. I think that's it."

"There's only one High Alpha, man." Jakobe crosses his arms and smirks. "Your info is wrong."

"How would you know? And why are you here?"

"'Cause, Beta Dude, I'm joining your pack!" He slaps my shoulder jovially and gives it a squeeze before crossing his arms again. "I heard all about the Rigdis prophecy from my dad. He's obsessed with it. High Alpha is mated by the Rigdis, the Rigdis does some sort of transformation, the High Alpha does some sort of thing, and then boom, they're, like, whole or something, I dunno. I didn't listen all the time, it's boring in most parts. But I do remember there's only one High Alpha."

Cyan scowls. "We'll talk more about this later, when I'm not scared shitless that something might happen to her. Shift. Let's go save my girl."

They both call up their beasts, and even though I have a sinking feeling it won't work, I try again. Still nothing.

There's not even an echo of a beast inside me anymore.

"Aeon," Cyan grinds out through his fangs. "Shift."

"Uh, about that." They both glance at me as I chew my lip. "I think I lost my beast."

JAKOBE

I gotta say, Aeon is yet another fine-looking dude. Cyan picked really well. But how's a guy lose his beast? And did he really die? He sure looks alive to me. That ghost werewolf was cool as hell, too. I mean, scary a little, but I actually dispelled a ghost! Can't wait to tell Veikko.

I'm tired. Really tired. Probably from running and swapping form so much already today, so I stay like I am. Reanne's energy line is only just starting to fade, so they haven't been gone too long yet, we just have to hope we get there before anything gets real bad. Crazy to think I'm about to meet the lady from the actual Rigdis prophecy. Dad would freak. Probably should have paid more attention to all that stuff but I didn't think it was real, even though, according to him, I have some part in it. Well, a Tracer does. I don't know if I believe that, I only want her to like me.

Cyan drops his beast again and stares at Aeon. "What?"

Aeon shuffles his feet, crossing his arms. "It's been gone since I woke up. Or came back to life? Whichever."

"You're…tired. That's all it is." Cyan's brows are pinched, jaw clenching.

"Whatever the reason, I should stay here, I'll only slow you guys down."

"I told you already," Cyan hooks his hand around the back of Aeon's neck. "I'm not letting you out of my sight again."

"You have to find her. I'll be fine."

"You already weren't fucking fine, Aeon. No, you're coming with. I'll carry you."

He snorts. "That's not a good idea, what if you have to fight?"

I huff a breath as I drop beast. We don't really have time for all this.

"You could take him back home to the village, and I'll run on ahead and find Reanne. We'll be back before you know it. No worries at all." I grin, winking at Cyan. "Tell Honeybear I'll be a bit late, but I'm bringing him a gift."

Aeon's brows twist, eyes wide as he glances between us. "Honeybear?"

Cyan ignores him though, and is focused on me. "What if you get attacked? And you're not bonded yet, I won't know if you're in trouble. Fuck, I don't like this idea."

But the way he clutches harder to Aeon's neck lets me know the thought of leaving him is even worse. I pat his shoulder.

"It's all good, I've got this. I was made for this sort of thing, literally. I'll find her, I'm careful. Your man Jak's on the job, remember?"

His expression softens and he snatches me into a choking hug. "Hrk—"

"Thank you," he mutters near my ear.

I soak up every bit of the Alpha energy coming off his skin, storing the feeling just in case. He lets up on the pressure and I laugh as I push back. "No sweat, my man. You're welcome. Now, you two crazy pups run along home." I slap his ass and hop back out of possible reach. I'd tap Aeon, too, but I get the feeling anything resembling a pass would get my arm chewed off. Besides, even I know better than to mess with an Alpha's partner.

"Literally twice your age, Jak." Cyan scowls, but I'm starting to pick up on when he's really angry and when he's making a big fuss. This is a fuss time.

I grin and bite the tip of my tongue as I call up my beast. My legs give a little, but I manage to keep anyone from noticing.

Cyan pulls Aeon into another short, hot kiss, then shifts and throws him over his shoulder. Aeon's smile is sad, strained, and

Cy gives me a nod as he takes off back for the village. Once he's out of sight I drop down to my haunches for a second, just to breathe.

I'm really happy for them. And I'm really glad I didn't tell Cyan how drained I am, or he'd have never taken Aeon to safety.

Another win in my book.

Alright, I've got a job to do. I just have to remember I can rest when I find Reanne, so the faster the better.

The stark quiet of the forest crawls up my back. Not a big fan of being alone, but I shake it off, grab hold of her energy line, and follow it as stealthily as I can.

Her line jumps all over the place, but the wolves are in a pretty steady pattern. Were they throwing her? My lips pull back in a snarl. Man, that's not a nice thing to do. I guess they weren't really concerned with being nice, though, since they tried to kill Aeon.

I bet if they knew what she really is they would have been more careful with her.

Two of the wolves split off to the left, but I stick with Reanne's line, following it over two creeks and around the edge of a bone pit. I finally see the outlines of tents up ahead in fog that hasn't burned off yet.

I try to slow, but I guess I'm too tired, and I end up flopping a little and rolling to a stop. Man, that did not feel good.

I can tell if I drop beast now, I won't be able to get him back for a while, so I just lay on my side for a minute, panting.

Why am I this tired? I slept like a newborn pup last night. I know I only had one thing of jerky, but that should have been enough for at least a bit longer. Did dispelling the ghost dude do something? Ugh, he did say I couldn't handle it, maybe he was right.

'sall good. Just gonna rest here a—

My skin pricks. Damn, someone's coming. Someone with a similar energy as the guys who took her, must be the same pack.

This blows my whole plan of sneaking into some back door and sweeping her away in silent heroics.

Okay, Jak, think. Oh. Easy.

I dump all the energy from Cyan, Aeon, and Reanne. I don't want to dump Veikko's, though. Maybe I can...yeah. I shove it deep inside. I can hide it well enough, no problem. I stay right where I am, playing up the tired bit. That doesn't really take much playing up, though, I am seriously drained.

The energy gets closer, footsteps shuffling through the leaves until I'm spotted. Then the sound stops. I don't lift my head, but I do cough.

There's a growl, followed by a whispered, "Hey, are you okay?"

The guy moves closer, and I cough again, tilting my head until he comes into view.

Holy hell, it's Corbet! I almost jump off the ground before I remember to play it cool. There's no way he doesn't recognize me in wereform. I'm the only red werewolf I've ever heard about. Man, this could be bad or good. What's he doing here? I want to drop beast so bad and ask why he picked this pack, but if I do, it could be a day before I can shift again. And I'm so...so tired.

He gives me a wink, sniffs the air around me, and frowns over my head as another guy approaches from behind. Even though my reflexes tell me to run, I stay still.

He growls, low. "What's an unbonded wolf doing lying here, about to die?"

Corbet shrugs. "No idea. Maybe he's on a Pack Hunt? Got injured?"

Nice thinking, Corby! Wonder if I can convince him to help me even more. After I rest.

The other guy nudges me with his foot and sighs. "Take him to Yuli, we'll let him decide what to do."

"Okay." Corbet smiles. "But you have to finish hunting alone then."

The other wolf grunts, and his footsteps retreat as Corbet calls up his beast and grabs me. Man, I don't remember him being this big the last time I saw him. Maybe all that time up north did him good. He's careful with me. Either because it's me, or I look worse than I feel. If so, that'll only work in my favor.

I'm in the center of their camp in no' time. The whole place feels heavy, like the general mood isn't very bright. I don't like it. They're set up differently than Cy and his crew, with animal hide tents instead of cabins, but the fire is a bit more defined, with a big rock border and a tripod thing above it.

There are way more tents here than SteelTooth has cabins, though. That makes me a little nervous, but it's nothing old Jak can't handle. Corbet lays me down on a bedroll near the fire, and drops his beast, giving me a pat on the scruff.

"Warm up a bit, pal, I'll be right back with some water."

Off he goes, out of sight. There are lots of guys milling around further into camp, chatting. But it's just me right here that I can see. Now to find Cyan's gal.

The real trick is opening up to feel for Reanne's energy without spitting any of Veikko's out. Should have dumped it, too, but I didn't want to be completely alone. Good news is, if there's a Tracer who can do this, it's me.

It's all a useless worry though, because I don't even have to search for her line. The second I open myself up, I'm hit with tendrils of her energy, pouring out of the biggest tent near the back of the camp. There's a lot. Like, way more than there should be. Could be she's hurt? Maybe her body is calling out for help, but...to who? Whatever. Someone else can worry about that, I just have to figure out how to get to her without getting myself killed in the process. No worries at all.

"Here we go." Corbet trots back and sits right by my head. "It's better if you shift back to drink."

I heave the biggest sigh. He's right. Which means I can't get her out today. And means I won't get to go back home to SteelTooth as soon as I hoped. I hope Vik isn't too sad.

Corb stares at me, wiggling the water cup. No help for it, I guess.

I drop the beast and groan. Every muscle I have hurts like I was stomped on. Corb helps me sit up, pushing on my shoulder until I'm righted, and hands me the cup.

I down it in one go, cracking my neck as I exhale.

"Hi, I'm Corbet." He's being extra loud as he juts out his hand, way too obvious if you ask me. "This is the BriarMaw pack."

More than a few eyes turn our way. Man, the pack's gonna think I'm deaf if he keeps that up.

"Chill," I cough under my breath, and take his hand. "Jakobe."

"Another young man, finding his way to us on Pack Hunt, at such an important time."

A low, unamused voice comes from a tent to my left, and I turn in time to see him emerge. Black hair, glowing blue eyes, and a sneer I don't like all that much, being honest. A shudder speeds through my body. His Alpha energy is dark. Explains why the camp feels so, I dunno, grim. Everyone feeds off an Alpha's baseline wavelength, and this guy is practically a hunk of rotting meat, energy wise. I really don't like how there's residual of Reanne's line around him.

"What are the chances?" He stands right in front of me, tucking his hands behind his back.

Time to shine, Jak.

I grin as best I can, which probably isn't much since I'm so damn exhausted, and stick my hand out to him. "Jakobe, I'm a —" I cough. "I'm glad to meet you."

Can't believe I almost told him I was a Tracer. Here I am, telling Corb to chill.

The Alpha stares at me a moment before he steps forward and clasps my hand, jerking me to my feet with no effort at all. I sway a little but manage to find my footing. I figure what's coming, so I bury Vik's energy even deeper, and open my wall just a little. I need to be completely packless as far as he can tell.

He narrows his eyes and sniffs, studying me as he sends his Alpha wave through. I fight the grimace, but man oh man, I do not like this guy's vibe at all. Finally, his smile turns sincere, and he pumps our clasped hands once.

"Yuli," he says, releasing me to pat Corb on the shoulder instead. "I suppose we'll need another welcome dinner."

Corbet grins at him and nods. "Great! I'll go let Pell know. See you around, Jakobe." He runs off, but I can't get a good look where because Yuli steps into the line of sight.

"He's spoken for, so I wouldn't get any ideas. Pell isn't into sharing."

I blink and refocus on him. "Huh? Pff, me and Corb—oh. Right. Man, that is…a bummer. I guess I'll keep my options open then."

He gestures for me to sit as he lowers to another bedroll nearby. "Wise choice. Now, tell me. Why are you here?"

17

NEO

"What are we going to do?" I whisper shout at Veikko.

Vik and Korey are flanking my prep table, worried faces matching mine. Well, Vik's face is still stoic as always, but I know he's worried. He should be. I mean, this is probably it for all of us.

"We're not going to mention Lazaros at all, firstly," Korey growls.

I nod, rubbing my neck. He's right, that would be awful. Laz is hiding out in Korey's cabin right now. Apparently, Mishka had the guy prisoner. It would have been good to know that before I had my tiny grumpy fit all over him.

"Did you tell him I'm—"

"Sorry? Yeah. He's not upset with you."

"Okay. Okay, great. That's great. Good."

My skin hurts. Even Korey is rubbing his arms. Mishka has scratched out one of the territory markers, and Cyan's energy is already fading since he's not here. Now, Mishka's overloading the SteelTooth grounds with his energy instead.

This is so bad. Our Alpha is gone, another one is inside our territory, and we're only a pack of three as far as it sits right now. Completely vulnerable.

This is really, really bad.

I whimper and pace to the fire and back again. "But what are we going to *dooo?*"

"Calm down." Vik's tone is frustratingly even.

"I would, if we weren't in danger of being taken over!" I can't stop whisper shouting everything, but it's the only way I can emphasize how utterly fucked we are.

I miss Cyan. We need Aeon. I desperately want to hold Reanne. I even miss Jakobe.

I'm hyperventilating, I think. Am I breathing? I can't feel my face.

Korey grabs my shoulders and shakes me, forcing my focus. "Neo, breathe."

I suck in a lungful and hold it. Guess I wasn't breathing after all. It escapes in a rush like I was punched.

"This is so bad. What if he's here to kill us, like he told Reanne he would? I think I'd rather him do that, than claim us for his pack, but I don't want to die, either!"

I've graduated to straight shouting now, this is no time for whispering.

Veikko's hand closes tight around my neck, and he holds my gaze, a faint ochre glow simmering deep in the eye that isn't damaged. I still, blinking in disbelief. Why…he shouldn't have a glow…

He steps behind me, loosening his hold, and ducks to my ear.

"Calm." His breath is hot, sending a chill across my shoulder. "Down."

I want to be calm, I really do. But this is the end of SteelTooth by one method or another, unless Cyan shows up, and I love this place, and I didn't get to see Aeon again, and I might die before he knows how I feel, and—

"Damn it, Neo, breathe," Korey mutters, lightly slapping my cheek.

I suck in another breath, the spots clearing from my vision, and give him a nod. He smiles softly and ruffles my hair before stepping back. Hmph. I reject the implication that's supposed to placate me, I'm older than he is.

I adjust my glasses, fix my hair, and breathe again, oddly comforted by Vik's hand still around my neck and his heat on my back.

"We just have to play it cool, right?" Korey stares off into the woods, thoughtful. "If he's here for Reanne, and we tell him she's gone, maybe he'll leave."

And I'm panicking again.

"Did you forget he somehow coerced Agnar into helping him poison Cyan?!" I whisper shriek. "You haven't spoken to him, he won't leave. No. He'll want to wait for her. Maybe kill us for fun while he does!" I whimper and try to step forward, but Vik's hand tightens, and he tugs me back flush with his body. I'm about to go into full white-out mode because I can't escape, can't run for my life, when needle sharp teeth sink into the spot where my shoulder and neck meet, freezing me in place.

My eyes widen as thick, heavy energy slides down my spine, relaxing every muscle it touches along the way, spreading around my sides like seeking fingers. Alpha energy. Part of me recoils at the foreign attack, but the rest of me melts like candle wax.

I groan, eyes closing, slumping fully against Veikko, inviting a deeper bite without even thinking. The swarm of heat is dangerously delicious, undeniable, tempting me, asking me for my soul in exchange for safety, pulling me into a cocoon of warmth and promises.

One of my eyes manages to crack back open and I see Korey's confused expression. "He's mated to Reanne, not you. How is that…working?"

More importantly, how do I keep him from stopping? I need to stay like this. Suspended in a happy, protected, relaxed, sensual state until Cyan comes back. If…he comes back. Panic tries to well again, but Vik's teeth burrow further, coupled with a soft growl that sends a burst of pleasure through me.

I fling my arm behind me and grab at his hip, pushing back against his obvious erection. He grunts, just a light rush of air down my collarbone, the fingers around my throat spreading, and his other hand snaking around to rest on my stomach.

"Shit, you guys are making me need my mate," Korey mutters, his throat rippling. "We don't have time for this."

Neo, he is correct. If I release you, are you going to be alright?

Veikko's voice in the link sends the energy into overdrive. I whine, digging my claws into his skin. My bond with Cyan is stronger than the force that pulls the moon through sky, so I'm not worried about how hard Veikko is wooing me. I'm worried I might fall completely apart when he stops. I'm also confused at how he's an Alpha and no one knew.

Wait. Is this...is this why he was biting Aeon? That would explain it. He was healing him, or calming him, or something along those lines probably. Heh. It really *wasn't* what it looked like. I was mostly focused on him anyway.

Neo.

Oh, uh. No. Probably I will not.

Vik chuckles against my shoulder and flicks his tongue against the raised skin still clamped in his bite.

"Oh, fuck," I moan. That's not part of Alpha wooing, that's just Vik licking me. Vik being...sexy.

I don't know what's going on anymore. My dick is throbbing like a broken limb, Alpha waves are making my bones weak, and all I can think about is when he shoved my head down on Aeon's cock. This is Cyan's fault. He didn't want me last night. Then, left us both high and dry this morning without so much as a goodbye, and now Vik's massive hand is giving me weird sparks and we're all about to die!

Vik growls louder, biting deeper, and my panic wanes again as a breathy whimper slips out. Blood leaks from the wound, running down my chest and back in small streams.

Korey is staring at us with a slight snarl on his lip like he doesn't want to enjoy what he's seeing, but he's also hard as stone, and could have looked away at any point.

This is a problem.

Ugh, his voice. I claw Vik's hip again, rocking against him.

Korey snorts. "You think? Dug in pretty deep, there. Much further and you'll take a chunk right out of him."

"I'm sorry, okay. I'm a wreck. I know it. The grass knows it. I had no idea how bad off I'd be without Cyan here. I've never been away from him."

Tears hit my cheeks, and I let them stay there. Korey's expression is pure sympathy, but thankfully he doesn't try to soothe me again.

Neo, I have to release you. We should present a strong front to Mishka. No indication of anything amiss. And since I am not an Alpha, nor your mate, this would be cause for suspicion.

Not an…Ohhh. It's a secret. Well, this is just great. I'm the absolute worst at keeping secrets.

Neo. Breathe.

"Okay. I'm breathing. I'm ready. I'm not but do it before I —gah!"

He unlatches, and the rush of sensation at the bite, compared to the complete void of Alpha energy has my skin crawling and my knees folding.

But then he laps at the wound, and his healing energy seeps in. He's still holding me by my stomach, hand still on my neck, but his thumb is smoothing along my jawline, lulling me. It's nice. Vik would be a great Alpha, I think.

After the holes on the back are closed, he spins me around and holds me a little farther away, leaning more to reach the front.

"La—My mate is so upset," Korey mutters, staring at his cabin, rubbing his chest. "I'm worried. He's still bonded to Mishka."

Vik stops mid lick and swivels to face him. "I thought Cyan… You are right. There was no time. Cursed sun, I should have made him another set of bracers."

"Bracers?"

But Vik gives me a hard lick, closing the last bit of skin, and runs toward his clearing, leaving me and Korey alone.

We stare at each other.

I cough lightly. "So."

"So." He raises a brow at me and smirks. "Feeling better?"

"Yes. Surprisingly."

It would have been better if Cyan had been here so I didn't need any of this in the first place, but that's not how my life is going right now.

"I didn't realize you were into pain. I thought that was Aeon's thing."

"I am *not* into pain, Veikko is…" I chew on my tongue before getting my words back in order. "Good. At it?"

Korey grins wider, crossing his arms. "Is he? Was it just the depth of the bite that did it?"

"Oh, you know. That. The…other things." I swallow and fidget with the arm of my glasses.

"Uh huh. I know he's an Alpha."

All my air explodes out of me. "Oh, thank the moon, because there was no way I'd keep that a secret. How'd you find out?"

"My mate felt a quick wave coming from Jakobe's cabin while he was getting some air. He's sensitive to that sort of thing. I didn't think he was wrong, necessarily, but I couldn't see it. This proves it. Can't wait to tell him he was right."

Yes, yes, you're adorably in love. Rub it in everyone's face.

I scrunch my nose. Turns out, I'm not such a nice person when I'm under extreme stress. I need to work on that. And Cy needs to get home.

"Okay. It's supposed to be a secret, so don't tell anyone else."

Korey mimes zipping his lip and we share a smile.

I'm not sure why he wants to keep it a secret. Cyan probably wouldn't care. Even I've heard of an Alpha staying in someone else's pack, never seating their own territory. Doesn't happen all that much, but it's certainly nothing worth being hush-hush about in my opinion. It's not like he's planning a takeover.

Veikko is on his way back toward us with something small

131

clutched in his hand, when he stops cold and widens his stance, facing the woods behind Jakobe's cabin.

There's a muggy stall in the air around our village, like that moment before a tornado hits and the sky turns green.

Korey and I work our shoulders, fighting the sensation of a million insects biting us. Cyan's residual energy is being flattened, slowly pushed outward from the fire pit by the invading Alpha.

I clutch the back of Korey's arm, and he mutters, "Holy shit," as the source of all our discomfort emerges from the tree line.

He stands straighter than Cyan, shoulders squared, chin tilted so he's looking down on us. But his eyes are the same, his lips, his ears, his jawline, everything. All that's missing is the large neck scar and slightly longer hair.

"They really do look almost exactly alike," I whisper. My eyes are telling my heart that Cy's home, but my body can tell I'm looking at a snake in a Cyan-skin suit.

Mishka smiles, tucking his hands in his pockets. "The SteelTooth pack. At long last."

CYAN

This is a waking fucking nightmare. I should be searching for Reanne, not sending a guy who's practically still a pup. Even if I respect the hell out of him for doing it. But I also can't let Aeon get hurt again, and now that something's wrong with his beast, he's basically helpless.

Another wall of blinding agony collides with my body, almost taking me out. I stumble a step and manage to set Aeon on his feet before I brace on a tree. I should have let Neo take care of me last night. Can't even tell you why I didn't at this point, there's too much pain digging into my muscles, fuzzing my brain. I drop the beast, huffing harder as I rest my forehead on the scratchy bark.

Sometimes this part of being an Alpha sucks ass. Seems almost too good to be true that Reanne can make it go away forever.

I'd want her even if she couldn't. I'd want her even if every time we were together, it hurt worse.

I miss her. I don't know what to make of this High Alpha bullshit. Or the fact that Mishka might also be one, depending on who's right. Probably why he's been jacking my body, to get closer to her since she's a part of some fucking prophecy. I huff a breath.

I mean, if I'd ever met someone worthy of being in a prophecy, it's her. But the me changing, her changing parts, I'm not sure about. Once we get her back, I'll take her to meet Zaid, since he apparently knows it all or some shit.

No matter what else happens, prophecy or the moon crashing

down on top of us, she's mine. She feels right. She's supposed to be with me. And I'm running in the opposite fucking direction from where she is, leaving her fate in someone else's hands.

"God damn it," I mutter with the breath I have left.

Aeon wraps his arms around my midsection, hands flat on my lower stomach, warm body curled against my back, forehead between my shoulder blades. I'm hard in less than a second, my body angry with need.

He sends his perfectly subtle Beta wave through me, and I exhale, soaking in the comfort, letting my head fall back against the top of his. Fuck, I missed that. I know I wasn't that long without it, but Betas are supposed to be with their Alphas for a damn reason, and it's not just to talk to. Everything I've been through wouldn't have been nearly as bad if he'd been home.

The needling anxiety fades, but it just clears the way for more pain, drawing a grimace.

Aeon's fingertips glide lower, until he cups my balls with one hand, and traces the veins in my cock with the other.

A groan slips out, but I growl, "We need to get back."

"Just a few minutes won't hurt," he murmurs against my skin, running his tongue along my spine.

Chills chase his movements, and when he changes from teasing touches to his strong grip and fluid stroking, I thrust almost mindlessly.

My claws spring up and dislodge bits of bark as I strain to maintain control. He pumps faster, twisting his palm over my head, fondling my balls, licking my back, fanning me with Beta energy, and it's not long before my first load splashes his hand. My roar is nothing but pure, bone-deep relief. The agony dulls as I pant, everything starting to come back into focus.

His mouth curls against my back, and he keeps going, coating my cock with the cum, not changing pace or motion at all.

I reach between our bodies and run a claw up and down his length, mashed against my ass. He moans, pressing his cheek to my back, his strokes turning less rhythmic as his breathing increases.

"Y-you don't have to—fuck, yes!"

I dig my claws into his balls, tugging, sending an unchecked wave of my energy. His long, pleasured whine and the shudder through his muscles is enough to push me back to the edge. He squeezes me harder, stroking faster, whimpering against my skin. In a chorus of heavy groans and moans, we both come, my lower back painted with his thick cum, mine landing somewhere on the ground.

We stay like this a moment longer, slow loving strokes, his hot breath on my back, until I can't take it. I spin and hug his neck, crushing him to me as I kiss him, speaking against his lips.

"You're in my bed tonight."

He nods, gripping my hips as he happy sighs into my mouth.

"So is Reanne if we find her."

He nods again.

"And Neo."

His eyes pop open and he pulls back. "Are...you sure that's a good idea? It could be, you know, hard on you. Splitting the energy."

Yeah, I'm not dumb.

"What's your problem with Neo?"

"No problem. There's no problem."

He's gone cold from his head to his feet, and he steps away, smiling as he gestures to the woods. "We should hurry back in case something goes wrong."

That's the fakest smile I've ever seen on his sexy face. I could have died happy after finally having them both at the same time, so whatever this shit is, it's going to end immediately.

"What else could fucking go wrong today?" I grumble, calling my beast.

Aeon eyes me, his brows pitching in the middle as he deflates. "It still won't come."

My heart hurts. I couldn't imagine not being able to shift, it's an integral part of everything. What the fuck are we if we can't do that? I'd never say that to him, though. He'll be perfect to me no matter what, but hopefully, for his sake, we can figure this shit out and fast.

I gather him in my arms and mash my muzzle against the center of his chest. He tugs on my ear with a sad half grin, and I take off running. It's slower to travel holding someone, but we should make it back before nightfall.

Hopefully.

JAKOBE

I glance past Yuli, catching sight of five guys leaving the tent in the back. I'm trying my best not to let my mind race with what they were doing in there, but it's hard. Damn hard. I gotta answer this Alpha's questions like the pro I am, when all I want to do is run through here setting fires so I can grab her.

"Gotta be honest." I nudge one of the stones around the fire with my foot as I refocus on him. "I didn't have a single clue where I was."

He leans back on his hands, studying me. "We are a bit out of the way. Where are you from?"

"DuskFall."

I track where the other guys split off, but one with blondish hair is coming this way. Something is wonky with his energy.

"Corbet is from there. You didn't recognize him?"

All chill. I am all chill. I've got this.

I smile sheepishly and rub my head. "Funny story, I told him to act like we were strangers. See, I didn't know if you were a cool Alpha, or one of them really uptight ones who would be all, whoa, hey, you're from the same pack what gives, ahh! Murder!"

He snorts, and a couple of nearby guys shoot him confused looks. "And you determined I was...which?"

"Oh. Cool, man. You have a really, you know. Steady...vibe."

The pro-est of pros. When I get us out of this, I deserve at least three days of meals, set up in my cabin so me and Vik don't even have to leave. Need a bigger bed so Reanne can hang, too.

No, man, you know what? We need one giant bed and we can

all be together. Yeah. I like that idea. Wouldn't mind some snuggle time with Glasses, if it wouldn't get me killed by Cyan.

"I see." Yuli smiles faintly, and shrugs a shoulder slowly. "It is unusual for you both to be from the same pack, but I know he hasn't sent word home, and Zaid has no qualms with us. So, in this case, you're correct. I'm cool."

"Right on," I grin.

He readjusts, crossing his arms. "Still. That's pretty far. You passed several packs before you got here. Corbet said you were injured, but I don't see any wounds."

The blond-haired guy is closer, and I'd think my skill was broken if I didn't know better. He's a complete void, there's nothing coming off of him, and…nothing getting in. My eyes widen.

I'd bet all my back teeth that man is a Tracer.

"I said what happened out there?"

"Huh?" I refocus on Yuli's stern expression. "Oh, sorry. Well, you might think this is dumb, but since this was my first time leaving home, I wanted to see how far I could run before I—" I cut myself off with a laugh at his widening eyes. "I told you, man. Dumb. Plus, all I had to eat this morning was a single piece of jerky I, uh, was carrying with me."

The blond guy's eyes snap to mine, and I quickly adjust my energy. He stops walking for a moment, glances to his left, and continues toward us, gaze focused.

Shit. I think he made me.

"You ran…from DuskFall to here."

I swallow thickly and nod.

"On jerky."

"I passed a bunch of rabbits and stuff, scared a grouse near to death, but I haven't tried eating anything in my beast yet, and, well, I didn't know."

"You really are fresh off the nipple, aren't you?" Yuli glances up with a determined expression. "Agnar, my friend. This is Jakobe. A potential member all the way from DuskFall."

138

"Nice to meet you, Jakobe." His voice is pleasant, even if his gaze isn't.

He sticks out his hand, but I don't move. I remember that name. Vik said he'd betrayed them and left. And now Reanne is here, in the same place as him? I don't like this, not one bit. Aside from that, I've never been this close to another Tracer. Hell, I've never even met one. What happens if we touch? Are we gonna blow up? Set each other on fire or something?

Yuli eyes me. "Aren't you going to shake his hand?"

"Huh? Oh, sure."

I grin, wipe my palm on the bedroll a few times, stand slowly, and face Agnar.

"Still pretty worn out, sorry about that. Nice to meet you, too, man."

Yuli stands and steps beside Agnar, watching me closely as we clasp hands.

Nothing happens at first, but in seconds, energy leeches into my skin, crawling through my body, invading me. I keep my grin in place, even though I'm screaming inside. He goes straight to the deepest part of me, through my wall like it's water. I can't block him out.

There's a static pop when he finds Veikko's energy. And I see it in his eyes. Recognition, fear, sorrow. His own wall cracks a little, bright energy flailing behind him like a flag only for a heartbeat, but long enough I can see threads of Reanne's on him. Then he's a void again, all energy gone, all signs of life erased from his eyes.

He releases me, and nods to Yuli who claps my shoulder. "You passed, Jakobe. Come, let's get some food in that worn out body."

Agnar leaves before we do, ducking into the tent behind me. I stare after him, stunned. I thought I knew all about my skill. Knew I could control the energy coming and going in my body and find people and memorize their energy…but I didn't know I could keep my vibe clean, even if the stuff coming in was dirty.

That's awesome. I wonder how, and if he has any other tricks he can teach me.

Yuli wraps his arms around my shoulder and tugs me along.

"Uh, that's great news, man. Passed what exactly?"

We step into a tent that's open on both sides, housing a long table in the center with benches. There's tons of food on the farthest end, and about twelve other werewolves in here, spread out along the seats.

"My test. See, for many…many years, I've been studying a prophecy that could destroy everything." He hands me a plate. "And a Tracer is supposed to be the key to it coming true. Since that's the last thing my fellows and I want, I've been taking steps to ensure it doesn't happen."

I chuckle, gripping the plate tighter. "That sounds like a lot of boring reading."

"It is, for the most part. But I feel the time invested will ultimately be worth it. Lamb?"

"You bet, load me up." We share a smile as I glance around. "So, that was you…doing what?"

"Checking to see if you were a Tracer. It's a good thing you aren't." He pops a potato wedge in his mouth. "You'd be dead."

My blood thins. It would have been over just that fast, if Agnar had outed me. Why the heck didn't he? What's his game?

"Really good thing. Have you found a bunch or something? I haven't heard much about them, other than they are rare."

There's a vicious cold in the gaze he levels at me. "They're rarer now."

"Heh." I stretch my neck. "Good work, I guess. And I guess you are a little 'ahhh, murder,' after all, huh?"

He chuckles this time, stopping several wolves in their tracks, and shrugs. "I suppose so. Everyone has something they're willing to kill for."

Man. I have got to get her out of this place, and fast.

We make our way through the room, him acknowledging pack members with a nod as he passes.

"Must be a helluva prophecy. You'll have to tell me about it someday."

"Well," he gestures for me to sit across from him, "if all goes according to plan, you'll never hear about it. Ever again."

Yeah, that settles it. Able to shift or not, we have to escape tonight. I don't like how any of this sounds.

"Then I guess we'll have to find other stuff to talk about."

I take a huge bite of lamb, because goddess knows I'm about to waste away. I think she'll forgive me for eating. Can't do any saving if my stomach moves out in protest.

I force the bite down under Yuli's stare and smile. "Like, for example, did you know there's a pack way down south that flat refuses to grab supplies from the human world?"

His brows lift as he hands me a cup of something. It's a dark reddish liquid. Smells really strong and fruity. He chugs his cup and sets it down with an exhale. I fake taking a sip and set mine down. I don't know what poison smells like, but I don't wanna learn by dying.

"I had heard of them. Purists I believe they like to go by."

"Yeah! If you ask me, I say, grab whatever you can, man. They can just make more, we can't."

He nods, as do a few guys near us. I'm selling it and they're buying it, but that ends when Agnar comes in and locks eyes on me. I choke on another bite of food, pounding my chest to clear it. All I've got to drink is this possible poison. Guess I'm about to find out if he's still trying to kill me or not.

I take a gulp, clearing my throat finally. "Whew! I'm good. I'm...wow, this stuff tastes pretty good. What is it?"

Yuli smiles. "Wine."

"This something from the humans?"

"Pell makes it, actually. Along with all the food you're eating. We found a recipe a few years ago."

"Thanks to the cook then." I take another small sip, warmth spreading down my throat. "Man. Makes my tongue feel funny. Does it do that to you?"

141

He smiles, but it doesn't look friendly. "Yes, sometimes. It's good at helping you relax."

I almost spit it back in the cup. Relaxing too much is not a good idea for me and my mouth.

"Agnar, join us," he calls out, still staring at me. Agnar stiffens near the food and glares at the side of Yuli's head. He grabs a plate and claims the seat beside his Alpha.

I can't help staring at the guy, but he won't even look up from his food. He's about my size, less muscle-y, broader shouldered. He could definitely do some damage if he needed to. I wonder what he did to Cy's crew.

If I could just get him alone. I have a bunch of questions.

"You know," Yuli eyes me, "Agnar doesn't have a partner."

Agnar and I both freeze, food midway to our mouths.

"I don't need or want one," he mutters, shoving a bite in, still not glancing up. "Especially not him."

"Your cock says otherwise," Yuli smirks, slapping Agnar's thigh. He jumps, swearing under his breath.

My brows lift as I chew slower. It's all I can do not to sneak a peek under the table.

"This is good. You can both join the pack officially at the same time, and you can show him the ropes while I deal with other things."

"I'm not a mentor," he growls at his plate.

"You're whatever I say you are."

I flinch at the Alpha wave and the glare Agnar sends to Yuli's smirking face.

"You swore—"

"I'm not going to command you, Agnar. Calm down. I can't yet, anyway. I am, however, going to strongly suggest you do as I've said. And remind you, like your father, you're useful to me right now."

There's a dark emphasis on the right now part.

The stare down continues another second before Agnar huffs a breath and refocuses on his plate. "Fine."

"Good decision." Yuli drains the rest of his wine, slamming the cup down. "See, this is why you need a partner. You're so tense."

I grin from ear to ear. I'm gonna need a new book for all these wins I'm racking up.

"Hey, man, that's great! I guess I wasn't hiding my interest too well, huh?" I wink at Yuli who chuckles.

"Not in the slightest." He stands and, without warning, sends a pulse of Alpha command through the room. I nearly don't get my wall up in time. I know I'm not pack, but I don't wanna take any chances. Agnar's grey eyes snap to mine finally. He gives me an almost imperceptible head shake.

The command ends, and he glances around as other pack members clean up their messes and file out. I have no idea what the order was, but Agnar's jaw ticks, worry crinkling his brow.

Yuli grips Agnar's shoulder. "Why don't you show your new partner where our territory lines are, our marking, the basics."

Yet another non-request. Agnar is majorly conflicted, so I stand first. "Sounds good to me! I need the lay of the land for sure. Don't want to go falling off a cliff or something like that."

Yuli blows a soft laugh through his nose and gives me an obvious once-over. "We'll settle around the fire in a few hours." With that, he strolls through the doorway and hooks to the right.

It's just us, but Agnar doesn't speak, still chewing and staring at his plate.

I lean on the table and clear my throat. "So, partner, we should—"

"No." He continues chewing.

"What do you mean no?"

He doesn't answer, so I swipe his plate. "There we go, now you have to look at me."

I grin and he levels a stare at me, tongue jammed in his cheek.

"At least the view's good, right?" I do a turn and am shocked at the slight smile crooking the corner of his mouth.

"Very good. That's not the point."

"Very good, he says. Alright," I laugh, "I like that. So, what is this 'no' you're throwing out?"

He stands slowly. With a quick move, he grabs the back of my neck and meets me over the center of the table, mouth pressed to my ear. "Whatever you're planning, no." His whisper sends heat down my side. "It won't work. You won't survive."

I chuckle. "Well, you'll have to let me know what it feels like to be wrong. 'Cause your man Jak is gonna live forever as a hero."

Agnar's cheek pulls back in an obvious smile, brushing my skin. "You're insane."

"Nah, I'm just that good, man."

He pulls back slowly, scrubbing his stubble across my cheek before locking eyes with me a breath away, hand still on my neck. "Is he okay?"

It's barely audible, but there's so much emotion in it, my throat closes a little. It's the same look he had when he found Veikko's energy. All I can manage is a nod at first, then grin. "He's better than okay. He's a fantastic kisser."

Shock is followed closely by blind rage as he digs his fingers into my scalp. "If you hurt him, I will destroy your body and scatter your energy to the eight points, so that not even the goddess herself could put you back together."

"Holy shit," I laugh. "That's an awesome threat. I'm totally gonna remember that! But, no worries, man. My Honeybear is gonna have to pry me off with a stick."

His hand falls away like it weighs a thousand pounds. Wide, blinking eyes stay glued to mine as he drops back down on the bench, dumbfounded. "Honeybear," he mumbles.

I'm not sure what to do with his reaction, but I can't help whispering, "Was he the one you betrayed? 'Fore you left?"

That snaps him to attention, and he shoves the entire ten-foot bench back as he stands, snatching his plate from me and tossing on the pile with the rest.

"No. Come with me."

He storms out, with me scrambling to keep up. I crash into his back, though, once I'm on the outside.

"Oof. Hey, man, what's…"

He's watching men file into the large tent in the back. Or, he's watching what I can see, which are all the iridescent waves of Reanne's energy, soaring now, up to the clouds and beyond.

"Shit," he mutters, grabbing the hair on the back of his head. "Was afraid the command had something to do with her."

"Yeah, I was worried too. How're we gonna get her out?"

"We?" He spins and finds me too close for his liking, apparently, and rears a step back.

"Well, yeah, partner." I grin. "The more teeth, the sharper the bite. Four ears are better than two. You know, all that teamwork stuff. I don't mind sharing the glory."

He huffs and glances around the camp before grabbing me by the arm and leading me away from everything, out toward the woods.

"What're you doing? She's the other way."

He doesn't talk but keeps shoving me forward until we are at the trees. "Go."

"What?"

"Go back to him."

"Are you out of your mind?"

Anguish crosses his features as he grinds his teeth. "If he opened up to you, that is a gift beyond compare. What he went through would have driven lesser men to fling themselves into the Quay." There's water on his lashes as he jams his finger into my chest. "And I'm not going to let you cause him anymore pain by getting yourself killed. So, you go. Go back to him, love him while you still have time. I'll get her out like I was already planning to."

"Man, I'm not going anywhere. Did you not hear me say I'm living forever? This is just a short detour. Besides, how would it look now if I ran off and you stroll back into camp like nothing happened? It's too suspicious."

He sneers harder and harder until he growls and punches a nearby tree. "You don't understand. If you stay, there's no version of this where you come out alive."

"How many times do I have to—"

He grabs my arms and shakes me. "You're the one from the prophecy," he seethes and my heart stops. "All this time I thought it was me but...the Tracer who gives their life to secure the union. It's you."

Oh. Well, damn.

KOREY

N eo's grip on my arm is the only thing keeping me from tearing across the camp and lunging at Mishka. I know I couldn't win, I'm not a seated Alpha or his pup, and those are the only things that can kill another seated Alpha, but I'd damn sure feel better. At least for a few seconds.

"What? No greeting?" Mishka strolls toward the fire, pushing Cyan's claim away, ignoring Vik completely. "Surprised to find so few of you. And, do correct me if I'm wrong, but…" He glances around at nothing. "It seems your Alpha is gone."

Without turning, he points a finger behind himself at Vik. "Your seated Alpha, I should say."

My jaw creaks. If he knows, it's not much of a secret, is it? And it's weird how he sounds like Cyan, the voice at least, that same rough edged, deep, clear tone, but the accent is just like Laz's.

"I know what you seek, Harbinger," Vik rumbles.

"Excellent, bring them out and we'll be on our way."

Shit, he knows about Laz, too? My stomach drops, everything in my world threatening to collapse. Neo holds me tighter.

Veikko feigns ignorance, which is more than I'd be able to manage. "Them?"

"Oh, please, Spectre." He flicks his hand dismissively. "We've known each other too long for you to play games. I'm not upset. Well." He chuckles and resumes walking toward the prep table. "I was. Terribly. Once I discovered he was missing, the reason you were lurking in the woods became clear. Then I realized you saved me a step. Brought them together, connected them for me. I daresay, the most interesting thing of all is how you've switched sides entirely. If you hand them over now, I might even show you mercy."

I share a confused glance with Neo.

"Lazaros," Mishka calls, gaze sweeping the cabins. "Do come out and say hello."

"Reanne's gone," I shout, fists clenched, panic welling.

"Korey." Neo clutches my arm tighter. "It won't help."

I can't talk to him right now. I can't see anything but the guy threatening my happiness.

Mishka's progression halts. "What?"

"That's why Cyan isn't here. He's looking for her."

Mishka's eyes widen as he twists back toward Veikko. "You let her out of your sight? Knowing what's at stake?"

"It was her choice. Good or bad." He crushes the grass bracers and lets them fall, the pieces swept away by a low breeze. "Just as it should be."

"So, all I must do is find her before Cyan does?" He grins and nods. "Only a small delay, then. I know where your brethren have likely taken her."

"What?" Neo gasps. "You don't think she's with Aeon? Is she in trouble?"

"Most assuredly," Mishka cants his head toward Neo, knowing smile spreading. "And it's the Spectre's fault entirely."

Vik's face pales. "That is impossible."

"Have you forgotten the venomous few you left behind? The ones determined to carry your banner until their dying breath?"

I have absolutely no idea what's going on, but the energy around us is changing, something stronger pushing in from the back.

Veikko's gaze flicks everywhere, like he's searching his memories.

"I…"

"Did you think they would simply give up? That your rallying words would vanish from their minds? Without your guidance, the Sentinels have taken to extreme measures." He steps closer to Vik's heaving form. "Any distress, any damage, any discomfort she endures is your doing as much as theirs."

Holy hell, Veikko was the leader of the Sentinels?!

"It…matters not. It is already done."

Do you think if we ran to another territory, we could get help? Neo's question spikes my adrenaline. I'd rather fight for love than run from danger, but fighting would mean dying, and if I die, I won't see Laz again until we're joined in the stars.

I don't know any pack that would do that.

Cyan would, Neo sniffles.

I take a deep breath and nod. He would. He's a really great Alpha. But that doesn't help us right now. I know if we live through this, Veikko has a ton of questions to answer.

"You are as infuriating as ever. But I haven't a worry, and would you like to know why? For one, though they may be zealous, they're too stupid to do any real damage. And second, she's your mate. You wouldn't have waited your entire, miserable life only to mate someone you intended to let die. Ergo, you must also know where she is, and there's some trick, or last-minute rescue, or…"

Mishka trails off as Veikko's expression dissolves into deep sorrow.

Power explodes through the space. "How could you be so idiotic!?" His shouts sounds even more like Cyan, unchecked emotion bubbling through him. "What if he doesn't find her in time? What if I don't?"

"Then the cycle starts again, and you stay as you are." Vik steps closer, anger renewed, jaw clenched. "A dead end. A mistake whose death is long overdue."

"A mistake, is that so?" Mishka laughs almost hysterically and faces us again, speaking over his shoulder. "Do they know who I am? Who their precious Alpha is?"

"What you seek isn't here," Vik growls, "Leave, before I—"

"Before you what?" Mishka smirks. "You can't hurt me. And you can't stop me from taking over this pathetic little pack."

He sends a small pulse of his energy, pushing Cyan's farther away.

Wait…Vik. Vik, you can, though. Take command first. You can give us back to Cyan when he gets here!

Veikko only shakes his head.

Korey knows you're an Alpha, no one cares, please don't let him take us!

Neo wipes his cheek with shaking hands.

Veikko works his fists. *I cannot assume control, even to protect you. Reanne is my mate. If I become seated, she'll be mated to an Alpha. The wrong one. Her cycle will be forfeit. It will be at least two hundred years before another Rigdis is born, who might be far more susceptible to the darkness, and the next High Alpha could be infinitely worse.*

Is he…is he saying the pack doesn't matter? And what the hell does he mean the next High Alpha?

So, that's it then? You care more about that than you do us? We're—we're done? Neo stares at me, tears pooling before spilling over.

Something crackles in the tree line, gone in a flash as Veikko straightens.

No. That is not it. I am not without a costly plan.

Mishka continues, oblivious to our conversation. "And you can't keep Lazaros from me for much longer. As soon as Cyan's miserable energy is gone and I can command hi—"

"Enough," Veikko shouts, a roll of thunder rumbling behind it, even though the sky is clear. Neo and I glance up in confusion. "You will release Lazaros. You will not take over here, and you will leave, never to return again."

Mishka's expression quickly morphs to utter amusement. "Delightful. Absolutely delightful. I wondered how many years it would take for your sanity to peel away, wondered if I'd see it with my own eyes. Indulge me in further lunacy, Spectre. Tell me why I would do any of that?"

"I know what you seek. What you…truly seek. I will show you where it is."

Mishka's eyes gleam, but the set of his mouth is pure malice.

"If you're bluffing, I will slaughter them one at a time while you watch. Starting with your Zed."

He glares at Neo, and I can barely take a breath. Barely stop myself from racing to Laz. Neo is shaking, a moment from collapse, but Veikko is as steady as he's ever been.

"I do not bluff. Release him, and we will set out immediately."

They stare at each other a moment and Mishka smirks. "It doesn't matter, I suppose. Once she and I are mated, I'll have him back regardless. Very well."

As if it's the least important thing he's ever done, Mishka lazily pushes up his sleeve and carves into his arm with a chuckle. "I hope you've prepared him, Spectre. He's so terribly delicate."

Prepared...oh no, the drop.

Mishka slashes through the carving, just as I race toward my cabin. Lazaros's wail is gut-wrenching, heartbreak stabbing through our bond so fiercely, I stumble. But it's the sudden spike in Mishka's energy, the fade of Cyan's, that pushes me to my knees, unable to move further.

Veikko growls in pain, grabbing his temple. "We...had a...deal."

"My agreement was with Reanne. And she hasn't upheld her end."

Neo hits the ground with a whimper and crawls closer, until he finally grips my shoulders with trembling fingers.

More of Mishka's energy swells, a suffocating, invisible cloud, thinning the bond that holds us all together.

Worst of all, my mate is writhing in pain, mere feet from me, and we can't get to each other.

"Laz..." I try to shout, but all that comes out is a whisper.

I can't—Neo's grip slips, and he hits the grass behind me, while I crumple forward, bracing on the ground.

I lock eyes with Veikko, who staggers slightly.

I am sorry. He groans in pain, and another clap of thunder sounds in the distance. *I cannot.*

Mishka is thrilled, grinning, hands tucked in his pockets like he's barely doing anything at all.

"It's been so long since I've overtaken a pack, I'd forgotten how exciting it is. GrimBite was nothing before I swept in, you see, and their Alpha was weak, barely put up a fight. Don't worry, gents. I've decided killing you myself serves no purpose. If you're alive, Reanne is far more likely to submit, adjust to her new home. So, under my command, you'll be given new jobs. And if you'd rather not perform the functions you're assigned, well, there is a robust dungeon where you can live out the rest of your time. Lazaros is quite familiar with the area, but, of course, I'd have to keep him separate from you. A mate can be so distracting. I suppose there is also the much more permanent way of avoiding either place, but I've heard tell the bottom of the Quay is quite jagged. Not a pleasant way to go, I'd imagine."

Rage boils inside me, and with every ounce of willpower I can muster, I force myself to my feet.

"Oh," he tuts. "So brave. Will you make it to me before you lose consciousness? I think not."

He doesn't move, doesn't drop his taunting smile as I trudge forward, each movement laced with agony.

It's too much. Too heavy. I drop down again, and Lazaros wails anew. Veikko staggers backward into a tree, gripping his temple.

I manage to twist my head enough to see Neo, who is completely still, laying just as he fell. I know he's only passed out, but he truly looks dead. I can't help thinking how heartbroken Cyan's going to be, if he comes back and we're gone. How sad Aeon will be that Neo is—

A lashing, thick wave of Alpha power blasts through the camp, sending a warm, wonderful buzz across the link. Cyan in his glorious beast form explodes out of the tree line and slams into Mishka.

Laz's pain stops, his cry leaving a sad echo in the air. But he flings the door open and runs straight into my arms. I clutch his trembling form so tight, I'm surprised his bones don't break. "It's okay, little pup, I've got you."

"I know where she is!" Mishka shouts. I glance over to see him pinned under Cy's massive wereform, claws pressed against Mishka's jugular. Droplets of blood form under the points.

"Do it, Alpha," Veikko rumbles. "We will find her on our own. End him."

"Time is of the essence, you can't afford to search everywhere." Mishka's voice is thin, grasping.

"He-he needs to know they're hurting her," Laz whispers in my ear. *"I want him dead, b-but..."*

I nod, grinding my teeth.

Neo gulps air, and pushes to his hands and knees, head hanging.

Where is...Aeon?

Even his thought is breathless. But Cyan doesn't answer, too focused.

Laz tucks into my embrace even more.

Alpha, Laz felt her pain, we might need him. You can always kill him later.

Cyan's vicious growl echoes through the camp, raising gooseflesh on my skin. Before anyone can react, he hauls back and cracks a blow across Mishka's face so hard bones crunch, knocking him unconscious.

All the invading energy fades, replaced quickly by the blessedly familiar hum of Cy's as it covers everything. Neo sobs in relief, and even my eyes water.

Veikko straightens, refusing to meet my stare. I hope he does feel guilty, and I hope it haunts him forever. If everything Mishka said had come to pass, it would have been completely his fault.

Finally, Cy lets his beast drop and shakes out his hand, shoving to his feet using Mishka's chest.

"Someone," he heaves breaths like he's been running for hours, "better tell me why this fucker has my face."

REANNE

My neck aches from the arched position, my throat dry, stomach empty.

There've been hands on me constantly for what must be hours. Taunting me. No one is talking, my whimpers the only sound. It started with teasing, testing touches, claws and fingers smoothing along my spine, down my thighs, across my breasts, like they were afraid of me. Now it's much more insistent, purposeful. I've determined they're under orders not to give me an ounce of release, but other than that, I'm fair game.

All I can do is whine, tremble, leak, and silently beg, on the edge and praying for someone to let me come. Only, they never do.

One of the men has been under me for a while, barely tickling my sides, stroking my stomach, plucking my nipples, licking me all over, his scruff stinging. My skin is tight, this curling heat inside an inferno. He dips a finger in and drags my slick across my clit every so often, just enough to keep me insane with desperation, while the other men cover me with their cum. The one under me has already come on my stomach twice and cleaned it off with his tongue. I nearly came from that, so he had to move excruciatingly slow.

His fingers trail down the backs of my arms next, light, too light, my body painfully aware of every touch. I moan on the edge of a cry. This is torture.

I'd promise him anything if he'd make it stop, if he'd just let me go back to my mates. I force their faces from my mind and blank it as best I can.

His hot tongue hits my clit and I jerk, violent with sensitivity.

God, please, please let me, just this once.

But he doesn't. One lick, only the barest bit of pressure. One finger. In slow, out slow. That's all any of them have done. In, just to feel me, murder me with desire, and back out again, followed by a load of cum on me somewhere.

I whimper in the back of my throat, wriggling my hips, mumbling sounds that aren't even words, because what's the point?

He drags his fingertips down my ass, sending chills all over my body and flicks my clit again, then once more. I'm dangerously close to an explosion. I hold my breath, hoping he messes up, that he doesn't notice the way I'm basically vibrating. Maybe I'll get to come, and the Alpha will kill him and that'll be one less asshole I have to deal with.

But he stops. I scream in frustration, completely muffled, as tears fall straight to the floor.

He slides a finger in slow and holds it there. I try to buck against it, panting, but can't. He withdraws, and suddenly spreads me wide with a harsh grip on each side, exposing my wetness to the cool air.

Panic hits. They haven't done that yet, and I don't know what to expect. There's soft groaning, heavier breathing behind me. I jump when a spurt of cum lands inside. The next hits my clit, the next my ass cheeks and a final one inside again.

I'm shaking, throbbing. Everything aches with endless need, too on edge to even breathe properly. I'd rather be dead than this alive. The man under me lets go and pushes his finger in, shoving the nut deeper. I want to throw up, I don't want anyone inside me but my men.

Don't cry. I can't cry.

There's no light here, no joy. And with none of the glowing, loving energy from my mates to combat it, the darkness feeds. It swirls, tendrils wrapping around cells until my mind clears, and only one thought remains.

I'd rather they be dead. All of them.

My darkness swells, energy pricking my skin. The one under me sucks in a breath, yanking his hands off me. "What the hell," he mutters.

He touches me again, and again withdraws with a pained inhale.

"We need to tell Yuli," someone behind me says before many feet file out.

I'm alone again, and the relief is almost painful.

It doesn't last.

Someone comes in silently, but I feel...something. A weird change in the air or...an energy wall? No, that doesn't make sense, but I guess it doesn't matter. It's just another person determined to make me suffer.

They move closer, close enough I can feel their body heat. I expect more of the same torment, but I don't expect the rope on my neck to go slack. I nearly pass out from the rush of blood, my joints twinging. My still-bound hands are unhooked next, ankles after that, and I collapse to the ground from fatigue.

"I'm going to take off the gag. It's important you don't speak." It's a pleasant but urgent male whisper.

I think I recognize his voice, but I'm not sure from where. At the very least, it's not Yuli. Confusion, fear, adrenaline, and excitement fill me, and I hold my breath again, keeping the tears at bay as I nod.

Fingers graze the back of my head, and the gag falls away. My mouth is a desert. I can't make saliva to force a swallow. He quickly lifts me, cradling me close, and even though my skin is still buzzing, he doesn't react at all. I don't know if that's good or bad, but I can't stop the tears any longer, soaking in his body heat as I sob into his chest. Whoever it is, even if this is a cruel trick, it's comforting right now.

He carries me somewhere else in the tent and sits, positioning me on his lap. Something hard touches my bottom lip, and I flinch.

"Drink," he murmurs. I'm not sure I can at first, but I take the glorious water in my mouth and hold it, letting it soak in until I can swallow. After that, I gulp all I can, draining the cup. I gasp, desperate to ask him questions, but I won't.

"Jakobe caused a distraction so I could come in, but it's not enough to get you out, yet. I know it's hard, but you can't let the darkness win," he whispers.

I don't know who Jakobe is, but it sounds like I might have two allies here, and that gives me a huge burst of hope. However, this darkness is the only thing that made the torment stop before, I have to keep it close. I don't know what to do.

Tears fall again, and he wraps me up tighter, pressing his stubbled cheek against my temple.

"I'm sorry about before. I wanted to help, but I have to behave as though I'm on their side."

Before…

"The rag?"

He nods against my head. "Not quite the same as in the woods, I know."

My mind spins in a thousand directions. When was I in the woods with this person?

"I harbor no ill will toward you for killing my brother. It was a shock, but I realized it would earn Yuli's wrath, and needed to take steps to ensure I could be here. I didn't aid in poisoning Cyan. Given what I've learned, I'm pretty sure Fen set that into motion, framing me."

Agnar! My emotions scatter everywhere, too many questions, too drained. I'm so glad to know he wasn't a bad guy, I almost burst into sobs again. And he must mean the woods on the night this all started, after the frat party. I had no idea. Honestly, I hadn't given any thought to who that was. Everything afterward happened so fast. Now I wish we'd had time together, but maybe we can after this is over.

He cuddles me closer, rocking me slowly. "I think you're genuinely our savior. I believe in you, believe you can ascend and master the darkness. I know you and Cyan will rule fairly and love deeply. That you'll gift our kind with your blessed pups, over and over. And I would have welcomed you as a mate. It's important you know these things, in case…in case I can't escape with you."

What? He has me now, why can't we leave?

"Did you hear me, my gorgeous queen?" He murmurs in my ear, and I'm lit on fire. My body is hyper-focused on his skin touching mine, this need bursting back to the surface. I curl into him, rubbing my cheek against his chest. He lets out a low, almost inaudible growl that has my nipples peak instantly. His cock hardens under me, every breath electric.

I'm too desperate to think clearly, and the ropes around my wrists are chafing, digging in, but I scratch at the side of his neck, begging.

"I…can't." It's a long breathy groan, just as desperate sounding as I am.

"Please," I manage, barely recognizing my own voice.

"You'll be loud, they'll find out, likely kill me, then they'll finish the ritual, and you'll die. Is it worth that? For one orgasm?"

Right now? Yes. I'm a breath from running through the door and begging Yuli to do it.

"The gag." I shiver, panting, arching.

He mutters what sounds like a swear under his breath and stands, setting me in his place. I fleetingly try to remove the blindfold, but my arms are too weak, only lifting halfway before falling to my sides.

His warmth is around me again, strong arms holding me close as I'm placed back across his lap, his lips at my ear.

"I soaked it with water. Hopefully you won't dry out as fast. Open your mouth."

Lust erupts with a frightening speed, and he affixes the cold, wet rag inside, securing the strap back around my head. He kisses my temple, wrenching my heart into a thousand pieces, before teasing my ear with his lips again. "I'm so sorry. You deserve much better than this."

A tear breaks free, sliding down my cheek as he cinches one arm around my waist, and trails the other hand up the inside of my thigh.

I'm already shaking, already panting and dizzy by the time the pad of his middle finger slides over my clit in a slow circle.

My head falls back, and I can't tell you what sounds come out, but the gag is the only reason this entire camp doesn't know what he's doing.

He never increases his speed, but the build is instant, a cracking explosion of ecstasy, sending my exhausted frame into convulsions. His tongue runs a path along my neck, finger still circling, and I'm slammed with another tidal wave of release, incoherent praises in the back of my throat as I writhe.

"Goddess have mercy...your energy is stunning." His reverence is too much, too caring and loving for what I've been forced to endure, and I burst into choking sobs.

He removes his finger, and hugs me tightly, stroking my head. "I have to return you, but be steadfast, hold on to your light."

I'm barely aware of anything but heartbreak as he quickly puts me back as he found me. He leaves me with a tender cheek stroke, and the tent falls into silence.

The boiling, near-deadly level of need has faded to a low simmer. It's only now I notice my skin isn't pricking anymore. Did he take my power somehow?! Panic wells until I scour myself and find the darkness, coiled, waiting like a patient pet. As if my search was a call itself, it unwinds, eating at the edges of what little light Agnar had managed to give me.

Despite Agnar's belief in me, I don't know if I hope I'm freed while there's still good left inside, or if I hope this darkness overtakes me and they all get what they deserve. I only have two mates left, and Yuli's threat hasn't left the back of my mind. Even if I die, taking him out might keep them safe, and that's becoming a more attractive cost by the minute.

JAKOBE

" 'm telling you, man. I saw it right here. Was like a giant scary ghost thing, and it asked for you!"

Yuli and six of his pack lackeys are searching the woods with me, flipping leaves over and checking in knot holes.

"Did this ghost give you a name?" Yuli steps up beside me, scanning the distant trees.

Man, I figured he'd ask that. I've been wracking my brain hard since Agnar and I came up with this plan. If I hadn't won the frog toss, we would have been setting something on fire and hoping for the best.

Yeah, not the greatest plans, but when we saw the black waves tangling around her energy, we were out of time to argue about me leaving or staying. Had to work together and fast.

If you ask me, this one's way better. Or it will be if I can get my thoughts in order. Aeon said something right after I sent the ghosty back underground, but I can't—Mother of the moon, I've got it!

"Kas…Kasimir, I think."

Everyone stops moving but me, still kicking leaves like I expect a twenty-foot-tall undead werewolf to be tucked under one.

"Kasimir appeared here?"

Something in his tone stops me mid-swish, and I pivot to face him. He's a weird off-color, like he might throw up. "Woah, are you okay? Was it the lamb? Maybe you had a bad chunk."

He doesn't seem to hear me, staring at nothing. I'm not sure

161

he even knows I'm here anymore. Maybe I should have said the ghost was named Brother Joe or Walter.

Finally, Yuli swallows, and a smile creeps up on his face as he cuts his eyes to me. "I'm better than okay. This means we're on the right path. The ritual proceeds as planned. Tagrin, stay here in case he comes back."

"Yes, Alpha."

Yuli spins on his heel, headed toward camp and his lackeys follow. Man, I had wanted to keep him out here longer! I run a few steps to catch up.

"Ritual?"

"Do you remember the prophecy I mentioned?"

I nod. Not like I could forget something I'm supposed to die in. But I don't care what Agnar or that dumb old thing says, nothing's taking me out.

"We're going to stop it from happening once and for all by destroying the main focus."

"Oh, okay. What's that?" I have a pretty good idea, and now I feel like my lamb was bad.

He eyes me sideways as we near the camp. "Not what. Who."

Yeah, that's not gonna happen. No idea how Kasimir factors into whatever he's got planned, but I don't think I want to know. All I have to do is focus on getting us all out of here.

Corbet comes rushing at us right as we clear the forest.

He stalls a little when he sees me, eyes Yuli, and stiffens. "Good to see you again, Jakobe."

"It's okay, Corb," I grin, "Yuli knows all about how I told you to pretend like we didn't know each other. It's cool."

He doesn't miss a beat. Good old Corby. "Whew, good. I'm sorry Alpha, it seemed like a good idea at the time, given what he is—"

"Prone to think about new people!" I interject, hooking my arm around Corbet's neck and ruffling his hair. "I'm a doubter. Anyway, what brings you out here? Did you hear about the ghost, too?"

Man, I can't give this guy an inch. Absolutely no chill in his body.

He cuts his eyes to me as they widen. "G-ghost?"

"It's nothing." Yuli frowns, glancing between the two of us. "What did you need, Corbet?"

"Uh...right. Something happened with her skin. She shocked me, while we were, you know. Her ropes even started smoking."

I snatch my arm back and stare at him. I thought I knew this guy. I guess it has been a while since we've seen each other, but taking advantage of a helpless—never in a million years did I expect he'd take part in—damn, I can't even think it. Yeah, this lamb is coming back up.

"Her?" I stifle a gag. Come on, Jak. Keep it together.

Yuli watches me closer. "The main focus."

Good thing I can perform under any kind of pressure. Even possibly puking.

"Wait, so you've got a Nikta tied up somewhere and she's shocking people with her skin?! That's crazy!"

"Not a Nikta. The Rigdis, and," he faces Corbet again, seemingly mollified, "tell Tayron to move ahead with purifying the dagger. We finish this tonight."

"Yes, Alpha. Hey, Jak, you should go check her out if you get a chance. She's really pretty. Tastes good, too. See you later."

He waves and trots back toward camp, while I hunch over and lose every undigested bit of my dinner.

This is exactly why you don't join a pack with such bad Alpha waves. They get in your brain, mess with your sense of right and wrong. Now I'm wishing we'd set everything on fire after all.

"Oh, damn." I cough. "Sorry, I guess I'm the one who," I cough again, "got the bad chunk."

Yuli pats my upper back. "Clean yourself up. See you at the fire."

"Yep, you got it. Looking forward to meeting everyone else. Thanks, man."

They leave me braced on my knees, eyes blurry, mind racing. I thought we'd have more time. I'm not sure I'll be able to shift by tonight. No worries, I'll…come up with something.

I shove back to standing and trot through the last trees until the camp is in full view. Her energy is still fanned out around the tent and butting against the clouds, but it's mostly back to the subtle, shifting iridescence, barely any black threads at all.

Good, whatever Agnar did, helped. I grin and continue through, on the hunt for him. After grabbing a cup of water from a stool and swishing/gargling until I'm pretty sure my jaw will lock if I do it again, I stalk along the main path, scanning.

Wait, was that…I skid to a stop and take two steps back, spying him through the open flap of a tent. He's sitting on a chair, elbows on his knees, head in his hands.

I stroll right in. "Hey, partner, what's wrong?"

He doesn't even look up, just heaves a huge breath. Hm.

"This your tent?"

He grunts. I guess that means yes?

I drop down on his cot with a satisfied sigh. "It's not so bad. Hey, good work, on the…thing. Darkness was almost gone."

"I saw," he mutters, scrubbing his face now.

I push his knee with mine, dislodging one of his elbows, but he puts it right back. "Then why are you so glum?" I add with a whisper, *"It worked, he bought the whole deal."*

"That's good." Another mutter.

Man, I dunno what's wrong but it's killing me. I stand and crowd his space, my knees against his knees, my hands on his shoulders. "Hey."

I try to sense his energy the way he did, but instead of hitting a wall, mine gets swallowed up. Not sure that's really a Tracer skill, but then again, he's been one longer than I have. I'm still the best, though.

He growls and finally lets his hands fall, tilting his tear-streaked face up to mine. I can't help myself, cupping his cheeks like we've known each other forever. What can I say, I'm more of a lover than a…well, than anything else, really.

"Is this from how she's being treated?"

"Yes, but not just that." He stares into my eyes. "Accepting my coming death is harder than I expected."

I almost laugh, because it doesn't make any sense, but he's serious. "What're you talking about?"

"You'll need a much bigger distraction to get her out."

No, that can't be right. I bet we can come up with another way.

He exhales forcefully and leans away from my touch, giving a soft, rueful laugh. "I waited for him. Gave him the time and space I thought he needed to heal."

Does he mean Veikko? Aw, man. I don't like it when my heart hurts like this. Why can't everyone just be happy and love each other?

I cradle his face again, not letting him retreat. "Then help me get her out in a way that doesn't involve you dying, and we can all be together. Together, together. Jak is nothing if not a sharer."

"No," he swallows. "I'm not sure he can think of me like that. I remind him too much of…everything." He smiles even though a tear spills down his cheek. "Despite how many times I told him, it took someone like Reanne and you to convince him he was worth more than he thought." His throat bobs again, only a whisper coming out now. "Worth everything. So, thank you."

My own eyes water. I knew my Honeybear was a gift from the second I shook his hand, which means I know he deserves to hear this from his friend's mouth directly, not from me in a tribute around a ceremonial fire.

"Sounds like I need to be thanking you, for being there. But the good news is, once we get out of here, you and me and Vik and Reanne and Cy, we can all do a whole lot of thanking each other." I grin, and he laughs through his nose, but still sad.

His energy flares again as he tentatively pushes his cheek into

NATALIA PRIM

my palm, but it vanishes just as fast. I quickly send mine after it, but, again, it gets gobbled up.

"How do you do that?"

"Do what?"

"You keep eating my energy."

His mouth quirks, just a little. "That's easy. Was one of the first things my father taught me."

"Pff, you're lucky. All my dad did was talk about this stupid prophecy."

He nods. "Mine as well. Life was full of nothing but preparation. I found out he wasn't my real father, but I still call him that. He's all I know."

That's sad. Thank goodness my dad's mine, no question.

"So, teach me. What do I haveta do?"

With a hefty exhale he straightens his head, my hand falling back to my side. "What you did with Veikko's energy, it's the same idea. Only, you have to grab the end of the line, before it hits you. Once it's on you, it takes another tactic, but you can still do it."

"Okay. Seems simple enough." I rub my palms together and brace. "Hit me."

He quirks a brow. "You'll never know when it's coming. You have to open your awareness and keep it open all the time. Otherwise, you won't catch it."

I drop my stance and frown. "Man, that sounds exhausting."

His chin bobs once, and his energy lashes out at me. I rear back, but it's on me before I can do anything. "Dangit. Try again."

The energy retreats, but flares at me again before I'm ready. "Damn! Again," I growl.

He chuckles and pulls it back slowly, but he's taking threads of mine, too, winding them around each other. My pulse kicks up, throat drying. Shit, that's hot.

The distraction works, and he drops mine and hits me with his in the same breath. I nearly shout in frustration. "Again!"

"Focus, Jak."

All I do is growl, staring at him, waiting.

"Open your awareness."

"I don't even know what that means, man. I'm doing my best."

With a huff he points at my head. "Pretend you have eyes everywhere, and you can see through them all the time. Each one has an energy receptor."

I blink, struggling to picture that, but what I come up with is freaky as hell.

"No, don't *think* about it. Just do it."

His energy lashes again, but it goes around me, and I swear to the goddess I *see it*, behind me, I see it as clear as—

"Got it!"

Agnar nods, pure pride in his eyes. "Good, now bury it."

I do, right beside Veikko's, grinning. "Like a pro!"

He nods again, slower, a knot traveling his throat. "Will you keep it...there? With his?"

My breath whooshes out, heart twisting up. I wish I could convince him there's another way, but I don't exactly have a plan to offer. I step back into his space, the same as before, and thumb his tear away. "Sure thing, partner. As long as Jak's alive, you two will never be apart."

He seems both relieved and sadder than ever. I seriously hate this. Maybe I should change the subject.

"So, were you this down when you were in SteelTooth?"

He considers me a moment, scratching his cheek. "No, actually."

"That fits my theory then. I think—" I glance over my shoulder as a werewolf passes the tent opening, and lower my voice. "I think it's Yuli's energy, man. Even I've been feeling less like myself, and I just got here."

"He is the Alpha, so that makes sense. His soul must be as evil as they come, so that bleeds into the pack..."

167

But his brows knit, because he just remembered what I know, and that's one big fact—neither of us *in* his pack.

"Hmm."

"Yeah, man. That's what I'm saying. Why do you think it's like that?"

He frowns and shrugs. "No idea. My father probably knows. Maybe…and this is a big maybe, if we all make it out of here, we can ask him."

"That's the spirit!" I grin and jostle him.

"We should head to the fire." He stands, pushing me back with his body, only I don't budge, so he mashes himself against me.

I'm not complaining. Since I'm not holding his face anymore, I put my hands on his hips instead.

"What're you doing, Jak?" He frowns.

"Standing here."

"With your hands."

"Nothing at the moment." I wink, and even though he frowns deeper, there is a definite hardening going on. "You're cute when you frown, anyone told you that?"

"No."

His frown flattens into a highly unamused line, and that's even cuter. It's probably the worst time to be horny, given what we've got to do, and all the emotions everywhere, but just like his cock was speaking for me earlier, mine's trying to have a whole conversation.

"You," his eyes widen as he glances down, "that's for me?"

I shrug with a nod.

"Why?"

"You're emotional, hot, and available. Do I need to carve it on a tree?"

He blinks at me like I've just spoken some bird language he's never heard.

"You know, for a guy who went out of his way to tell

someone else how much they were worth, you don't seem to realize you're worth a lot yourself."

He makes a click of disapproval, but chill bumps race up his torso as I trail my fingers higher.

"We don't have time for this," he murmurs, chest rising and falling faster, his hard length hitting my hip.

Just as curt with his answers as someone else I know. A shiver twangs my spine at the thought of both he and Vik in my bed at the same time.

"Sure we do," I murmur right back, gripping his face again and tugging until he meets me in a kiss. It's quick, but soft, and there's a pulse in my chest, an echo from his energy.

He scans my face, grabbing a lock of my hair and giving it a gentle pull. "Not a color we see a lot. I like it."

"Thanks, man." I grin. "Feel free to pull it any time you want."

He cracks a real smile, his eyes crinkling, and two deep smile curves hit his cheeks. "Yeah?"

My heart swoops, dipping to my toes before hitting me in the throat. Gorgeous.

"Hell yeah, especially if it makes you smile like that. Man, you could use that as a weapon."

His skin flushes and he laughs, running a hand down his face.

There's a commotion outside, voices shouting in the distance, dumping cold water over our moment. We stare into each other's eyes, serious expressions falling into place.

"Jak, all that matters is saving Reanne. Swear to me you'll do that, regardless of what else might happen. That you'll always do that."

"We'll do that, not just—"

"Swear it." His jaw jumps.

"Alright, man, I swear. I'll save Reanne."

With a solemn nod, he leaves the tent with me right behind, heading toward literal and figurative fire.

CYAN

This guy could be my twin. Uglier twin, but still, I don't fucking get it. Did my mom have us both or something? Pass him off to the GrimBite? Doesn't seem likely but otherwise, it doesn't make sense why we look the same. Someone better start talking soon before I—

Neo's need attacks my nerves like a howl in the dead of night, but first things first.

After eying the fresh pack cut on Mishka's arm, I glance back at Laz, trembling, clutched in Korey's grip. I send out a thick wave of Alpha energy, as much as I can spare, and stamp my claim all over him. His muscles relax as his sexy mouth lifts in a small smile.

One of these damn days I'll get to actually woo a fucking member again. But right now, I need Neo.

I cut my gaze his way, twisting to face him as I point at the ground in front of me. He bites at his lip, worry crinkling his brow, and heads over. I shove everything down inside, leaving only the barest amount, and once he's a step away, I cup the back of his neck and brush my lips across his.

I expect him to be cold with me, I fucking deserve it, but he whimpers and throws his arms around my neck, opening for me first, clawing at my shoulders. I get hard so fast my head swims.

I worship his mouth, living for the way he leans his whole body into the kiss, until he breaks away, flushed, flustered and smiling. Exactly how he should always be.

Takes all I have not to fuck him over Mishka's passed out body, because my beast has had a seriously miserable day.

There's no way I wouldn't hurt him right now, though, so I trail nipping kisses down his smooth skin.

Staring in his eyes, I settle on my knees in front of him. It's reckless, and damn sure not something Alphas are supposed to do, but I can tell he's seriously not okay, above how he was before I left.

Korey and Laz both inhale, and yeah, I shouldn't be in this position, let alone in front of anyone, but you know what? Fuck convention and fuck anyone who tries to tell me I can't take care of my Zed.

"C-Cy," Neo whispers, eyes wide, cheeks turning a deep maroon as he glances around. "You don't..." he buries his hands in my hair. "We haven't done this before, are you sure?"

"Do I fucking look like I'm unsure?" I bark it out, but give him a slow wink and a smirk. "Anyone who doesn't wanna watch is welcome to turn around, but I'm taking care of you, right here."

Weirdly, no one but Veikko moves. And he doesn't seem too sure whether he wants to watch or not, but ultimately he faces the other direction.

Neo stares at me in awe and sniffles, stroking my cheek as he nods. His cock is hard and ready, already leaking. I flick my tongue along the tip, my stomach flipping at how sweet, how good he tastes. As if I didn't already know he was my fucking match, now I know he tastes like this? He only thought we had too much sex before.

I take him all the way in my mouth, pulling back slowly, grazing him with my teeth, toying with his balls as I glance up.

His eyes practically glaze, hips working in time with my motions, gripping my hair hard as his lip locks under his teeth. Fuck, he's beautiful. How did I forget how utterly damn hot it is every time he loses himself to me?

I growl, gripping his ass harder than I intend, but he doesn't suck in a pained breath, or push away, or indicate it's a problem in any way. He moans louder, egging me on.

Holy fuck, I could explode just from that. Maybe seeing me with Aeon changed something in him, I dunno, but I'm sure not gonna question it. I send a little more Alpha energy, just a tiny bit, and he smiles, head falling back.

Goddess, I just fucking love him.

I suck his cock like it's the last time we'll ever get to, dragging him to the edge once before letting him calm down, and dragging him back again. It doesn't take long, as far as suck-offs go, but it's the sexiest orgasm I think he's ever had. His muscles quiver under my touch, his moans raw, and there's so much love in his gaze it's almost choking.

He comes right in my mouth, and I drink him down, overwhelmed with a weird sense of accomplishment at how content he looks. Wonder if that's why he and Aeon like doing this to me?

After I give him another hard suck just to hear that hiss of overstimulation, I let him go, giving his ass a final squeeze as I stand.

"I'll take care of you better soon. I'm…sorry," I murmur against his jaw before nipping it.

"That was amazing," he breathes with a lazy smile. "I forgive you, and it's me who needs to take care of you. I'm just so happy you're back, and we're safe, but…" His smile dives into a frown. "Did you find Aeon? Where's Jak? And Reanne?"

I open my mouth, but Vik interjects.

"Alpha. He may wake soon."

"Good point. Slap the Shift Collar on this fucker and tie him up."

Vik nods and heads toward his clearing, to his secret stash of stuff.

Neo's face pales and Korey sucks in a breath. "We have one of those?"

I feel a little guilty for keeping one, since they're so fucking awful, but evidently, I needed it for a special occasion, like capturing a psychotic look-alike.

Vik returns with a coil of rope and the nightmarish metal band. There are a couple different versions, but the one we have is lined on the inside with large, barbed spikes, and the sides are cantilevered so when the person shifts, depending on how tight you make the band, it can range from bad to dead. A shudder speeds down my back as he clamps the collar into place, fixing the bracers on Mishka's shoulders.

"Don't cinch it too tight," I grumble. "Don't need to cut his head off." I know I hate the guy, but I'm not a monster like he is. I just can't take any more chances with him where my pack, my family, is concerned. After Vik ties his hands behind his back, he nods and gives Neo a gentle shoulder pat.

Good, great. Now we just have to solve all the other fucking problems.

"I-I've unfortunately seen one many times," Laz whispers, the sound barely carrying to my ears. "Fitting justice, as it is one of his preferred methods of, ah, compliance, is a safe word to use. Mostly the-the threat was enough, but he forced shift on a few and…well, he didn't have to do it many more times. N-never on me, thankfully, but on others. I-including your daughter, I'm sad to say."

"He put a collar on Suzette and forced her to shift? Are you serious?" A sniping wave of anger comes off of Korey as he stands and storms toward us, fists clenched. I step in his path.

"Don't get too close to him."

"Blast, I'm s-sorry, I shouldn't have said that." Laz glances back and forth between Mishka and Korey, clearly wanting to comfort his mate but not wanting to get near the other. He settles on sending a Beta wave, but it doesn't have much effect.

There's a standoff, and I'm genuinely worried I'll have to Alpha Command him to keep his stupid self from getting hurt by a spike, or accidentally decapitating Mishka before I'm ready. Finally, he exhales long and slow.

"Just promise me," Korey seethes through clenched teeth, "when this is all over, that piece of shit is going to die."

"I'll kill him with something stupid." I smirk and clasp his shoulder. "We won't even light a candle, let alone a fire."

He nods several times, spits on the ground near Mishka's face, and walks backward to Laz, pointing at me. "If he doesn't die, we're both leaving."

It feels like he punched my heart, but I nod.

"W-what?" Laz says, turning wide eyes up at Korey.

"Korey, when has Cy ever lied?" Neo's voice is gentle, but I can pick up the underlying irritation.

"S'fine. It won't be an issue, and we've got other shit to deal with."

"Where is Jakobe?" Vik's eye bores into mine, almost accusingly.

"He went to find Reanne, since Aeon…so Aeon and I could come back here."

Not sure if he wants me to tell everyone else, or not. I'll just leave it to him.

"Then why isn't he with you?" Neo's anxiety is ramping, but we don't really have time for me to deal with it adequately.

"He's in the woods. I told him all he had to do was head straight and he'd get here eventually."

Neo stares at me, paling again as he clutches his neck. "You know that means he's probably lost again."

"Yeah, but I had to get back here." I stroke Neo's hip, earning myself a blush, even though he's still scared.

"So," I exhale, "we have to go find him. We'll leave now, and you guys can fill me in on everything else."

"I, too, advise leaving straight away," Mishka grunts as he pushes to his knees. "We can locate your wayward Beta on the way."

I almost knock him out again on sheer principle, but that really would be torture because his head would loll right into the rusty spikes. He's lucky as fuck I'm not that kind of guy.

"On the way to where?"

He smiles and unease dribbles down my back. It's so fucking weird to see my face do things my face doesn't do much of.

"It's like gazing at a broken mirror. I expected more, I think, from the one who finally brought a Rigdis into being. Though, I suppose, it was due entirely to idiotic providence and a slumbering Sentinel. What say you, Spectre? Is he the perfect version?" He bounces a glance between the two of us, smile widening. "See, I think not. And you don't truly think so, either. That's why you haven't shown him yet, isn't it?"

Vik's jaw clenches. I don't know what he's talking about, but I don't like this ass-hat talking to anyone else. Hell, I don't like him talking at all.

"The only reason anyone has or hasn't done anything is 'cause you keep fucking interfering, you body snatching brick of shit. Just answer the question." I kick his knee and he grunts in pain. "On the way to where?"

"What does she possibly see in such an oaf?" He sneers, struggling to his feet with a huff. "He," his chin juts toward Veikko, "is going to reveal the location of something inaccessible to anyone, save those to whom it currently applies. Something, it turns out, we'll need to save my precious queen."

"She's not your fucking anything. Reanne is mine, and if I have to rip your throat out to prove it, that's what I'll do."

My beast explodes to the surface, more than ready to do just that. *Must kill. Must protect.*

"Yes, I'm certain that will win her eternal love," he chuckles.

"I…already…have it," I growl, baring all my teeth.

That hits home, twisting his features in an all-too-familiar rage. We're both blasting Alpha waves, only mine are winning, thanks to my territory.

Alpha, we need him a bit longer.

I glare at Neo's almost glowing outline and allow his hesitant touch on my elbow. It calms me just enough to shift back.

"Stick something in his mouth so he can't talk. We need to find Aeon."

175

Vik nods and heads back to his stash.

"Predictable. You'll ask for my help soon enough." Mishka sneers. "Don't forget, I know where they've taken her, and if you sent one, lowly pack member there, he's surely already dea—"

His word ends on a sharp inhale as Vik grabs a giant handful of Mishka's hair, craning his head back just enough that the spikes push into his skin before releasing it with a push forward, so the same happens to his throat, leaving small threats all around his neck.

"Jakobe is not dead," he growls as he ties a strip of cloth around Mishka's mouth. "Once I have brought you to the hidden dwelling, you will reveal what you know."

Mishka doesn't respond at all, simply glaring ahead.

"Are we all going?"

I glance back at Korey, and Laz behind him. I know they'd rather stay here, far away from the me-wannabe, but I'm not risking anything anymore.

"I can protect everyone if we're together. Plus, I don't know when we'll be back, and I don't want to miss joining you to the pack because you stayed here to fuck."

I quirk a brow as Laz ducks behind Korey.

"That-that's not entirely why…"

"I know. Grab a bit of jerky, shift, and let's roll. Goddess only knows where the hell Aeon is by now."

AEON

I t's no big deal. No big deal. I'll walk back into camp in man form like nothing has changed. Hello, everyone. I'm completely normal, what's up with you?

Ugh.

I try to call my beast for the hundredth time. Try and fail. I've never been this empty in my life.

Am I even a werewolf anymore? That thought freezes me in place. The fact I've got no way to protect myself makes me realize how alone I am out here.

Telling Cy to run ahead was the right call, no doubts. He felt something weird in the territory claim and I've never seen that look in his eyes before.

Rage and fear and a glow so bright it was like two moons shining on the forest floor. Honestly, I don't think his beast would have let him stay any longer.

But it leaves me walking alone with my thoughts, which, turns out, I don't like doing. Especially not for this long.

The faint whisper of pack link chatter draws me to the present. I'm too far away to pick up anything substantial. I wish it worked no matter the distance, that would be so much simpler, but at least it means I'm almost home.

I think.

He said I literally only had to walk in a straight line, and I'm pretty damn sure I did that.

The main problem is, without my beast, I can't see in the dark. That didn't occur to me until the sun started setting. After Cyan was gone.

Something scuttles across the forest floor nearby and I flinch. Given that Cy's rough affections with me earlier still haven't healed all the way, hours later, I think I have to be way more cautious. Things I wouldn't pay attention to before might seriously hurt me now, because clearly, I'm worthless and fragile and who even am I?

An angry tear slips out as I call the beast again, uselessly.

...re you?

I cock my head. Weird snippet to pick up, but I walk faster, because even if they all pity me or don't want to be around me, it's still home and I've missed it.

Aeon if you don't answer, I'll kill you myself!

My eyes widen. Why does Cy sound so scared?

Uh, what?

Aeon?!

Neo's voice causes an avalanche of emotional and physical reactions, from my heart lurching, to a lump grabbing my throat, to a cold sweat breaking out, to bursts of nerves, excitement, and dread. I don't know how I'm going to handle this thing with him.

Rustling and thudding footsteps get closer and closer. I try to shift again, even though I know it's pointless. I can make out vague shapes, the outline of a werewolf before it shrinks drastically and collides with my body, knocking me on my back.

"Ow, careful!" I suck in a breath, something sharp jabbing into my shoulder blade. I adjust until it pops out, and wince, wrapping my arm around the man lying on top of me. I thought it was Cy at first, but this doesn't feel like—

"Sorry, I thought you'd move! I'm so glad you're okay. I know this is going to sound weird, but I really missed you. I was so worried." He laughs derisively and nuzzles the hollow at the base of my throat, his tickling breath sending blasts of heat through me. "I had planned to not say any of this, but you're finally here and I thought the pack was done for, and I figure it's stupid to keep it all in. It's been such, such a shitty day."

Neo.

My system shorts out, hand freezing in place on his lower back. It feels way better than I expected to have his weight on me, his muscles pressed against mine. I can't stop myself from remembering how his tongue tasted, or how his mouth felt on my cock. But I force it all away, focusing on how he's nuzzling, rubbing his cheek on my collarbone, like he's convincing himself I'm actually here, memorizing my scent. It's so tender and sweet my eyes start to water.

I don't even know what end is up anymore.

"I know why Vik was biting you, by the way, but Cy still doesn't know, and I feel ridiculous for being jealous about it, yes, I'm admitting that. Mishka's tied up and gagged after Cy knocked the stars out of his eyes, but Laz is finally free of—Wait, did you say 'ow'?" He jerks his head back, but I can't see his face, it's too dark.

"Mishka is in the camp?" I push up to my elbows before he can spot my tears, and he rocks back on his heels. "Wow, he really did come for her."

I'm blatantly pushing his jealousy comment out of my mind and ignoring the flutter in my chest. I wasn't sure how we'd work before I lost my beast. I have even less of a clue, now.

"Well, he's not in the camp anymore. None of us are."

"Huh?"

He grabs my arm and tugs me to my feet. "We came looking for you. Cy was worried you were lost, which you clearly were. We're making a trip to some invisible house."

I blink at the darkness.

"Invisible house." I deadpan, though, I did get brought back to life by a ghost god, so I should probably keep my mind open and my trap shut.

"Aeon…I'm over here," his voice is small and unsure as he steps closer, his heat leeching into my skin. I orient on the sound, but I'm still looking in the wrong place, apparently.

"Can you, can you not see me?"

"I lost my…"

179

The words fade. Telling Neo makes it too real, too quickly. I'd been thinking about it, pretending I was fine, pretending I was processing, while still constantly trying to shift. Hours of calling for a beast that won't come. I've been in denial.

It's really gone. I'm broken.

"Lost your what?"

I can barely breathe, but when he touches my jaw, I crumble in on him. "It's gone," I whisper, tears clogging my throat.

He wraps his arms around my back, squeezing me tight.

"Whatever it is, it'll be okay. You're Aeon. The favorite."

There's a subtle bitterness there I can't deal with right now, but I shake my head anyway.

"You're still bleeding." Fear clings to his words as he touches the skin on my shoulder blade. "Is this why you said 'ow'? What happened?"

"I died." It comes out on a sob, everything hitting me all at once as I wrap my arms around his waist, hanging on for dear life. I almost never saw him or anyone else, ever again. I've cried more in the past two days than the sum of all my days before. "I died and I-I lost my beast."

"You—" His breath leaves in a sharp burst, and he holds me just as urgently, fingertips digging into my skin. He holds me while my heart breaks, while my cries echo against the trees, his own silent sobs hitching his chest.

Once I've calmed a little, he leans back, and wipes my cheeks before gently cupping them.

I freeze again, even though he's sending explosions through my chest.

"We could have lost each other today," he whispers, full of emotion. "I don't want to wait until something else happens to—"

I close the gap, claiming his soft lips, devouring his whimper, because he's right.

He breaks with a gasp, but keeps his mouth on mine as he

says, "I know we don't make sense together, and I have no idea how this will work, but I can't stop thinking about you."

The rush of relief is staggering. It hasn't been only me stuck in my head, questioning everything.

"I can't either," I rasp, grabbing the sides of his neck and angling his head with my thumbs as I delve deeper, tasting him, just him.

It's everything I hoped it would be and nothing like I imagined. It's different than when we were with Cy. Rawer, scarier. I can't help but be urgent and hard with how I kiss him, because I want to consume him.

But he's so gentle it's messing with my mind. Why would I want him so bad if it's so hard to be with him?

He pulls back, tucking his lips in for a second. "I have an idea. On how to maybe, what if you kiss me like you'd kiss Reanne?"

I blink into the darkness again, my mind working overtime. It seems so simple. It can't be that easy. But it's not like I have anything to lose.

"Okay, sure, we can try that."

Not being able to see him makes this both easier and harder. I adjust my hold on his face, fingers tangling in his hair, thumbs caressing his cheeks.

His breath stutters as I brush my lips across his, teasing his bottom one with my tongue before dipping inside. I slide it along his as our mouths meet in a slow dance. A deep moan escapes his throat, and he melts against me, grabbing my waist. It's a heady feeling. And it might be because my emotions are all over the place, but I think it might be one of the best kisses I've had from a guy. I'd never tell Cy that, but damn, this is hot.

Neo pulls back, gasping again. "Wow, no wonder she likes kissing you. That was…"

"Glad you two worked it out. I could seriously fucking unload just from watching that, but we have to move."

Knowing Cy saw us does nothing for my aching cock. In fact, it makes it harder, but nothing to be done about it, I guess.

Cy stalks up to both of us, kisses Neo first, then me with a softness I'm afraid might be my new normal, before pushing past. "Gonna be a long walk in man form."

"We do not have time for that. I will continue to carry Mishka, someone will need to carry Aeon."

There's a muffled grumble of disagreement, I can only guess is Mishka, and a deeper, authoritative growl I feel in my stomach.

"Hey Vik, good to, uh, see you."

There's a snort farther off. "You're looking at a tree, Aeon."

"Thanks for that, Kor. Always helpful."

He chuckles and grabs me in one of his bear hugs, releasing me with a shoulder pat. "I'm glad you're back, you messy fucker."

I can't believe he manages to pull a laugh out of my wrecked body, but he does.

"Why can't Mishka shift?" I ask no one in particular.

"Pretty obvious, Aeon," Cy chuckles from up ahead, near Vik's voice. "I thought everyone had seen a Shift Collar before."

Holy shit, we have one of those? They're such nasty pieces of construction.

"Guys," Neo says, clearing his throat. "He can't see in the dark anymore. And his healing is off."

Damn it, Neo.

"What?"

Cy's bark hits my fear center hard. I should have told him.

He's against my body in less than a heartbeat, holding my face in his big hands. I wish I could see if he's mad or scared.

One hand drops down to my balls, and he grazes the scratches he left before, forcing me to draw in a pained hiss.

Heavy anguish pours out of Cyan's body as he grips my face again.

"I hurt you?" His throat is tight, the words strangled, pulling even more emotions out of me.

"You hurt me all the time," I mutter, heat rising to my cheeks.

"Don't get smart with me, Beta," his tone dips, angry. "This is different."

A shudder slips down my spine as he lances me with energy. I don't know if he's being more Alpha because there's another one here, or if he's just feeling the pressure today.

I send my wave out as far as it will reach, and his grip loosens, his nose finding the sensitive space under my ear.

"I'd heal you if it were just us, and we had time." He whispers, flicking his tongue over my lobe, letting me know exactly what he means. "And I guess I'll have to find another way to punish you for your damn mouth, now, huh?"

A full body shiver hits me in a wave.

His cheek lifts, brushing against my jaw, and I grin too. "I guess so. Alpha."

"Hmm."

He releases me with a shove and a semi-firm slap on the cheek that lights my bones on fire, before his energy moves away.

Fuck, I don't know how I'm going to survive if I can't take his pain anymore.

Fingers dance across my palm before lacing with mine. Neo.

Sparks and turmoil twist inside me again. I don't know what I want, or what I can have, but that feels...nice.

"I'll carry you," he says sweetly.

Cold water dumps over my head and I snatch my hand back. "No."

It's one thing for, well, whatever the hell this is, but for him to carry me like I'm, like I'm...

I rake my hands through my hair harshly.

But that's exactly what I am. Weak. Pathetic. A liability. A burden.

My stomach hollows, breaths coming shorter, until Neo grabs my hand again, gripping it hard. So hard it shocks me right out of my panic. I didn't know he had that much strength.

The next second, he's in wereform, and I'm cradled in his arms.

I'm about to yell at him, but his beastly tongue slides along my cheek slowly, and damn it all, the claim thrills me down to my marrow.

Still. I don't like this. Never mind what my cock is saying. I cross my arms, and his chest bounces, growls chuffing out in laughter.

I can't see where we're going, but Neo doesn't seem to have any trouble carrying me the entire run.

It should be nearby.

Good. I'm so fucking tired of running I could puke.

We run a few more miles before I decide to breach the silence.

What does it look like?

You will see. We are here.

"Are you fucking kidding me?" Cyan has obviously shifted. "Why didn't you say we were going back to the creepy fucking ghost's house?"

Neo sets me down and drops beast, following Cyan's lead.

"This place again?" Fear hits me. It's hard to be back where I died.

Mishka urgently mumbles something, but we're not paying him any attention.

"You have been here? On your own?" Veikko's voice is incredulous.

"Yeah, this is where I ran that night."

"It remains shrouded at all times. You should not have found it. In fact, you should not see it now, at all."

I shrug. "I thought I was running in the right direction, and this was a cabin in the woods, where I thought you said yours would be. There was nothing hidden about it."

"You know, Jak said it was like your energy line was being led here. And the energy he felt here was the same. I didn't like the idea then and I sure as hell don't like it now."

Mishka is practically shouting through his gag, growls mixed in with it. I kind of wish I could see him, it sounds like a fantastic fit.

"Guys, a little more information would be great." Korey rumbles from behind me. "Because there's nothing here. Trees and sticks and shit, but no cabin."

"Yeah," Neo sighs. "I'm fairly confused myself."

"I, uh, also see nothing out of-of the ordinary."

"What the hell are you guys—it's literally right here!" Cyan slaps something, wood from the sound of it.

"You literally hit a tree." Neo's smile is evident.

Veikko rumbles a hum, and all I hear next is scraping on the ground, rustling, and shuffling of feet.

What's he doing?

I ask anyone, but Neo answers.

I have no idea, it seems like a weird time to be drawing a picture.

Vik chuckles.

"Cyan, there's a lantern on the table inside, maybe if you turn it on, they'll be able to…oh, shit."

The whole house starts to glow from the ground up, brighter until it's almost daytime, illuminating Veikko's unreadable expression, Mishka's sheer twisted joy, and everyone else's wide-eyed confusion.

"Woah," Korey moves farther away, followed by Neo and Laz.

"This dwelling guards the soul, the heart, the energy, of Kasimir." Veikko's voice is slow, reverent, as he presses his palm to a wall. It glows brighter under his touch, ebbing when his hand falls away. "Our first, and only, true High Alpha."

My mind fills with the memories of him tearing into me, giving me an amazing orgasm with ReeRee, repairing our mate bond, and saving me.

"Huh," is all Cyan says.

"I know, we met. To say the least. We did…things. He's the one who brought me back to life after…after those werewolves attacked me and took Reanne."

185

Both Veikko and Mishka snap their attention to me.

The rest of what Vik said rattles through my brain next. The only High Alpha. Jak said there's only one, as well. But everyone also thinks either Cyan, or Mishka, or both are High Alphas, too. It doesn't make any sense. Are there three or is there one?

Mishka's eyes glow as he steps my way. Even with a gag, that huge torture collar, and his hands behind his back, it's still intimidating to be stalked by an Alpha.

"Impossible." Vik monotones. "No one has that power. Except potentially the Rigdis, but nothing is known for certain."

"Oh." I scramble for the words, palms sweating. "Maybe I wasn't, totally dead then. That's probably it."

I'm so damn confused. Maybe I'm the only one, because no one else is asking anything. Mishka's glow fades, eyes narrowing before he refocuses on the cabin itself.

Vik hums and strokes the wall again. "He should have emerged by now."

Cy snorts. "Doubt he'll ever come back after what Jak did."

The wood under Vik's hand creaks as he slowly twists his head toward Cy. "Explain."

REANNE

It's been quiet in here for what feels like hours, but now there's activity again. At least no one is touching me. Yet. I'm thirsty, but Agnar soaking the gag worked for a while. I never needed so much water before, but I guess existing in a near constant state of arousal means I need to replenish my fluids more. Who knows? Maybe I'll live to find out, maybe I won't.

I'm exhausted, mentally and physically. However, emotionally... I don't know. Something is off. The darkness is still here, still slowly spreading, but it almost feels like it's waiting for some sort of trigger.

I hope I find it and I hope I don't. Here, away from my mates, it's easier to locate that odd second version of me that came to life when I almost died. She's not tangible, I can't even see her in my mind, I just know she's here. Whether she's tied to the darkness or not, I don't know either.

"Where did this flower come from?" A full, smooth, languid voice sounds near where I was first tied up, random sounds of shuffling boxes or bags following.

I continue breathing as quietly as I can, hoping like an idiot they'll forget I'm here.

"No clue, we're not here to worry about flowers. Just get the stuff."

"It's a moonblossom."

"So? They're rare flowers, so what?" Something heavy thuds onto the dirt.

There's a pause. "Growing inside a tent."

Another pause. Longer.

"Hey, what are you doing?" The other guy whispers urgently. "You're going to get in trouble!"

My blindfold is snatched off, and I suck in a breath, blinking in a combination of fear and desperation.

The man inches from my face is strikingly beautiful. Medium build with muscular shoulders, angular, lilac eyes rimmed in long, dark lashes, smooth dark skin dusted with pale freckles, dark stubble, a fully defined mouth, and dark brown hair shaved short on the sides, with a shock of soft curls on top.

I scarcely believe it, but there's a heavy tug in my belly, a call inside. That other version of me curls closer, and as if he can feel it, as if he can see her, that sumptuous mouth of his pulls into a smile.

He leans closer, brushing his lips along my ear, lighting my body on fire in an instant. "By the stars…it worked. Hello, little one," he whispers. "Though the hour is late, your faithful servant Evrik has not forsaken you."

Evrik. Something snaps in my chest. Awareness. Familiarity. Hope. A ray of blinding white light pierces the darkness so fiercely, I'm convinced if my mouth wasn't covered, it would shine out like a beacon.

Evrik leans away, gives me a slow wink, and pushes back to his feet, speaking over his shoulder. "Come help me tighten her ropes, she's loose."

"Fine." The other man storms over. "But then we have to get back to wor—"

It happens so fast I don't have time to react. One second the guy is glaring at me, the next, his head slides off his neck, blood gurgling out as his body slumps to the dirt.

There's a weird buzz in the air for a second, pricking against my skin, then nothing.

Evrik flips a bladed weapon of some sort in his hand and stashes it behind his back as he crouches in front of me again.

A scream tries to escape, but the longer I stare into Evrik's eyes, the calmer I get, until there's nothing but peace inside.

I cut my gaze behind him and catch sight of the most beautiful flower I've ever seen. Eight brilliant white, crescent shaped petals curve inward, each with a pulsating, glowing vein down the back. A intricately twisted double stem is capped with drooping, frail, translucent leaves.

Evrik strokes the apple of my cheek with the back of his middle finger, sending a cooling, oddly musical sensation through my cells as he draws my attention. I can't explain it, but it fills me with a deep, bittersweet longing.

"I've waited so long." My gag falls away and his gorgeous smile widens. "Now here you are, surrounded by water hungry moonblossoms in a dry tent. Just as the prophecy foretold."

There's a knowing glint in the curve of his mouth, but I don't understand why. The words are beautiful, pulling tears to my eyes, even though it doesn't make sense. He quickly unties my neck and smooths his icy fingers across the rawness, soothing me to the core.

"Thank you," I rasp as he frees my wrists next, followed by my ankles. "What...worked?"

He winks. "Making you human this time."

"I don't understand."

"I can't explain, I'm afraid." He holds out his hand, and I rest my palm on his without a second thought, insides warming as he strokes his middle finger down my tendons, one at a time. "Am I the first of your court to make contact?"

"My—" I blink at him, shaking my head, swallowing the dryness.

His brow wrinkles a moment before smoothing. "Forgive me, I didn't realize I was so early. Time is endlessly fickle. Allow me to help."

As far as I'm concerned he's helped a whole lot. I've already got feeling back in my hands and my neck doesn't hurt in the slightest. In fact, my wrists are perfectly healed. I'm pointedly ignoring the fact it sounds like he can time travel. I don't have any space left in my brain for a freakout.

He gently guides me into an upright position. Once I'm steadier, he bows his head, pressing his tightly closed fist to the center of his chest.

"Forever in your service, forever by your side."

The oath is thick with old energy I can't begin to understand. It also strikes a chord which makes me wants to wail with happy tears, like I've been reunited with someone I thought I'd never see again, which doesn't make any sense. Still, even as damaged, used, and abused as I am right now, I want to stand before him like someone worthy of that loyalty.

But I can barely stay upright.

He lets the salute drop and catches me when I sway forward. "Sorry," I rasp.

"Never apologize for letting me touch you," he murmurs.

I open my mouth to ask him how he'd feel about touching me a whole lot more, but he cuts my line of thought off with a finger trailing Veikko's mark.

"You've taken mates already. Correct? That's what this is?"

I nod. "Three."

He doesn't seem upset at all. If anything, the bob of his chin feels like a check mark. His gaze crashes into mine. "Are they treating you well?"

God, I'm such a mess right now. Tears prick my eyes again, but I nod again.

His jaw ticks. "Good."

We stare at each other through air heavy with heartbreak and light with the joy of falling in love.

"Five remain."

Adrenaline shoots through me as I blink at him. He can't be serious. "Five...mates?"

"Indeed. Eight total. Just as it was written."

Again, his mouth curves into a smile that says ten million things without making a sound.

"How do you know that?"

"I was there at the making, little one. Just as…someone else was."

The smug smirk tugs at my belly the same time annoyance taps along my neck. If he was there when the prophecy was made, he should have all the information I'm missing!

"Evrik, do you…know what's going to happen to me?"

"Ah," he grins, baring his stunning teeth, "I do indeed. I know everything, more than anyone. But before you ask, I cannot tell you more than I can say. Prophecies are as fickle as time. One fact a moment too soon could ruin everything."

"Okay." The word is shaky, excitement battling with disappointment. "What can you tell me?"

He considers me a moment, the hand on my lower back making light circles. "Each mate will make you stronger. Not in the way you expect. You have allies everywhere, as well as enemies hidden in the familiar." His gaze drifts higher. "The…dark one with green eyes straddles that line, while the thin one with multicolored hair will be the glue they seek. There is more than one trial coming. Since I'm not entirely sure *when* I am, I can't reveal much more." He refocuses on me and grips my hips, flexing his long fingers. "I will add that you have been loved…since your creation. It was impossible for me to show you, until now. And that I'm glad you—"

Someone slices into the back wall of the tent and slips inside. Evrik steps in front of me, with scarcely any visible movement, and I clutch his arm in long-forgotten instinct, struggling to burn all his words to memory.

"Hey man, I don't want any trouble," the intruder says in a laid back, playful lilt. "Mm, wait I take that back. I could definitely go for some trouble with you."

I peek around Evrik. Red, wavy hair, hard muscles, a sly dimpled grin, and bright green eyes flick to mine.

"Wow," he breathes, a knot traveling down his throat. "You're…" he trails off, gawking at me, mouth hanging open.

"A Tracer," Evrik rumbles with a hint of reverence, sheathing his blade inside a hidden leather holster under his waistband. "Your arrival was foretold."

No clue what a Tracer is, but I guess that means he's a friend. Good, I can always use more of those. I give him a smile, and he blinks several times, clacks his jaw shut, and grins.

"No wonder the guys are so crazy about you. And look how tiny you are!"

I'm not tiny, and not sure which guys he's talking about specifically, but—

"Behold," Evrik says, gesturing to me. "Your charge. Her transition nears. Are you prepared for your task?"

As if the words kickstart my body, it buzzes again. I guess he's not wrong.

"Pssh. Obviously." The red head clears his throat. "That task thing is the whole reason I'm here, man. Me and tasks are, like, you know."

I quirk a brow, because that was the single worst bluff I've ever heard.

"Good." Evrik continues, oblivious. "They're preparing the dagger. Make sure they don't use it. Fate is in your hands."

"You got it. I mean, I've got it. No worries at all." Red says with a big nod. "Dagger. Yep."

Evrik's hand twitches at the base of his back, fingers brushing his weapon. "You mock me?"

"Not even a little, my man. Especially if that's what made you kill this guy. It's just," he inches closer scratching the back of his head, grin turning sheepish. "Truth out, I didn't really pay all that much attention to the prophecy. Wishing like heck I had. But, hey, you tell me what to do, and I'm your guy."

Evrik's sigh carries the weight of all creation as he tips his head back and glares at the ceiling, his voice thin and weary. "Test after test. How many must I endure?"

I can't help the soft giggle, because all of this is comforting and weirdly familiar. Evrik twists back to eye me, his frustration melting into a pleased smile. With a gentle move, I'm fitted against his warm body, skin to skin, one arm tight on my lower back, while he traces my lip with the pad of his middle finger. My nerves flare to life, his energy skittering along mine, ramping everything sky-high.

"For another of those, I'd endure them all."

There's a choking amount of adoration in his gaze, and it chases even more darkness away.

"So, you're the one making her energy flare. It's really something, I've gotta say." The red head circles, eyeing us both. "But dude, you're practically giving off lightning. Who are you?"

"Evrik." He doesn't break our gaze, my pulse riding higher and higher.

"Like the constellation?"

My awareness pings again, and I flick my eyes to the red head. "What do you mean?"

"So, when a bunch of stars form a pattern—"

"I know what a constellation is." I grin. "But I haven't heard of one called Evrik."

"Oh. I think we have different ones here than you do in the human world. I dunno. I haven't been there yet. But anyway, yeah. Evrik. It's up there almost always. Means 'the one who watches', I think. I only know that because of my dad and the proph…ohhh. I get it. No wonder you look like you're covered in stars."

Evrik smirks, changing his face completely, making my knees weak. "On the nights I couldn't be found, I was hunting. I've watched you die a thousand times, so to finally see you live is…" His jaw ticks again, emotions clearly running high.

Ah, my heart. I cup his cheek, and he leans into my touch, closing his eyes.

"Makes sense, I guess. Man, I really wish I'd listened more. But it was all he ever talked about. After a while it's just noise, ya know? Anyway. So, not that either of you asked, but I'm Jakobe. Your hero. You can call me Jak. Or Kobe. Or anything you want, really. I'm down for whatever makes you happy. Anything, if you get my meaning. Just as long as we get out of here before they find us."

Oh God, that's right.

The weird haze in my mind clears, present reality crashing down. Not only are they planning on doing something bad to me, my mates might be in trouble, Mishka could already be there. I have to get away.

Evrik pulls back, frowning as he strokes my hair. "The troubles of this plane dim your light."

Jakobe crosses the tent and stands right beside us, his calming, gentle scent doing wonderful things to my insides.

"I know something we can do to make her glow again." He winks at me and juts his chin up at Evrik, smiling. This feels right. Both of these men are safe, but it's deeper than that.

Evrik's eyes flash, brow lifting as he scans Jakobe's body. "If the queen so desires."

Oh, I desire alright. But my adrenaline wanes, a tremble hitting my bones.

"Right after we get you out," Jak says, giving my shoulder an awkward pat. "We'll all take care of you."

The friendly gesture quickly turns to something else as his hand lands heavy, like it got caught in glue, his smile falling.

I glance down, grinning as a small laugh bubbles up. "What are you doing?"

He blushes full on, sending butterflies exploding inside me. "Might seem weird, but I've never touched a female. You're... really soft. And...delicate. N-not in a bad... Man, this is..." His hand glides along the outside of my arm, and a small gasp escapes my now parted lips as those butterflies turn into full-on lust. It's not just the skin on skin, he's doing something with my energy, soothing it, twisting it around himself somehow. I can't help but melt, leaning toward him. It's intoxicating.

He's lost in clearly erotic thoughts, heated gaze locked on my stomach. Skipping my chest entirely, he cradles my tummy, stroking his hot palms in soothing motions. It reminds me of what Cyan did, only more intense, and my heart hiccups.

A deep, loud growl rumbles up from his chest, and he jumps back, covering his mouth. "Wha—sorry. I wasn't growling at you, I dunno why I did that!"

I blink out of the haze yet again, laughing. "It's okay, I've heard it plenty of times."

"That was your beast, young Tracer." Evrik's eyes dance with amusement. "He approves."

Jak grabs his chest, brows mashed together. "I haven't, well, he hasn't done that before. I mean, I can't even talk shifted yet, and he can just growl out of me whenever he wants?" Jak juts out his bottom lip.

"Would that I had time to teach you what your beast, and your body, are capable of." Evrik eyes Jak with hunger.

"Now that's the kind of learning I'd pay attention to." Jak grins and bites his lip. "You can teach us both, and I can show you being young doesn't mean I dunno what I'm doing."

Evrik breathes a soft laugh through his nose and refocuses on me. "I'm beginning to see why you love these creatures. What a life you'll finally live." His smile falls, throat bobbing as his brows tilt. "I'll miss you so."

Finally live? Something claws at my mind, trying to break free, but it's too hazy.

His sadness vanishes, replaced with determination. "Follow the Tracer to the end. He will never lead you astray."

"Whoa. Thanks, man, but, I wouldn't be so—"

"Wait…follow—you aren't coming with?" Panic rises in my throat, and I grab his wrist, but his skin is different. Colder.

He shakes his head and strokes my cheek again. "I am too early. And my time is up."

His body shimmers until I can see the tent through him. "No, please don't go!"

"I have no choice, my shining jewel," Evrik murmurs, wiping

my cheeks with his thumb. "You've shed enough tears to cover the universe a hundred times over. Soon, you will cry no more."

I believe him. I don't know why, given all the crap I've been through in my life, but...I do.

"Will you come back?"

We gaze at each other, and it's so charged I can barely breathe. "If that's what you wish, I'll return each night I'm able, for you."

Overcome with emotion, I lean in. He's tentative, but meets me halfway, and when our lips touch, heat blisters through me, my heart soaring. Both versions of me are one for the smallest fraction of time, and in that moment, everything is crystal clear. It's over too soon to remember any details, and Evrik pulls back. He scans my face before whispering, "I've longed to do that since the beginning of time."

He glances at Jakobe. "I cannot say much, but it's imperative you find her amplifier before the mating is complete. And it's an unexpected source."

"Amplifier. I'm on it." Jak gives a small salute.

I have so many emotions, so many questions, but I can't force anything past the lump in my throat.

There's a crackle in the air moments before a tidal wave of energy blankets the camp. Startled shouts ring out, followed by running footsteps and clattering sounds.

Evrik's expression hardens. "Your mate approaches, my queen. Prepare yourself, Tracer."

And he's gone, leaving nothing but sparkles floating to the ground. I catch one, and it's like a tiny ball of ice, needling my palm but soothing my soul until it fades completely.

"Dude," Jakobe breathes, "that's the coolest thing I've ever seen."

I sniffle, closing my fingers around nothing, squeezing until my knuckles go white.

A court. My queen. Moonblossoms. Stardust. And all of it related to this prophecy, to...me.

Am I some sort of royalty?

"I'm still so confused," I whisper, glancing toward the gorgeous flower. It glitters a moment, but slowly fades. The petals dry, curling in on themselves as the middle fronds wither to dust. With a small pop, it's gone. Little sparkles float down to the dirt, still raised from where my fingers dug in around my tears. It doesn't make sense while at the same time feeling completely normal. I seriously might be losing my mind.

"That was cool too, but not as cool as the hot dude vanishing. We should go while we can." Jak touches my arm, and I crash against him, hugging him tight. It might be weird, but I need a friendly, safe touch so bad right now.

"Aw, it'll be alright." He wraps his arms around my shoulders and rocks me side to side. "Man, oh man, I think I could hold you all day."

I agree, it feels good. He's warm, and solid, and whatever he's doing with my energy is wonderful. It's like I'm nearly balanced.

"But, hey. No reason to be sad, right? I mean, you heard the star man. Cyan's here."

I suck in a breath and step back, excitement blasting through my veins. "You know Cyan?"

Jakobe laughs. "Uh, yeah. He's only the best Alpha ever. Can't wait to join officially. That's who sent me to find you."

"Oh, my God! I thought you were a member here."

"No way!" His face contorts in disgust. "Nope. Proud soon-to-be member of SteelTooth."

I want to laugh. To cry in joy and sadness. To fuck. My God, do I want to fuck. But something big hits the side of the tent, making the whole structure shudder, and I'm shocked back to the present threat.

Jakobe holds out his hand. "Time to go, beautiful."

He'll never lead you astray.

With a nod, I follow behind as he tugs me through the flap, toward chaos.

VEIKKO

I've waited to return for so long, and yet hoped I never would. I planned for how it might go, fretted over what I might say.

But I certainly never expected Kasimir not to be here in any scenario.

Cyan glances at Aeon before refocusing on me. "After the ghostly fucker appeared, Jak did some sort of hand thing, got his attention. He said Jak wasn't strong enough for his power and said we had eleven days to find the Queen, which, Aeon says is Reanne. By the fucking way, I'm pissed at all of you for keeping shit from me."

Everyone tucks their chins in, save for Lazaros. And me, even though I've kept more from him than anyone.

Eleven days. I'd always known the full awakening would be on the new moon, but it feels frighteningly close.

Cyan eyes me a moment before continuing. "Then Jak threw him back into the ground, and that was that."

That was most definitely not that. Nothing can fully dispel Kasmir, but I'm oddly proud of Jakobe's mastery of his skill.

"I will call him home."

"What do we need him for anyway? He's fucking awful to look at."

Irritation swarms me from nowhere and I glare at Cyan, huffing, "He's been dead for thousands of years. He looks far better than you will after you're buried."

He blinks at me, the pack falling silent. Even Mishka's brows lift, though he seems more pleased than surprised.

"What the absolute fuck, Vik," Cy growls.

I exhale slowly, drawing another rune. "I...apologize. It has been a stressful day."

"You're telling me, I literally died. Uh...maybe." Aeon coughs and shrugs.

Neo touches Aeon's shoulder and they share a smile. I'm happy for them, truly. But I miss Reanne and...Jakobe. Never in a trillion years would I have imagined this path for my life.

I begin tracing the required symbols, the ritual bringing back deeply buried memories. How many times did I summon Kasmir to speak? Until I finally got the answer I'd been seeking. My jaw clenches.

They watch, expressions varying from unease to awe. They've never seen me do this before, for good reason. One in a long line of secrets I carry.

The final rune in place, I close my eyes, calling on his familiar energy. Though faint, it's here, and I will it closer, brighter, stronger, sharing my magic with him. Magic no one else can offer.

The ground rumbles and gasps ring out, fading as the pack shuffles backward.

My eyes peel open slowly, adjusting to the growing glow surrounding him. Odd feelings roll through me, but mostly, all I feel is a sense of duty and determination. He's likely the only one who can save Reanne, now.

"Dear god," Neo whispers.

"Yeah, literally. But don't be scared, he's not evil or anything."

I cut my gaze to Aeon, who's staring at Kasimir with a small smile in place.

Hmph.

Kasimir's growl vibrates through the earth. "You..."

I hold my breath as he stares at me, cracked, decayed hand raising, claws curling into a point. After all these years, these centuries, I have no idea what he might say.

"Are…late."

My jaw clenches anew. It doesn't surprise me those are the first words I hear, but it does annoy me.

"How is he talking without talking?" Korey steps closer, less afraid and more curious.

"He's Kasimir," Aeon says with reverence. "First Alpha. He can do that sort of thing, I guess."

I squint at him. While I understand Kasimir returned him to life, likely at great power expenditure, I don't understand the affection. Why is he defending as if he cares— Oh. Oh, perhaps I *am* late.

Aeon!

He jumps in his skin, facing me with a wild gaze. *What? Damn, you didn't have to shout.*

Did he bite you?

Um…

Everyone, save for Mishka and Laz, orients on Aeon, who squirms under the scrutiny. Before he answers, light flashes from Kasimir's body, shocking us all to attention. He doubles in size, looming over the house.

"Remove," he hisses, pointing the claw at Mishka, "his…restraints."

No one responds at first, and I open my mouth to explain, but his Alpha wave explodes outward, and I cannot help but comply.

The Shift Collar comes off first, then the rope around his hands, and lastly the gag, revealing the most self-satisfied smirk I've ever seen.

"Thank you, great Kasimir. I've waited for—"

"SILENCE!"

My ears whine, and Mishka drops to his knees, wincing. Korey clutches Laz tighter, and Neo does the same to Aeon. Cy simply stands tall like the proud Alpha he is, fists clenched, watching.

"You…have interfered…for the last…time."

"Wh-what? Interfere? I've done nothing but try to fix what *he* broke!" He points at me, then himself. "It should have been me, it was my time, and now—"

"Your time...has long since...gone. You killed...her. You...are no longer...deemed worthy."

Mishka blinks, before letting out a soft laugh. "You're joking. You—Do you know what's been going on here? He," Mishka jabs a finger in my direction, "created an entire army, whose sole purpose is to kill—"

"I am aware," Kasmir booms, casting a dark glance my way. I can feel the pack's scrutiny, but I stay focused ahead.

Did you really do that? Korey's stare burns the side of my face with its intensity.

Yes. I fear now I may have received faulty information. I am not the same as I was all those years ago.

No wonder you were so quiet, Neo says. *That's a lot of guilt to deal with alone.*

I glance at him and give him a small nod.

"Then," Mishka rises to his feet, "you surely understand I'm not to blame. They lied to me, convinced me she was a monster, and I didn't realize until it was far too late. I've spent my whole life since that day—I nearly saved the last one, but yet again, Veikko interfered. If you're mad at anyone, it should be him! I've prepared everything for her, my followers know what to expect. They wait at this moment to teach her everything I've learned. What has this one done? She still has no idea what her true role is!"

"You...are no longer...worthy."

"And he is?!"

Mishka gestures wildly to Cyan, while centuries of hope, purpose, and life, drain from his eyes. His mouth works, silent until words finally form, starting small and quiet. His arm drops in defeat.

"I didn't know who she was. I didn't know how much it would hurt, how every single minute of every day I'd miss someone I never even spoke to. I tried—I wanted— T-tell me, is she there? Her star, is it as brilliant as it should be?"

There's a heavy pause, as Kasimir tilts his head to the sky. We all follow his seeking gaze, until there's a glint. Mishka shudders a breath.

"Good."

"Your time...is over," Kasimir rumbles, more caring a tone than I've ever heard.

There's an odd calm that sweeps Mishka's face, a resignation, a gleam in his eyes. Finally, he focuses on me with the only thing he has left, rage, even though it seems calculated. "You. This is all your fault! I believed your lies, you and your twisted Sentinels, you ruined me!" He growls, transforming to his wereform, and I don't have time to react as he lunges for me.

In a swirl of choking power, Cyan shifts and tackles Mishka mid-air, tangling with him on the ground. Blood and fur fly everywhere, snarls and bone-chilling growls filling the forest.

It's a battle worthy of the celestial record to be certain. The past, fighting for position in a future that doesn't want it, desperate to claim something that isn't, and hasn't, been his since the start. He has been fighting a war he lost 400 years ago.

I almost feel bad for Mishka. He is not wrong, this is my fault. But...that was a version of me that no longer exists. I will not apologize. He proved me right, and himself unworthy over and over, though, he doesn't believe that to be so.

It is still hard to watch a werewolf be destroyed, even one who deserves it, but I'm transfixed.

Cy rips into Mishka's chest, bones cracking, splintering as he peels him open. There's no fight left in Mishka, but Cyan can't stop. It is the same Alpha drive that compelled me to pound Fen into dust.

With a horrifying wet noise, Cyan rears back, clutching Mishka's tattered heart in his fangs. He swallows it with a single gulp and lets out an emotional victory howl.

A pulse of pure, white energy radiates from Cyan's upper

body. Mishka's beast fades from existence, his portion of Kasimir's soul floating back home, sending a surge through the First Alpha's decayed form.

Cyan drops beast and glances down at the barely recognizable mass of bloody tissue and organs under him. His expression is grim, haunted.

"No one threatens my family." He wipes at the blood on his face and steps back.

"Cy," Neo murmurs.

They lock eyes, and I can feel how badly he wants to go to his partners. Fatigue and pain ripple through his muscles. He needs a release, but I also know he will not allow time for that. It is a dangerous game to delay the urge.

Kasimir rumbles in satisfaction and floats higher.

"Where…is…my…?"

"Just a damn minute." Cyan barks, wiping the blood from his mouth.

The behemoth being turns slowly.

"What the fuck did he mean, asking if I'm worthy? Worthy of what?"

A throaty rumble, like a distant chuckle, fills the air. "Me."

"What the fuck does THAT mean? I'm so sick of these vague ass fucking answers from everyone. I wanna know, right now, why this weasel licking windbag thought he was worthy of something I wasn't—"

Chest heaving with adrenaline, Cyan stops a moment, staring down at Mishka's smear. "Wait. Is that why we had the same face? Are we the same—Hold up, hold up. Wait. Everyone fucking WAIT!" He grabs his head and whimpers, while the whole forest breathes in silence. "My twin, right? Long lost or some shit like that."

"Not your twin, Alpha." I mutter, the sound carrying through the stillness like a thunderclap.

"Well, I sure as fuck didn't kill myself!"

Kasimir looms closer to Cyan, a weighted sigh hefting his frame. "When the moon...descends, we...will become...one."

"I'm done with this bullshit. You." He points at me. "What am I? No fucking sideways answers, don't make me command you."

I bristle, but crack my neck. "You are a reincarnation."

"Of *who?*"He shouts it at the top of his lungs, blasting his amplified Alpha wave across the whole forest floor.

Kasimir hooks a claw around Cyan's neck with a whip fast movement, snatching him into the air. "I...was never... this...abrasive."

Of all the things I've heard in my immensely long life, that's the funniest. I snort, loudly, and by all the stars I didn't mean to let it out. I quickly clear my throat when Kasimir flicks his gaze my way.

Cyan quits struggling, hands hooked around Kasimir's claw to keep himself from choking as they stare at each other.

"You? So, we were both..."

"Yes, Alpha," I interject. "Every two hundred years, a reincarnation is born, with the potential to house—"

"Is that why that fucker could hop in my body?"

Kasimir tilts his head slowly. "Two potentials...overlapping... perhaps caused...issues."

"You don't say." Cyan glowers. "Put me down or snap my fucking neck."

Kasimir chuckles again and lowers Cyan back to the ground. After he shakes out his shoulders, stretches his neck, and scrubs his face in frustration, he eyes Kasimir again.

"Eleven days."

Kasimir nods.

"And then you and I..."

Another slow nod.

"Am I gonna change?" There's not even a hitch in his voice.

"I don't...believe so. We will...simply...become one."

Cyan blows out a long, loud breath and plops his hands on

his hips. Unease filters through the pack link, and though Neo and Aeon twitch, it's Lazaros who reacts first.

He leaves the safety of Korey's shadow and, with his small fists clenched, eats up the distance between them. Cyan eyes him with one brow lifted, even as his throat bobs.

Laz collides with his waist, hugging him tightly. "E-even if you were to change, I think, no, I know, that you will always be Cyan. The most wonderful, attentive Alpha I've ever had the pleasure of m-meeting."

Cyan tilts his head to the sky and holds it there, swallowing again. Neo, Aeon, and Korey close in next, placing their hands on his shoulders. I would go, too, but I oddly feel this moment shouldn't include me.

"Thanks. Okay, enough mushy stuff." He sniffs, shouldering them all off, though he squeezes Neo's hand before releasing it. "None of this will fucking matter if we don't find Reanne."

"You…lost her?"

I step forward, craning my neck as Cyan stares at the rest of the pack. "Someone took her, and she is likely in trouble. Mishka knew where, but did not tell us."

"I will find…her."

Life and awareness bloom in Kasimir's dead eyes as he scans the horizon. The ground shakes again, trees groaning as they lean away from the force of his seeking energy.

A terrifying roar cracks across the forest, and he soars above the canopy, flying away, plunging the cabin back into darkness. My vision only takes a moment to correct, the landscape visible again in shades of grey.

"He'll lead us to her, but we have to follow him, or risk losing them both."

"You heard 'im. Shift."

The energy Cyan sends as he calls his beast again is supercharged, chafing my skin, unwelcome. That shouldn't happen, ever. Have I been too careless with my own Alpha energy? Or is this just because he's amplified from killing Mishka? A problem for another time.

Aeon's knees buckle, and Neo's shift is instant. Korey and Laz both shift next, as Neo scoops up Aeon and they all stare at me.

I nod, shift, and in less than a second, without a single parting glance at The Harbinger's dead smear, we race after Kasimir.

It's quite simple to follow the tendrils of power he's left in his wake, because, unfortunately, he's being reckless with it. No one speaks for a few moments, until Korey breaks the silence.

I can't even see him anymore, how do you know we're going in the right direction?

His glow is still visible to me.

Cyan growls. *How? And how do you fucking know to do all this, Vik?*

I don't answer immediately, only because I've never said the words out loud. There was one who suspected. I could laugh at how close he came to confirming. Despite living as long as he had, it wasn't quite long enough, and now he'll never know. Even my old friend Eoghan never made the connection.

Veikko.

I sigh and duck under a branch before glancing back at Cyan.

Because…Kasimir is my father.

JAKOBE

I thought her energy was something special before, but having been in the same room, and then holding her? Man. She blew my mind right outta my skull. Who knew human females were so soft and little and squishy? Nothing at all like a Nikta. Her little hand feels nice, too. I could seriously get used to this. And star dude was super easy on the eyes. Can't wait to see him again.

I duck through the tent flap, her vibe pinging off my back as I glance around. Guys are hurrying all over the place, someone's taken down one of the three tents by the fire, and in its place, they're building some sort of raised thing. That big guy, the one with Corbet when they found me in the woods, is carrying a massive flat rock toward the newly cleared area. I've got a bad, bad feeling in my gut.

It's all good. I've got this. We just have to get out of here, meet up with our pack, and get to living the best lif—

Dark energy seeps out of the nearby tent.

Aw, man.

There's no time to hide before Yuli appears, his glare practically slapping me even though he's ten feet away.

"Jakobe. Who told you to bring her?" His gaze dips to our joined hands.

Alright. Time to work the brain muscle again. I should have planned for this but, well, I didn't. The only thing I can think of is pinning it on the dead guy.

I point over my shoulder, back into the tent. "The one with the bald head."

There's a beat of tense silence, the rest of the ruckus muted under my slamming heart. For the first time in, huh, I guess ever, I'm actually worried I might not pull this—Wait a minute…ha!

I grin and brandish our hands. "Corb was right, she feels amazing. So, where do you want her?"

I do my best to send her calming waves, while keeping my own energy in check, and Vik's buried out of Yuli's reach. It's a balancing act, like I'm one of them flying rats, going from branch to branch in the winter.

She stares at me, her vibe shifting from the stunning pearly white, blue combo, to the scary glossy black and back again.

C'mon, Reanne…

"Please," she whimpers, yanking on our hands. "Let me go."

Atta girl!

I halfway expect him to grab her and take her himself, which wouldn't be good for anybody, but he grunts and gestures off toward the stone thing that guy put down.

"Tie her down on that, then go help Pell get the rest of the food sorted."

"You've got it." I give him a salute and pull Reanne behind me, while she shoves at my hand.

Once we're out of ear—and energy—shot, I give hers a gentle squeeze and she stops fighting.

"You're a natural, beautiful," I mutter. "Sorry about that, but good work."

"Thanks, I was a little worried until I felt your wave," she whispers. "We're going to make a run for it, right?"

There are guys criss-crossing our path, zipping through the camp, watching our every step. My beast is still totally knocked out, so, there's no way I could get her outta here without getting us both killed in the process, even though the tree line is right there.

Besides, I have no idea where Agnar is and I'm not going without him.

"Uh, not yet."

"What? Why?"

We reach the stone and someone tosses an armful of rope at me before he dashes off to some other place. I barely catch it with my free hand, and twist to face her.

Man, I can't stand those tears in her eyes. I just wanna cuddle her under a blanket until she's a boneless puddle of happy.

"I'm really sorry," I whisper. "But I swear, it'll be alright. We'll get out of this. I've, well, we've got a plan. Sort of. You just gotta play the part a bit longer."

"We? Who is the—"

Agnar choses this moment to make the best dramatic entrance in werewolf history, and flings open a tent flap. "Me."

If I had my hands free, I'd give him a round of applause. Dude had to be waiting here this whole time. I'm sort of jealous, being honest.

Her energy clears a bit, and my own responds, which is weird as heck, because it shouldn't do anything I don't tell it to do. I try not to dwell on that, because, man, she feels so good right now I could lay down and die happy.

"Agnar," she whispers, her lip trembling. "I really want to hug you right now."

He nods with a small smile, though I can see the pain in his eyes. "I'd like nothing more, but that can't happen."

"Not yet anyway," I murmur. "Let's just focus here and then we can do that other stuff."

"O-okay. I trust you guys. Just…please. Don't let them hurt me again."

"No way." I help her onto the stone, and as she situates on her back and stares up at me with those shining, doe eyes, it's all I can do not to kiss her.

Apparently, I'm staring too hard, 'cause Agnar clears his throat, snapping me out of my trance.

Together, we tie her to the stone thing, making sure it's not too tight.

"Agnar, where's Cyan?"

"What?"

"Evrik said my mate was here," Reanne whispers, wincing as she adjusts her shoulder.

Agnar's gaze lifts slowly from her to me and then off to the tree line. "No one's here yet," he mutters. "And who is Evrik?"

I chuckle. "Let's just say the man has stars in his eyes and leave it at that."

Agnar focuses on me now, brows knitting a whole sweater. I wave my hand. "Never mind. Listen. I figure we can make a break for it soon. You shift, grab her and run, and I'll—"

"I told you." His expression drops into that determined thing he's been rocking. "That's not how this goes," he snaps.

"And I told you I wasn't leaving you here," I snap right back. We stare at each other until Reanne's energy sizzles and pops, drawing our attention.

She glances between both of us. "What?"

"Tell us what you're feeling right now." As if Agnar doesn't know.

Her cheeks turn a stunning shade of muted pink. "N-nothing."

"Nothing, huh?" I quirk my brow, a smile spreading before I can stop it, and lean closer. "I totally promise, between me and all the others, you won't be able to walk for a full cycle, just as soon as we get out of here. Hang on a bit longer, okay?"

She nods, a tear slipping down her temple and darkening the stone below. "I'll hold you to that," she whispers, gifting me with a tiny smile. My heart throbs, and I want to risk it all, take her and make a break for it right now.

"Jak, are you coming?"

My skin bunches, and I shoot a look over my shoulder. Corbet is standing at the entrance to the food tent with a tall, stick-thin guy who I guess is Pell. He looks like he hasn't touched a thing he's ever cooked.

Nothing for it but to do it.

"Yep, on the way."

I pat her shoulder, give Agnar a slow nod, and head toward Corbet's weird grin and Pell's deathly serious glare. Ducking through behind them, I'm greeted with quite a sight.

The tent is full of half-complete meals, which Pell flits between, muttering to himself. Corbet clutches my waist in a side hug. "I hoped one day you'd get to meet each other. He's upset about the short notice, but normally, he's great. I think you guys will get along."

I slink out of his grip and face him. The guy I knew has to be in here, somewhere. And that guy would have wanted the chance to leave a burning tree, for sure. "Corb, you've got to get out of this place."

His smile slowly falls. "The tent?"

"No, I mean—" I grab his wrist and pull him behind a giant barrel, giving his shoulders a shake. "Snap out of it, man," I whisper. "The vibe in this pack, the energy, it's eating at your brain."

He stares at me a second before laughing and patting my shoulder. "Still joking around. Hey, did you get to go see the abomination? She's something, huh?"

Every memory of my carefree, good-hearted friend melts away before my eyes, leaving a BriarMaw lackey, through and through. Whatever happens to these awful werewolves, he'll share their fate and probably be happy about it.

Damn, this hurts.

"Uh," I swallow and force a smile, "yeah, man."

"Corbet," Pell calls with a thick accent. "I need this deesh plated."

"Be right there." He gives me another friendly pat, and I watch how he interacts with Pell, but more I watch the dark energy coming from him. Even Pell has his own darkness. I couldn't see the subtle color variation before, but sure enough, Yuli's dark energy has a different tint. Dang. Why can I spot that now all of a sudden? Agnar! Has to be. I must have picked up more than just a new trick from him. Heh. That's awesome. I can't wait to tell him and show Vik. Good thing we'll have a long time to figure it all out. I'll be an even better Tracer. As if that were possible.

Corbet snickers and bumps Pell with his hip and I frown. Maybe the guys who joined here were already prone to being bad, and that's why they chose to stay with such an obviously evil Alpha. Or…does being around such a bad source change you so much, even if you left you'd be ruined forever? And why didn't any of them break pack when they realized Yuli was so dark, or is that something only Agnar and I can see?

I trudge over to the pair of them and take the plates as Corbet passes them off.

I hate this. I wish I knew more about any damn thing. I rub at the ache in my chest. I swear I've been through every emotion that exists in the past day. Far cry from feeling dead inside like when I was DuskFall. I still don't regret leaving. Even though… even though it's not near as much fun as I thought it would be.

REANNE

J ak swaggers toward the tent, all confidence and adorableness. I shouldn't be noticing his ass, or thinking how you could probably bounce a quarter off of it, or wondering what that long, thick cock of his would feel like, but I'm boiling inside.

Once he's slips behind the flap, I straighten my head, my hair snagging on the chilly rock, and find Agnar staring at the tent, too, still as a statue.

"I agree," he murmurs. "He's quite nice to look at."

"It isn't just that. I mean, yes, but, I really need…" I clench my thighs, shifting my hips under the ropes.

"I know." His throat bobs, nostrils flaring. "I'm sorry."

God, knowing it's affecting him is only turning me on more. This seriously sucks.

"Agnar. I wish we'd…"

I can't finish the sentence, but his eyes meet mine, and there's a charge in the air between us before he forces a sad smile. "So do I." He glances around the camp before stepping slightly closer.

"Jakobe is too optimistic. You should know, I will die here. Soon."

I suck in a gasp, staring deep in his crystal blue gaze.

"Why?" The word barely makes it out of my squeezing throat.

"So you'll both live." He shrugs a shoulder like his life for mine is no big deal.

"...No! I don't want that. You don't need to sacrifice yourself, there's another way. There *has* to be!"

One side of his attractive face lifts in a smile. "I see you share the same trait. It's not a sacrifice, it's a gift. Truth out, you are far more important than me, Reanne. Than anyone."

I shake my head as furiously as I can. "That's not true."

He's already focusing on something else, lost in his plan I guess, or whatever dark thoughts have convinced him that he's got to martyr himself. I can tell by the look in his eyes, he's committed. Nothing I say will change anything.

It's weirdly quiet, even with the sound of feet shuffling around me, there aren't any nature sounds, like crickets or anything. Just endless night around me and endless stars above.

"Agnar."

I jerk, Yuli's commanding voice startling in the worst way. Twisting my head, I track his measured approach, but he doesn't look at me.

"Get the dagger. We're going to start now."

"Now?"

Agnar's voice is tight, panicked as he glances between the two of us.

"You're not going to stop being useful, are you?"

He pauses by my head, one wide hand braced on the stone, his body heat radiating straight to me despite the slight breeze. His tendons jump, a vein throbs with his pulse, and I follow the path of several more veins traveling his forearm. Desire washes over me before I can stop it. Damn him. My breaths come shorter, and I can't keep from remembering his touch in the tent, or noticing the faint swatch of dark hairs leading down, or how perfect his stomach is, or how utterly bite-able his chest is, or how muscled his shoulders are, or—

My exploratory gaze collides with his cold, assessing one, and I quickly refocus on Agnar.

God, I need to get it together. This is utterly ridiculous.

There's probably a psychosis around wanting to be banged by the guy about to kill you.

"No…Alpha." Agnar growls, and storms away, fists clenched.

I lift my head and try to follow his path, but a scalding finger presses on the middle of my forehead, flattening me back down.

Yuli and I lock eyes again, and my stupid heart flips. Even though he seems like nothing but darkness, there's something, buried deep in him, I can feel it. A tiny light, faint, nearly dead, but it's there.

"Looking at me like that won't stop this."

I blink rapidly forcing my eyes to the sky. "I wasn't looking at you like anything."

He leans all the way over until his face fills my vision, a smirk twisting his mouth. "What did I say I'd do if you lied to me again?"

I suck in a breath, brows pitching as I stumble over my words. "I didn't, I mean, I was, okay? Fine. You're attractive and I…"

"Say it." There's his twisted, desperate tone again.

A tear slips free as I whisper, "I hate you."

He seems more relieved than anything, the corner of his mouth twitching. "It's the cruelest form of torture, isn't it? To lust after someone you can't stand?"

We stare at each other for too long. So long, my heart skips beats and my palms sweat. His gaze roams my face, jaw jumping before he jerks backward, out of my line of sight.

"Luckily, neither of us have to suffer much longer."

I shake loose another tear and press my cheek to the stone, eyeing his impatient posture, as he glares off into the camp. This is it for me anyway, apparently. I know Jak and Agnar thought they could save me, but that was before. Now, Yuli is right here, and since I'm going to die anyway, I might as well speak my mind.

"I'm only suffering now because you're making me."

His blistering blue eyes snap to mine. "If I'd succeeded before, you wouldn't be suffering at all. It would have been a quick death."

Tears fall again as I fume. "How on Earth can you say that? Those frat guys were going to rape me first. They were literally starting when…"

The utter shock and pain on his face eats the rest of my words and ties my stomach in a knot.

"That," he swallows, "was not what I told them to do."

Sheer insanity forces a laugh free. "Is it so shocking that someone who'd agree to stab a woman to death might also just use her body first? And-and how is that any different than what you told all your guys to do to me in there?"

He's at the side of the altar in a blink, and I squeak, recoiling in fear. But all he does is hover his hand at his side before flexing his fingers and curling them into a fist.

"Did one of them enter you?"

I blink. "No. They just…" I squirm, highly uncomfortable with reliving it. "Touched."

"What is it," he seethes under his breath, "about these impulsive, smelly, ignorant creatures that you find so desirable?"

That's sort of what Evrik said, only the opposite. My pulse kicks into high gear for a whole other reason. It's like I'm struggling to fit pieces of a puzzle together, but the picture is upside down, and none of the shapes make sense.

"They don't listen unless I command them, they take what I say and twist it. I said keep her on edge. That was it. I cannot wait to finally, *finally,* be free of this fucking place." He steps back. "And these awful monsters."

"Why, though?" I sniffle. "Why do that to me? And what do you mean? Aren't…you're a werewolf, too."

"Because you deserve to feel a fraction of my torment. And obviously I'm a werewolf," he barks with disgust. "The issue is you're not this time."

I don't quite understand the feeling his torment part, other than he's clearly lost some marbles along the way, but "this time." That's something else Evrik said.

"Yuli."

He looks like his name on my lips is the worst offense possible and the most amazing gift he's ever received.

We stare at each other for a beat before I continue.

"Have I…been here before?"

I can't decipher his expression at first, but it quickly turns to contempt.

"Would it upset you if the answer was yes?"

"I…"

Would it? I take stock of everything, and the idea that I might have been hurting like this, or even worse, makes a ball of fear grow inside. I nod.

He takes a step closer and glares. "Then, yes. Every two hundred years. I've been here as many times as you have. The difference is no one ever remembers me. I'm not in the original prophecy, because no one cares about me. Or didn't until this time, but you saw to ending that. It's always, always about you," he sneers. "How anyone believed they could create endless second chances for you and that hideous monstrosity, but forget we're connected, forget that we'd share the same, miserable fate is—"

Rage explodes in his eyes, but he breathes deeply through his nose, straightening his shoulders. Second chances? Monstrosity?

"The biggest difference is, I used my time wisely. Made moves to end the cycle. Veikko was the easiest one to corrupt," he whispers, scraping his nails across my hair splayed on the rock. "A few well-worded lies, a nudge in the wrong direction, a friend he needed more than anything who just happened to hate the entire idea of you. And the best one, a command from an Alpha he couldn't disobey."

My heart lurches, adrenaline spiking through my veins. "That's horrible!"

217

"Is it? Worse than being forced from my home continuously against my will? Forced to inhabit some other body? I think not."

I open my mouth but nothing comes out. I don't think I'd like that either. If I have been reincarnating, at least I don't have any memory of it. I can't imagine remembering every time, and not being able to avoid it.

My jaw clacks shut, and I can't help my frown. I may understand—slightly—where he's coming from, but it still feels like I'm missing something big. The picture is fuzzy, the pieces are making a little more sense, but his answers feel…

"It doesn't matter what you think, in all honesty," he continues. "I made a way to end it all."

Agnar storms back and hands Yuli the dagger without a word. We lock eyes and he twitches like he wants to come to me, but quickly casts a furtive glance at Yuli and stands his ground.

"Excellent. Now we can begin." Yuli comes to my side and twists the dagger above me. "You don't mind, do you?"

The grin that spreads across his face is pure delighted malice as he puts his scalding, heavy hand over my mouth, the altar's rough stone surface scratching my skin. I don't have time to take a deep enough breath to properly fuel my scream as he drives the blade upward, under my ribs.

I arch, nearly blinded by the pain.

"So dramatic," he tuts. "This won't kill you unless I cut off your head." There's a gleam in his eye. "But…it will make a certain someone very upset."

The blade twists, agony spreading through my system at break-neck speed. I shred my throat, every nerve searing, my brain wanting to fight, to escape, but at the same time, too afraid to move and cause more injury.

Out of nowhere, a single thought drowns out every other impulse.

I'm really fucking tired of being stabbed.

The tiny ball of anger and blackness I've been nurturing grows so quickly, it fills me to the brim, exploding outward.

Yuli yanks the dagger free and ducks as it smothers the camp in a blanket of black, knocks Agnar over, pushes smaller tents off their bases, threatens to snuff out the roaring fire, and blots out several of the stars which had been twinkling above me.

Yuli laughs, of all things, hands creeping over the edge of the altar. "There it is, let it all out."

I get even madder.

"I…have had…enough!" I shout, but it doesn't sound like me. It doesn't even sound like the other version of me, hiding inside. It's something else entirely.

Fear permeates the air. Good. They should be afraid. Everyone should.

Werewolves are shouting, scrambling in all directions, and every time I catch movement, I lash out a web of my darkness, tripping whoever it is.

Yuli's laugh echoes in my head, and I shouldn't like the sound of it, I shouldn't like how it makes the darkness stronger, makes me feel more powerful. But I do.

"What the heck was that?" Jakobe comes rushing toward me. I snap my attention to him, and he skitters to a wide-eyed stop, slowly lifting his palms. "Hey, okay. Let's just take a nice deep breath."

Thunder rolls above the forest, getting louder and louder until I realize it's not thunder at all, it's a growl.

The other werewolves freeze, sending their attention to the sound, but Jakobe stares right at me, inching closer.

He blasts a wave of his sweet, clean energy, but I don't want it. I need the darkness, it will save me.

His brows twist as he pushes harder. "Come on, I get it, you're sad, but—"

The growl changes to a snapping snarl which vibrates through the whole camp, wrenching shouts and screams from most of the other werewolves, but Jak keeps his focus on me, pushing, pushing, pushing.

"I know you're still in there behind those…freaky new black eyes, beautiful."

"No," I growl and lash an arm of my darkness around his neck.

He grabs at the invisible noose, choking sounds barely audible. "You…don't…want to…do this."

But he's wrong. I want them all to die. I only wanted to be happy, to stay home, that's all I've ever wanted, and these awful creatures—

"Mate."

The voice is so loud, so commanding, like the heavens themselves opened up, and I can't help but flinch. Thick, heavy, warm energy pushes the air out of my lungs as a shadow looms above me, blocking the entire sky. The sounds of panic fade from my mind, and I twist my head, locking eyes with the terrifying form of Kasimir. He's glowing and at least ten times the size he was before. He's beautiful.

Sobs of joy burst free, the dark arm falling away from Jak's neck and recoiling like a scolded pet as it climbs back inside my chest.

Yuli snarls something, sounding a million miles away, but I can only focus above me. Kasimir rumbles deeply, soothing me as he runs the tip of one claw down my torso, slicing through each rope like it's a spider's web.

I try to tell him Yuli is still here, to be careful, but my mouth isn't working.

Jakobe stumbles forward and flicks the ropes away before grabbing my hand. He blasts his energy through me, and the last dregs of darkness shrivel back into dormancy. I cry even harder because I never wanted to hurt him, I never wanted to hurt anyone, he's not the slightest bit angry at me, and I don't deserve someone so wonderful in my life, especially after I tried to strangle him.

"Man. Good timing, big guy," he pants, squeezing my fingers. "Sorry. About the whole…dispelling thing. Before."

Kasimir lets out a single chuckle, and my heart leaps around, kicking my ribs.

But his focus lasers in on my body. He runs his claw along my stomach, tenderly stroking the now healed wound, crusted with dried blood.

I'm a furnace in an instant. I sniffle and touch his absolutely massive claw, squeaking when he darts his face closer to mine. But instead of giving me another soul-shattering orgasm or two, he shifts his attention to Agnar, a snarl curling what's left of his lip.

"They...will pay."

Finally, my thoughts reach my mouth and I shake my head. "N-No, he's a good one. It's Yuli who—"

I twist my head, trying to find him but a wave of dizziness sweeps through me, and I close my eyes. With Jak's help, I sit up, the world spinning around me. I'm drained, which...I guess is from the darkness. I wish I knew why it was different each time it came out. There has to be a common thread. Jak cradles my stomach too, heartbreak flashing in his eyes.

Kasimir steadies me with his claw until Agnar groans, easing to his feet.

"Shit. Where did he go?"

"Who, Yuli?" Jak stretches taller and twists in each direction. "I dunno man, let's just get out of here."

"We've been over this, Jak." Agnar growls.

Kasimir orients on him and Agnar bows his head, clapping his fist to his shoulder. "I offer my body as a vessel for your revenge, Alpha Kasimir."

Kasimir rumbles in agreement, his eyes lighting, and reaches his claw toward Agnar.

"What?" Jakobe's jaw drops. "Wait, is that what you meant—no! Hey, man. I, uh, do that, too. C'mon, we have history, right?"

Kasimir's head twists around, and he eyes Jak for a moment, before darting closer.

"We...do."

There's a brilliant flash, an instant of blindness, and when I can see again, Kasimir is gone. Jak staggers a bit, wincing. He clutches the side of his head and groans.

"You fool." Agnar says, but it's a strangled, emotional whisper.

"Jak? Are you okay?"

He opens his eyes and I gasp. The green is gone, swallowed by Kasimir's umber glow.

"No," he growls, but it's three times as deep, and pained. "Something…is…wrong. Too…inexper—"

At that moment Agnar lets out a sharp, pained breath.

I turn in time to see Yuli's triumphant, crazed grin behind Agnar's shoulder. "Thank you for playing your part so dutifully, filthy Tracer. May you both rot away into nothing."

Agnar grunts as he drops to his knees, revealing the blood-soaked dagger in Yuli's hand.

"No!" My scream feels empty, no matter how much force I put behind it.

Jak staggers, trying to move, but it's like he has no control over his body, like he's fighting with it.

I reach for my darkness on instinct, determined to send Yuli to meet his disgusting mate in whatever their afterlife is, but it's…not there. Kasimir's light and Jakobe's sweet energy are too powerful. I'm helpless.

Yuli quickly approaches, nothing but insanity and glee etched on his face.

"Now that your horrid obsession is finally dead, it's your turn. Time to go back home for good. You'll thank me someday." Clarity hits his eyes for a brief second. "Maybe even forgive me."

Everything happens too fast, yet feels like slow motion. Yuli steps behind me, wrapping his arm around my shoulder as he presses the blade to my throat.

Jak lets out a deranged roar, panic evident in his eyes, and ineffectually dives for Yuli. In the span of a blink, Agnar shouts and races toward the two of them.

Jakobe's expression swaps from angry determination, to utter confusion as Agnar closes his hand around Jak's shoulder. The blade pierces my skin at the same time a blinding light fills the sky, a crack of thunder shaking the earth and plunging us into the fire-lit darkness.

The dagger skitters down my side, loose, landing with a clatter against the stone as I blink the blur out of my vision. Yuli is gone, Jak is on his back a few paces away, and I'm faced with a bloody, shaking, glowing Agnar.

Jakobe jumps to his feet. "Damn it! I told you, I could have handled it! I had it, man! Why did you…" Emotion chokes his words, and tears race down his cheeks. "You—I could have—"

"Peace…young Tracer." Agnar speaks but it isn't him, it's the same deep voice that was in Jak. "You will…be ready soon. But this—" He cuts himself off with a groan and stumbles into the stone platform. I clutch his face, scooting closer and force his gaze to mine. Even though I know, I still have to ask.

"Kasimir?"

That beautiful umber swims to the forefront of Agnar's eyes, overtaking the blue.

"Who…else?"

He smirks, and I let out a watery laugh, wrapping my arms around his neck.

One of his huge hands grips my waist and I'm content to soak up the contact, until his hand is suddenly on my jaw, twisting my face skyward.

"Oh," I whine as his wide, hot tongue slips across the cut.

Around us, Yuli's pack is in a blind panic, like if a spaceship had landed in the middle of Times Square and made the mayor vanish. But I can only focus on this feeling, this closeness and care. It's so right and perfect.

"I…I think I love you," I whisper, and his grip tightens, thumb bruising.

"You do," he murmurs, flicking the tip of his tongue on my collarbone. "And I love you."

Tears spring to life, dripping on their own, even as I smile. "Can we go home, now?"

He pulls back, letting his palm skim up my skin until he cups my cheek.

"Couldn't have asked any better myself," Jak grumbles, frowning at Kasimir. "How about you hop out of Agnar, back into me, so they can run?"

Kasimir sighs and tugs a lock of Jak's hair. Tears spill over Jak's lashes, and he roughly wipes them away with his arm.

"That…is not…possible."

"Worth a shot, I guess," he whispers.

"They…must pay. And you…must prepare."

Kasimir nods at Jak, and even though something unspoken passes between them, Jak isn't any happier.

"Could prepare a lot better if you didn't take him." Jak's eyes flood, but he chews his lip, keeping it all inside.

Kasimir rumbles that soothing frequency and stumbles around the altar, wincing with each step, until he's between me and Jak.

"If you have anything—" Kasimir shouts in pain, knees buckling, as he braces on the altar. "Stupid wrong body," he growls, pushing back to an upright position. "If you have anything to say to this vessel, do so now. This is your only chance."

The umber vanishes, Agnar's clear blue gaze meeting mine as his brows pitch. "Did I…did I do it?"

I nod, biting my lip as my tears fall again. "Yeah. He said I —mmm!"

He cuts me off, searing his mouth to mine in the most heartbreaking kiss I've ever been fortunate enough to have. He pulls back, slowly opening his eyes. "Promise me you'll never stop loving him."

"I promise, I—wait, which one?"

We stare at each other a moment, before the adrenaline takes over and we both burst into laughter, though his ends in a sharp pained grunt. Fresh blood pours down his back, despite the hand he presses there.

"Dagger," he's half speaking, half gasping. "Destroy it. Jak. Jak!" He spins in a panic, and exhales in relief, snatching him into a nearly violent hug. If that bothers Jak, he doesn't show it.

Instead he cries, clutching at Agnar's skin.

"I'm gonna miss you," he forces out around a sob. "Sorry I wasn't strong enough, yet."

"You'll see me again."

That doesn't help. If anything, that makes Jak cry harder. "I know, man. I know."

Agnar pushes him back by the shoulders, "And you'll be ten times stronger by then."

He faces me as the brilliant umber swirls take over. He's gone. My heart breaks, for myself, and for Jak, who is clearly not okay, but quickly wipes his face and forces his feelings down.

Agnar's body glows, brighter and brighter until I have to shield my eyes. "We've almost won," Kasimir murmurs, an echo of the sound bouncing around me. "Only time separates us now, mate."

He growls the last word, making it vibrate through my bones the way only he can. I nearly shriek with unbridled joy. I have trouble keeping the sound in, honestly. I don't know what it all means, or why I'm so excited about that.

Oh. My brain fires with connections. Oh my God. Him. It's him. The monstrosity. Second chances for me and Kasimir. He calls me mate. I'm human *this* time. I must have been a werewolf or...something. And...and we were mates and something happened? Hm.

Though, how any of that fits with a court and being a queen or this darkness, I'm not sure. And even though this realization feels right, I still feel like I'm missing something important. But Kasimir has to know!

"Kas—"

"Time to go." Jakobe snatches me off the rock, cradling me

close as he mutters to himself what sounds like a prayer. "If this works, I won't be able to talk for a bit, but I promise we're gettin' out of here."

"Wait!"

But he's already running. He throws his arm behind him, grunting with effort. "Can't wait. Hold on!"

Some of the glow leeches off of Agnar's damaged body, hurtling toward us and crawling up Jakobe's arm, until he finally shifts into his monster form, sprouting absolutely stunning, blood red fur.

I clutch his neck as he takes off at full speed, hugging me against his chest. Whimpers cling to every exhale and it takes me a moment to realize it's not me, it's him.

I watch as Agnar's face tilts skyward, blinding light emanating from every part of his body. No matter how far away we get, or how fast he runs, it doesn't seem dimmer. Are we safe anywhere?

Suddenly Jakobe grunts and twists, skidding his feet as he tries to stop, but instead we tumble. He covers me completely, protecting me until we finally stop rolling and land at the feet of—

CYAN

H *e's your what?*

Most of the high from killing that satchel of shit Mishka is gone, and the adrenaline buzz from finding out I'm just a copy of some fucking old dude is fizzling out. So, I've got to be imagining that Vik said he was that same old dude's pup.

Veikko…Are you serious?

Right now, Neo's voice in the link is like a hug. A hug when the last thing you want is to be touched, even though it's the one thing you need.

Yes.

Frustration bubbles up past, and I snarl.

Just yes? Fuck, Vik. You've been with me for my whole life. I knew you were old but, shit.

We veer around a familiar pit of bones, close to BriarMaw. And that means, Yuli with his stupid face. Being here brings back far too many bad memories…Oh.

Sound vanishes as blood whooshes in my beast's ears. It makes sense now. The weird energy bursts I'd been feeling, his commanding tones.

You won your Alpha challenge, didn't you? Fuck a duck. I figured all this time, your scars were from losing. You're an Alpha.

…I am.

The rest of the link is completely silent. No sounds of surprise. You've got to be fucking kidding me.

Everyone but me knew this, too?! I'm so damn sick of secrets. Do I need to issue a command to get a little fucking honesty?

Everyone mutters a variation of, "No, Alpha," but at this point, I'm not sure I can believe anything they say.

I skid to a stop and the rest of the pack follows suit, Veikko growling as he slows ahead of us.

If you insist on talking about this now, we must keep moving.

Oh, that's fucking it. I've had it with this day.

"Quit. Giving me. Orders!" I stop blocking my beast, and he gleefully takes full control. I grow even larger, teeth extending, muscles swelling. He hasn't been let free since I killed my dad. Even when I stomped Mishka, I was still holding back.

"Show yourself!" My shout fills the forest, the growl under it reverberating in echo as my Alpha wave lashes out. The pack cowers behind me, watching, waiting.

Vik's battling the push, I can see it in the twitch of his shoulders. That's proof enough of how powerful he must be, ignoring a direct command from his Alpha.

I should probably rein myself in, because I'm hurting like crazy and tired as all hell. Not to mention, him being Alpha means he killed Kasimir. A god. Truth out, I might not win if it came down to it, but my beast is in control, and he's just as pissed as I am.

I send the command again in energy only. Vik's beast jerks at odd angles, each movement making him bigger.

"Very well," he growls, doubling his already massive size. He stomps toward me, claws extended, and even though I don't want to, I have to look up just to keep his maw in sight. My beast pauses, huffing breaths, unsure for the first time what to do. It doesn't want to hurt Vik, not even a little, and I have no fucking idea why not.

I try to lunge, but nothing happens. My arms aren't listening either, so our beasts just stare at each other. Sadness sweeps over mine, followed by what I swear to the moon feels like pride.

Alpha. We must hurry before it's too late.

Even his voice in the link is deeper, growlier. I get my thoughts under control, and sneer.

Why lie to me? After everything we've fucking been through.

I was hiding. He snarls, fists clenching. *From my past. From myself. From everyone. I assumed you wouldn't let me join if you knew, and I needed to be in your pack in case I had to...dispose of you.*

There's a sharp inhale from the entire pack, save for Laz.

I can't even process the feelings shooting through me now. Just one right after the fucking other.

Why would you have to do that?

Aeon's voice is weak, even though the beta wave he's sending is strong as hell.

After we won at The Obscurance—a battle between us, The Sentinels, and Mishka with The Vigils, there were only a few of each still alive. The Sentinels disbanded, but I vowed to take out the next wave of reincarnations myself. I'd see no more life lost because of me. The silence was a penance. He glances at Neo. *Out of guilt, primarily. And because my words, my fervor were the cause from the start.*

I narrow my eyes.

Well, why didn't you take out that prick before he became seated? You could have fucking chawed on his neck in his sleep.

Mishka got away, hid himself. I stayed isolated for many years, hunted for him and the others, but grew lonely. Then I heard of the BriarMaw pack. Once I did the math, I realized...it was likely you'd reincarnate there or nearby.

I can't help my growl. *How would you have done it?*

Pain flashes in his gaze as he takes a step back.

Just as you said. In your sleep. I would have...cut off your head.

My eyes burn, fur bristling, my Alpha wave sizzling through the pack. Aeon mutes most of the anger. Fuck, he's getting strong.

When did you decide not to?

He doesn't want to answer, taking another step back, breaking our locked stare.

When, Vik? I advance, pushing the command hard. *Fucking tell me before—*

The moment I saw you with Reanne.

I stumble a bit, clearing space between us.

You've wanted to kill me my entire…fucking…LIFE?!

This pit of heartbreak is swallowing me alive. Aeon blasts his Beta wave, and it's stronger than ever, which is probably the only reason I'm still on my feet at all.

No, Alpha. His beast whimpers, a long, morose note. *I never wanted to. I never could. You were different, better. I constantly watched for a sign that you'd turn like all the rest, expected it, feared it, but you never did. You're finally…the right one.*

I want to rage at him, but again, my beast is being a prick with a mind of its own. All it wants to do is hug Vik, which makes no fucking sense.

Veikko drops his beast and hits his knees, craning his head to the side. That snaps my beast back into action, and I take his throat in my jaw, restoring emotional order, snarling as I bite down.

"Much has been kept from you, I apologize. I am loyal to you, to seeing you take your rightful place, to helping you and Reanne in any way I can. I know I don't deserve your trust, but believe me when I say, we *must* get to Reanne before my father takes his revenge or she could die."

My beast whimpers and practically spits Veikko's neck out, stumbling back a couple of paces as he gives control over. Now, my body refocuses on pain, hunger, desire, and failure. I shouldn't have screwed up, should have made sure she was fine, then she might not have left in the first damn place. And now we're chasing a giant ghost god to save an Aruna, and hopefully Jakobe, though, if I'm being honest, I'm afraid he's—

A yowl tears out of my throat as a fresh wave of this nightmarish pain takes hold in my bones. My heart hurts more, and my body is barely holding together. Neo's right here. Aeon's just as close. I bet Laz would help, too. Hell, if it came down to it, Korey would do whatever I needed. But there's no time.

Then let's go find her.

Vik stands, nods, shifts, and leads the way again.

We're not okay, but we're not broken, and that's something at least.

Father. The word rattles around in my head as we run, but I can't get my thoughts in line. It's taking everything I have to keep it together through the agony. I should be unloading in someone, right fucking now, and it's my own damn fault I'm not.

There's a glow on the horizon, and Veikko slows at the familiar tree line I swore I'd never see again.

He drops beast and grabs a nearby trunk. "Agnar?"

"What?" I follow suit and storm up beside him. Sure enough, Aggy is near some altar, glowing like a zap bug. "Why the hell is he here?"

Vik mumbles something, shaking his head, then he orients on a fuzzy red blur, zipping toward us. Before I even have a chance to call my beast back up, the blur stumbles, and I recognize it.

Jakobe! Damn, I'm glad he's not dead. And if he's still alive, maybe that means he found—

He finally stops right in front of us, and out tumbles the single most beautiful thing this whole fucking universe has ever made. My lungs catch, my body twanging, because the one person I need most of all is finally here.

She locks eyes with me, and everything is perfect.

"CYAN!"

I've never been so happy to hear my name in my life. Happy doesn't cover it. I snatch her off the ground and mold her to my body, breathing in her scent like it's the first bit of air I've had in a damned year. The twenty million razors ripping at my muscles stop, all of my pain fading away. Even though that's happened before, and I should damn well be prepared, I get dizzy.

I wrap my arms tighter around her shoulders and bury my face in her neck. "Fuck," I whimper, clutching her tighter as she sobs. "I missed you."

"I missed you, too," she cries.

"You okay?"

"Sort of," she mumbles against my collarbone. "And no, not at all."

She nearly strangles me as she mashes herself against me even more, her nipples hardening. I fucking love it.

I love her.

Grabbing her face, I push back just enough to claim her mouth, fighting the urge to throw her down and knot her for the rest of eternity.

Nothing seems as world-shattering with her in my arms. And I know we have a million other issues to deal with, but my dick is hard as stone, and she's fueling my fire with her little moans.

It's the worst time, but she needs a release almost as bad as I do, I can feel it. I grip the back of her neck and press our foreheads together, holding her gaze. I know she can see what I'm thinking as I slide my fingers home.

"You need something from me, little slut?"

Tears spill down her cheeks, though she's grinning. "I thought I'd never hear that again, and I love you, too," she whispers, ending on a gasp as I hook my fingers.

That's the first time anyone's said it back to me. There are too many things happening in my body at once, and I'm kind of at a loss, until she nods rapidly, clawing at my neck. "Please, Cyan." The tears flow faster. "Make it go away. Make it all go away."

"Hey, I've got you." I bite at her lip as we kiss, nipping down her jaw and back to her mouth, her skin getting hotter, my fingers soaked. I ease in and out, faster and faster. She whimpers a "yes," on every exhale, digging at my skin until I grip her neck harder. "Eyes on me."

They fly back open.

"You don't leave my side again, do you fucking hear me?"

She writhes in my hold, riding my hand, as she nods. "I w-won't. I'm s-so sorry."

Her words are broken by sharp breaths, which vanish as I steal the rest of her air. Her tongue is so sweet, her mouth a literal fucking drug.

We break with a gasp, pressing our foreheads together again. "I'm the one who's sorry. I should have fucking talked to you first." I grip her neck even tighter. "But you don't leave again." My throat closes on the emotion, so all that comes out next is a strangled, "You can't."

"Oh, Cyan," she clutches my face, kissing me over and over, muttering, "I won't," between each one, until she can't talk through the moans. Her stunning orgasm tears through her, and the most amazing scream fills the air. I catch Neo's concerned expression out of the corner of my eye. I know he can tell how bad I'm hurting, how much worse this is making it, but it doesn't fucking matter.

My girl needed me. My mate.

I slow, letting her wind down before I pull out completely. Then I suck every bit of her juices off my fingers with a growl. "Fuck, I can't wait to eat that pretty little kitty."

She lets out a weak laugh and nods, holding on to me. "Me either. Thank you," she breathes, giving me one of her heart-stalling slow kisses.

But out of nowhere she freezes, her body going ice cold, and shoves out of my grip.

"A…Aeon?" Her whisper sounds like there's broken glass stuck in her throat, which she grabs.

Neo sets him down, before he falls on his ass, and turns him to face the right direction.

"Reanne, I'm so—"

She crashes into him, wrapping her whole body around him, legs and all.

"You're not dead! I saw you, saw what they—I thought I felt you die! But you're not dead?"

He shakes his head, tears in his eyes. "I'm here, I'm okay. I love you."

They squeeze each other tighter as she cries her love in return.

Then he does what I can't fucking wait to do—sinks his teeth into his mate mark, relief bursting through the pack bond.

She throws her head back, letting out the most spine-melting cry-groan I've ever heard. It's practically orgasmic all on its own. Neo drops beast and latches on to his mark as well, squeezing her breast at the same time.

"Oh, God," she moans, grabbing his head, her other arm hooked around Aeon's neck.

Together, they drag her through another orgasm, chills springing up along my body as I watch. I'm glad they're tending to her, not like they could ignore their mate's need, but I'm also so jealous I could kill Mishka all over again.

She's still desperate, soaked, and panting when they set her down. Literally every guy here is hard and ready, but there's the not-so-fucking-small matter of Agnar glowing like a miniature sun.

Laz steps closer to her, and they stare at each other, weird energy going off between them. Eventually she nods and gives him a friendly hug.

What the fuck was that?

I mentioned it before, Laz and she are connected somehow. He felt her pain.

Oh, I do vaguely remember him saying that. Little focused on getting my territory back at the time.

Korey grabs her in a bear hug, swinging her a bit before claiming her mouth in a deep kiss. She melts in his arms, and I swear they're all about to go at it without me.

Veikko looks like he can't decide what to do, until Jakobe finally drops his beast and fumbles to his feet. Everyone's attention snaps to him.

"Hey…big…guy…" He smirks and promptly passes out. Vik catches him right before he hits the ground again. The guy is dead weight in his arms, and Vik takes a moment to simply stare at him, possessive, before glancing at me.

"Hold him. There is something I must do." He takes a slow breath. "Please, Alpha."

I quirk a brow, my beast already stretched thin on patience and threats and pain. But I take him, mostly because I wanted to hold him anyway. The guy risked his life to save someone he didn't know, for an Alpha he wasn't even fucking bonded to.

Not to mention, he's seriously fine as hell. But more than that, it's his energy. Even unconscious, he's doing something to me.

Veikko traces symbols in the dirt and steps in the center of some sort of design, stretching his arms out in front of him, palms up.

Huge ass beams of light are everywhere, bright as the sun, forcing me to squint. Agnar crumples to the ground, and there's a mad rush of werewolves toward us. I'm braced for the attack, strained enough to kill them all right now.

The air in front of us shimmers, Veikko's hands emitting a faint whitish glow, like moonlight.

How the hell was he keeping all his damn powers a secret for so long? And who ever heard of a werewolf who could do all this shit?

The first group of bodies crashes into some invisible barrier, just a few paces away, and I grimace at the panic on the horde. No sounds get through, but they keep screaming, banging on nothing. They seem to recognize Veikko, some drop to their knees in clear reverence, pleading with him. One of them has the idea to try to go around, but it's solid everywhere. The shimmer continues growing until there's a dome covering the whole camp.

Jakobe stirs, wincing as he bunches his shoulders and rubs his neck. "Ugh, man...there's some crazy vibes whizzing around right now."

He cracks his eyes and grins at me. "Mister Alpha! What are yo—" His expression falls like dead leaves, that fresh face aging right in front of me. He leaps out of my arms and lands on wobbly legs, facing the barrier.

One of the werewolves inside stills, locking hopeful eyes with Jak. They stare at each other through the weird wall, clearly reliving some damn history. But the other werewolf's hope melts to fear and then something else as Jak slowly steps closer to Veikko and presses against his side, resting his hand on Vik's lower back.

"Don't worry, Honeybear," he whispers. "Agnar's already gone and no one left is worth saving."

VEIKKO

The moon above dims as I send more power to the protective barrier, fatigue inching in. All I can think of is how I will allow an entire pack to perish while I watch my oldest, dearest, and truest friend fade into memory. The one who knew my state of mind often before I did. Who could tell when I was hurting, no matter how well I hid it. Who listened to all the words I never said, and never left me alone when I needed to heal. Who showed me what true friendship meant, in the small, quiet moments of nothing.

Gone. With no chance for goodbyes.

One of the werewolves tries to get Jakobe's attention, desperate to escape. Instead of asking me to let him through, or anything in his usual playful style, Jakobe turns his face, digging his chin into my arm as his fingers sear my skin.

"He wasn't a bad guy," he says on a choked exhale. "He loved you."

Twin tears fall, his and mine, because I know who he means.

And I know he was good. I know who Agnar is...was. I may not have always understood his motives, but his heart was pure, and, I...I knew he loved me. But I did not, could not feel the same, for him or anyone. Then Reanne and Jakobe unlocked something. I hoped to see him again, to tell him fear no longer rules me, to ask if he would return. Beyond that, I hadn't planned, but it was all pointless. I'm glad they met each other, however.

Reanne's arm slips around my back, her cheek pressed on my other arm. "He helped me. When they were...he left so he could be here because he knew Yuli…would…" She fades into a small sob as the glow reaches the highest point and Agnar's body is no longer visible. "It was Fen who planted his bucket," she cries, "Agnar didn't do anything wrong."

Ever self-sacrificing. There is truly no other way he would prefer to leave this world. And that explains what Fen was doing in the camp to begin with.

I swear Agnar's eyes meet mine, swear I see his smile one final time before the light explodes, blinding everyone as a wave of destruction rockets outward. Tents flatten, trees burst into flame and float away as ash in mere seconds. Reanne shields her eyes as the werewolves turn to face their doom, calling their beasts so they die with honor. And then they're gone. Fur to flesh to bone to dust. The barrier vibrates slightly as the whole dome fills with light.

Reanne shudders, gasping, clutching her chest, and Jak lets out a pained whimper.

I cannot lower my hands, or the spell will fail, but all I want to do is hold my mate and Jakobe, close my eyes, and pretend Agnar is still alive, still roaming the forest. Still offering advice and being a solid shoulder.

Everything blurs, my lungs hitching. The light vanishes, taking Kasimir's energy with it, but I don't move.

"Is he…is Kasimir…okay?"

I nod. That's all I can do.

"Hey," Jakobe murmurs and grabs my left wrist, "it's…it's over." He tugs until my hand drops, the barrier falling in tandem. Smoke billows to the sky, bits of ash finding a breeze to carry them home.

It might be beautiful, were this any other circumstance. But tonight, it is nothing but a landscape of pain.

Reanne steps in front of me, smoothing her palms across my cheeks, and when I finally lower my eyes from the devastation, meeting her wet gaze, I crumble.

"Veikko, I'm so sorry." She collides with me, wrapping her arms around me as far as they'll go.

I drop to my knees and hold her close, Jakobe hugging my neck from behind.

After a quiet moment filled with tears, Cyan steps beside me and puts a heavy hand on my shoulder. His contact is nearly too much after our standoff. I don't deserve anything but contempt and anger from him, yet he continues to prove he's the one.

"We'll build him the biggest fucking fire The Glade's ever seen."

I want to be much stronger than I am, but I can still only manage a nod. The fire will be heartbreakingly final, confirmation of death in the dancing embers.

I rest my hand on Cyan's, because I am eternally grateful for his support, and that he accepted my deference. It would complicate things far too much for me to be cast out now. Luckily, I was able to resist my full Alpha size being revealed. I don't believe anyone is prepared for that.

"Let's go. Grab the bones, if there are any."

Cy squeezes and slips free of my grip. He snags Reanne in a cradle carry, smothering her surprise with his mouth as he walks, leaving Jakobe and I to watch.

She buries her hands in his hair and her still-vicious need blasts through the link, wrenching an answering growl from her mates, myself included.

Jak swivels a glance over his shoulder then back at me. "Man, I can't wait to join officially. You okay?"

He trails the back of his finger down my cheek, so sweet and caring I nearly lose control of my emotions again.

"I…will be. I was worried I might not see you again."

Some of his swagger bubbles to the surface. "I told you I'd be back. I'm unstoppable."

I stare into his eyes, fully believing him. "I am very glad."

"Me too." He tips his chin toward the camp, toward Cy and

Reanne, and smiles, though there's a hint of sadness in his eyes. "Only reason I'm still alive is because of you."

"Me?"

He nods, biting his lip. "I didn't wanna flush your energy, because...ah, well you know why." His cheeks tint. "But he recognized it, since he was a Tracer, too. And Yuli was using Agnar to flush out other Tracers, to uh, kill. So," he bumps his nose on mine, sending my pulse into a whirlwind, "thanks."

"Tracer..."

It cannot be. How could he have hid something so important from me? Why?

"Yeah," Jak sighs, frowning. "I was hoping he'd teach me more of his cool tricks. Guess I'll have to learn to be awesomer on my own."

All this time, under my very nose. Now it's clear how he could read me, how he knew me when no one should have. But Yuli's involvement to this degree is the most troubling news I've heard in four centuries. The only good thing is nothing could have survived my father's attack.

The faces of those werewolves I let die flash in my mind again, and I study Jak's tight features.

"Are you okay?"

"Pff. Of course I—" he chews his lip when our eyes meet. "That was Corbet."

Pain lances my heart. I let his friend die. "I'm so sorry."

"Nah, I'm okay. He...wasn't who I thought he was. That's really all that's buggin' me."

The shadow that crosses his features doesn't make what happened hurt less.

"Agnar made me put his energy by yours." A small laugh leaves his plump lips. "Taught me how to do it, just so I could. I told him, as long as I was alive," he winks at me, "which will be forever, that you guys will always be together."

I stare at this male, who blew into my life a mere day ago and made himself at home in my heart without any effort at all. I can't imagine how I would have handled this moment without him here. And without Reanne's warmth, my mate, wrapped around my soul.

"Jakobe. I'm...very glad I met you."

He grins, some of that infectious luster coming back to his eyes. "Yeah? You mean it?"

"Yes."

"Well, I hope it's pretty clear I feel the same way."

We share a slow, tentative kiss, nothing more than affection and reconnection. Something I desperately need to do with Reanne, as well.

After he pulls back, he gives a lock of my hair a tug, sadness dimming his light.

"What do you say, Honeybear? Ready to set some stuff on fire? Agnar deserves a helluva send off."

I force my attention back to the present and nod because, yes, he truly does.

Jakobe holds his hand out, and though I take it, I let go. "I will join in a moment."

"You got it, HB." He winks, stealing a kiss, and warmth spreads through my chest. He saunters after Cy and Reanne, as I breathe deeply. Despite my protestations...I like the nickname, even this shortened version. I've never had a good nickname before.

Aeon and Neo flank me, sending an odd sensation under the warmth, almost as if— My eyes widen. Oh no. It can't be.

I launch to my feet and face them. Aeon takes a step like he wants to lunge at me, but holds his place, while Neo chews his thumbnail and paces.

"I knew it," he mutters, "I knew this was going to be a problem."

"Vik, tell me you feel that. You feel it, right?"

The last thing I wish at this moment is to feel anything else, but...

"Yes."

Neo dissolves into a whimpering mess, crouching as he holds his head. "You broke me. I didn't want—I love Cyan, he's my Alpha, not you."

Aeon is not as distressed. He glares at me, and if I didn't know better, I would think there was challenge in the air.

I take a slow breath. "When Cyan forced my beast, my Alpha, fully to the forefront, it must have…triggered something from the bites."

Neo whines, and Aeon growls, "Fix. It."

"There's nothing to fix." I nod toward the center of the BriarMaw camp. "Cyan is still Alpha of SteelTooth, of which we are all members. I am not breaking pack to form my own. I will do my best to bury the energy again, and you two continue as you were. He needs be none the wiser."

"No. No way. We already tried keeping stuff from him and you saw how that went down." Neo pushes to his feet and steps into my space, jabbing his finger at my face. "Besides, he deserves better. We're telling him and we're telling him now."

"Stop that," I growl with far more command than I mean to.

His arm falls in response, like the bones melted. Both our eyes widen.

"Oh, bleeding moon. I'm—I can't breathe. No. No! I hate this. What now? Do I, do I have to ask you to break pack? Grovel myself to Cyan?"

He turns various colors, flitting around, until finally Aeon breaks his concentration on me and grabs Neo's face, claiming his mouth.

Neo freezes, his shoulders slowly dropping as he closes his eyes and leans into Aeon's touch. Every time he breaks away and stutters a panicked sound, Aeon claims him again, until there's nothing left but kissing. It works brilliantly. If only this had been an option before I bit Neo.

Aeon floods the area with Beta energy, further soothing Neo, even me. But the energy is clearly different. Much, much more powerful. He's reflecting the strengthened Cyan, yes, but also… me. Blast the stars, how is this even possible?

I run my hand down my face and send up a small prayer for guidance. There's a distant rumble of thunder somewhere past the horizon, but that tells me nothing. Though it does give me pause. I…could command Neo not to say anything. I wince, my stomach souring. No. He's right. We should be honest. And I should be the one to take the brunt of the wrath.

Leaving them to their quickly heating kiss, I turn and find an utterly silent Korey and Laz, staring at us with wide eyes.

31

REANNE

O nce I break from the kiss, I cling to Cyan's neck, soaking up his warmth as he carries me over the smoking ground. I expected the air to be heated from the blast, but it's eerily chilly, random nips against my skin. The closer we get to the center of camp, the tighter I hug him, and the tighter he hugs me back.

There's nothing left. No bodies, no bones. The broken altar is blackened with char and what look like ice crystals, oddly enough. Worst of all, it's disturbingly quiet.

"I can't believe they're all dead."

"They fucking deserved this just for laying a claw on you, let alone whatever else they did after that. Plus, what they did to Aeon."

I nod against his shoulder, whispering, "How is he alive? Cyan, I saw his body, he was practically in pieces. There's no way." My throat closes, and I bury my face against his neck, fighting the memory.

Cyan squeezes me even tighter, kissing the side of my head as he sends a wave of power. What they went through while I was gone obviously had a big effect on him. He's different in a good way. More open with his affection, and his Alpha energy is so intense, but smooth, like I'm being wrapped in a warm blanket, rather than smothered by it.

"Kasimir apparently brought him back to life."

My brows lift, but it doesn't seem unbelievable. I've felt his power, in so many ways, and we all just saw at least some of it.

Cyan's throat bobs. "I searched so fucking hard for you guys.

When I felt him die... Just really fucking glad you're okay," he murmurs.

"I'm glad *you're* okay!" I pull back, holding his gaze. "Did Mishka get to you?"

He snorts as he slides me down his body, keeping me tight against it. "Yeah, but I killed him."

Killed?

I stare up at him, processing. "You—wow."

"Was pretty easy, actually. Fucker just gave up. 'Course, he learned some pretty tough news."

My body is a whirlwind of reactions. I'm glad he's gone, and they're alright, plus knowing Cy handled the threat is hot and makes me feel stupid for thinking I had to make a deal in the first place. There's so much going on with this darkness and Kasimir's words about only time separating us, and Yuli's whole conversation, and Evrik's weird words about— Oh, right, Cy needs to know about them.

"I...learned something today, too. I think."

"Yeah? That makes all of us, apparently. You first."

Exhaling slowly, I catch his gaze. "Yuli told me I've... I've been here every two hundred years, and that he's been forced to come back, too. He remembers, but no one else does."

Cyan scans my face a moment. "Well, ain't that some shit. That lines up with what I learned, too. The two hundred years part, not the Yuli part. Wanna know mine?"

I nod, holding him tighter as his expression falls. "What's wrong?"

"Apparently, I'm not even who I thought I was."

"What? That's crazy. You're Cyan. The sexiest, growliest, strongest Alpha in the world."

His mouth hooks in the most adorable smile. "Thanks."

My heart leaps around, until his expression sours again.

"But I'm evidently just a fucking reincarnation of a creepy ass ghost god."

Excited little fireworks go off all over my body. I can't help the twist of my mouth. "I think I'm supposed to be his mate."

"That's not gonna happen," he snaps, "you're mine even if I have to figure out how to kill a—what the hell are you laughing at?"

I grab his face and kiss him, but he jerks back. "Reanne."

"Your mate, silly. The other part I heard. Well, I think I've figured it out. Anyway, I keep coming back for second chances with Kasimir. And if you're supposed to be him, and you keep coming back, too, then you're coming back for second chances with me, and I just love you."

Some of the possessive rage fades from his body, half-snarl morphing into a half-smirk. "That so?"

I grin. "Which part?"

He nips my chin, and when I squeak, he trails another nibble up my jawline, warming my blood. "The only part of that whole fucking sentence that matters," he whispers, sending chills darting down my arms.

"I love you," I gasp out as he bites my lobe.

"Yeah, you do," he says with a clear smirk. "I love you too, my gorgeous little slut. And yeah, if something happened that cut this short I'd fucking rip apart the sky over and over again to make it right. Just as long as you remember you're mine."

I nod, and even though I feel a little silly doing it, I nip his jaw. "Yours."

"Fuuuck, that was hot. Do it again."

I giggle and nip a little harder, losing my breath as he squeezes my body tighter, his hard length mashed between us.

"I want you, right here, right fucking now."

I'm on fire, aching in an instant. "I want that, too."

"But if I slide into that tight heat," he growls, wincing, "there's no stopping me. My beast will mark you so hard, they'll feel it on the other side of The Glade. And I know you're not ready. Fuck, I don't even think I'm ready. This shit about the prophecy and High Alpha and you taking some sort of power...I get it. Just wanted you to know, I guess."

Tears spring up, and I hop, wrapping my legs around his waist with the aid of his grip. It's a dangerous position, I know, but I can't get close enough.

"Thank you," I cry. "I'm sorry I didn't stay, I'm sorry I didn't trust you to listen or wait. I'm sorry I put you through so—put you all through—"

"Hey." He cradles my head with one hand, his arm supporting me around the waist. "You didn't do shit but try to save us. It's not your fault you didn't know everything. The rest happened because of other pieces of trash. Fuck, I probably wouldn't have listened, truth out. But I hear you now. I'm not mad, just happy as hell you're back where you belong."

I sniffle, fingers digging into his skin. The longer we hold each other the more it feels like everything is going to be okay. Bits of Evrik's conversation overlap, sending yet more adrenaline spiking through my system.

"I met someone in the tent, someone I think I'm supposed to mate."

He frowns. "Then he died before you got the chance."

"No, no he was gone before all this happened."

"And left you there?" His voice rises in disbelief. "Fuck that guy!"

"It's not like that, he's... not from here. He," I wince, "turned into stardust because he said his time was up. But he'll come back every night."

Cy blinks at me. "Stardust."

I nod, biting my lip.

After he scans my face, he exhales and cracks his neck. "Probably the least fucking weird thing that's happened. Okay."

"He said he was there at the start of everything, and he knows I'll get five more mates."

That delicious chuckle of Cyan's fills the night air. "You're gonna be busy. When I let you out of my bed, that is."

247

Not going to lie, that thought makes me insanely hot.

I clear my throat and continue."He also called me his queen."

Cyan grunts. "I've heard that, too."

"Did you hear anything else? What am I?" All that comes out is a whisper. "Some sort of royalty? And I was apparently not human any of the other times. I can't make it make sense."

"I dunno, but we'll figure it out, I can promise you that. Together. Hey," he nips my chin playfully, "thanks. For telling me, dove. Swear to the damn moon, you're the only one who respects me enough to fucking be honest."

My blood goes cold, burrs of ice spearing my heart. It can't be. "What did you call me?"

"S…lut? Guess I could give you a different—"

I grab his face and mash our foreheads together, exhaling in relief at the very Cyan thoughts.

"What the hell?"

There's clear confusion in his eyes but also a little amusement. Maybe I heard him wrong. Besides, he said Mishka was dead. Clearly, I'm exhausted.

"Sorry, I guess. No, slut's fine."

Cy groans and grips my ass in both hands, grinding his hips into mine, shocking me out of my thoughts. "Someone's tryna get fucked. Hearing you say that is…mm."

He wraps my hair around his hand and tilts my head back, first kissing away my tears, then trailing down my jaw, down my neck, each of my breaths getting harder.

"Fuuuuck," he snarls against my collarbone, grip tightening and sending a delicious burn through my scalp. "This is going to be hard as hell."

"Uh huh," I whimper, scratching at his shoulders. "We need," I pant when his tongue slides up my throat, "someone else, I guess."

"Mmmm, like we did with Neo?"

I nod, cinching my legs tighter around his waist. "Or a different pers—"

"Hey, hey, that looks like fun."

Both our eyes pop open, our chests heaving as he slowly relaxes his grip. I level my head, and I swear we both grin at the same time before he dives at my mouth, sending sparks through my blood.

"Don't mind ol' Jak. Just keep right on going. It's gotta be around here somewhere," he mutters.

He's by the singed altar, and that's when I realize what he's looking for.

I break from Cy's kiss with a gasp. "The dagger."

"I'm on that, beautiful, you just hang out with Mister Alpha there."

Heat roars through my body as he crouches on the ground, his thigh muscles twitching, calves tightening.

"Dagger? What—" Cyan cuts his gaze to Jakobe, then back to me, smirking as he whispers, "You like him?"

I nod slowly, chewing at my lip. "Is that okay?"

"Fuck yeah, that's okay. I thought you might when I met him."

I hold Cy closer. "He's great." I tug on his neck until his ear is at my mouth and whisper, "I think...I'd love to watch you fuck him."

"Holy shit," he hisses, taking a long, slow breath before stealing another kiss. "How'd you know that's what I was thinking?"

I bite my lip again and we both tilt our heads to the side when he stands. He doesn't have his shorts on at the moment, and he is legitimately packing a serious cock.

"Mm. Or, maybe you...sucking him off."

"Fuck, I'm not saying I wouldn't," Cy mutters with obvious appreciation, letting me slide down his body to my feet. "But I think I like option one better right now. Jak!"

"Yeah?"

"Get over here."

"Sure thing, Mister Alpha."

He trots over, and it's like I'm watching a slow-motion porn. "Damn," I whisper.

"Fucking seriously," Cyan mutters.

He stops in front of us with a little hop, and a playful salute, giving me a wink. "Whatcha need?"

Cy's mouth kicks up in a smirk, hand tightening on my outer hip. "You. On your knees."

Jak's breath leaves him, eyes widening as he glances between the two of us. "Uh. Totally yes. For which of you?"

The lust that rolls through me is murderous, and I slide my hand down the front of Cyan's thigh, his cock jumping. "Both?"

"Talk about the best day ever," Jak murmurs, dropping to his knees in the same breath. His warm, wide hands glide up each of our inner thighs, until he teases my lips and grips the base of Cy's cock.

Cyan's chin tips up, a groan of appreciation escaping as his muscles vibrate against me. Jak grins and flicks his tongue across Cy's tip before taking him in his mouth.

I gasp at the same time, because he slips a thick finger inside me, letting out a groan of his own. He pulls off with a pop and stares up at me in wonder.

"What the—it feels amazing in there! Did you know you have ridges and—" A breathy chuckle escapes my lips before I whimper, his finger seeking, and finding, its mark. "Oh, man, tell me I can get in there at some point."

I nod, grinning, and Cyan grips Jak's hair, putting him back to work on his cock. With his other hand, Cy clutches the side of my head, claiming my mouth in a deliciously punishing kiss, and as he thrusts, I writhe, riding Jak's hand to orgasm.

He mutters something around Cyan's cock, working me faster and deeper, as I break from Cy's kiss and brace on Jak's shoulder.

This is somehow hotter than any of the other things I've done so far. I can't stop watching Jak worship Cy's cock, his head bobbing, twisting, his tongue twirling, all while he absolutely rocks my world with his magic fingers.

"Fuck," Cyan shouts, holding Jak's head in place as he unloads. After he gives a shiver of relief, he lets Jak go, who sucks in a breath, releasing a sexy growl.

"Yo, I thought you'd taste good, but let me tell you what, Mister Alpha. I could die happy down here. Just strap me to this thigh."

Cy's breathy laugh sends a chill down my spine. "Lay down, Jak."

"Anything you say, man."

He's quick to situate, taking his fingers back and flattening, his thick, long cock standing at attention, tip glistening.

Cyan grips me by the shoulders and maneuvers me until I'm facing him, a foot on either side of Jak's hips. "Your turn on your knees, little slut," he murmurs against my lip before biting it.

My eyes widen. I glance down, and with Cy pushing me, Jak's hands clamp on my waist. I grab his cock, lining it up before I slowly fit it inside me.

"Oh, hell," I whine, and Jak lets out the sexiest groan, bucking up before I'm ready. Stretched and full, I shiver, letting my head fall back.

"Goddess on high." He sucks in a sharp gasp when I'm finally seated, my knees pressed to the dirt. His hands move from my waist to my back, smoothing everywhere he can touch like he's mapping me. He's twisting my energy up as well, sending pulses through me that end at my clit.

"Knees up, Jak."

He does, and I grab hold, thankful for something to brace on as Cy lines his cock up with my face.

I dive on it, moaning as he fucks my mouth, cradling my jaw. I imagine I can taste Jak's mouth on here and that's even sexier. Jak bumps his hips again, hitting every place inside that desperately needs the pressure.

"Holy," he moans. "She like—it's like," he cuts himself off with another deep groan as he bucks harder.

I lavish Cyan's cock until he's losing himself in the pleasure. He pulls out too soon and hits his knees in front of me. Glowing eyes locked on mine, he grabs Jak's thighs and lifts us both like we weigh nothing, lining his cock up.

He holds his fingers in front of my mouth, barking, "Spit."

I do, flashes of need spiking through me as I watch him tease Jak's entrance.

Cy holds my lust-hazed gaze as he slides in. Once he's fully seated, I wrap my arms around his neck, kissing him for all I'm worth as Jak lets out the longest, most satisfied sound I think I've ever heard.

"Damn," he whimpers, "I wish you guys could see how good you look. And feel how good you feel, plus your energies, unhh." He bucks when Cyan thrusts forward, and we all moan at the same time.

I can't see what Jakobe's doing to our energy, but I can feel it, all through me. Cyan's thick, commanding line mixing with mine, running through Jakobe like he's a conduit of some kind.

Wait. I lock wide eyes with Cyan, who's staring back at me just as shocked.

It feels like we're actually together, or at least, as close as we'll be able to get until the actual time.

Desire blazes through my limbs, and Cy lets his hands wander down my back, smoothing along my spine until he has a firm hold on my ass. He moves his mouth to my neck, sucking hard on my skin, bruising as he lifts me and shoves me back down so Jak's cock drives even deeper.

"After you're mine," he purrs, biting as he talks, lifting and dropping me again, "I'll fuck you so much, you'll pass out with my cock in you and wake up coming."

I moan, desperate beyond reason as he repeats the lift and drop.

"I'll fill you up until you're swollen with it. Until you can't fucking move. Until all you can do is lay there and take my knot and scream my name."

"Shit, that's hot," Jak whimpers, and I lose control, the most insane combination of words and sounds escaping as Cy drops and lifts me again, and again, faster. Jak's hands ghost my skin on each pass, his appreciative moans sending me over. I break apart around him, and he seizes, shock and reverence laced with each of his breaths.

"That…feels amazing," he groans.

"You're so fucking sexy," Cy growls in my ear, biting my jaw, overflowing my heart, as Jak starts meeting Cy's motions with his own thrust up, each one spreading splinters of glorious aftershocks through me. Finally, Jakobe shouts his release, filling me with his superheated cum, waves of energy licking along my skin.

Cyan lets me go and wraps his arms around Jak's thighs, lifting again, and pounds him while I watch. I grab Jak's balls, toying with them, which earns me a deep groan of satisfaction, before I trace up Cyan's chest.

Jak's cock throbs inside me, his fingers curling around my waist as I tease Cyan's nipples. Cy's head falls back, thrusts picking up speed, until he stills, grunting and groaning, shooting into Jak's ass, each sound echoed by Jak and a cock twitch.

After a moment, he laughs. "You guys are trying to kill me, aren't you?" The word cuts off on a groan as Cy pulls out. I glance down at the growing puddle, a mixture of what's leaking out of both of us. Longing hits my heart out of nowhere, and I'm suddenly aware of every spot on my body not covered in a loving mark. They feel empty in contrast.

And because Cyan is the best Alpha ever, he senses it.

"You need him to mate you?" Cy murmurs, and I barely hear it over the thump of my pulse, but I nod, throwing an arm behind myself and reaching for Jak.

"C-can he? Even though he's not pack yet?"

"Mmhhm. You can mate anyone you want."

"Then yesss, please!"

"Really? You want me?" Jak cups my forearm. "Man, I might cry. I love you guys. So, how do we start?"

My next breath is cut off by Cy's hand around my neck, eyes boring into mine as he growls, "Fuck her, Jak. Hard and fast."

Jak's grip tightens, bruising, and it's like someone took off his leash. He drives into me, over and over, slamming his hips up as Cy suspends me in place by my jaw, hungrily watching.

With his other hand, he grabs my nipple and tugs, while Jak does a particularly punishing series of thrusts, growling and shouting his pleasure. Pressure builds in my head and in my clit, panic welling the longer I go without air, twisting with the rapture. Cy loosens his hand in time for me to suck in a breath and explode in the biggest orgasm I've ever had. Every muscle trembles, stars form in my vision, joy and relief spreading through my cells. There's not a single speck of darkness in me now. Nothing but light and ecstasy.

I don't even feel Jak's teeth slice into the back of my arm, but the union consumes me. His soul rams itself into every corner of my body, setting my heart on fire. Each beat sends a new zing to my other marks, but it's even stronger than before. I'm so filled with love, appreciation, and happiness that tears drip down my cheeks.

"Fuck!" Jak mumbles against my skin, unlatching with a single lick before jackhammering into me. I barely catch my breath when his body starts to change. He's...shifting.

"Ohmygod ohmygod," I gasp and moan as claws dig into my hips, his cock swelling, growing thicker and longer, each thrust hitting a new place. His muscles define against my ass as he slams me, my eyes rolling back.

Cy hums in approval. "Such a dirty little slut, you really fucking love that, don't you?"

I can't answer, but I manage a nod, floating closer and closer to another explosion. Jak's brilliant red fur pricks and tickles, his huge, meaty thighs twitch with each thrust, and I'm so full. Fuller, I think, than when Veikko fucked me in the bathroom.

I'm shocked nearly to death when a giant hand closes around my throat. It's massive, the claws reaching each other and able to interlock.

My eyes pop open to see Cy's erotic half smirk-half snarl, his arm fully shifted from the shoulder down. He's being careful, not choking, but absolutely showing his ownership. That alone is almost enough to send me into a tailspin.

"Faster," he growls, so deep and predatory, his teeth sharpening to needled points as I watch, eyes glowing.

There isn't enough time or enough air, as Jak finds a new rhythm so intense I get no break at all in the pleasure. What sounds I do manage to make are staccato, like his cock is hitting my lungs from the inside.

I'm dizzy by the time the orgasm nearly detonates me, and I ride one wave straight into another as he blasts me with another load, bathing my insides like lava.

All I can string together is "fuck," a hundred times in a row, as he finally slows. Cy's hand shifts back and smooths my hair away from my sweaty face.

Each of my breaths is high pitched, my limbs weak as I cling to Cy's neck, forehead against his shoulder. "I love you, I love you so much. Thank you."

He chuckles. "Love you, too, but it wasn't my cock you came all over."

Jak's body quickly shifts back to man, and his grip loosens as he smooths his palms over what are no doubt scratches, and places a kiss on his mate mark.

"Thank you, Jak. That was," I pant, "amazing."

He gives a thumbs up, his arm quickly falling back to the dirt. We're a tangle of heavy breaths and contented chuckles, mixed with claiming kisses from Cyan, each one stamping him on my heart harder than the one before.

Cyan grips my hair and tilts my head back for a deeper kiss, giving Jak's thigh a pat.

"Nice work, Jak," he eventually murmurs.

"Thanks," a long breath, "Mister Alpha."

When Cy's grip loosens, I lay back against Jak's chest.

"Well, hey there, my pretty mate," he murmurs in my ear.

My grin is sleepy and so satisfied. "Hey, yourself."

"This sure is a funny feeling, huh?"

"Yeah," I chuckle, stroking his hip. "I love it."

"Me too. Me too."

He wraps me in a tight hug for a second, then nibbles my neck as his hands slide down my body. One hot hand rests gently on my stomach, while the other travels farther down, covering my mound, fingers on either side of his cock, playing with the wetness pooling where we're joined. He groans, bucking a final time, his cock pulsing.

"Wish I could see it leaking out of you, so I could shove it all back in there," he whispers, tonguing my ear.

Jesus, that's hot. I shiver with a gasp and grip his hip tighter. How my body could have a fraction of desire left is a mystery.

Cyan appears in my line of sight and hooks his hand on the back of my neck. In one motion, he lifts me and takes me off Jak's cock with a wet noise. He falls to the ground, setting me on his lap instead, my back pressed to his chest as he circles me with his arms. My deliciously possessive Alpha. I soak up his warmth, breathing through the dregs of my arousal, letting this moment chase all the bad memories away.

Jak fumbles to his elbows with a wheezing laugh, rubbing his face. "You guys can use me any damn time you want. Especially you, beautiful. Literally, you don't even have to ask. You need a piece of Jak, you come and get it. Day or night. Asleep. Awake. Both of you. Any of you." He falls back flat again with a softer laugh. "I'm gonna pass out when we get home."

I chuckle, resting my head back on Cyan's shoulder. "Me too. Are we, I mean, am I—"

"Mmhm," Cyan nibbles my jaw. "Like I'd let you out of my fucking sight."

My insides warm again, and I twist my head to steal a kiss, stroking his cheek.

We press our foreheads together when we break. "I feel selfish, keeping you to myself."

But what he's showing me in his thoughts is not at all what I imagined.

"Oh, you mean…all of…"

He smirks, and I flush red, which at this point doesn't make any sense to do.

"You know, I was thinking we should make, like, one big bed." Jak bumps my foot with his foot, stroking it. "Just a big ol' fluffy crash pile."

Cyan grunts. "That's a damn fine idea. Then I could just… mm. Yeah, we're doing that."

Based on the way his cock twitches under me, I'd have to agree. But that's later down the road, if…I don't destroy everything before then.

That dark version of me may be quietly tucked in a corner right now, but it's still very much alive and waiting.

I bump Jak's foot back. "Thanks, by the way."

"Mm, don't mention it. Like I said, ya don't even have to—"

"I mean for saving me."

His expression falls, and I can almost see the memories playing in his eyes. He gives me a small nod. "Anytime."

"So, do you have a bed yet?"

His expression falls even farther, and he sits fully up. "Yeah. Uh, maybe, I…"

"He's sleeping with us, for a while."

Cy gives Jak a small nod, and Jak's answering smile is tiny and painful. It only takes me a second to figure out what cabin was empty.

"Aww, don't be sad." Jak rocks forward on his knees and kisses my cheeks. "Can't be sad after the greatest sex in the history of ever. There's a rule against that, I bet. Plus, I got to mate you. We should celebrate. I mean, yeah, I know you didn't get to feel how amazing his cock is, but you will soon!"

Cy lets out a single laugh against my hair, hugging me tighter. "She had a preview before we brought her through the barrier."

Jak's eyes bug and he drops to his ass. "What? You had se—what? Out there? You can do that?"

"Yeah…" There's a thick pause. "Wait." Cy slides me to the side and leans forward, scrutinizing. "Jakobe," he growls, and it's scarily deep, menacing, wrapping genuine fear around my throat like a vice.

"Uh, I have to find that dagger." He scrambles to his feet.

"Sit!" Cy barks it, and Jak drops again like his ankles broke. "Tell me again how old you are."

My breath leaves me at the utter terror on Jak's face.

"Nn…I…am pretty sure I said 27."

Cy is on his feet in a second, me clutched in his punishing grip. "You said 29. You better come clean. Right. Fucking. Now!"

LAZAROS

I'd say I was confused, but given that's my general state, it seems pointless to do so. Well, confused or utterly terrified. Glutted for choice, really.

We've been quiet, my mate and I, watching and talking to each other since Mishka died. A spark of joy flashes to life in me again, and I have to work to keep from inappropriately laughing. The whole scene of his utterly humiliating annihilation will live in my brain as one of my happiest memories. Funny how the few I have are all since meeting Cyan. And by funny, I mean blisteringly pathetic.

The darling Reanne's connection with me has gone inert since our conversation, but that's quite literally the least of my concerns right now.

Neo moans into Aeon's mouth, and I'm doing my very best to pretend it's not happening, but oy. It's terribly erotic. Never fancied myself a watcher, but with Korey here, also doing his best to avoid staring, I think, well, yes. That could be something we explore someday, possibly. If we all live that long.

Thankfully, or maybe not thankfully if you ask my cock, my very smart, very handsome mate speaks, breaking the moment.

"Can you do that? Bury the energy?"

Veikko doesn't answer right away, but I know he can. The fellow stood up to Mishka and gave me energy-blocking bracers and turned in to the largest, most fearsome werewolf I've ever seen and has genuine magical powers. Not to mention, quite surprisingly, he's the son of a god and I daresay, though I'd never do so out-loud, he could best Cyan with minimal effort. Yes. Yes, Veikko can do anything.

"I…am not sure."

I blink and blink a hundred times more. Surely, he misheard the question.

Aeon growls and steps in front of Neo, glaring. "I hope for all our sakes you figure out how."

Neo grips his shoulder. "The good news, if there can be any, is you only have to keep it together for a little longer."

"Yeah," Korey rumbles. "Once she and Cyan mate it won't matter what you do, the connection or whatever will be done."

Veikko considers them both with a nod. "That is true."

"Well, that's the bird's beak then, innit?" My voice sounds loud to me, however minuscule it might be in reality. Everyone stares at me, and I slip partially behind Korey's arm, clearing my throat as I continue. "I, uh, simply m-mean that, given what, and who, we know, it should be, well, ehm, easy. F-for you."

His eyes light up, and by all the stars I feel thirty-two and a half feet tall. "You're right," he mutters. "Jakobe could help."

Korey grins down at me, giving me a slow wink and I nearly fall over. Oh, I love him so. I could never imagine my life without him in it. Rubbing his mark, part of me hopes Aeon and Neo decide on another impromptu mouth-love session.

Instead, they all glance off toward the circular wasteland and Korey squeezes my hand. "Cy wants us to 'hurry the fuck up'." He juts his chin toward the others. "You guys go on, we'll be right behind you."

Ooo, potentially salacious. Maybe he's going to—No, no I certainly don't need to let my mind run away and then have Korey say he saw a fancy snail he thought I might like, not that he wants to suck my—Never minding that I would absolutely love to see a fancy snail, and he knows that. And now I hope it's a fancy snail. Blimey, I'm hopeless in every blasted way.

Neo grabs Aeon's hand, not taking his sound of protestation into any sort of account as he pulls him gently along.

They're such an odd duo, but hot. Very hot.

Veikko follows, and it's just my mate and I and whatever snails or other oddities he might have spotted for my collec—

"Lazaros," he drops to a knee in front of me, holding my gaze, "we have to decide if we're staying in this pack or not. Before…things go down."

My poor blood-lacking brain can't quite process. "Wh-what? But…the snail…"

"Huh? Snail, what?" He looks around my feet. "Well, we'll find it in a minute, wherever it is. This is also important."

I haven't even joined this pack proper, and he already wants me to scamper away. This is the second time he's mentioned it, and it's just as shocking as the first.

"I-I don't want to leave," I whisper. "Cyan saved me, I would-would have still been trapped there, miserable. Korey, if he hadn't convinced me to follow Veikko into the unknown, you and I never would have met. I certainly wouldn't have ever gotten brave enough to tell someone I didn't agree with them, let alone someone as-as attractive as y— Why don't you want to stay?"

He takes a deep breath, stroking his finger down my cheek, threatening my stability. "My job is to protect you now. I'm… worried. There's some crazy shit happening, and I just don't know if it's a good idea to be right in the middle of it all."

"But, what about Reanne? Our connection? And-and everything? Veikko is my friend. Well, I assume he is, I suppose I could be wrong. I usually am, you understand, wrong. Snail for example. Stupid Laz, thinking you—"

"Pup," he growls, and I whimper as he tugs me closer. "Stop talking bad about my mate."

I know what's coming and I'm already leaping toward insanity like a blind deer.

"You're not stupid," he croons in my ear, gripping my waist. "You're smart." He presses hot kisses along my neck as he shatters me. "So smart. And sexy. Mmm. Caring."

I can't control my lungs any more than I can control the sounds I'm making or the flush on my skin. I cry out when he grazes sharp teeth across his mark, the shock of half-shifted contact nearly sending me over the edge.

"Damn, I always start this thinking it's only for you," he growls, falling back to the forest floor and fixing me so I'm straddling his massive erection, "but every time, I get so hard I could die."

"Same," I gasp as he nips my jaw. "Very hard."

He chuckles, his hot breath and beard eradicating the last of whatever resolve I'd scraped together.

"I just want this, Laz. I want this all the time. Without drama, or ghosts, or spells, or weird Alpha battles." He teases my cock through my jeans and it's the utter end of me. "Don't you want that?"

"Yes," I hiss as his grip tightens. "Of-of course I do. But…"

He sighs and glides his hands around my waist instead, hugging me tight. "Alright. Just think about it. Someplace quiet, full of our stuff, where we can be together forever without any interruptions." He frowns and gives me a quick kiss. "Like Cyan, now shouting in the link, wanting to know if we got lost or just can't follow directions."

Well, in his defense, he is the Alpha, and he gave an order. Not a command, no, but they should be regarded as one and the same, if you ask me. No one does, but that's beside the point. What good is having an Alpha if you don't listen to them?

But his vision of our future is perfect, and I would truly love nothing more. I don't know what to do, so I nod, and Korey smiles, though it's a bit sad. "Sorry to leave you wanting."

"O-oh, it's okay. Before you, that was my entire state of being."

I forgot to include that in my status choices; eternally horny. I had intended it to make him feel better, but it doesn't, so I quickly add, "It's fine, truly. It'll…only heighten it when we do get to, ehm, finish."

His smirk slides back into place, doing nothing to stop my arousal, mind you, and he stands while holding me.

"I guess if that's true, I should keep your perfect cock hard and ready all the time, little pup."

That squeak noise, which I've determined at this point is in fact me, escapes. "Y-you…whatever you want. Sir."

The smirk falls away, replaced with a lusty snarl, and it occurs to me, now's not the best time to pull the tiger's tail. Yet, I think I get the same thrill, the one he gets from praising me. We genuinely, without a doubt in my mind, are made for each other.

And as he kisses me I also have no doubt if he leaves, I'll go with him, because I could never, ever lose this. I sincerely hope he doesn't force that choice, though.

CYAN

I'm going to kill him. Him and his damn dad. Jakobe stumbles back a few steps, palms raised.

"I had a real good reason, Mister Alpha."

I snarl, ripping into beast form. "ANSWER ME!"

His eyes widen, throat bobbing. "I ever tell you how sexy you are in your wereform?"

My beast and I both feel sick. I whimper, gripping my muzzle, and Jak finally rubs the back of his neck.

"I'm, uh, 23. But, look, like I said before, age is just a—"

I roar, completely consumed with guilt, rage, and…and…I don't even fucking know what.

"Hey, I get it, you're mad. Totally understandable. But I did still save her, and I'm, you know," he clears his throat gesturing to Reanne, then me, then the puddle, "experienced. Heh. A whole lot more experienced now. Sorry, not the time for jokes. Listen, it's no big deal, my man."

Reanne's delicate hand lands on my arm, a small smile hooking her mouth, and I can't for the fucking life of me figure out what's funny about this situation. He's a pup. A literal pup. I had a pup mate my Aruna. No…worse. Oh my fuck. He mated the Aruna Rigdis. I might throw up.

"Cyan, I'm 23."

"That…doesn't matter," I growl, barring my teeth at her. She's not in the least bit scared. "You…are…human."

It would be easier to talk if I was in man form, but every part of me is losing it.

"Even if you guys age differently, he's proven himself, right?"

She continues stroking my arm like I'm some furry creature she scooped off the forest floor. I hate that it's making my beast happy, because we're supposed to be united.

Jakobe takes a small step closer to her. "It's not like I was on the nipple last week or something, anyway."

My beast gives up and retreats, because the man form is close to heaving. I brace on my knees as the world spins.

Reanne scratches the back of my head. "I mean, that really was amazing sex, and he's clearly full grown." I glance up in time to see her cheeks tint as she eyes him.

"We're physically grown by 18, and obviously he's fucking gorgeous, that's not the point!" I shout, squeezing the bridge of my nose with a wince. I fucked a pup. I swear to the moon, someone's going to pay for this.

"What is the point?" She rubs my upper back, and as hungry as I am for the contact, now's not the time.

"He's too young to be away from his pack, he hasn't even been outside The Glade yet! And now you're mated! I didn't sign up to be a fucking mentor or some shit, and neither did you. Werewolves aren't supposed to do anything but learn until 29 because once you leave, you're on your own until you find a pack. It's dangerous as hell in The Glade, and he fucking knows it."

"23 is prime, though. And I'm not on my own, I'm with the best Alpha ever. The best pack ever! Besides, you know how stupid the rules are, you were a pup once. Like, why can't we leave if we're not happy? Grown werewolves get to break pack if something's wrong, why not the younger ones?"

There's pain in his eyes. Fuck, that's right. The whole shit with his pack because he lost the Challenge. Ugghhhh! Yeah, okay. I get it. If I could have left before I was full grown, I would have too. But, I wouldn't be who I am today, wouldn't have found Reanne. Who knows who Jak might have been if he fucking stayed?

"You lied to me." I shove upright and point at him.

265

"You're right, Mister Alpha. And I'm real sorry. I won't do it again. I'm sure you can come up with some way to punish me for it." There's the faintest smile on his plump lips.

Why the fuck is my dick getting hard? I glare at it and shout, "What is WRONG WITH YOU!"

Reanne bursts into laughter, hugging her waist. I whirl on her, wild eyed and angry, but...I've never heard such a stunning sound in my whole life. Even Jak is looking at her all moon eyed. Not to mention, it's making those plump breasts jump around, which isn't helping my dick in the damn slightest.

"I'm...sorry," she cackles, wiping her eyes. "You liter... literally screamed at your cock. I can't even." She laughs harder, and Jak starts chuckling, too.

"Okay. Okay I'm...I'm fine. God, that was funny. I needed that."

I growl, even though I'm grinning, and call up my beast again for a whole other reason. I dive at her, scooping her tiny body into my arms before she can finish the squeal. But whatever I had planned, I couldn't tell you, because the second I have her, she grabs my muzzle, mashing my jowls in with another giggle, and when we lock eyes, time stops.

I can't fucking explain it. This is familiar. There's this weird ass ache, deep in my chest, and it hurts so bad my beast whimpers. Wind kicks up around us, dust and bits of ash floating in a million directions.

Her smile softens, and she runs her fingertips along my brow ridges, my ears, my nose, exploring, memorizing. She bumps them along my teeth, absolutely no fear in her at all.

"You're so beautiful," she murmurs, giving the top of my muzzle the softest kiss.

My beast whines this time, and I drop to my knees, setting her down in front of me. As I shift back to just me, she holds my face through the whole transition, watching, smiling, the moon glowing behind her.

This is the perfect damn moment to mate if ever there was one, and we can't.

"Fuck," I rasp, launching to my feet and cradling her face in the same move. I claim her mouth like I can't get enough because I seriously fucking can't.

It turns heated in less than a minute, and I yank her against me, dragging my biting kiss down her jawline, lapping Veikko's mark on my way to an empty spot on this shoulder. One bite. Just lay her down, pick a spot above her slit, and sink in. That's all it would take.

She's gasping for air, grabbing at my arms, and I'm a heartbeat from just taking her right now, when I catch Vik, Neo, and Aeon out of the corner of my eye.

It shocks me back to the present, the weird feeling, the weird wind, all of it dying at the same time. I lap her shoulder again and spin to face them.

"There you fucking are. What took so long?"

Jak quickly steps up behind me, setting all my nerve endings on edge, and whispers, "Please don't tell Vik. I really want to be with him. I mean, I wanna be with everyone, but you know what I'm saying. Please."

All I can do is growl, louder and louder until he steps back, all my happiness melting away. "I don't like secrets and I fucking hate lies."

The approaching trio stalls, each of their eyes widening. Neo clutches Aeon's hand tighter, who isn't even looking in the right direction. Reanne eyes him curiously. That's right, she doesn't know he lost his beast. I bet he wants to keep that from her, too. Fucking ridiculous.

Neo drags a stumbling Aeon past us, and sets about starting the fire, while Vik and I stare at each other. An Alpha. Still can't believe it, even though the signs have been here, I guess.

Jak takes a few quick steps and presses against Vik's side, smiling up at him. Fuck's sake. I let out a forceful exhale, scrubbing my face as I head toward the fire.

We've all been through so much shit, and before I tear away the one thing that seems to make the viking happy, we should at least get through this damn Ceremony.

Aeon and Neo are situated around the existing BriarMaw firepit, and it's a painfully familiar scene. It all started here for us. I suppose it's fitting for an ending here, too.

Neo scrapes a claw across one of the starter rocks, sending sparks onto the horizontal kindling, which ignites to a blaze. Ceremonial fires are prettier than the upright ones for cooking or heat. Like a blanket of flame, stretching from rock to rock.

My gaze trails to the right, where the Alpha's tent used to sit. I can almost see my dad in the dust, see his red eyes in the flickering embers. Hate this fucking place.

"L-Lovely fire, Neo." Lazaros and Korey make their way toward us, hand in hand, but stop a few feet away.

"Yeah, can feel the heat from here. Good job."

Neo smiles, pushing his glasses up with a finger in the center. "Thanks."

He's still sad about he and I, and I swear I'll make it up to him, I'll make it up to everyone, there just hasn't been any fucking time!

Reanne threads her fingers through mine, resting her cheek on my arm. "How do we start?"

Taking a slow, deep breath, I squeeze her hand and release it as I step toward the fire. Neo and Aeon stand, stepping in line with Reanne behind me.

"When Agnar showed up during his Pack Hunt, he was a smug shit."

The guys chuckle lightly, and there's a loud snap as one of the logs break, sending a plume of sparks to the stars. It's quiet for a moment, before I continue.

"Him and his damn brother. They knew everything, knew they wanted to be in our pack, and wouldn't take no for an answer. Even though they never told us where they came from, Dad was happy to have them. Loved Agnar especially." I let out a humorless laugh. "Hell, that's probably why I hated him so much to start with. But mostly it was his holy attitude. Then…he changed. I couldn't have told you when or why before today."

I twist my chin over my shoulder as Vik steps beside me.

"But now I can point to the second it happened and who caused it."

After another quiet moment, we nod at each other, as Vik swipes his thumb under his eye.

"He was an anchor," Vik murmurs, "in the storm that had become my life. I don't believe I could have stayed in BriarMaw, or SteelTooth, without his calming quality. He—" Vik chews at his lip, fists working as he glares at the flames.

Jak fits himself between Vik and I, hooking an arm under each of ours. "He was a damn good werewolf. And a helluva teacher. I only knew him a short time, but I'm already better for it."

Reanne wraps herself under Vik's other arm, and Neo slides his arm around my waist, Aeon clutching his other hand.

"He tried to teach me how to know where I was by the stars," Aeon chuckles. "It didn't help, but…yeah, he was good at it."

Korey steps up beside Reanne, holding her hand, Laz on his other side. "When he came hunting with me, he always kept an eye out for things to bring back to Vik."

"Ohh," Neo says. "I always wondered where that stuff came from."

Vik swallows and blows out a breath. "He was patient and kind. Loving and thoughtful. And the sky doesn't deserve him." The last word chokes out, and everyone's eyes flood.

No one adds anything else, because it would hurt too damn bad. There's a long stretch of silence, everyone reliving whatever they want to with him.

For me? It's the day I won the Challenge. How he held me while I cried my damn eyes out, finally free of my abusive, shithole dad, but shackled with the Alpha power I never wanted. He swore he'd stay with me, to help guide me. And he did.

"He may be gone, but he'll live forever in our memories." I clear the emotion, making sure my words will reach the goddess. "May the moon bless his star to shine brightest."

"May the moon bless his star to shine brightest," everyone echoes.

Flames kick up, higher and higher while we watch in somber silence, only broken by occasional sniffles.

It's a sad, beautiful moment, one I think Agnar would have been proud of.

Neo hums a soft note. "Cyan. There's…something we need to tell you."

"Okay." I swallow. No fucking idea what it could be. "Reanne?"

"Yes?" She leans forward out of the line. As soon as our eyes meet, she breaks formation and is at my side in a heartbeat, squeezing between me and Jak.

I breathe easier, and nod at Neo. "What's going on?"

"So, when you were gone, I needed calming and Veikko, uh, took care of me."

I chew the inside of my cheek, gripping Reanne's hand tight as I manage a grunt of acknowledgement.

"And," Aeon mutters, "After you—after Mishka didn't heal my bond, I…had Vik do it."

"…okay." My pulse races, temple throbbing, while my stomach bottoms out.

They exchange a glance, and Veikko steps in front of me. "When you forced my Alpha to the forefront, it…affected things."

"Things."

I'm hollowing out inside. Are they planning on leaving?

"You're an Alpha?" Reanne eyes him. "How come—but you feel different. That sounds weird, I mean I don't get the same energy or whatever from you."

"I am not a Seated Alpha. Without at least one pack member my power is, or should have been, mostly dormant."

"Oh. Well, why is it a bad thing you're an Alph—"

"We're linked to him," Neo blurts far too loudly as he steps in front of me, beside Veikko. Beside his…Alpha.

My mind blanks, nothing but white light and heartbreak.

"But we're still linked to you, too! I know you can feel it. Or, at least I hope you can. And we're, I for sure, am never leaving you, Cyan."

"I'm not either," Aeon says. "Uh, again."

"It was something beyond our control, and we wanted to be honest with you, that…it happened, but you don't need to worry about it at all. Vik says he doesn't plan to…are you…say something. Please." Neo's voice gets small.

I can't. What could I even say? I'm the one that forced his Alpha, I'm the one who left Neo alone, unattended, I'm the one who upset Aeon, I'm the reason Reanne left…

Am I a bad Alpha?

It hits me like a kick in the stomach, so vicious, it thrums through the entire pack. Neo's lip trembles, Aeon's eyes glass again, Vik's mouth twists to the side, and Korey sucks in a breath.

"You can't be linked to more than one Alpha," I whisper, sound barely able to make it through the noose around my neck.

"We are though, I can prove it." Aeon blasts his beta wave at me, and he's right. It's my energy. But it's not just mine in there anymore. It doesn't make any fucking sense. Nothing does.

I drop to a crouch, cradling my head. Neo hits his knees in front of me, stroking my shoulders, cupping my hands, pawing my neck, pressing his cheek to my hair.

"I'm sorry, I'm so sorry," he whispers, "please don't be mad."

Mad? I might be feeling everything under the fucking moon right now, but not that. I wrap my arms around him, pulling him closer, burying my face on his shoulder as he cries.

"I'm not mad. It's all my fault. I failed you guys."

"No!"

"Hell no."

"You didn't fail anything, Mister Alpha."

"Cyan." Reanne's voice is the only one that cuts through the white noise in my brain. "If it's anyone's fault, it's mine. I ran away, I took Aeon." She sniffles. "So, don't blame yourself."

"You only left because I'm a fucking asshole!" I shout into Neo's shoulder.

She folds herself over my back, hugging me tight. "It wasn't just you, though. Mishka was in the mix, too. Look, can we all just say we're sorry, and promise to stay together forever? Please? People fuck up, say stupid things, but I don't want to lose the only family I've ever loved. The only one I've ever had."

Neo reaches above my head and cups her cheek. "We don't want that either, baby bird."

"Ugghh," I groan, leaning back and scrubbing my face. Reanne clings to my neck, kissing the back of my head, while Neo strokes my chest.

"So sick of these fucking emotions."

She laughs into my hair, squealing when I stand and she's forced to hook her heels around my waist. My mouth twitches into a smirk as I twist an arm back to support her.

"Listen up," I bark, everyone's eyes snapping to mine. "Thanks...for being honest. That's all I've ever fucking asked for. Honesty and loyalty."

I cut a glance at Korey directly, who averts his eyes.

"No one is leaving this pack. I don't give a fuck what else happens, this is it. None of you shits are allowed to die, either."

Reanne blows a laugh against my neck again, which relaxes my shoulders, and I soften my tone. "I love you guys too much. So."

I'm attacked on all sides by hugging bodies, and a chorus of "I love you's." I hate to admit it's not the worst thing. I even enjoy it.

Right up until foreign Alpha energy pricks my senses. I quickly pick up countless other signatures behind us, and twist, claws out, followed closely by Vik wearing the same wary, protective expression. Reanne slides down my back and retreats, keeping just her palm between my shoulder blades, as we form a protective wall.

It's Jak's shock and excitement that confuses me the most. But, as the horde of werewolves silently exits the tree line, I understand.

Jakobe

"Dad!" I can't even believe it. I figured I'd never see him again. I mean, we're not supposed to! How does this work?

He bows his head as the fire crackles. "Blessings on those who passed, for their spirits strengthen the moon."

Every werewolf with him repeats the phrase, and I swear The Glade hums.

"Alpha Zaid."

He refocuses on Cyan with major relief. "Alpha Cyan. I hoped it would be you."

Cyan's chest rumbles. "Yeah, glad to see you, too. Got a few things we need to discuss."

Oh, man. I try to catch his gaze, imploring, but he ignores me. Damn. I guess I need to come clean before Veikko finds out.

It'll break my heart if he decides he hates me, or never wants to talk to me again. But…right is right, and I owe him the truth. And my new Alpha wants no lies. Can't have a relationship built on a lie, anyhow.

I step in front of Vik and take his hands, lowering my volume as I draw in his energy. "Truth out, I'm only 23, and I'm sorry I lied, but I really want you to be mine, and I promise, I'm not too youn—"

He ducks and presses his mouth to mine, hot tongue diving deep as his giant hand cups the entire back of my head. I swear my heart dips down to my toes before it blasts out the top of my skull, headed straight for the stars.

When he finally pulls back, it takes me a second to open my eyes.

"I have lost too many to lose you, as well. My truth out," he lowers his voice, barely a whisper, "everyone alive is significantly younger than I am." He winks and my knees give a little.

I knew he was older, but that's a serious fact to be throwing around. My dad is, like, over 200... Man, I couldn't be any luckier. I wanna tell him I got to fill Reanne up, because that was so damn hot, but I guess now's not the time.

"For starters," Cyan continues, cutting a glance my way and back, "why're you here with your whole pack?"

"May we approach?"

Both Cyan and Vik growl in low warning, but I pat his arm. A bunch of them may have been mean to me, but they're all good guys deep down. No real darkness coming off of any of them.

Dad holds up his hands. "We didn't come to fight."

I finally take a good look at everyone behind my dad. Huh. Why are they all carrying so much stuff? My eyes widen as I figure it out the same time Cyan does.

"You're...migrating?" He drops his stance, claws retreating as he scratches his head.

"Essentially."

"That's dangerous as hell."

"It is."

"Something happen with—"

"The territory is fine. Someone will make good use of it, I'm sure." Dad takes a few slow steps closer, waiting until Cyan nods, and then the whole pack shuffles forward.

I frown, weirdly sad. I mean, it's not like I could ever go back there while he was still alive, but now there really isn't anything to go back to. And it's also hard to see everyone again. I don't think Garrin will slip up with Vik backing me, but that don't mean I have to be happy he's here.

Ugh. I'd forgotten how much energy there was in DuskFall.

My skin hurts, all my nerves on edge because they are all still familiar. I bet Agnar never had this problem. If he was still here, he could teach me how to handle it, but…he's not.

I'm not even in this pack yet, but Cyan picks up on my anxiety and throws out a blanket of his Alpha energy, catching my eye again. Aeon sends an answering Beta wave, covering the whole fire pit, and I feel better than ever. I had no idea he was so strong!

"Man, I love you guys," I sniffle.

Veikko chuckles softly from behind me.

Cyan jams his tongue in his cheek, a smile fighting to be freed, before he faces Dad again.

"Why the hell are you migrating to BriarMaw? You're lucky everyone's dead because they'd have killed you on sight."

Dad smiles again, stopping just a few feet away, as close as the two of them can get, the rest of the pack forming a wedge behind him. "Very lucky."

Cyan squints. "You gonna answer the question?"

"We aren't. Migrating here, I mean. Our destination is The Spire. But, light from the explosion reached even us, and I needed to see with my own eyes."

"See what?"

Dad's smile widens, a weird glint in his eyes. "That you're alive. That she is. That everything is proceeding as it was written."

"The prophecy, huh?"

Dad nods. Why hasn't he even waved at me? It's not like I'm invisible here. Wait…am I? I slap my chest, and glance up at Vik, who quirks a brow and meets my gaze. Okay, no I'm not. Maybe it's just how dads have to act if they ever see their pups again? If so, I don't like it at all. I'd never do that if I was lucky enough to get someone pregnant. 'Course, I'd never let it out of my sight, either, rules be damned. When Reanne gets pregnant, I'll be glued to her side like a second skin. My cock is starting to twitch, so I grit my teeth, pushing the thoughts out of my mind. I'll just...remember how much I hate Garrin. Yep. That did it.

"Ya know, that works out. I had wanted to bring her to meet you. Figured you could help fill in some blanks. Based on what Jak said, anyway." Cyan steps to the side, clearing the line of sight to Reanne. She gives a shy wave, covering herself a little, and every DuskFall member drops to one knee at the same time, heads bowed, including Dad.

"Aruna Rigdis," he whispers to the dirt, "is it really you?"

"It is her." Veikko's voice booms. "Verified by my magic."

The murmured word, "Spectre," floats through my old pack, and that's when it hits me.

Spectre. Ghost.

I whirl and stare up into his wide eye. "Are you...Kasimir?"

"No," he smiles, mouthing, "his pup."

"Back to this migration shit," Cy growls. "Why The Spire?"

I can't look away. Mainly, the idea my enormous Honeybear was ever a pup, ever waist-high to a deer is funny as heck, but if he's Kasimir's pup...he's the first-born of the first Alpha, and I don't remember exactly why, but I know that's mega important.

"We were hoping to be of assistance to you, High Alpha, and you." He nods at Reanne. "During your transition to power."

"Why'd you think we'd be there?"

Dad's brow scrunches. "Where else would you be? I assumed..."

He trails off, and that's when he finally looks at me, but it's not with anything friendly or happy. It's disappointed and downright cold. Familiar in the worst way. "Have you remembered *anything* I taught you?"

I open my mouth to say one of a billion pre-made defusing responses, but Cyan growls louder.

"Hey," he snaps the word out with a clack of teeth, stepping in front of me and pointing at my dad. "He's not yours anymore, he's mine. Watch your tone."

Dad takes a slow breath and works his jaw before nodding. "Sorry."

"It's fine." I swallow, smiling. "He's right anyway, ol' Jak's not good for much."

"Got that right," someone snickers from behind dad, and I know who it is, I know. But I'm not looking.

It's Vik's turn to growl. "The next one who speaks ill of my partner will not take another breath."

There's almost a tornado of gasps, flowing through my old pack. Even Dad's face is nothing but shock.

I puff up just a little. That's right. Your boy Jak has the oldest living Alpha on his arm.

"You're disrespecting one of my mates," Reanne's voice rings clear. I glance at her and she's showing off my mark like she's just as proud of it as I am. Her energy is brilliant, sparkles floating above her like tiny stars. My heart's gonna burst right out of my chest.

Cyan smirks and crosses his arms. "And if it wasn't for Jakobe, you wouldn't have an Aruna Rigdis to be worshipping right now, so I'd calm the fuck down, if I were you. Should probably give them a command so they don't do something stupid. I'll wait."

Dad spins and glares daggers right at Garrin's annoying face. I can't hear the tirade anymore, thank the moon, but boy, can I see it, reflected in everyone's falling expressions.

"Yes, Alpha," everyone barks in unison, and a chill hits my back. Man, oh man, I don't miss that at all.

Dad turns again and smiles, bowing his head. "Sorry again. It's been a tough journey for us, plus all the hours of preparation. And training."

He starts to cut his eyes to me but stops. I know he's upset, I can tell. And yeah, I do sort of wish I'd paid a bit more attention, but it was so boring!

Maybe if I hadn't begged to leave, stayed a bit longer and learned more I'd—Well, no. If I hadn't come, none of this would have worked out the way it has. And Dad wasn't putting up much of a fight anyway. Most of that was for show, just for Cyan.

Vik squeezes my shoulder, and Cy nods, cracking his neck. "Makes sense."

"If it's alright with you, Alpha Cyan, we'd like to rest here a moment before we continue."

"Sure. It's neutral ground now, so help yourselves."

The pack relaxes and moves in slow groupings toward the fire, none of them glancing my way as they make a wide arc around us.

"I also apologize for interrupting the ceremony. Was it for the fallen BriarMaw?" Dad offers a skin of water to Cyan, taking a draw himself when Cy shakes his head.

Cyan snorts. "Hell no. It was for Agnar."

Dad chokes, coughing water everywhere. After he settles his lungs, he wipes his mouth and stares at Cyan, unblinking.

"Agnar…is dead?"

"Yeah. How'd you know him?"

The rest of the guys are watching the DuskFall members warily, while Reanne steps over beside Vik and I, curling her hand around mine. She gives me the cutest little smile and truth out, not a damn thing else matters. I saved this female's life, I got to mate her, I got to fuck her, I got fucked by the Alpha, and if I read my stars right, I can keep doing just that. Not to mention, my Honeybear just claimed me as his partner in front of everyone who matters and a bunch who don't. Life is good as hell.

"I raised him. Same as I did Jakobe."

My heart stalls, static crackling in my head. Vik's grip on my shoulder tightens the same time Reanne's hand crushes my fingers.

Did he…does that— "He was my brother?!"

I had wanted to shout it, but all that came out was a weird gaspy whisper.

Dad glances at me. "No, don't be silly."

279

"But," I stumble forward a step, "if you raised us both, then we're both your pups, and that means he's my—"

"I raised you both, yes." He strolls closer, and I feel like I'm going to pass out by the time he puts his hand on my shoulder. "But neither of you are my pups. My only legitimate pup was named Fen."

Everyone freezes, heavy sadness soaking the air, and Dad's expression slowly twists into concern. "What?"

The static crackles louder, and I can't breathe. He's not my dad. Bits of the conversation with Agnar hit my brain one after the other. His dad talked about the prophecy, taught him Tracer skills, spent his whole life preparing him...

But his dad was my dad, so, why didn't I get taught?

"Hey, woah," Cyan spins and faces us all, blasting his wave out, and grabbing hold of Aeon's and Reanne's hand. "Everybody take a fucking breath." Aeon sends his Beta wave, but it's wobbly. I know I'm not pack, but he's strong enough now that it should have worked on me. Maybe I'm broken.

"That monster was yours?" Reanne whispers, wrapping her other arm around Vik's.

"Monster?" He frowns. "I had hoped separation from me would..."

I'm sure they're all real concerned about this Fen guy, but I only have one thing I wanna know.

"Who is my real dad?"

"I—"

"Did you steal me?" A tear breaks free. "Did he give me up? Did my mom live? Where am I from? Why didn't you tell me?"

I expected someone to grab me, but I didn't expect it to be Reanne. She mashes herself against me, hugging so tight my lungs hurt. Or maybe that's because I'm crying, who knows. I bury my face on her shoulder as she wraps her arms around my head. Love comes exploding through our mate link, thick and warm and like nothing I've ever felt before. Her energy flares behind her and I grab it, curling it around us.

"It hurts, I get it, I really do," she whispers, "but you're not alone."

No idea how she knows exactly what I'm feeling, but, man, she hit that frog right on the head. I hug her back, nodding, breathing her scent in as I get myself back together.

I guess it's pretty clear why I don't look anything like Dad… Oh, man. Guess I have to call him something else now.

I turn my head, pressing my cheek to her shoulder, and eye Zaid. What the…weird. For a second, I swear there's black energy around him, but it's gone before I can really focus on it. Probably just my emotions going all sideways. Taking a deep breath, I straighten as best I can, since Reanne doesn't let me go.

"What about my real dad?"

If making the point that he's not my dad affects him, he sure doesn't show it.

"He was long gone by the time I found you. And yes, your mother had lived, though she's now also dead. Killed by the one who came looking for you."

Mom. I had a mom who lived after birthing me, and I don't even remember her.

"Did…did she look like me?"

Zaid nods. "A living flame if ever there was one." He laughs softly. "Thinking back, I should have known you were the one. It's pretty clear now."

"Who even…am I?"

"You're Jak," Reanne whispers, kissing my head. "The best you that's ever lived."

My heart hurts just a tiny bit less.

"I apologize. I didn't expect such an animated reaction." Zaid sighs. "Agnar took the news much better."

"Yeah?" I sniffle. "That's probably because you bothered to tell him a helluva lot sooner than this."

Zaid hums. "Probably true. He knew from a very early age. There's no reason to be so sad, though. I gave you a good life."

"A good—" I unwind myself from Reanne's arms and stare

him down. "If I'm not yours, then I'm not Alpha bloodline. You let me challenge, for absolutely no reason, man. You scarred me, for no reason! Then you let me live out my life as a sad failure, you treated me like an idiot. 'Jak go move those rocks.' And it turns out, you taught Agnar how to use his skills, but all you did was teach me to pretend I didn't have them! If I'd been better at it, I could have...I might have..."

I can't even make myself say it. Everything just hurts.

"I had a reason for that, Jakobe. It was to protect you."

"How's that protecting me?" I finally do shout, and the whole Glade falls quiet. Not even a bird squawking as my fists tighten at my sides.

"By the time I discovered a Tracer was at the heart of the prophecy and decided to take action, someone had already begun killing them off. Your mother loved you, gave you to me to save you. She...called you her little sunbeam. She'd also heard about the killings, and knew you were a Tracer the second you were born. Because she was also a Tracer."

He keeps talking but I can barely listen. My whole life coulda been different. Or, I guess I could have died, and maybe I should be thankful, but man, he could have treated me better. Not that he was the worst. I mean, I've heard stories that would burn your tail-fur clean off. And I don't know how I'd be different if I knew earlier, but it sure would have been nice.

Reanne wraps me in another hug, squeezing me as my da—as Zaid carries on.

REANNE

J ak wraps his arms around my waist, muscles trembling, so I hold him tighter. I may not know this exact heartache, but I do know what it's like to have your reality broken. I know it's crazy fast, but I do feel love for him, a wonderfully sweet, heart-warming love. He saved me, stayed with me, forgave me for almost choking him, mated me, gave me insanely good orgasms, not to mention when you share a loss with someone, it does bring you closer. I just wish we could have done all this under less heartbreaking conditions.

Zaid paces a small circle. I had initially thought he was kind of handsome in a rugged, mountain man sort of way, but now I hate him with all my bones.

"When I first started searching for Tracers, I was years late, then months, then mere days, until I finally found Agnar—alive. I spent so much time and attention training him, I...neglected Fen. I knew it, but I was convinced Agnar was the one, which meant little else mattered, I'm afraid. Fen grew resentful of his 'brother,' while at the same time becoming obsessed with him. When I sent Agnar to BriarMaw, I hadn't intended Fen to go, but he begged...just as you did. I thought perhaps spending time away from DuskFall would be good for him, but if just saying his name has such an affect, it seems I was wrong. Regardless, when I found you, I decided to do it differently. To hide you and your power, in case something went sideways."

Jak jerks his chin off of my shoulder with a snarl. "Well, something did go sideways, you trained the wrong one!"

Zaid's face falls. "I can see that now."

"Wait…" Cyan slowly turns. "You sent Agnar here?"

Zaid nods. "Positioned him with who I suspected to be the next incarnation of the High Alpha."

A growl rumbles in Cy's chest. "So, you knew who I was when I ran up on DuskFall."

"I…had a feeling. Despite the fact I had planned to keep Jakobe safe with me forever," he spreads his hands with a sad smile, "the prophecy had other plans. It looks like it's all worked out, though."

Worked out? Ugh, this guy and all the prophecy talk. It's no wonder Fen was as obsessive as he was. Like father like son, I guess.

"First of fucking all," Cyan steps closer, forcing Zaid back a few steps, "you're a real piece of shit. The greasiest smear I've ever seen, and that's saying something."

Zaid's face blanches. "What?"

He advances again, and Zaid stumbles back to keep his distance. "You let your pup—and I don't care what you say, you raised him, he's your fucking pup, end of story—you let him challenge, when you knew…" Cy's beast ripples threateningly under his skin. "But worse, you attacked *back*. You could have just taken it like a true werewolf, but you hurt him. You mauled a pup, Zaid. A really young one, based on how fucking young he still is. And yeah, I found out about that, too."

Jak lets out the quietest whimper, and my eyes water as Veikko wraps his frame around both of us. How completely horrible. I get this is their life, and they aren't human, but still.

Zaid at least looks apologetic, though it doesn't change anything.

"I shouldn't let you live at all," Cyan continues on a growl, "let alone whatever the fuck you thought you were gonna do at The Spire. But since I don't want to be Alpha to those rat-tailed assholes, you gather all your junk, you finish your migration, you stay away from my pack, and stay the FUCK out of my sight."

Zaid doesn't say another word, or glance at our sad hug trio as he trudges to the crackling fire. Within seconds, the rest of his pack is on their feet, readying to leave.

"Thanks," a sniffle, "Mister Alpha. I'll be okay."

Poor Jak.

I hug him tighter. I guess no matter what world I'm in, there's always going to be abuse. It's hopeless. I tilt my wet eyes to the moon, and the longer I stare, the calmer my soul gets. I glance at Veikko's good eye, and it flashes at me, just a blip of his Alpha side. That's when I decide. It doesn't have to be hopeless. I have to take the power, whatever it is. I can't let this whole race die. And if any of what Mishka said was true, maybe…maybe I can make them all stop doing things like that. Just force them to be nice and take care of their children, and not give them up to a system full of neglected, forgotten kids and strung-out social workers who are just doing their best to—

"Hey," Cyan appears on my left and presses his nose to the space behind my ear, inhaling as he sends another wave over us. He rumbles a deep, commanding growl that lingers, burrowing all the way to my bloodstream, shaking every cell in my body. Almost like a vicious purr.

Aeon appears next and nuzzles his mark as he tugs me back a step, sending thrills through the mate link.

But it isn't until Neo slides against my back that I realize why they're all doing it. I'm sobbing. I quickly clear my throat and swat at my face. "Sorry! So sorry. I didn't mean to. It's close to home is all."

"Don't be sorry, ReeRee." Aeon kisses my neck. "It's been a heavy couple of days."

I nod, letting out a watery, "Yeah."

Jak thumbs one of my tears away. "Anyone ever told you your hugs are the best? No offense, Honeybear."

"No," I laugh, sucking in a sob, as Veikko chuckles.

"Oh, hey, whose is this?" Neo rubs the mark on my arm, sending a jolt through me.

"That's mine!" Jak grins and it's so proud I almost start crying again.

"Nice. Did you see mine?"

"The one on her chest? Hell yeah, I did. It looks great. They all do."

They share a smile and my heart hiccups, because they both send a burst of love through me. Jak's is heavy handed, and Neo's is a smooth, warm hug to my soul. My skin just starts to heat when Neo clears his throat.

"What's our next move? Do we get to go back now?" Neo strokes his fingers through my hair, clearing tangles. Which reminds me I desperately need to get clean.

"I could use a shower. And sleep."

"Sleep sounds fucking perfect." Cyan hums and nips my shoulder, breathing deep through his nose. "Don't know why you wanna fade your scent, though."

If I think about it too long, I'll start crying again. And I don't really want to talk about it, either. It helped, having Jak come in me, claiming me for something beautiful again.

Despite wanting to ask for more, I settle on the harsh truth, "I need to wash away…what they did to me."

Everyone grows quiet.

Great, I guess I ruined the moment.

But Aeon wraps me in his calming, safe Beta energy. Korey glances around and heads in a different direction, Laz staring after him. Neo's fingers push deeper through my hair, rubbing my scalp in soothing circles, while Cyan runs his nose along that spot again, weakening my knees.

"We've got you," he murmurs, sending chills across my skin.

A rogue tear drips down my cheek. "No, it's fine. This doesn't need to be about me. Jak's whole—"

"Jak's all good, beautiful, don't you worry." The werewolf in question steps closer and strokes my stomach tenderly as he gives me the softest, most soul-stealing kiss I've ever had. I exhale harshly, chasing more as he pulls back.

"Oh, she liked that," Neo muses by my ear with a sultry tone. "You must be good at it."

"Maybe I'll show you someday." Jak winks and glances higher, his dimpled grin growing.

Veikko's massive hand cups my chin, twisting it to the side until our eyes meet. He rubs his thumb over my cheek and leans in with a hungry kiss. My bones get light and heavy at the same time, skin tingling as he sends a zing through our mate bond. It's laced with faint Alpha energy, too, forcing this need of mine straight to the surface. And Jak's hand hasn't left my waist, making slow passes across, slightly lower with each one.

God, this is all way hotter than I expected.

I whine when they step away, the air meeting my sensitive body cold in comparison. But when I open my eyes, here's Korey, holding a bit of fabric and a big bowl of water. My heart plummets.

He holds up the cloth and lifts his brows. "What do you say, sweetheart? Want a little help?"

Damn these tears, and these memories. I nod, chewing my lip to keep from crying out loud.

Neo gathers my hair away from my face and shoulders, thumbing Aeon's mark. The sensation makes me moan slightly, and Aeon's attention snaps over my shoulder, cheeks blooming in pink.

"Let's start here, okay?" Korey gently wipes my face first, paying attention to my eyebrows, my hairline, behind my ears, my lips, the tip of my nose, and every tear that falls while he's doing it.

Once he reaches my chin and skims down my throat, he gives me a series of kisses, one on each corner of my mouth and two in the center. "All set, ready for the rest?"

A lump travels my throat, even as slickness forms between my legs. "Yes," I whisper.

Cyan gives Korey's shoulder a squeeze, holding out his hand, which Korey plops the cloth into. I grab his wrist before he steps

287

away and put it on my cheek. I don't want any of them to wander off.

He chuckles. "You're running out of places for hands to go, sweetheart."

"Just wait 'til she's got Cy's pups in her and that belly gets all swollen." Jak runs his pinky finger along the top of my mound, groaning. "Plenty of room then. Man, I'm telling you all now, it's gonna take a command to keep me away from her."

There is a collective spike of arousal, not just through the mate link, but in the air itself. Neo's cock hardens against my hip, Jak's juts out even farther, Aeon bites into his lip, brow furrowing like the thought is so hot it hurts him, and Korey mutters something under his breath, running his fingers through his hair as he glances back at Laz. Even Veikko groans appreciatively behind me. But it's Cyan's smoldering gaze I can't look away from. He takes my hand and wraps it around his massive, solid length.

I don't know why the idea of me pregnant is so hot to them, but I honestly don't care. I always wanted to have kids one day, and I never thought I would, so to hear that they all want me to is incredible. Sounds like I'll never have a lack of attention at any point, and that's exciting, too.

"Time to wash this gorgeous body." He leans in, lips pressed to my ear as he barely whispers, "Ready for that, my needy little slut?"

I whimper, nodding, squeezing my thighs together on reflex, but it does nothing at all. Cyan stays right where he is, lips moving along my lobe as the cloth glides down my throat. I lazily stroke him while he circles one breast, then the other before cupping it fully in the cloth. He massages gently, the textured surface dragging along my nipple. Jak's fingers inch lower, slipping down the outside of the lips, while I tremble.

Cyan moves to the other breast, giving that nipple the same treatment before moving to my stomach. He doesn't spend long there at all, and since Jak's silky touch is still driving me crazy, Cyan moves to my legs.

He gently taps the inside of my knee. "Open up for me."

I quickly shuffle until he can reach everything.

His groan lights me on fire. "Fuck! How can one person be so sexy? Someone take this." He tosses the cloth up and drops to a crouch in front of me. His arms cage me in, a hand gripping the back of each thigh, spreading me wider.

Veikko apparently caught the cloth, as his massive hand starts cleaning my back, but my focus is fully on Cyan's head as he positions between my knees.

"I-I won't be able to stay upright if you're doing that."

"Not a damn person here is gonna let you fall, Reanne. Ever. You're coming on my tongue and that's fucking it."

My heart swells with love. Jak drags his hand higher, fondling my breast instead as Cyan runs his tongue along the length of my slit. My head falls back, and both sides of my neck are lavished in tongue-heavy kisses.

Veikko uses his masterfully along his mate bite, while Neo teases Aeon's mark and the rest of my shoulder. Aeon groans and steps to my side. With a quick move, he fondles and sucks my right breast, dragging his teeth along Neo's mark.

Neo's breathy chuckle is cut off by a sharp grunt of pleasure, the same pleasure Aeon, Jak, and I feel when Veikko's fang slightly pierces his mark.

"HB, you're gonna kill me." Jak chuckles.

Kill him? I'm already a hot, wet mess, and this is just four mates. Eight touching me at the same time? I might not survive. I'm not sure if I'm making words at this point or not. I know sound is leaving my throat, but that's about it.

Cyan's tongue finally slips inside, gently flicking my clit. My body jerks as the tidal wave of need hits me. I'm aching, pressure rising with every pass he makes, while my mates drive me crazy with their lust.

Something cool and damp brushes my lips, and my eyes pop

open. Korey's in my glazed line of sight, hovering the middle finger of his other hand over my mouth. He mimes opening, and I do with a whimper.

"There we go," he murmurs and glides his first two fingers over my tongue. Part of my brain registers that they're wet because he made sure they were clean first, and I can't express how much just that small thing means to me. Mostly, because words won't come as Cyan gets hungrier with his movements, stronger with his grip.

I suck on Korey's fingers, heat and need and overwhelming love ricocheting through my marks as Cyan brings me to the brink.

My hands clumsily reach back on either side, the right one finding Aeon's cock, left one, Veikko's. They both exhale in a burst against my skin, Veikko's kisses becoming firmer, while Aeon's tongue on my nipple is replaced by teasing grazes with his teeth. Neo's arm snakes around my waist as he moves his kisses to the back of my neck, his cock nestled against my ass.

Cyan groans and moves his head side to side, gentle flicks mixed with an occasional quick one, grip beautifully merciless on my thighs. Heat spreads through my core, but again I'm at the point of almost too much pleasure for my body to make the leap.

I...can't believe I want it, but I miss Cyan's grip on my neck.

My desperate whine is muffled by Korey's fingers, but it no sooner leaves my mouth, than Cyan's cheek hitches against my skin and Aeon freezes, his head tipping back, cock pulsing in my grip.

Someone's fingers dance along my shoulder and slowly wrap around my throat. Neo! Lust explodes through me so fiercely I shiver from head to toe. Moans come on every pinched breath, and he squeezes the sides with exactly the right amount of pressure.

I'm lost in euphoria, sucking Korey's fingers, supported by Neo's other arm, pressed against his body, while stroking two cocks.

Jak crouches beside Cyan, his hand abandoning my left breast, trailing down my body and around my thigh under Cyan's hand. He teases my opening once before slipping two fingers in just as Cyan increases his speed and I'm undone.

The orgasm erupts, tremors racking my bones as I buck. Cyan holds on tighter, fighting the clamping of my legs, moaning against my skin and sending slight vibrations through my clit. Jak pumps faster as I clamp down, twisting my energy into his again, and my scream rises in pitch, the ecstasy burning every nerve ending.

I'm surrounded by groans, love and desire blasting through the mate links, and it's too much. Static fills my head, my vision whitens, and I go limp. Neo's grip on my neck loosens as he holds my waist tighter, keeping me upright.

Korey removes his fingers, stroking my cheek instead, and Cyan slows finally, pulling back.

"Lay her down." His voice sounds distant.

I'm on my back by the time the static subsides, but not on the ground. I'm on top of Neo, his arms wrapped gently around my stomach. Veikko is between my knees, lightly rubbing my calves, and Cyan is pressed against my side, nuzzling that soft spot under my ear.

"Welcome back, baby bird." Neo mutters in my other ear.

"Holy…shit," I whisper, ending on a laugh.

Cyan chuckles low in his throat, sending his warm breath down my neck. "We're gonna have to work on your endurance, moonbeam."

Oh, my heart! I think that's my favorite nickname yet. Love in its purest, most beautiful form spreads through my body, and I adjust my head, claiming Cyan's mouth. I would cup his face, but I can't exactly feel my hands yet.

Deep growls cover me. From Cyan at my side, from Neo, vibrating through my back, and from Veikko as he massages.

"Tell you what," Cy murmurs against my lips, "I'm gonna let

these guys help you through the next one. There's another cock I'm dying to get my hands on."

Next one? That can't be possible. Every muscle I have is deliciously weak, my core fluttering.

Cy bites my bottom lip, tugging it a bit until I give him the gasp he's looking for, then he lets it go with a pop and a smirk.

I hungrily watch him stand, his cock hard and throbbing, as he stalks toward my feet. Aeon quickly takes his place, his gorgeous, kind face smiling down at me.

"ReeRee, you okay?"

I nod with a lazy grin. "Yeah, way okay."

Finally able to move my arms, I bury my fingers in his hair and pull him in for a kiss. A tiny flame of need flickers to life out of nowhere. Neo thrusts up, grinding his cock against my ass in response, and Veikko's hands move higher, to the backs of my thighs. I break from Aeon's kiss and catch Vik's gaze, tilting my brows with a small nod. His pupil darkens, a slight glow forming as he strokes higher and rubs his blunt, wide thumb across my clit.

My eyes roll back, muscles twitching. "That feels so good," I moan.

"He's probably not wrong," Jak chuckles, kneeling by my head, slowly stroking his huge cock. "I hear the mate cycle is like this, times a hundred. Easy."

I don't have a response, intelligent or otherwise. That's both exciting and, frankly…terrifying.

Veikko swaps hands, keeping murderously light contact, and pushes Jak's hand out of the way, taking over.

"Aww, yes," he hisses, rolling his neck to eye Veikko. "There's my Honeybear. Harder. Like that, yeah." His head tips back, a shiver spreading through his toned body. He moulds my breast instead, grip teasing and fierce in alternating waves.

A whimper peels out of my throat, and I reach over my head, grabbing at Neo's face.

"What do you need, baby bird?" He kisses my cheek.

"I don't...I don't know."

"She wants your cock, Neo," Aeon rumbles against my shoulder.

"Mmm. Is that what you want?"

Heat blasts through me, and I nod, watching Vik's hand as he works Jakobe.

"Okay, you might have to help. Can you lift your hips, Reanne?"

God. Can I?

I push down on my heels, willing my body to work. It sort of does, at least enough that Neo can get his hands under my lower back to lift the rest of the way. I feel a different hand bump against my ass, dragging the head of Neo's cock along my opening.

"Holy damn, Aeon," Neo whispers. I expect him to lower me, but he keeps me lifted, groaning with every pump of Aeon's hand.

I wish I could see everyone at once. It's all so erotic. Eventually, Neo bucks up when his head lines up again, and slowly, so slowly, he lowers me on his length.

"Oh, my goooood," I groan, everything tightening again.

"Shit, that's hot," Aeon's breath hits my thigh, and I tuck my chin to my chest. He's watching Neo's cock vanish inside me inch by inch. Veikko's thumb still circles my clit while he makes out with Jakobe over my other leg. They're stroking each other now, and I can see glimpses of Cyan's body farther away, shrouded by the shadow of firelight.

"Watch out, Vik," Aeon mutters, batting his hand away and leaning further over. He runs his hot tongue down my slit until he's lapping at my opening, getting both me and Neo at the same time.

Neo groans in my ear, thrusting slower, but farther out each time, earning more of Aeon's tongue with each pass.

"Veikko," I whisper. His eyes snap open, attention on me as I reach for him. After glancing at Aeon's head, he hikes his knee over mine, straddling my leg and pitches forward, braced on his massive arms over me.

His hair falls forward, the moon behind him and I'm struck again by what and absolute monument he is. And I get to have him.

I cup his face and pull him down, sharing a slow, sensual kiss while Neo picks up speed. Vik swallows my moans, our tongues dancing.

"Hey, you know what that position is good for, don't ya?" Jak's voice tumbles down over the two of us, and I pry open my eyes, greeted by his handsome smirk.

"Stars above," Neo rasps out, grinding into me. "No way she's ready for that."

"Ready...for what?" The words are broken by gasps, as Veikko laves my nipple instead.

Jak's smirk spreads into a delicious grin as he holds up two fingers. My eyes bug, but scalding heat hits my core like a freight train. I have no idea if I'm ready for that physically, but dear God, I'm ready emotionally.

"Let's try."

Neo stills, Aeon and Veikko both leveling a heavy stare at me.

Aeon quickly cups my face, taking up the space at my right side, while Jak kneels on the left, stroking my stomach.

"You sure, ReeRee? It might hurt. Neo's probably the best for that, though, of all of us."

I nod, placing my hand on his. "I trust you guys. And now it's all I can think about, so we have to."

Chuckles and smirks greet me as Veikko situates himself fully between my knees again, pushing them a bit wider.

He grunts, staring at where Neo is sliding out of me bit by bit. "That is a nice sight."

"Right?" Aeon grins, reaching over my hip and grabbing Neo's shaft as it pops out. He pushes it between my lips and Neo thrusts up again, applying brilliant friction against my clit.

He ducks suddenly, stubble brushing my inner thigh as he all but swallows Neo's cock, coated in my juices. Neo's moan sends a chill down my back, but he reaches around my hip and grabs Aeon's hair, pulling him off.

"I won't be able to last long in her if you keep using your magic mouth."

Aeon stares at Neo, lips glistening, slightly open, with Neo's grip tightening in his hair, and I see it happen. I see the moment it hits Aeon what he's feeling. And I feel the moment he accepts it, through both of their marks. They sizzle my skin like I'm being branded, the burn running deep, all the way to my soul. I arch, my torso lifting as everything inside turns molten. I can't even scream, I'm nothing but emotion from one end to the other.

Veikko groans, hands finding my hips, but Jak presses his palms to the center of my chest. He sends his energy through me, and it feels like I'm being electrocuted one second, and covered in silk the next. The relief is jarring as the pain subsides. My breath saws in and out as tears pool in my eyes.

"Shew." He shakes his head, dazed a bit. "You guys need to be more careful. She might be ready for a double dose of dick, but she sure wasn't ready to hold all that."

Neo hugs me tighter. "So sorry, baby bird!"

"It's fine, totally fine," I gasp.

"What did we do?" Aeon's gaze is so full of concern and sorrow.

"Well." Jak juts out his lip in thought. "Felt like you mated inside her, like, your souls linked up. Through hers. I tried to separate them, but they weren't budging."

"That is not possible." Veikko mutters, but Jak shrugs.

"Just telling you what the energy is doing, my man. Possible or not, that's what happened. They're mates"

The leftover emotions from the apparent bond boil inside me. My core throbs, lower stomach fluttering.

"It's really, *really*, okay," I growl, grabbing Vik's hand. "Can we talk about this later? Fuck me, please. Both of you."

"Oh, yo, that was sexy," Jak chuckles, planting a kiss on

Veikko's mark while running his fingertips along the back of my arm, along his own mark.

Aeon takes a moment to collect himself, chewing his lip while he helps Neo line up with my ass.

Veikko plants his scalding hand on my mound, thumb finding my clit again. "Relax."

I nod, whimpering and shifting my hips as Neo eases in. Thankfully, it's wet enough down there to drown someone, so there isn't much resistance at all.

They soothe and stroke, kiss and lick, distracting from the stretching pinch, until he's in. It's a weird sensation at first, but with Vik working my clit, I'm panting again in seconds flat.

Neo breathes harsh against the back of my neck, winding an arm around my ribs. "Your turn."

I hold Veikko's gaze as he pushes the huge head of his cock into my opening, spreading me thin.

"Oh, fuck," I whine, already feeling full and he's not even in me yet. Maybe Veikko and his giant cock weren't the best choice for my first time at this, but there's no way in hell I'm backing out now.

Neo swears under his breath, moving his hand to my breast. He adjusts his shoulders, sliding his upper body farther out from under mine as Jak holds my face and melts my heart with another of his kisses.

Veikko pushes in a bit more and Neo and I both moan, mine muffled by Jak's mouth, Neo's by Aeon's apparently.

I keep getting hit with swells through my mate links which fan my heat into an inferno.

With another gentle, insistent shove, Veikko is farther in than feels possible, and he pitches forward, braced on the ground by my ribs, looming over us.

Jak pulls back, taking his delicious kiss with him, and runs his thumb on my bottom lip. "Time for the fun part, now. Ready, beautiful?"

KOREY

There's a slight breeze winding across this flattened camp. The rest of the guys are taking damn good care of Reanne, that's for sure. I'm glad I was here for it this time, though I sure as hell don't regret why I missed the last one. And that adorable reason is standing off near the edge of the firelight, half watching, half not.

Cyan and I close in on Lazaros, and even though I can tell by the flush on his skin he's more than a little excited, I'm worried.

We've worked up to two fingers, but Cyan and I are both much bigger than that.

Alpha, he hasn't...he's still...unused.

Cyan gives me a sidelong glance. *That right? He sure seemed ready to take whatever I had when we met in the forest.*

Oh, he'll do anything, probably, to make you or me happy, but that doesn't mean he's ready for it. I don't mean to growl, but it's out before I can stop it.

His lip curls in a snarl. *Do you seriously think I'd hurt that tasty fucking snack for any reason at all?*

No.

That answer is at least easy.

Cyan stops walking, and claps my shoulder, drawing my gaze. *Do you trust me or not, Korey? Answer me right now.*

Damn. That's a jarring question.

I—

I guess even though I've felt like an outsider for a while, and now I'm scared of something happening to Laz, Cyan hasn't given me any specific reasons to doubt him. Either as an

Alpha or a person. He killed Mishka, protected the pack, and brought everyone back together. Yeah, shit's a bit weird right now, but…

I nod.

Great. He smirks. *Then let's go fuck your mate.*

Shocking lust zips down my spine, and I stall as Cyan stalks closer to Laz.

"Korey," Laz breathes, arms tight around his waist, "what, ehm, what are—"

"Time to come out of those damn clothes, Lazzy boy."

His mouth forms an O, before his jaw clacks shut. "Right, I should have gues—one moment, I'll, ah but, here? With-with all of…*blimey*!"

Cyan stops in front of him, cock angry and throbbing, not an ounce of shame in him.

I shouldn't like seeing my mate flustered, staring at another guy's cock like he wants to eat it, but I'll be damned if I'm not harder than I've ever been.

"Shirt," Cyan barks, though, it's pretty quiet for him.

"Y-yes, just a second."

Laz grips the hem and wrenches it free in one move, twisting like a snake.

Cyan ducks and without warning, runs his tongue along Laz's nipple.

"Kah!"

Laz makes one of his non-word sounds, gaze crashing into mine, and my cock jumps.

I move closer as Cyan glides his tongue to Laz's other nipple.

"He likes that on his stomach, too, don't you, little pup?"

Laz loses his breath, eyes wide. He tries to make a word that clearly starts with F, but Cyan mumbles, "was already headed there next," against his skin and his eyes almost roll back.

My grin spreads from ear to ear. This is…fun.

Cyan makes slow drags down Laz's chest, biting kisses along his stomach to the waist of his jeans.

He tucks a finger inside and jerks Laz forward against him. "These next."

"Bleeding hell," he whispers, fighting to undo the button with trembling fingers.

I step behind Laz and lean over him, sliding my hands down his sides and along his waistband, pushing his hands out of the way. He quickly leans against me, death grip on my forearms, as I thumb the button free and ease the zipper down.

Cyan grins and flattens his palm against Laz's stomach, inching down as each bit of new skin is exposed.

I know when Cy makes contact, because Laz's hips snap forward, that needy gasp of his setting my blood on fire.

The jeans slip off his hips, and he steps out of them, while my eyes are locked on Cyan's hand, working in slow, teasing circles.

"Look at this beautiful fucking cock." Cy smirks. "Were you planning on keeping this thing a secret forever?"

It bobs, the tip glistening even more as he writhes.

"No, S-Sir, ah, sorry. Alpha."

I groan, gripping Laz's hips and duck to his ear. "Pup, you can call him sir. It's sexy as hell every time you say it, apparently even if it's not at me."

His gaze snaps up, neck craned, eyes searching mine. I lean in, brushing my lips across his.

"You want to call him that?"

"Yes, sir," he whispers back, and I nip his lip playfully, earning myself a gasp.

Cyan growls. "Fuck! The way you say that. You tryna make me bust all over the place?"

Laz smiles, full of so much awe and desire I nearly can't take it. "No, sir."

"That's a damn lie," Cyan grumbles with a wink, and hovers his face right by Laz's cock.

It's the second time in Cyan's life he's been on his knees, and both in the same day. It was weird to see the first time, like he was less of an Alpha somehow, but I can tell now, it's a powerful move. It means he truly has no fear of anything. That he knows, without a doubt, nothing can touch him. Kinda hot, really.

Laz inhales sharply, all his muscles trembling as Cyan drags his tongue through his sweet precum, flicking over the tip.

"Oh, my life," Laz groans, holding on to me tighter.

Cy chuckles and does it again, eyes locked on mine this time. It sends a weirdly possessive zing across my neck, followed by a flash of heat.

Laz's hips snap up, another needy whimper filling the air.

"You tryna fuck my mouth, pretty boy?"

He moans something about dying before clearing his throat. *"I d-don't know. No, yes? I just need—"*

I grind my cock against his back. It's way too sexy seeing him such a mess like this.

"I got what you need," Cyan smirks. "Your problem's I ain't in a hurry to give it to you."

Laz moans, the desperate sound hitting me right in the dick.

One of my many favorite things about Laz is how sensitive he is. I've seen a lot of blow jobs, we all have. Sex is nearly the only thing to do other than learn before you're officially a fully recognized adult. For the most part, everyone reacts about the same. It feels amazing—no question, sometimes better than other times, and there's no such thing as a bad blow job, but Laz…

It's a whole other experience for him. I don't know why, I just know I'm lucky as hell to have him.

"Gimmie your hand, pup," I order, twisting his arm behind his back and thrusting against his palm. He grips me hard, right as Cyan descends on his cock.

A groan rips from my throat. Fuck, why is that so hot? Maybe I like watching way more than I realized.

My gaze drifts to the group when Reanne arches off of Neo's body, clearly enjoying herself. I love her body. More than a little excited for when we officially start prepping her for the mate cycle. That thought has my jaw clenching, thrusting again in Laz's hand.

He's utterly lost in pleasure, other hand partially covering his face with the fingers spread so he can see. I make small circles on his chest and stomach, lightly tickling his skin.

"You like us both?" I lick his cheek, biting his jaw.

His breath races out of control as he melts farther against me, bucking into Cyan's mouth.

"Yessss," he hisses, "I bloody well do." Then uncertainty washes over him and he quickly twists his head, seeking my eyes. "If-if that's alright with, meaning, of course if you—"

"I like it too," I whisper in his ear, tonguing his lobe, and nipping it before straightening.

I still don't know if it's a good idea to...

Cyan quirks a brow and tilts his gaze up, slowly pulling Laz's cock out of his mouth. Damn! Pleasure sweeps through my stomach like fireworks.

Why don't you ask him instead of assuming?

Oh. Suppose I could do that.

Ducking again, I rest my chin on his shoulder and reach under Cyan's chin, grazing Laz's balls. "Do you think you're ready to take one of us, little pup?"

He shivers so hard it's like he stepped on a bolt of lightning. "H-here? Now? You mean in my... am I? What if I don't ah, like it?"

Cyan and I both laugh, Cy's deep in his throat as he swallows Laz's cock again, all the way to the base.

"Trust me, you'll like it. You like my fingers, right?"

He nods, hovering his hand above Cyan's head, but thinking better of it and snatching it back against his chest. "Very much, sir. I just...I'm, well, fair to say scared, though that word hardly covers it, really."

"I'll go slow," I rumble, gripping his hips firmer. "Take you a little at a time."

"Damn all the—" he whispers, biting into his sweet bottom lip as he nods again. "A-alright. Yes. Korey." He finds my eyes again. "You, if that's okay with," he refocuses on Cyan, "you. Sir."

Cyan growls, giving him a hard suck that has him dragging air in through clenched teeth. He pulls off with a pop. "As long as your mouth still works while you're riding him."

"My," he exhales every scrap of air in a wheeze, managing a nearly inaudible, "mouth."

The smile that spreads on Cy's face is nothing but pure happiness. "Sit down, Korey. Ease him on."

I hit the ground in a heartbeat, my own thudding in my ears. Never thought we'd do this the first time in front of literally everyone, but it's apparently not an issue for anyone, including us.

Cyan stands, slowly stroking his cock, as I pull Laz down on my lap. He whimpers, wiggling with nerves, until I shove my fingers in his mouth. He watches Cyan's hand as he works his tongue over them like a mini-god, and it's so hot I'm pretty sure my first load in him is gonna be damn near instant.

When they're more than wet enough, I pull them free. "Lean forward a bit." He does, and I slowly work them in his tight hole.

"Oh, fuck," he whines, arching a little. He relaxes into it after a few pumps, and then it's time. I grab his hips and position him, angling my cock against his opening. He's tense as can be, so I place a soft kiss on his spine.

"I've got you, little pup. You look so sexy right now, and I can't wait to feel you wrapped around me."

The words heat his skin, and he curls a bit, his head dropping forward for only a second before he snaps attention back to Cyan.

I'm about to pull him down, but he does it himself, reaching between his legs and gripping my shaft to guide it in.

"There you go, fuck," I whisper as he sinks lower, gritting my teeth against the roar building inside. "That feels amazing."

This is the first time I've fucked my mate. My beast is on the verge of frantic, the urge to pound Laz's small body nearly driving me insane.

Cyan rumbles the same soothing tone he did against Reanne's ear, a low vibration, and we lock eyes as his Alpha energy washes through me. The burn in my limbs and itch in my skin to shift subsides, and I'm back in control.

Thanks.

I really hadn't given him half as much credit as I should have. Though, he's changed a whole lot since Reanne showed up.

Cyan shrugs a shoulder. *That's what I'm here for, you know. Alpha shit. Not just to rail sexy little newcomers, though that is fucking literally one of the best parts.*

I breathe a laugh, wrapping my arms around Laz's chest as I huff against his back. He groans, neck rolling to the side a bit as he fully seats.

"Open up, Lazzy boy."

I pick my head up to find Cyan standing between my legs.

"Mercy," Laz murmurs, letting his jaw fall as he reaches forward with trembling fingers.

"Not gonna bite your hand off." Cyan smirks. "You can touch me."

Like it was a command from the moon herself, Laz practically dives forward, taking Cyan as far in his mouth as he can, both hands circling the base.

"Shit," Cy groans, tipping his chin up.

I reach around Laz's hip and lightly stroke his cock while I drive in deeper. He moans loudly around Cyan's shaft, pushing back against me, and I can't keep from moving. It's all too sexy.

"Brace on whatever you need, little pup."

He nods, lavishing Cyan, and I lift his hips, bringing him down slow, the friction nearly killing me.

"Daaamn," I moan. As if just being in his tight ass wasn't hard enough. This is…

I do it again, and he lets out a soft whimper, gripping Cyan's hip with one hand.

The next time is a little faster, the next a little deeper, the next, harder, until Laz is practically bouncing—not just because of me.

He abandon's Cyan's cock and takes a deep breath, reaching his arm back to touch my face. I kiss his fingers, and snag one in my mouth, sucking it hard.

"Oh, my fuck," he whines, bouncing harder.

"Guess you like it, huh?" Cyan chuckles, shoving his thumb in Laz's mouth. He freezes a second, like he's not sure if he likes it—or should like it. I stroke his cock harder, and he gives up, sucking and losing himself to all the sensations we're giving him.

He mumbles, moaning as I stroke faster. After a few combined down strokes of my hand and upward thrusts of my hips, he unloads with a relieved shout. Splatters hit his chest, dripping down.

"Such a good pup," I grunt, slamming him harder, as Cyan takes his hand back. "You can take it all, can't you?"

"Bloody damn apparently," he exhales on a fast breath.

Cy and I both chuckle, Cy lining his cock up again with Laz's mouth. He doesn't even hesitate this time, taking Cyan as far down his throat as it'll go.

"Look at that," Cyan croons, "that's a sexy sight. Keep it nice and loose, just like that."

Laz's cock twitches in my hand, and I grip his hips instead, pounding him to my end while Cyan fucks his throat.

I moan, the orgasm exploding through me as I fill up my mate. I know it's just in my head, but this feels complete, like he really and truly is mine, now.

He manages to make satisfied sounds, one hand reaching back to grab my waist.

Cyan snarls, chin tipping again as he stills. Laz's throat ripples, and the hand he slaps to Cyan's hip erupts in claws. He digs in, little trickles of blood appearing under the cuts, and Cyan's expression softens.

With a slow undulating move, Cyan pulls back until Laz

gasps a breath. He crouches and grips Laz's jaw, holding his panting face still.

"S-sorry, so sorry for the—blast, you taste fantastic! I didn't mean to—"

"That was fucking perfect, Laz." He leans in and licks Laz's face, cleaning it, showing him tenderness I'd only ever seen him give to Neo. Through a window, not even in public. Private level tender.

It kind of hits me right in the heart.

When he's done, and Laz is mostly breathing normally, they share a short, tongue heavy kiss before he straightens.

"Good work, Korey."

I nod, expecting him to head back toward the group, but he leans down and grabs my face the same way.

It shocks me immobile, and when he laps my cheek, I realize that's...all I've ever wanted. Him to accept me the way he does everyone else. I have a job. He appreciates it, sure, but I wasn't a partner by my choice. Never occurred to me that choice was hurting me all on its own.

Fuck.

Cyan...

You're good, Kor. He Alpha waves me, wrapping me up in it, like he...loves me. *Take care of your mate.*

I open my mouth to reply, but nothing comes out. He pats my cheek and steps over my leg.

The others are getting Reanne to her feet, laughing to themselves, all of them wobbly, but especially her.

I hug Laz tighter, my throat closing. Not really ready for this moment to be over, but I guess there's no choice.

He scrambles to get off of me, so I help, and he spins in my arms, hugging my neck so tight I can hardly breathe.

"We should stay with SteelTooth," I whisper.

"Can we please stay with Steel—" He says it the same time, jerking his head back to search my eyes. "Do you mean it?"

I nod, kissing the tip of his nose.

"Oh, I love you more than anything at all," he whimpers kissing me hard.

I clutch his face, wincing to hold back my emotions.

Jak's voice sounds above the rest. "Man, you could probably get another one in there with some practice, that's all I'm saying."

Laz breaks from the kiss with a soft laugh and stands, quickly gathering his clothes.

Reanne laughs. "Uhno, not so sure about that."

"Would certainly be something fun to try," Veikko rumbles, kissing her hand. "Do you feel better?"

"I feel like my bones are all broken, and I couldn't be happier about it." She glances over at us and waves, biting her lip. "The finger thing was really hot, Korey."

"Anytime, sweetheart."

And I actually mean it, since we're staying. Neo and Aeon keep passing odd glances at each other, but I don't know why. Maybe they're still upset about being linked with Vik.

"Thank you, guys," she says. "So…do we just…leave?"

Jak shrugs. "No reason I can think of to st—oh! Man! The dagger!"

He squeezes out between Vik and her, dashing toward the broken rock. Veikko smiles and she crashes against him, completely engulfed in his huge, warm embrace.

"Jak's wrong," she whispers, "your hugs are the best."

He rumbles a soothing note and squeezes tighter.

"Hey," Aeon pouts.

"I'd have to disagree, Baby Bird."

"Not a damn one of you hugs better than I do," Cyan grumbles, hands cinching around her waist. She laughs as he pulls her away from Vik and cradles her in his arms.

"I would suggest t-that, ah, Korey's hugs are, well, supreme."

Laz catches my eye, tugging his pants on, and my heart nearly explodes.

"Oh." She grins and glance around Cy's head at me. "That's true his are really, really great."

I smirk and wink at her, as Cyan growls, deep and loud. She cackles and kisses him again.

You know, as weird as it all may be, this *is* a family. One I'm glad I'm a part of.

"I don't mean to be the bubble buster," Jak calls out, grunting as he slides a bit of the altar to the side. "But the dagger ain't here."

"Are you sure?" she calls out as I shove to my feet.

"So what?" Cyan sets Reanne down but catches her when her legs give.

She stares at him, fear stealing all of her happiness. "Agnar said we had to destroy it, it's spelled or something. And Yuli said there's not a werewolf alive it can't kill. They used it to…stab me. More than once."

The twist of horror on his face, and the shock on everyone else's makes her eyes water.

"Shit, Reanne." He hugs her so tight her bones are probably hurting.

She's clearly fighting tears as she taps his shoulder. "You're right, your hugs are the best."

He only holds her tighter. Each second of the hug makes my heart ache. Laz steps up beside me curling his hand around mine.

At least Yuli's dead, and we never have to see his face again.

Finally, Cy steps back, grief and Alpha waves trickling through the pack. "Everyone. Shift and search. Find that fucking hunk of metal."

We all spread out, everyone but Laz and Aeon transforming. My beast is happier than it's ever been. Whether that's because of the sex, or the sex and being accepted by Cyan, I don't know.

Shouldn't something like a dagger be easy to spot? I ask, flanking Cy.

You'd think. Fucker probably painted it black or something.

Yeah, I'm not seeing anything shiny, Neo adds with a chuff.

Aeon steps beside her, linking his fingers with hers as Cy calls his beast and starts swiping at large chunks of ground.

"Thanks for staying with me." She turns and hugs his neck, smiling when he winds his hands around her waist. "I really missed you."

"I missed you, ReeRee. There's something I need to—"

"Guys?" Jak's voice pierces the moment, slight panic tightening the sound. "You need to see this."

We converge around Jak, dropping our beasts one at a time.

Cy's rumble is low, tense. "That shit wasn't here when we left."

Neo tilts his head before cutting his gaze to Aeon.

Oh. Damn. I purse my lips and glance at Laz, who quickly focuses on Reanne. Probably trying to send her something through their connection.

Tentative steps across the cold ground draw her closer, as she tugs Aeon along like a lifeline.

This is going to be bad. Veikko sighs, eyes lifting to the moon.

Aeon. You think you can Mate Blind her?

Holy shit, are you serious? His eyes are as wide as the Quay.

Woah, I say, facing Cyan dead on. *Is that safe? For her?*

If she freaks out, we're not gonna have a choice. I can't stay to keep her calm. I'm counting on you all.

That silences all the protest, Aeon giving Cy a firm nod. *I'll do my best, Alpha.*

She steps around the broken altar and freezes, her gaze landing on the partially uncovered hole. Jak shoves an earth-camouflaged board farther back, revealing a crude ladder descending into the darkness.

An escape hatch.

"He didn't die." Her words are strangled, pitch rising. "He… he's not…"

"Aeon." Cy nods at him and drops straight legged to the bottom of the hatch, no hesitation at all.

"On it."

He blasts his Beta wave directly at her, but it's different. Thicker, three times as strong, sending a tingle across my skin. A quick look at Laz, scrubbing his arm, lets me know he feels it, too.

Then Aeon steps in front of her, one hand on her face, one arm around her waist, and bites into his mark before she has time to spiral completely.

She goes limp in his grip, her expression completely relaxed. He fits his thigh between her legs, holding her closer.

Hurry.

"I'll bring back his fucking head, if I can," Cy calls out from the hole.

Laz inches closer to Reanne, eyes on mine, and lays his hand on her arm. Any leftover tension in her muscles leaves completely, and Neo rushes over to hold up her head.

"I hope she doesn't get sick," he says, glancing at me.

"Me too. She's strong, though. Don't worry."

He gives me a small smile and refocuses on supporting her, scanning Aeon's face.

Jak peers over the edge of the opening and stares at his hands for a second.

Veikko passes a glance my way before he sighs and searches the sky again. I dunno what he's looking for up there, but I hope he finds it.

And I hope Cy finds Yuli.

CYAN

Why the hell is this thing even here? The scrape marks in the dirt are still sharp, not worn by time, as if I didn't already know Yuli did it at some point in the last decade.

This exact spot is where my hut used to be, and you can bet your ass, if I'd had an escape route, I'd have taken it way more than once.

Dunno what kind of fuckery this tunnel is supposed to lead to, but it's too low for me to shift. And since there's not a window in sight, and no moonlight, I can't see shit beyond right here.

There's only faint firelight coming down the top of the hole above me, and that ends in a sharp line.

Guess I'm running blind.

The ladder behind me creaks, and Jak hits the ground behind me with a grunt. "Been put through it today, Mister Alpha, let me tell you. Oh, dang. It's dark."

I ain't got a fucking ounce of energy to devote to being annoyed right now. "Yep."

"Good thing you asked ol' Jak to come."

I quirk a brow and step against the dirt wall as he pushes past. "I did, huh?"

"I mean, I'm pretty sure I heard you." He grins over his shoulder, way too sexy for his own good. "Something like, 'Jak is the best, I'm sorry I yelled at him earlier, I wish he was down here helping me'."

I don't want to laugh, but I can't help it. Finally, I rub my cheek. "Yeah, not a chance. Get your ass back up there. No telling what's in here and I can't risk you getting hurt. Besides, they could use your help with Reanne."

"Trust me, they've got that totally under control." His smile doesn't falter at all. "I think I can help here, though, for real. Well, at least, we're about to find out if I can."

He refocuses and slowly aims his palm at the darkness. "Come on," he mutters, and a faint, twisting glow leaches out. "Yes! That's right, Jak to the rescue."

"Woah, what the hell is that?"

"A little leftover energy I might have swiped from Kasimir. I don't think he'd mind. He didn't like Yuli, either."

"You're just full of surprises. Fine, get behind me."

It's awkward as hell, half-hunched, shoulders scraping the curved ceiling as we make slow progress across the cool, sticky ground. Jak keeps his arm outstretched, so it's by my side, but the energy barely highlights roots and pits in time for us to avoid them.

"So, hey, thanks again. For standing up to my da—to Zaid."

"That hunk of shit." I fight the beast from surfacing, a take a slow breath. "I'm sorry he put you through all that. No one, and I mean no one, should challenge if they don't have to."

"Yeah. Well, it's not like he made me. Though, I was goaded a bit by some other…anyway, thanks is all I wanted to say."

"You're welcome, Jak."

"So, biting the mark, what's that do?" He grunts when he kicks a stone.

"That's how you access the part of your soul you gave her. Good for lots of things. Calming, or making sex feel deeper… emotionally." I sniff. "Or whatever."

I dunno which I'm looking forward to more, that, or the days of endless fucking.

"Heck yeah, I'll have to remember that. And what's a Mate Blind?"

I exhale forcefully. "He flooded her system with energy,

through the mark. She might get a little sick, but we won't be gone long. Just needed him to distract her while I rip this shitbrick's head off."

"Oh. You sure that's all he did? That felt like a whole lot of energy for just a distraction."

I frown. He's not wrong, but Aeon was probably being extra careful. When I don't answer, he continues.

"Hey, how many mates can someone have?"

"No limit. Stop asking questions." I take a long step over a gnarled root. "I'm still fucking pissed you lied, don't think I forgot. Fucking 23. You probably don't even know which moon cycle is for binding new members."

"Youuuu would be right, there, Mister Alph—oof!"

I slam back into his chest, narrowly avoiding a crude stick trap which lodges itself in the wall by my shoulder. Jak's energy fizzles as he lands on his ass.

"Traps. Are you serious with this shit?"

I grab in the darkness for his hand, colliding with it, and yank him to his feet. The light is back the next second.

"Yo, we should be careful." Jak examines the pointed end without touching it. "If he has one super deadly dagger, he might have more than one. Or at least some deadly sticks."

"Fucking hell," I mutter. "Hate this guy so much. Come on. Eyes open."

The tunnel goes for what feels like miles, and we avoid eight more traps before the faintest bit of moonlight appears in the distance. Good thing, too, since Jak's energy beam is getting dimmer.

Right when we reach the end, he shakes out his wrist. "All gone. Least I was good for something, huh?"

"You're good for a million things, Jak. Wait here."

It's gonna take a long time to erase the shit Zaid fed him. But he's worth the effort.

I step into the moonlit section and call my beast, leaping out onto a worn-bare swath of ground.

Empty. Dead silent. No scent on the air at all. Fuck, he's not here.

Growling, I reach down into the hole and grab Jak's hand, lifting him out with no effort. I plant him beside myself and drop beast, taking a deep breath.

That's when I smell it. Mud. Sharp, overly muddy mud. The wind changes, just the slightest movement against my neck, and I duck, shoving Jak a step to the left.

In the half-second it takes me to stand back up, there's a solid black hand, caked with mire, tight around Jak's neck, one around his mouth, and a spear lodged in the ground where he'd been standing.

I call up my beast, but two more spears appear on either side of my neck, pushing in. Like that'll stop me. I step toward Jak, but he makes a choked sound, eyes widening as the hand tightens.

"Let...him go," I growl.

No one responds, but the one holding Jak does loosen his grip.

Motion from a pitch-black space behind a nearby tree draws my attention, but I quickly realize the pitch-black thing is the motion. It rises, finally opening glowing eyes. Alpha eyes.

"Shit," I mutter.

There's only one pack I've heard of that can move with the darkness, and they're the last fucking pack you ever want to run into.

He's a ShadowMane, has to be. But there's no way that stupid tunnel was long enough to get us around the world. Why are they here?

There's a thud in my head, crude Alpha energy demanding access to my link. I can't tell if he means it respectfully or not, but I open the line and stare up into the neon green eyes peering down at me. His wereform is fucking massive, bigger than Veikko by two or three feet, easy. Pisses me off that I have to look up to hold eye contact.

Speak your intention.

His voice booms, rattling around in my skull. I flinch.

Damn, no need to shout. I'm chasing an Alpha named Yuli, he tried to kill my…partner.

No idea how much is too much to tell these creepy bastards.

The ShadowMane Alpha gestures slowly to Jakobe with his inky claws, but I shake my head.

Nah, not him.

He drops his hand and refocuses on me, as Jak's mouth and neck are freed. "Man, you guys should be careful with those things, you almost hit us!"

Leave. This one stays.

Better fucking try again, I growl, baring my teeth.

He stays. We will escort the unbound.

This bitch. I call my beast back up, not even wincing as the spears pierce each side of my neck, going deeper and deeper as I grow. By the time I'm chest level with the ShadowMane Alpha, which is as tall as I can get, the spears are hanging on their own, blood pouring down.

He. Is mine. Where do you think he needs—

It hits me all at once as I glance around; what his dad said, where we are right now, what we're near, where we're apparently supposed to be. This is the Crossmark, which puts us at the neutral conjoined edge of GrimBite and TalonWhisper, and the only thing nearby that could mean a damn is—

The Spire?

The Alpha nods, advancing a step. *He should be in place. Before the vessels arrive.*

That sounds a hell of a lot like prophecy talk. I smirk, which in beast form is just a wider snarl, snatching the spears out and flicking them into the darkness. *Vessel. Who the fuck do you think I am?*

We stare into each other's eyes, feeling the energies out. Finally, he tips his chin higher, sniffing the air, followed by all the others.

High Alpha?

Apparently.

"Hey, Cy, Yuli went that way," he points toward GrimBite. "If you guys are done chatting, we should probably get back to the pack."

There's something off with his voice, but I can't tell quite what it is.

Brave Tracer. The ShadowMane Alpha rumbles. *It will serve him well until his end. If you will not accept our aid, and you intend to see this through, hurry. Let nothing keep you from The Spire. The Rigdis is rising. She cannot be kept waiting.*

Who can't be kept waiting?

His throat rumbles. *The other vessel. Your...partner.*

You already knew that was who I meant, huh?

We have eyes everywhere.

Yeah? Did you see when they took her? I snarl. *Did you see when they stabbed her?*

He doesn't say anything, which in my mind, is a fat fucking yes.

If you were just gonna let her get killed, why does it matter if we're late to The Spire?!

She was not in danger.

An angry laugh barks from my chest. *Okay, so not only are you scary, you're stupid. Got it.*

The Tracer was with her. As well as her guardian.

Her what? Who is that?

His gaze shifts toward GrimBite and back. *Time wears thin. You must hurry.*

No, you need to answer me.

I answer to no one. He looms over me. *I have been here since since the beginning. I am nearly one hundred times your age. Be grateful I am on your side, for now.*

Holy shit, is he serious? He sniffs the air again, gaze narrowing.

You are intended to keep her darkness in check. I hope for all werewolf kind you are stronger than you appear.

The fuck?! Rage bubbles under my skin, my beast taking over. *First off, if you really didn't think I was strong enough, you'd have killed me.*

Is he shrinking? No, I'm growing. Good.

Second, I growl as adrenaline tears through me, *you should be grateful I don't rip your eyes out for laying a claw on my pack member.*

He is not bound to you, yet. However, he leans closer, giant teeth on display, *it seems the goddess may have a chance, yet.*

Goddess?

My pulse slams. He can't mean—

To answer your question, it doesn't matter to me. Either way it goes, we were here before, we will be here after. I offered to help the Tracer out of curiosity. This is the first time the vessels have created life, and it could change things. Even though it is unlikely she will complete her plan to finally live among the werewolves…she is nothing if not persistent.

A goddess. My Reanne? I want to shout at him that it's a stupid thought, that it makes no sense, but it doesn't feel wrong. All I can picture is how fucking beautiful she looked with that moonlight around her, and my heart flip tells me everything I need to know. It doesn't matter what she is, or who, she's mine.

How'd you find out about all this?

We were made by her hand.

Yeah, yeah, I know all that, legend and whatever.

You are not listening, High Alpha. He steps closer. *We. Were. made. By her hand. I remember life as a wolf. I remember that life ending and the agony of change. I remember being haunted by the shame of being declared a failure by my own creator. She wanted more than this.* He gestures to his chest. *We cannot become men as you can. We cannot talk, as you can. We are this, nothing more. It was not enough for the goddess, so she attempted it again. And again.*

There's an angry curl of his lip and flash in his eyes.

And again. Until she created a version she was happy with. One she could love.

He pokes the center of my chest, and I'm too lost in the story to even react.

The one for whom you are a vessel.

Bits and pieces that feel like memories hit me again, but they're all blurry.

"Hey, uh, Cyan? What's going on? What's he saying?"

Jak's voice snaps us both out of the past.

We will watch the path after you go, as the TalonWhisper are under our protection, but pray you never see us again. If you do, it will spell doom.

He closes his eyes, hiding his location, and in less time than it all started, they're gone. Even the spears have vanished, without a single sound. The area around us is brighter, even though the moon hasn't changed at all. Shit, how many of them were there?

Jak stumbles toward me, and I snag him in a hug without a second thought. I'm so sick of people threatening my family. He squeezes my waist, digging his fingertips into my skin.

"Those were the…Shadow something, right?"

I grunt and release him, checking his neck for damage. "ShadowMane."

"I thought they were just a story." He steps back, scanning the empty area.

Hm, maybe he's still worried. "Very real. And they're gone."

There's so fucking much to process. I rub my temples and crouch, resting my elbows on my knees. Jak matches my position and cups my shoulder.

"Whatever you said to him worked, Mister Alpha. Thanks for saving me."

"You're welcome, but he wasn't gonna hurt you. They wanted to help you get to The Spire so you could be in place for the vessels. Reanne and me."

"Oh."

I glance up just as his expression falls. I lift my brows. "Got anything to add?"

"Heh, pff, not a thing, man." He quickly grins, gifting the world with his dimples again. "Should head back, though. Good news is the traps are all triggered, so even though I can't make more light, we'll be okay."

But neither of us move. He looks like he's lost in his thoughts, and I can't shake what the Alpha said. It's one thing to have a whole dumb story that explains where we came from, but to hear it differently, firsthand... I don't know what to think.

"Hey, what's wrong?"

"Apparently," I exhale loudly, "Reanne's going to be a goddess. That's what her change is, I guess. I don't fucking know. He also said he was made by her, but they weren't perfect, so she kept trying. That I'm the vessel for the one she got right. Which, we know who that is."

"Yeah, Kasimir."

I nod, "Said this is part of a plan to live among us. I'm just... confused as hell."

"I didn't know there was anyone before him," Jak says, frowning.

"More than one, if he's not lying."

Jak's gaze drifts again, the frown deepening until he pops up.

"That's all in the past anyhow. No sense being sad over it. The future's sad enough." He mutters that last bit, before he thrusts out his hand. "Whatever else happens, man, I'll make sure you're both where you're supposed to be when the time comes. Jak's on the job. Now, whaddya say we go get our little goddess?"

Warmth spreads through my chest like a wildfire. He's damn right. She already is a little goddess.

NEO

What a messed-up day. We've all been through a hell of a lot, but the sex was honestly worth it. And Jak... holy hell. Ugh, I'm getting hard again.

"Laz," Korey calls, walking backward away from us.

"Yes?" He lets his hand slip away from Reanne's arm.

"Come sit with me, pup."

"O-okay. Are you good?"

Aeon utters, "Mmhmm," flicking his thumb up.

My chance to try and make things right with Lazaros is finally here. I clear my throat. "Thank you for helping, Laz. You're a great guy."

He gives me a genuine smile and nods a couple of times. "Ah, you are, oh, and you, not to say one and not the oth—though anyone can see you're both—"

"Pup," Korey chuckles.

"Right." Laz waves and all but dashes toward Korey, taking his outstretched hand.

I breathe a laugh, shaking my head as I catch movement by the hatch. Veikko. He's alternating between staring at nothing and staring at the moon.

An annoyed huff escapes.

Veikko has no right to be as sexy as he is. I could have lived the rest of my life without knowing how attractive he looked, grinding and lost in pleasure while hovering over me. Yes, he was technically fucking our mate, but I felt his cock. What am I supposed to do with that knowledge, kicking around in my brain?

I have no idea what we're going to do about the bond with him, either, but more important than that, what the heck are Aeon and I now? I mean. I know how I feel about him. I think I know how he feels about me. I guess there's only one way to find out.

One hand cradling Reanne's head, I hook my other arm around Aeon's waist and rest that hand on his hip. He flinches. He actually flinches.

Okay, obviously we need to talk.

About what? How you mated me without asking?

I snatch my arm away like he burned me. *What the hell? You mated me, Aeon.*

His lip curls around Reanne's skin. *No, I didnt. I'm mated to her, why would I want to mate anyone else?*

So am I! What makes you think I would want anyone else, either?

I almost say, especially a jerk like you, but I don't mean that. I take a slow breath instead.

Look, I continue, *I think it's clear what happened.*

Clear as mud.

I ignore the snipe and touch his lower back again. He growls but doesn't say anything else. He also doesn't jerk away from my touch.

What are you so mad about?

I don't… his eyes close, harsh air shooting out of his nose. *I don't know.*

His skin heats just slightly under my touch before he snarls again.

No. You know what? I do know. We're supposed to get one chance to share our soul with a mate. One. And I gave mine to Reanne, who doesn't remember a single second of it. I got no rush of love, none of the contact buzz, nothing. I don't regret it, I love her, and I came to terms with it. Then, by some miracle of fate, something in her damn blood I guess, I'm able to mate again, but guess what, I didn't have a say in who it was, or when!

I stare at the tear clinging to his eyelid, surrounded by a low grumble. My heart squeezes, pain leeching through my blood.

And you wish it wasn't me.

The grumble stops, his eyes widening as he stares into the darkness. *That's not what I said.*

It's what you mean, though.

Damn it. I take another slow breath. This could spiral fast. I don't want to hurt his feelings. He died, and lost his beast, so I know he's stretched thin. I also don't wanna piss him off enough he lets go of Reanne too early, and we let Cyan down. Time to switch tactics.

Are you forgetting you can't mate by force? Reanne might not remember it, but she agreed on some subconscious level. Deep in her soul, she welcomed you. But that also means whether you admit it or not, you wanted to mate me as bad as I wanted to mate you. I don't understand how it happened, but I don't really care. We're mates, so…fucking deal with it.

He blinks the tear free as he flicks his gaze to me. *You wanted to mate me?*

I don't know why that's so hard for him to believe. I lean in and drag my teeth across his neck.

Yep. Guess what else? I love you and her and Cyan. Not a damn thing you can do about that, either.

He blows a breath against her skin, swallowing a lump. *It's just hard. You were my friend. I guess I'm worried that's gonna change, now.*

Why would it? I grin. *You're still a numbnuts who can't cook.*

He barks a startlingly loud trio of laughs, warming my heart. *And you're still a food obsessed perfectionist.*

I'm a hot, food obsessed perfectionist, though.

I trail up to his jaw, planting a firm kiss on his now pinker cheek.

Yeah, he says with a smaller swallow. *You are.*

I wasn't lying about the magic mouth, either. No wonder you're Cy's favorite.

Don't do that.

I shrug, even though it feels like nails are lodged in my throat. *It's true, you can't deny it. He said he talks to you.*

Yeah, you wanna know what about? You!

My pulse soars. *Me?*

Yes. Neo this. Neo that. There hasn't been a single fuck where you haven't been mentioned at least once. And he takes everything he can out on me, so he can be softer with you. If anyone's the favorite, it's you.

I blink at him. I could argue for the rest of my life that he's wrong, but... Cyan mentioned me. It sucks it takes so much work for Cy to be with me, but at least now I have Aeon and Reanne. I won't tell him Cy never talked about him, because he never really talks at all. Why would I? It would only hurt him, and that's the last thing I want to do. Especially now.

Okay. Maybe neither of us are the favorites. And this is probably not healthy. Based on how he reacts to seeing us together, I think separate might be a thing of the past, anyway. So, I hope being with me isn't a problem.

His brow bunches. *It's not a problem. I'd suck your cock right now if I could.*

Lust rockets through me.

The drive to give him what he needs is even stronger now that we're mated. Being submissive comes second nature to me, no doubt, but as barky as Aeon is, he's even more of a sub than I am.

I run my tongue over his lip, tasting both him and Reanne's salty skin. Having two mates may, or may not, be giving me confidence.

Too bad your mouth is occupied, then.

He whimpers, the sound barely skating on his breath.

When Cy told you to grab her throat, I literally thought I was going to pass out.

I laugh, reaching between his body and Reanne's, fisting his hard cock with a tight grip.

Were you jealous?

His pupils darken. *A little.*

I'll choke you later while I'm fucking you, how about that?

His lids flutter, the whimper turning to a deep groan. The sound of victory if you ask me.

Shit, are you trying to kill me? It's hard enough to keep this bite tight.

My grin spreads wider. This is going to be way more fun than I ever expected.

Hey.

I pick my head up, finding his gaze.

I...think I love you, too.

I can't help my laugh. *You think?*

Don't be an ass. He grins as best he can, and I grin right back.

Just so you know, we're gonna have to do something about your cabin. I'm not having sex in a pit of trash.

A flush explodes on his face, grin falling. Heat wiggles through my chest, my whole body warming.

Was that...was that him? I can't believe he figured out how to do that first! We don't even have marks, how did he—

I growl with a smile, settling my teeth on the side of his neck, and send as much love as I can through the contact.

His knees buckle, bite slipping a bit. Definite victory. Loving Aeon will be a constant competition, and I couldn't be happier. Reanne stirs and we both readjust.

Sorry, I laugh, as I kiss her chin. *You know, we're really lucky.*

Yeah, we are.

I rest my cheek against hers, staring at Aeon's handsome face.

If she hadn't come here, this would have never happened, would it?

He blinks at me, brows tilting. *Probably not. Things would have stayed exactly like they were for who knows how long.*

His expression saddens even more. I bet I know what he's thinking. I lay a gentle kiss on his shoulder. *We'll figure out how to get your beast back, don't worry. I'll help however I can, and you know everyone else will, too.*

I know. He locks eyes with me again, setting my pulse spinning. *Thanks, Neo.*

Anytime—Oh, hey. A wicked grin hits my mouth. *You need a nickname.*

He groans, rolling his eyes up and holding them there.

Yesss, this is happening. How about—

Immediate no. Any name at all-no.

I bust out laughing, drawing everyone's attention. With a happy hum, I pull my glasses off and rub my nose on his cheek, making a huge show out of it.

I hate you, he sneers, even though he's chuckling in his throat.

Sure you do. As soon as your mouth is free, I'm going to shove my tongue in it, right here in front of everyone. We'll see if you hate me, then.

He loses his breath, cock twitching, and I'm pretty sure life is going to be a hell of a lot better from here on out. For everyone. And it's all thanks to Reanne.

CYAN

I slap Jakobe's palm and clasp tightly. With a quick jerk, I'm on my feet.

"See ya down the rabbit hole," he mutters.

I frown at him as he drops into the darkness, before letting my gaze sweep up to the moon. I sure as fuck don't wish I hadn't met Reanne, but I do wish this wasn't all so damn complicated.

Heaving a sigh, I drop down after him, following into the pitch black. His falling expression flashes in my mind. I may not be able to read him like I can my pack, but I can tell he's hiding something.

Once we're out of the moon's reach, I grab his arm, lowering my voice. "What aren't you telling me?"

"Ah…it's nothing I don't think. I just… I swear I felt…"

He cuts himself off with a sniffle, so I loosen my grip a bit. "Felt what, Jak?"

"Agnar."

My stomach hollows out. Jak spins and collides with my chest again, hugging me tight as he cries. Here, in this damp, dirty tunnel, away from anyone's line of sight, I don't fight the tears that swell in my eyes.

"Grief will fuck with your head," I mutter.

"Maybe. It was so strong though, for just a second. I…I really thought I could save him," he sobs, "but I couldn't. Kasimir jumped in me, man. I had all that power and so what?" A big sniffle. "He left, went into Agnar's body instead."

With a heavy sigh, he pulls back. "Sorry, I'm okay."

His sorrow is almost filling this whole tunnel. He's nearly out of my embrace before I kick myself into action. I shouldn't, I really fucking shouldn't. For damn's sake, he doesn't even know if he can eat raw meat while shifted, but I grab his face and plant an energy heavy kiss square on his mouth.

He manages a muffled sound, before grinning against my lips and pushing back with more force than I expected. He grabs my face, too, and he's doing more crazy stuff with my energy. I can feel him tugging at it, taking it in huge gulps, or rejecting it completely, like he's...he's...ha. The little fucker.

I pull back and grip his chin hard. "You're playing with my energy, aren't you?"

"Just a tiny bit. Sorry. Energy's my—"

"Thing, yeah." I chuckle. "I remember. Here I am tryna make you feel better and you're frog-hopping in my damn wave."

He laughs, and since he can't see, I grin from ear to ear.

"I mean, it did make me feel better."

"Uh huh. Walk."

"It did, I promise, man. Made you feel better, too, though, right?"

I grumble and spin him, giving his shoulder a shove, sending him deeper into the tunnel.

"My man." He laughs again. "Whaddya know, kissing Jak is the official cure for sadness now, too."

"Stop talking, Jakobe."

"Alright, alright, but if you ever need another pick me up, Ol' Jak is here for you."

I stop replying, because I can't stop grinning, and he'd hear it in my voice. We go a few hundred feet or so in silence, before he sighs.

"Are we gonna tell Reanne?"

That sucks the humor away.

"Which part, that we couldn't find Yuli? Or that you thought you smelled Agnar?"

"...either."

I rub my face, deep in thought. With as much shit as I've

given my pack about keeping things from me, the fact I'm seriously considering keeping it to myself is making my skin crawl.

I guess Jak can tell I'm having trouble with it because he reaches back and pats my side.

"Just the Yuli part. Like you said, grief probably. No reason to make a big ol' fuss for nothing, right?"

"Right."

No matter how much I wish Agnar was still alive, facts are facts.

"There we go," Jak continues. "Now you can go back to thinking about kissing me."

I smirk and push him a step forward. "You wish."

"Heck yeah, I do. So, what about the goddess part? Are you gonna tell her that?"

"She needs to know."

Jak doesn't say anything at first, our steps through the dirt the only sound. Another bit of the conversation flits into memory.

"He said she wasn't in danger, because you and her guardian were with her."

I bump into Jak's now immobile body, backing up a step as he turns.

"She was in a ton of danger. Her energy was all over the place, flaring up to the sky. And she went full black eyed crazy there for a bit. It was bad."

"Who is her guardian?"

"I dunno, man. Unless he means the stardude, Evrik."

Evrik again. He and I have to talk.

"You met him?"

"I sure did. He's a good-looking guy. Coolest skin I've ever seen. And he loves her like crazy. Or...I guess, the old her? Huh. New her? Whichever. Hey, that would fit with the goddess thing, wouldn't it? Yo! Maybe he knows more about all of that stuff. He's supposed to come back, we should ask him."

Oh yeah. We definitely have to fucking chat.

Jak turns and starts walking again. "If he was an Alpha, do you think his pups would do the disappearing thing, too? Can't for the life of me picture that. Fuzzy little half monsters just popping all over the place."

My blood freezes right along with my heart. Blistering heat chases the cold away, burning me all the way to my damn soul.

Pups. Life.

He said—

Fuck, I might puke. Can you puke from excitement? I grip the back of my neck and brace on the cool, dirt wall.

New life. He said none of the other vessels had created new life.

Does…does that mean Reanne's pregnant?

I'm gonna be a dad?

My knees nearly give.

Okay, fucking breathe. How would that guy know anyway? Maybe he's wrong. But he's old as all hell, and apparently has different abilities.

I'm gonna be a dad.

I nearly laugh out loud but bite my tongue instead.

How though? We were outside of The Glade. We're not supposed to be able to get humans preg…

Fuck a frog, she's not fully human. Not if she's gonna hold a whole damn goddess. Holy shit! Reanne's pregnant!

All my happy feelings flatten. What if…she doesn't want to be pregnant? She might hate the idea of having my pups. Any pups!

My heart falls straight to my toes. What if she can't survive it? If this kills her I can't imagine how we'll all live without her now.

No, wait. She's not just an Aruna, she's the Rigdis, too, plus a goddess, and oh my fuck she's going to have my pups.

Light flares in my face, illuminating a concerned Jak. "Man, what's going on? Your energy is—" The light dims, flickering out, but not before I see his expression change. "Are you gonna be sick?"

Of all the fucking feelings I'm having right now, the loudest one is a burst of jealousy. I'm not telling Jak. Little sex fiend would tie himself to her, and I'd never get a second alone. And definitely not tell him before she even finds out.

"Did I say something wrong? Are you mad at me? Lemme see, what did I say."

Shit!

"Stop talking, Jak. Move."

"You got it, man. I can think and walk. Jak's got skills. So, I said something about Evrik's skin. And the disappearing thing."

"Jak," I growl, shoving him hard.

"No worries, Mister Alpha, I'll just think in my head, then."

"Don't," I snap, "don't think. Or… think about something else."

"Wait, was it the pup thing?"

"Jak, I will throw you into the Quay myself if you don't stop."

"Why would that—" He sucks in a deep breath. "Is *that* what I felt mixed up with her energy? I wondered what was up. Wow, I didn't know I could pick out a… Hey, maybe that's why Aeon and Neo—" His voice drops three whole levels, a deep growl underneath, "Reanne's pregnant?"

I hear bits of dirt falling, more and more, until it sounds like he's literally tearing the walls apart.

"Calm the fuck down, you can't shift in here."

"I'm trying," he snarls. "It's…not listening."

I swing in the dark until I connect with him. Shit, he's already furred out. Grabbing his throat, I force him down to his knees, blasting my Alpha wave as hard as I can. He's not pack, but Alpha is Alpha. Last thing I need is for him to destroy this stupid tunnel.

It takes only another few seconds for the muscles under my palm to stop rippling, replaced by heavy breaths. His skin returns to normal, and he grips my wrist.

"Okay," he gasps, "I'm good."

I don't let go.

"Listen to me. Don't you say a fucking word until I tell her. Am I clear?"

"Yeah, totally, you got it," he ekes out. "Not a word, I promise, man."

Slowly, I unclench my fist until he's able to wrench himself backward.

"She's pregnant," he whispers, getting louder as he continues, "She's pregnant. Cyan, you're gonna be a dad!"

"I…" A smile spreads on my face, and I can't force it away. Fuck, I don't want to.

"Yeah."

"We've gotta get back. Hurry up, man!"

He speeds away, and once I'm sure my legs will work, I follow.

"I can't wait for everyone else to find out."

Damn, that's right. Everyone else will be all over her, too.

"I want to tell her away from the pack."

"Oh yeah? I guess that makes sense, okay. Whatever makes you happy, man, I'm all for it." He adds under his breath, "Mmm. I can't wait."

"Have to tell her about Yuli, first. Which fucking sucks."

"Dang, that's right. Well, start with the bad news, end with the best news that exists ever. She'll be good, I know it."

I damn sure hope so.

We both fall quiet. My thoughts rage the rest of the trip, and when the exit is finally visible again in the distance, the silence we'd been in turns heavy. I grab his hand and squeeze reassuringly. For him, for me, who fucking knows. All I do know is it doesn't work at all.

Now it's not just her, and my whole pack I have to protect, which was more than important enough. Now, it's her, my whole pack, and my unborn pup.

If anyone thought they'd seen protective and possessive before, they're about to meet a brand fucking new Cyan.

VEIKKO

block Neo and Aeon's conversation out of respect. Their trials are not my concern. The burgeoning pack bond, however, is. I wish Cyan hadn't forced my Alpha to the surface.

I can't help but wonder if my interference had something to do with their unexpected mating. I don't know how it could have, and we are surrounded by one odd, reality-altering occurrence after another, but I still wonder.

I know Reanne and I share a mate bond, but now I worry about getting too close for this same reason. My love for her feeds a once non-existent desire to form a pack of my own, with her at the center. If I lose control for a fraction of a second, it could all be over.

Yet another way my presence proves a possible burden.

My gaze lifts again, and I tilt my head.

Hmm. I dare not point it out, because I doubt anyone other than me can see it, but the moon has…changed. It seems rounder, if by just a hair. There's a slight change in color, a wobble in the halo. What this spells for Reanne and Cyan, the coming ritual… I'm not sure.

A breeze curls in from the forest, leaves caught in the draft slithering through the camp. The quiet here is…unusual. Perhaps I just miss the gurgle of our stream, the croak of familiar frogs. Or, perhaps The Glade itself prepares for a new beginning.

I can't believe I lived long enough to see the new day I tried so hard to stop. Agnar should have been here with me.

Eoghan flits back into my memories, dragging the past with

him. His words laced with dark promises of what that day might bring, sounding in my head as if he's still here. *It isn't right, why does she get special treatment, death should be the end.*

I was barely over two hundred and fifty when we met. Alone. Lost. He was such a voice of reason. Much of who I am today formed around his mould, solidifying during the years we spent together.

I treasured those times for over a thousand years, but now… now I wish we'd never met. Because I never formed my own thoughts, simply clung to his.

With a huff, I track the leaves as they twist farther away, dancing over my runes.

You were changed without your consent, his voice whispers in my memories again. While true, and while I let that fuel centuries of unnecessary anger, my magic has proved useful. Even if I only have it because the goddess tried—and failed—to save my father.

Eoghan taught me how to harness the power, manipulate it. I still don't know how he came by that knowledge, but it didn't matter then, and it hardly matters now.

Damn. I wish Jak were here to quiet these thoughts. I've spent too many years in my own mind.

Life was easier after Eoghan vanished, before I rejoined pack life, before I met werewolves I cared about. Werewolves who inevitably leave.

My thoughts turn darker, turn toward my imprisonment in Fen's nightmare, and I can't stop the panic that rises in my throat. He's dead. He shouldn't still have a hold over my brain. I—

Jakobe appears when I most need him, yet again, his attractive, dirt-smeared face popping up out of the hole.

The panic ebbs, leaving just a tremble of adrenaline in my muscles.

I'm the first place he looks, the first recipient of his sunshine smile. "Hey, Honeybear. Miss me?"

"Yes." I shouldn't be surprised how quickly it comes out, but I am.

He drops the playful expression and hoists himself out of the hole. After a weighted gaze at Reanne, Neo, and Aeon, he clears the distance between us in two strides. Wrapping his arms around my waist, he whispers, "What's wrong?"

"Nothing now." I tip his chin up and kiss him, pouring my Alpha energy over him out of reflex. He hums, grinning against my mouth, before he somehow splits my wave in half. It goes around him, a stick in a stream, and I quickly stop.

"I get too much more Alpha in me tonight, I'm either gonna pop out a litter or set up my own pack."

The smile that forms on my face is his alone, but it falls when he grabs my arm and pulls me a few steps away from the hole.

Cyan hops out, and surveys the group, taking stock as he plops his hands on his hips and breathes.

Did you find him?

Korey asks as he and Laz move closer, but Cy shakes his head.

"HB, listen." I refocus on Jak. "I don't wanna tell you this because it's probably nothing, but I also wanna tell you because I wanna tell you everything."

He's visibly distraught, but also excited. A strange combination.

I cup his face. "What?"

"I felt his energy out there. I was thinking maybe some of his got mixed up with Yuli's, like Reanne's did. But what if maybe..."

Hope for Agnar doesn't live within me. I know what I felt.

"Kasimir using his body could have scattered his energy to the eight points. You may feel him for days. Weeks. Decades."

"Oh." Every bit of light drains out of him. "I hadn't thought about that. Y-you're right. Makes...total sense. Hey, thanks for setting me straight, there."

He tries to smile, but it wobbles.

"Today was hard, Jakobe." I tug him into a hug. "We are all missing him. Some, more than others. I'm sorry your grief is so raw."

"Pff, I'm fine. Jak is unstoppable. I know something else, something good, really damn good, but Cy made my promise not to tell anyone. Just know, if he hadn't done that, I'd have already told you."

I smile again, releasing him. "Thank you."

"Anything at all for my Honeybear."

"Aeon," Cyan exhales, cracking his neck. "Time to wake her up."

Jak squeezes my arm as he leaves, taking up position beside Cyan. They share a look, while my attention veers back to the moon.

Only a handful of days stand between life as we've known it and something completely different. I fear for us.

REANNE

I have no idea how long it's been, but by the time Aeon eases his bite free and licks the wound, Cyan is standing right beside us, dark dirt smeared across his body in various places, bloody areas on his neck, gaze fierce and shadowed.

My vision clears with each blink, and Jak comes into view, just as dirtied but staring at me with the hungriest stare I've ever seen.

Aeon stumbles a bit, releasing me and giving his head a shake. "Whew. I was starting to wonder if you guys were coming back. You feel okay, ReeRee?"

Not…really. I feel like it was the worst night's sleep ever, out but no rest at all. The don't need to know that, though. They're all worried enough as it is. I nod slightly, and he gives me a hungry kiss.

"Welcome back," Neo says, smoothing my hair away from my face. He takes Aeon's place in front of me and claims my mouth as well, sending love straight to my heart.

After leaving no doubt how he feels about me, he steps back with a smile and faces Aeon.

"Your turn," Neo mutters, grabbing him by the face and kissing him even deeper. Aeon groans, wrapping his arms around Neo's waist, their love for each other pinging through their marks again.

Cyan's gaze cuts to them, jaw jumping before he refocuses on me.

I swallow, feeling a little queasy despite how hot it is to see them together. "How long…"

335

"Don't worry about that." Cy's gruff, but his expression softens as he steps against me and cups my cheeks. My eyelids flutter, his intoxicating scent sweeping through me, his thick, brilliant energy settling in my bones.

"Fuck, I love you so much," he whispers.

Emotion clogs my throat, as I cover his hands with mine. "I love you, too."

"Bad news first." We both take a steadying breath. "He got away. But we know where he's going. Mark my fucking words, Reanne, I'm going to find him, and when I do, I'll shove that dagger so far down his throat he'll shit nails."

A shiver winds through my muscles, and my darkness bubbles back to life as a faint, familiar echo teases my ears.

"Okay. I...I believe you."

Cyan strokes his thumbs along my skin, drawing my attention, but when his mouth opens again, Veikko speaks instead.

"Where does it lead?"

"The tunnel comes out at, you know, that spot at GrimBite and TalonWhisper." Jak runs his fingers through his hair with a sigh, brushing dirt from his neck.

"The Crossmark?"

"Yeah," he smiles at Vik, quickly letting it fall. "Yuli's... energy was heading straight for GrimBite."

"Auch, that's good." Laz visibly relaxes. "I-I've met a TalonWhisper. Well, I've seen one. There's one in Mishka's, ah, collection. Orden. Lovely hair. Uh," he clears his throat, "r-regardless, I don't think they'd be able to fight off an ant, alone an Alpha like this Yuli chap."

"That must be why they're guarded by the ShadowMane," Cy rumbles.

"ShadowMane? Afraid I haven't heard of that lot. Are they—"

"Dangerous fuckers who can't talk, but get near them and you're face first with the darkness, and a spear digging into the back of your skull." Cy rubs his face, smearing a bit of dirt down his cheek.

If someone as strong as Cy thinks these guys are dangerous, I'm not sure I want to meet them.

"Listen, Reanne. I need to…" he exhales and glances around.

Something is weighing on him, I can feel it. I curl my arms around his neck, squeaking when he hugs my ribs and picks me up.

"Shit." He quickly sets me down, resting his scalding palm on my stomach, eyes as big as dinner plates. "Was that too rough?"

"Too rough for what?" I chuckle. "Getting railed by giant cocks counts as way rougher than a hug."

Jak snickers, the rest of the pack chuckling.

But Cy's face turns a weird color, illuminated by the crackling firelight behind us. Why is he so worried?

"I'm okay! Really. I was a bit tender, but since I've apparently got super healing, I'm all good."

He nods, hand still on my stomach.

I've never seen him like this, it's a little unnerving. I bunch my brows and rest my hand on his. "What's wrong?"

His yummy bottom lip disappears under his teeth, so I stroke his cheek.

"We'll be okay," I whisper, "whatever it is, I love you, we love you, and we'll handle it together."

He buries his face against my neck, under my hair, drawing an inhale along my skin before leaning back just enough to hold my gaze.

"Love you, too. More than you possibly fucking know."

He glances around again at the guys, pursing his lips.

"Is it something you want to tell me later?" I whisper.

Grateful is the best way to describe his expression. "Yeah. It's nothing bad, so don't worry. 'Least I hope you don't think it's bad. Fuck, I don't know. Never mind, don't worry."

I chuckle and tug him in for another kiss. "Okay, I won't."

"Good. Okay, so, you know how that shit stain Zaid talked about The Spire?"

I nod.

"It's in GrimBite territory. Yuli's probably planning something there. Besides, that look-alike fucker said his pack is prepared for you, too."

He pauses, and a sinking feeling hits my stomach, immediately followed by a small spark of hope.

"They'll have answers."

Cy doesn't say anything.

"You…want to go after him now, want us all to go."

He stares at me a moment, chewing his cheek. "I don't want that. I *want* to go home and fuck every one of you until we all pass out. But he doesn't get to live after what he did."

"I agree." Jak's voice is so haunted, my breath catches.

"Which means I'm going after him. And where I go, you go, and my pack goes."

He strokes my stomach of all places, and my heart lurches, that sense of belonging sweeping over me, chased by the choking fear of losing it all again.

Jak and Veikko are still staring at each other, like they're having a whole conversation with their eyes. He casts a furtive glance at me, then back at Vik.

Is he hiding something? No. Why would he do that? Grief and fear are probably clouding any judgement I might have been able to scrape up before finding out Yuli isn't dead.

Going after him feels like inviting a snake to bite me, but I know I need some sort of closure. Maybe I can find a way to send him wherever it is he wants to go back to so badly. Not that he deserves my help, but I feel guilty. Besides, if Mishka's pack is waiting for me, even if they're bad, I won't be alone this time. My family will protect me, I know it.

Cyan cups my cheek with his free hand, and I smile. Tilting my face, I snag the side of it in the same nibble he did the night we met. Reactions sweep his face, but ultimately, he settles into determination again.

"GrimBite it is, then. Alpha."

That gets a more defined reaction, his trademark snarling smile lifting his lip as he grips my face and steals my soul with a kiss. I'm panting and flushed by the time he pulls back.

"Everyone, stay together, no straggling. It's a helluva long walk." He gives my face a parting pat and holds my hand, tugging me along. "Can't take the tunnel, Vik won't fit. I barely did."

"W-wait, I, uh, Reanne. Please take this." Laz appears at my side, holding his white t-shirt out to me, one arm around his now bare torso. "I'm-I'm afraid you won't take to the snow without any clothes."

"Oh my God, thank you! Are you sure?" I release Cy's hand and hastily jerk the shirt on, letting out a happy sigh. It's not long on me, hitting only at my waist, but it's a shirt!

He grins and nods, adjusting the band of his pants a bit higher. "Least I can do, innit? We can get you lots more once we get there. All of you, in fact. Ooh, I can't wait."

He's so excited, I can't help but giggle. "That sounds fun. Thank you again."

"Very welcome indeed!"

He steps away but my gaze can't leave Cyan's heated one. He hooks his finger under the hem, using it to pull me closer. "And I cannot fucking wait," he murmurs hot in my ear, "to bury myself in you for the rest of my life."

My heart hiccups, and I cling to his shoulder as he glides scalding kisses down my neck. With a long growl, he pulls back, nipping at my lip before tugging me along again.

I glance back over my shoulder at everyone falling in line, eyes on the two of us. Well, except for Aeon, busy staring at random places, led by Neo's gentle hand.

"Reanne."

My nerves blister to life as I refocus on Cy's glowing eyes.

"I love the way you say my name," I whisper, swallowing as I squeeze his hand tighter.

He chuckles, wiping the smile away. "Ready to go?"

After meeting everyone's gaze one at a time, I finally nod. "Yeah. Let's get out of here."

Cyan shifts in front of me again, changing bit by bit, arms and legs first, body second, head last. I crane my neck to hold the golden glow of his eyes.

He picks me up, cradling me so gently I half think he's convinced my bones are brittle. God, I love how their fur feels. I know it's not soft, but it's familiar, and warm. I yawn, nuzzling deeper into his embrace as we begin the journey.

I wake up shivering. I'm snuggled in Cyan's arms still, warm everywhere we touch, but the weather turned cold at some point. There's a nip in the air, biting at my bare skin. The shirt is helping, but not nearly enough.

I'm utterly exhausted, even though I napped. And starving, oh my God. Dinner and about twenty-nine hours of sleep. That's what I need now.

A shiver hits every muscle in my body at once, prompting Cy to squeeze me tighter. "G-god it's cold."

"We're almost there, I'm sad, and glad to say." Laz calls from the back of the line with Korey.

"I recognize…these trees." Cyan growls, sending a different shiver through me. I scrape my nails over his chest, fighting the ache in my body.

He stops suddenly, holding me tighter still, so possessive I'll no doubt have bruises.

I twist in his grip until I'm facing the front, and suck in a sharp breath.

Hundreds of bodies spill out of the forest, various states of dress, all eyeing us warily. Neo and Aeon step to our right,

Veikko and Jakobe to our immediate left, and Korey clutching Laz beside them.

No one says a word, until Cyan almost drops me, and Aeon staggers a bit.

He shifts around me, adjusting me back into a fireman's carry once he's fully in man form. "Shit," he mutters.

One by one, every man drops to a knee, bowing their head. "Welcome home, Alpha," bounces from mouth to mouth, dancing across the snow, whirling around us.

There's something thick in the air, a feeling I can't quite—nerves. It's like an entire blanket of nerves, covering the forest.

Cyan sets me down, stepping in front of me, and takes Aeon's hand. With an apologetic glance my way, which I don't understand, he faces the crowd.

His Alpha energy blasts out, sweeping the forest floor, mixed with Aeon's hyper-loaded Beta wave. I stagger back into Neo's waiting arms, and he holds me gently.

Every expression changes from apprehension to wide-eyed wonder. They glance at each other, clearly unsure what they're supposed to do now.

"What's going on?" I whisper to Neo, but it's Cy who turns to answer, heartbreak deep in his eyes.

"I killed Mishka." His voice is haunted. "I killed their Alpha. They…this is now our pack."

I can't tell if that's a bad thing or a good thing, what that'll mean for us, for SteelTooth as a whole.

There's a beat of heavy silence, punctuated only by our breathing, little puffs of cloud against the frigid air, before Jak whistles.

"Gonna need more than one massive bed now. I call dibs on the main one, though. Wherever Reanne is, that's my new home. Hey, you think they have—"

I can't hear him anymore, all sound replaced by a whine in my head. Something's not right. Or…too right. I don't—I don't know.

There's a weirdly familiar energy in this group, hiding, and something is calling to me in the distance, a heavy pull.

Glancing around the bodies knelt in deference, my awareness snags on a pair of eyes aimed at me, a ball of heat blooming inside.

He's strikingly handsome, in a dark kind of way, with a strong, angled jaw, defined lips, thick arched brows, and sinewy muscles on arms visible under a fur-lined, leather-vest-style shirt, open at the neck, revealing a single tooth hanging from a black cord. Dark wash jeans, and cold-weather boots of some kind, topped with fur, complete his look. He quirks a brow at me but doesn't smile.

I don't get a good or bad feeling from him, just...familiar. And there's a definite curling toward him.

I frown, even though my body reacts again. Not really sure how I feel about any new mates. Can I ignore the call? Do I have to take a mate if I feel it? Does he feel the same thing I do? So many questions.

Severing the gaze, I scan the horizon until my eyes land on a stunning woman leaned against a tree—not kneeling for the new Alpha. She has the build of a barbarian combined with an amazon and a viking. Tall and muscular, broad-shouldered, with long, bright silver hair, running in a fishtail braid down the top of her head and flowing loose around her neck and back. The sides are shaved close, with a few strands framing her face, adorned with beads of some sort. There's a furry grey pelt draped over one of her shoulders, a plain white tunic-style shirt under that, cinched with a brown belt, over skin-tight dark brown pants. They lead to matching combat boots half-lodged in the snow, like she's been standing there for a long time.

Goodness. She's absolutely gorgeous.

My mouth dries. She shoves away from the tree, gaze locked on me as she tromps toward us with loud steps, making no attempt at masking her approach in the slightest. A low murmur travels the pack, but I have no idea what they're saying. Once she's closer, I can tell only part of her was the pull, there's still something—or someone else—out there.

"Oh, t-that's your—"

"Suzette?" Korey's voice is barely a whisper yet so loud it's like a crack against my skull.

She stops, breath leaving her as she finally looks his way, breaking the tension between us. "Dad?"

He rushes her, grabbing her in a bear hug, even though she's clearly uncomfortable with the contact. She hangs, stiff as a board in his hold.

"I thought you were dead. My pup, we looked for you everywhere."

"Not everywhere," she mutters, stepping back and fixing her shirt. "I've been in this bloody shit-heap the whole time."

That hits Korey hard. He hangs his head a little, rubbing the back of his neck. "I didn't think of anyone stealing you, we thought you'd just run off."

"It's fine." She smiles, but it's clearly forced, pain evident in her eyes.

"I'm sorry, Suzy."

"Don't—" She growls with a snarl, dropping it the next second. "Don't call me that."

She doesn't say anything else as she finishes her path to me. Air gets thinner as she looms over me, brilliant violet eyes burning into mine. She's almost as big as Cyan, and as broad and defined as Jak. An absolute monument. I've never been this close to a woman her size in my life. She snaps a strand on the pelt, and it falls into her waiting hand. I stutter a small gasp as she wraps it around my waist, her icy, rough fingers dancing along my hip as she ties it into place.

"There you are, poppet," she murmurs with a smirk.

Ahh, these butterflies are going to kill me. The old part of me wants to freak out that I'm feeling something for a woman, but the rest of me, the parts rooted in this new world, my new identity, are completely okay with it.

Each of my mates ping their marks like they're testing the connection. Even Jak, his a clumsy sort of thwack, but I love it all the same.

"Quite right, Nikta."

The deep, rich timbre of the new voice clings to the edges of my heart, winding me up further, but I'm shocked more than anything. I don't know why it hadn't occurred to me, but this is a female werewolf! Okay, yeah, we're about as different as night and day.

"They should all learn a bit of modesty."

That voice…

A chill vibrates along my spine. It's a harsh accent, not the same as the rest, sounding like a combination of Russian and British. I glance around Suzette as the striking man rises to his feet. He has a heavy walk, too, like a brutish soldier, but he threads through the kneeling crowd with grace.

He stops in front of Cyan, a slight sneer hooking his lip as he sizes Aeon up. Finally, he thrusts his hand out to Cy. He's the same height as Aeon, but far more cut.

"Romnyr. *Former* GrimBite Beta."

After eyeing him right back, Cy clasps his hand in a harsh grip. "Alpha Cyan. This is Aeon," he raises his voice, addressing the whole group, "your new Beta."

There's another low muttering, several more exchanged glances, and many more staring at Romnyr, like they're waiting to see what he'll do.

But he says nothing, simply tilting his head slightly. "Your rooms are prepared. Follow."

He turns, and panic forces me around Suzette. I grab his wrist, utter shock twisting his features as his attention snaps to me.

"How did you know we'd be coming?"

He composes himself, freeing his wrist with a fluid move. "All part of Mishka's plans. We felt him die," a shadow crosses his eyes, "which meant you wouldn't be returning with him, it

344

would be with…" he gestures lazily in Cyan's direction. "We were prepared in any situation. Come."

I don't know what to do with this information. I feel small, weirdly vulnerable, and like a spoke in a wheel that's racing downhill.

"He guessed you'd kill him?" I glance at Cyan, whose brows lift.

"No guess. He planned it all. Come, before your tiny feet freeze off."

He doesn't sound particularly upset by the idea, even though I feel something under his words. He tromps away, giving Suzette an odd sideways glance.

I don't realize how cold I really am until he says that. The pelt skirt helps a ton, but he's right, my feet and legs are absolute ice blocks.

Of all my mates, it's Jak who surprises me again.

He steps in front of me and pats his shoulder. "Hop on, beautiful. Nice and easy."

What is up with them? I squint. "Why are you both acting like I'm fragile?"

"Uh, no reason at all. Just helping my sweet, sweet mate. It's cold, we have to walk more, and I figured you're still tired."

"Oh. Then…thank you. Okay, hold still."

"Not moving an inch."

I brace on his shoulders and climb up, aided by his strong grip. He makes a seat with his hands behind his back, and I cling to his neck, my legs hooked on his waist.

Neo brushes the snow off my feet and legs, rubbing them a bit to warm them. "I guess this is why they all wear clothes, huh? Even my feet are cold."

"That, and mostly we—they—frown on nakedness."

Laz is planted firmly behind Korey, clinging to his hip.

Suzette spins, pinning him with a shocked stare. "Lazaros?!"

He smiles and nods, not retreating as she approaches. "H-hello again, wild one."

She grins, all teeth, breathtakingly beautiful as she crouches and holds open her arms. After a beat, and a furtive glance at the group still knelt in wait, he tucks into her hug.

"I worried about you," she says.

"Are-are the others free?"

"Yes!" She pushes him back gently by his shoulders. "When he died the compulsion to keep us locked away died, too. No one has been mean to me since. Or any of us."

Laz looks like she just told him unicorns could do algebra.

She chuckles and ruffles his hair. "You're smaller than I thought you'd be. The cage made you seem bigger."

"How very rude!" He's obviously aghast, but he's smiling. Korey looks angrier, clutching Laz's shoulder possessively.

She laughs in full, a rich, rough, belly laugh, and hugs him again before standing.

"So, you're mated with my dad I see. I'm glad. You should be happy. At least one of the collection should be."

All the mirth leaves the air, and he pats her arm. "I'm sorry."

She dismisses it with a wave of her hand and heads in the same direction Romnyr did, walking backwards. "He's right, if terse. We should get inside. There's a blizzard on the way."

Her gaze catches mine again, and that pull gets stronger. She gives me a small smile, and spins, touching a few of the pack members on their shoulders as she passes. They stand, others following their example, until the whole pack is at attention. Waiting.

Cyan lets out a forceful sigh. "Everyone back to their places. And we could use some food. Please."

It's the 'please' that breaks them. The ones who'd begun moving freeze again. Slowly, a few clasp their fists and beat their chests until the pack is drumming in unison. It's weirdly emotional, and Cyan seems affected more than anyone else. After a few more rounds, they bow, and race back to wherever they came from.

It's just me and the rest of SteelTooth here. Silent. Overwhelmed.

I guess this is our new home now. These people won't fit in the old houses. The clearing itself wouldn't even hold this many werewolves. I'm going to miss those cabins and the fire…

But I'm not mad at the prospect of clothing on a regular basis, that's for sure. Or of getting to know Suzette better, even Romnyr. I hope Kasimir is okay, wherever he is, and that Evrik can find me.

The pull hits me hard again, tugging toward a place behind the valley where everyone's heading. Cloud cover breaks, revealing the gorgeous moon, and a cluster of glittering stars to the left. My heart clenches, and I can feel him there, feel that he knows right where I am.

There's something else, there, though. Highlighted by moonlight, a twisting, winding pillar of stone nearly scrapes the sky. The top pulses as I stare at it, the flash strobing faster until it seems to match my heartbeat for a fraction of a second.

I blow a slow breath and hug Jak's neck tighter, burying my forehead against his back. He calls up his beast, and I grin as I sputter the fur out of my mouth, nuzzling into his warmth.

"I love you, Jak," I whisper.

He lets out a low rumble, pinching my butt in response. I squeak, and Neo chuckles.

Cyan grabs the back of Aeon's neck, giving it a reassuring squeeze. "You beat death. This is fucking easy compared to that. You've got this."

He nods, reaching back his hand. Neo takes it in less than a blink. Korey kisses Laz's fingers, and Veikko…

I pick my head up, frantic until I spot him. Why is he so far back?

I hold out my hand, but he hesitates. It stings like a rejection, even though I know it's not. Ugh, my emotions must be all over the place.

My mates, including Veikko, send their love to me, but it only stops hurting once he moves closer.

He threads his fingers with mine, pressing my hand to his scruffy cheek.

Yes, there we go. That's much better.

Whatever happens, this is how we'll handle it—together.

Me—whoever I actually am—and my wonderfully filthy werewolves.

TO BE CONTINUED IN...
PROTECTED FOR THE PACK

Get it here: http://smarturl.it/BuyProtected

Flip the page for bonus NSFW (not safe for work) art I commissioned of the Korey, Las, Cyan scene. There's more art on the way, so if you don't wanna miss it, be sure to hop in my facebook group (fb.com/groups/ primspack) or join my newsletter from my website (www. nataliaprim.com)

Follow the artist, Kaybee, on twitter: @KaybeeDrawsNSFW

AUTHOR'S NOTE & ACKNOWLEDGEMENTS

First and foremost, whew! You made it! I'm so excited for you all to find out what happens next. Protected for the Pack is likely going to be a CHONKA book. Bigger than this one. I was thinking I'd do 4, but I'm fairly certain I can just shove it all in one epic finale.

Super looking forward to exploring Suzette's relationship with Reanne. I know female mates are a rare commodity, so I promise I'll do my best not to let you down.

Enormous shoutout to my beta readers, Alexandra, Betsy, Lea, Mandy, & Verity. Your early insights were critical, and I can't thank you enough.

My arc readers, Jessicca, Ally, Nicole, and Jessica G., thank you so much for your time and energy!

Helena, you are an absolute diamond. Thank you, thank you for obsessing over these characters with me at all hours, for loving them as hard as I do, and for always being there for me. You're a joy to work with and be around, and I'm so happy we met.

M.J., I'm beyond thankful to the universe for allowing your precious soul to cross paths with mine. These beautiful idiots couldn't survive without their Auntie J. Your enthusiasm and quickness to offer kind, supportive vibes have gotten me over **many** a hurdle.

My hubby, I love you. Thank you for talking over plot foibles in the shower, for reading all my sex scenes and reminding me not to leave the jizz out of my descriptions, for snuggling me when this crazy ride gets overwhelming, and for generally just being the best husband ever.

To everyone reading this, thank you from the bottom of my heart. I hope you have enjoyed the ride thus far, and that you are as amped for the next book as I am. Feel free to email me any time if you have questions about my books, natalia@nataliaprim.com, or better yet, hop in my group and tag me! I love connecting with my readers, so please don't be shy.

Made it this far? A reward is in order, I believe. For your diligent eyes only...After Protected for the Pack, I have two spin-off books planned in this world. One features the ShadowMane Alpha and a pregnant human he rescues, and the other features a werewolf stuck outside The Glade, forced to masquerade as a human for a month. You might be asking yourself, how's either scenario possible? Well...you'll have to read Protected to find out. ;)

PROTECTED FOR THE PACK BLURB

Monsters are real...and I will rule them.

The SteelTooth pack is in new territory, physically and emotionally. With mere days until the Glade changes forever, Cyan struggles to adapt to the pressures of a different culture and the demands of fifteen times as many werewolves, while Aeon excels...concerningly.

Several new mates and a rekindled will to live give Reanne hope, as the struggle against the darkness grows more difficult by the day.

After the long-awaited joining ceremony, familiar faces, both friend and foe, reemerge bearing promises and warnings.

And when tragedy strikes, unlikely allies appear when needed most.

Death and life, future and past, heart and soul, all collide in this explosive finale where love proves it's the strongest force of all.

Grab it now!
http://smarturl.it/BuyProtected
(The release date you see is just a buffer.)

A Zealot's Guide to
The Glade

Packs Thus Far & Characters Met or Mentioned

SteelTooth — Cyan, Aeon, Neo, Korey, Veikko, Jakobe (not bound), Reanne, Lazaros (not bound)

~~**BriarMaw**~~ — Yuli, ~~Fen, Bertram, Filnir, Tagrin, Corbet, Pell,~~ Agnar (not bound), ~~et al.~~

GrimBite — ~~Mishka, Silvin,~~ Suzette, Romnyr, et al.

DuskFall (in migration)— Zaid, Garrin

???— Kasimir

???— Evrik

TalonWhisper — Orden

ShadowMane — Alpha

Purists — ???

Terms (As have been revealed & are currently understood by the characters)

Alpha — *Leader and protector of a pack. Receives the right to lead by eliminating his father and taking the Alpha energy into himself. Done during an official 'Challenge.' Can choose not to form a pack of his own, thereby not fully activating the Alpha energy. If this happens, an unseated Alpha residing in the pack has first right to lead, and must choose an existing pack member as his Beta.*

Aruna — *Uncommon. Alpha's true mate. A female, either human or werewolf, who is able to bond to all pack members, sate the Alpha urges, and if they survive mating the Alpha, they can produce offspring without dying.*

Aruna Rigdis — *According to prophecy, the one capable of ascending and ruling all werewolves as their Queen. As this has never happened, the Rigdis' ability to survive birth is undetermined.*

Beta— *Any werewolf whom an Alpha chooses. Tasked with releasing Beta energy to keep emotions and pain at a reasonable level. Uses Alpha energy to produce Beta energy.*

Born Beta— *Extremely rare. Werewolf who can produce Beta energy without an Alpha present.*

Full Moon Freedom — *The one night a month werewolves can cross to the human world.*

High Alpha — *According to prophecy, the mate of the Aruna Rigdis, and therefore King of the werewolves.*

Lake of Tears — *According to legend, where the moon goddess met the first Alpha.*

Mate/Mating — *Permanent & irreversible. When one werewolf bites another with the intent of transferring a portion of his soul to his chosen partner, and taking a portion of his partner's soul in exchange. Neither the recipient, nor the giver of a mate mark have a single soul, but a mixture of the two, and therefore cannot initiate a mate mark on someone else. Either can, however, receive additional marks/mates, though this is uncommon.*

Mate Guard — *Glade wide law that prevents an Alpha from ordering one mate to leave the other. Provided the Alpha is decent, it is usually adhered to. Strong mate bonds can occasionally override an Alpha command that is contradictory to the safety of either mate.*

Mate Blind — *Not particularly safe. When one mate floods the other with energy through direct contact with the mark. Has varied effects, but typically places the recipient in a hazy awareness state. The longer the connection, the more likelihood sickness will occur in one or both.*

MoonMare Cavern — *According to legend, a place often visited by the moon goddess.*

Migration — *When an Alpha severs ties with his territory, retracting his energy claim, and relocates his pack. Involves scraping their pack mark off the territory marker trees. Returns the land to neutral state.*

Nikta— *Rare. A female werewolf. Typically dies giving birth. Born to Alpha pairings only.*

Pack Hunt — *When a werewolf who has just completed Pup status leaves his home pack and roams The Glade, looking for a new pack. Fairly dangerous, because they're unprotected and could be killed, so most tend to stay with the pack they're born to.*

Pack Mark — *The marking each Alpha chooses to represent his pack. Applied to the border of their territory.*

Pup — *Name for the period of werewolf development encompassing birth to age 29. Werewolves mature slower than humans, as their life span can continue indefinitely if they aren't killed. They are not declared "grown" by their birth pack until they prove mastery over their shift.*

Seated Alpha — *When an Alpha takes his first pack member, typically a Beta, thereby fully activating the Alpha energy he obtained through Challenge.*

The Crossmark — *The neutral conjoined edge of the GrimBite and TalonWhisper territories. Patrolled by the ShadowMane.*

The Glade — *The protected realm where werewolves live. It weakens once a month, when the moon is full.*

The Obscurance — *A battle between The Sentinels and The Vigils, over the life of an Aruna Rigdis, 200 years ago.*

The Spire — *twisting stone pillar, considered to be the location where the prophecy will be fulfilled.*

The Quay — *A large chasm bisecting a portion of The Glade, the bottom is rumored to be littered with jagged stone.*

Tracer — *A werewolf capable of manipulating the inherent energies of the species. Reading, tracking, and storing are also skills. At higher skill levels they can act as conduits for powerful energies.*

Unseated Alpha — *An Alpha who won his challenge but chose not to form a pack. Able to bond to another Alpha as a pack member, or live alone, though that's uncommon.*

Zed— *An Alpha's Partner who has no other purpose in the pack. Can sometimes be used as a derogatory term.*

MATES & THEIR MARK LOCATIONS

—REANNE'S MATES —

Aeon (tendon between neck and right shoulder)

Veikko (left side of neck)

Neo (outer side of right breast)

Jakobe (back of left arm)

— OTHER MATED PAIRS —

Korey & Laz (right shoulder)

Natalia Prim has been fascinated with the broken and less-than-beautiful since she was a small girl. Now, not much bigger but definitely older, she writes s3xy stories where the rejected, misunderstood, or even downright evil get their happy endings and then some.

Sign up for my newsletter right on my website, or here:
Click here to join my email list!

Want more content? Check out my Patreon!
www.patreon.com/NataliaPrim

EVEN MORE?! Pop over to my discord server:
www.nataliaprim.com/discord

Click here to follow me on le Zon for release alerts.

For more k^nky shenanigans, hop into my reader's group: Prim's Pack
I do giveaways, write custom shorts, and am just generally goofy, so come hang out!
And follow me everywhere else by tapping the icons below!

facebook.com / NataliaPrimAuthor
twitter.com / AuthorNataliaP
instagram.com / author_nataliaprim
bookbub.com / authors / natalia-prim
goodreads.com / nataliaprim
tiktok.com / @author_nataliaprim
amazon.com / Natalia-Prim / e / B08VV7TSZY

READ MORE OF
PRIM'S BOOKS

You can see current books & their content alerts on my website:

www.nataliaprim.com

MATES OF ARTRIZIKAS

Kali and the King

Gilly and the General

& many more coming!

THE GODLESS GALAXY

Talini's Ship Mate

Victoria's Nightmare Mate

& more soon

CELESTIAL CLAIM SERIES:

Dark PNR Werewolf Poly/Reverse Harem

Abducted for the Pack

Hunted for the Pack

Protected for the Pack

VIE DE MORT SERIES: Cowritten with Helena Novak

Dark Contemporary MF Erotica

His Innocent Muse

His Christmas Muse

His Insatiable Muse

& more

One offs: Jupiter's Fantasy

Printed in Great Britain
by Amazon

16338100R00206